# THE DEMISE OF BOBBY MAC

## BY

## BARBARA LEACHMAN

Sandy,
you've been a loyal friend
for 25 years. I hope we have
twenty five more. 95! You're 95!
Thank you for being such
a wonderful friend.

Bloomington, IN    authorHOUSE™    Milton Keynes, UK

Love & Sunshine forever,
Barbara

*AuthorHouse™*
*1663 Liberty Drive, Suite 200*
*Bloomington, IN 47403*
*www.authorhouse.com*
*Phone: 1-800-839-8640*

*AuthorHouse™ UK Ltd.*
*500 Avebury Boulevard*
*Central Milton Keynes, MK9 2BE*
*www.authorhouse.co.uk*
*Phone: 08001974150*

*First published by AuthorHouse 6/5/2006*

*ISBN: 1-4259-2978-8 (sc)*

*Printed in the United States of America*
*Bloomington, Indiana*

*This book is printed on acid-free paper.*

# ACKNOWLEDGEMENTS

This novel wouldn't have been written without the encouragement of my husband, Reid Leachman, and it is to him that this book is dedicated.

Neither could it have been re-written and re-written without those who faithfully critiqued it for me: Ray Myers, my fellow author who never stopped telling me to "do it." My weekly critique group and wordsmiths Janeen Anderson, Dave McCarthy, Stephen Gregg and Jack Phelan. Writers on the Net students Betty, Gillian, Sue, Maribeth and instructor/author PhyllisPianka. To the final "reader," Roi Ann Archibald, thank you for taking the time to be sure I had dotted all my i's and crossed all my t's and got rid of the "junk."

A big thanks goes to those people who allowed me to "pick their brains" for information to be used in the story: Dr. David Leachman, Jean Aragon, Scott Conner, Terry Lilly, John and Sherri Atchison and Jill and Julia Critch.

*Hope deferred makes the heart sick;*
*But when the desire comes, it is a tree of life.*

Proverbs 13:12

# WEDNESDAY NIGHT

*Automatic light controls. They leave them on to fool people but they don't fool me.*

The owners left this morning. He saw them go.

His leg bumped a deck chair. He cursed and slid it out of his way then continued moving across the wooden deck. The man glanced over his shoulder into the moonless night. Inky blackness met his eyes. He pulled a pen light and a short hacksaw blade from his jacket pocket and started to spring the sliding door lock.

Startled by a loud yowl behind him, he wheeled around and faced two copper ovals shining in the darkness.

# ONE

Paige Lewis stopped reading.

Alone in the house, she heard it.

Outside the door.

A thud. Scraping.

Footsteps?

There! A faint rasping.

She waited, not daring to breathe.

The dimness of the room pressed in and gripped her with its invisible hand. She listened, illuminated and exposed in the circle of light from the floor lamp at her side.

Her eyes scanned the room and came to rest on the computer atop the mahogany desk. The lamplight cast a shadowy pattern on its blank screen and into that corner of the den. She shivered, an inadvertent reaction to the stillness that permeated the room.

Turning once more toward the drapes covering the patio door, she imagined what might be on the other side. A wide deck stretched along the back of the Tudor style house. Farther out in the yard set a rectangular in-ground swimming pool, its cover in place, ready for the long winter that would soon be upon Tulsa. With her mind's eye she could see the bushes and trees that could, in the darkness of the night, cover someone's presence. Beyond them, a secluded greenbelt rolled down into a dry creek bed. Paige imagined a shadowy figure out there, someone who... She struggled to quiet her mind.

Moments passed, the silence broken only by the quiet hum of the heating system and her pulse pounding in her ears.

Her dad always said she had a vivid imagination. Was this another one of those times?

Another scraping sound.

Was that a cry?

Scalp tingling and small prickles creeping down her neck, Paige lowered her book to the sofa cushion. The slow, deliberate movement was in contrast to the fear that threatened to paralyze her. She wished she were back in her safe dorm room on campus. Her first night here and she was already lonely and afraid with only Pepper around.

Pepper! A relieved sigh escaped her lips. Her brother's four-year-old Oriental Shorthair Siamese. The noises must have come from the cat. Maybe it *had* been her imagination after all, the result of the first-night-in-a-strange-house jitters.

Shaken by the scare, she approached the door and peeked cautiously around the edge of the drape. She flipped on the outside light. Nothing. She flipped it again.

*Drat! The bulb must be burned out.* She carefully pushed the drape aside allowing the faint light to shine onto the deck. Brad's ebony cat glided into view. Still apprehensive, Paige freed the lock and slid the door wide enough for Pepper to enter. She closed it quickly, her heart thudding against her chest. Hands shaking she fumbled with the lock, still unsure there was no one lurking in the darkness. Paige replaced the drape to shut out the black night, and greeted her feline companion. Pepper purred and wrapped himself around her legs.

"I'm glad to see you, too, buddy."

Feeling slightly more at ease with the door locked, Paige stretched to relieve the tension in her back and pushed a dark curl behind her ear. The grandfather clock in the hall chimed.

"Midnight," she whispered. "The witching hour."

Stop it, she told herself. It's all your imagination.

Paige switched off the lamp. "Come on, Pepper. Let's go to bed." A soft glow from the hallway lighted their way as they climbed the stairs to the second floor.

Paige and Pepper settled into the Lewis' king-sized bed. Pepper was nestled into his usual place at the foot, and Paige curled up within easy reach of the alarm clock. Quiet descended upon the house as the girl and the cat drifted into sleep.

---

Hidden beneath the drooping branches of a weeping willow Rob McGruder watched the house darken. He waited, counting the minutes until the occupants were in a deep sleep.

He lifted the tangled mass of sandy colored hair that hung around his face and massaged the back of his neck in an effort to ease his tension. He had been so sure the house was empty and remembered the noise he had made moving the chair. Only an amateur would make the mistakes he'd made.

Then that noise. Sounded like a wild animal. It took him a minute to realize he was looking into the eyes of a cat. Both the man and the cat froze, each waiting for the other to make the first move. It was Rob who made it. He stepped away from the door just as a sliver of light stabbed the darkness. He ducked behind a padded deck chair just before the door slid open.

Heart pounding at the close call, Rob stayed in his hiding place until he saw the light go out then he crept across the sprawling yard. Sinking to the ground, he leaned against the smooth tree trunk. Was he digging himself into another ditch? It had been like that when he got caught. A black, dirty hole and it was all because of his father.

Rob cursed silently.

Myrna's face rose before him. His sister. Her husband. Her rotten husband.

In the stillness of the night he waited, and his mind went back to the previous Tuesday evening.

He and his sister had one night a week when they could be together. One lousy night when Leroy wasn't at home. But when he drove up to her house and saw the white van in the drive way, he knew what it meant. His brother-in-law was there. He was preparing to drive away when he caught sight of Myrna on the porch motioning for him to come in. Thinking perhaps Leroy had ridden with someone else to the bowling alley, but still wary, he stayed. When he stepped on the small porch, he heard Leroy's voice from the living room, "Is that your useless brother?"

Rob stiffened and turned to go. Myrna gripped his arm. "Please stay."

"I can't," he said.

Myrna's eyes begged him. "Rob, I need you to stay." Unable to deny her, he entered the small living room.

The room always depressed him. A picture window covered with yellowed Venetian blinds, a couple of them angled toward the door like flat beckoning fingers. A worn floral sofa, the pattern almost faded from view, sat in front of the window. To the right of the door a 40 inch high-definition television set blared. Across from it a disheveled Leroy lounged in a brown leather Chinese Massage recliner.

*What a slob*, Rob thought. The tee-shirt the man wore stopped before the top of his wrinkled under shorts revealing an unappealing paunch. The few stands of graying brown hair Leroy usually combed across his balding head were standing awry as though they'd been caught in a strong wind. Rob fought down the desire to deliver a barb.

Rob's shoulders tensed as he and Myrna crossed the room between the television set and the chair, but Leroy ignored the pair as they went into the kitchen.

"Thank you." Myrna whispered.

"Is everything all right?" Rob asked her. "You said you needed me to stay. What's going on?"

"Nothing. I'm all right. I just wanted you here, like always on Tuesdays."

"Why is *he* here?" Rob gestured with his head toward the living room and jammed his hands in his jacket pockets.

"The bowling alley is closed for lane repairs tonight," she said. "I know it may be hard, but I told him this is our night together--yours and mine--and he could stay or go. It didn't matter to me."

Surprised she didn't cower to Leroy as usual, Rob asked, "And what did he say?"

"Not much." Myrna grinned. "He isn't used to me speaking up like that." She ran her fingers through her honey blond hair, patted it gently, and then washed her hands at the sink.

"Will it get you in trouble later, talking to him like that?" Rob worried for his sister. She'd never told him Leroy had mistreated her but he suspected the man had.

She hung the drying towel on a rack and began dishing mashed potatoes into a chipped ceramic bowl. "No more than usual. I'll be all right." She sat the bowl on the counter and pulled a plate of fried chicken from the oven where it had been warming. "I'm glad you're here."

Rob shrugged and shook his head. "If he starts anything..." He walked away from her and looked into the living room.

Myrna sat the plate beside the potatoes and pulled him back into the kitchen. "I know. Just please don't let it get out of hand."

It hurt to hear the anxiety in her voice. Rob loved his sister, knew he had never done enough for her, and he didn't want to cause her any more harm if he could help it. He nodded, his fists clenched. "I'll try."

"You can do it. I know you can." She smiled at him. "I'm glad you're here with me."

It was a strain being around Leroy at any time but having to eat dinner with him was an added stress. Leroy placed himself at the far end of the wooden table so he could continue to watch television. Rob and Myrna spoke quietly to one another. She told him about Oprah's television show that had been about women whose husbands had left them for another woman and then wanted to move back home.

"And some of the women took them back." She shook her head. "I don't know how a woman could face that," Myrna whispered. "Why would you take him back?"

Rob didn't say it but wondered why Myrna stayed with Leroy. As far as he knew the man had been faithful to his sister, but there had to be more to faithfulness than just not having another woman. He made no comment and turned his attention to his food. As much as he wanted to be a comfort to Myrna, he wanted to be away from Leroy and the anxiety he felt in his presence.

A commercial came on, the television volume rising. Leroy pressed the mute button on the remote. From the corner of his eye Rob saw him looking at him. He gripped his fork and braced himself. It was coming, a jab, an insult, something ugly. Rob hoped he could hold his temper when it did.

"Hey, Rob, when are you going to get a job?" Since Rob had quit working for the delivery service, this had been Leroy's constant question. He had tried to keep his situation from his brother-in-law, but one afternoon he had stopped by Myrna's and Leroy had come home. An argument ensued and Rob had left his sister in tears. He was ashamed of his behavior and had vowed to never let his temper get the best of him again.

Rob hesitated, pushed down his annoyance and didn't answer. Leroy, his eyes mocking, dared him to respond.

An idea took root in Rob's mind. He met Leroy's gaze and said, "I have a chance to make some money helping a guy move but I need a truck."

Leroy froze, a forkful of chicken and potatoes suspended in front of his lips. Then he pushed the food in, chewed noisily not bothering to wipe away the residue that hung on his bottom lip. "Your point?"

Rob pushed ahead. "I was wondering if I could borrow your van this weekend." If he could get Leroy's truck, he wouldn't have to rent one that could be traced back to him.

Leroy smirked "You've got to be kidding." He chuckled without mirth. "Besides my shampooer is being worked on and I'll have to make up for it this weekend. Guess that's a no-go for your move."

Rob heard Myrna draw in her breath and was surprised when she said, "Maybe he could help his friend tomorrow." She looked at Rob.

It would be better if he could get the vehicle today and do the deed tomorrow. The sooner it was done, the quicker he could get out of town and to his new life.

At Rob's nod, Myrna said, "It's only sitting there anyway."

What?" Leroy's round heavy face betrayed little emotion but the color rose in his cheeks.

Myrna continued, her speech quickening. "He isn't asking you for money, only a way to make some for himself." She hesitated, looking from her brother then back to her husband. "Give him a chance." Her voice was strong but her hands were clutched together in her lap.

Rob saw a ring of white around her mouth and knew she was frightened, but she didn't give up. "I'm sure he'll take care of it and bring it back filled with gas." She saw the hesitation in her husband's expression, and when she saw it, she hammered in the final nail, "You know he wants to start over and move out of Tulsa."

And because Leroy thought he might get rid of him forever, the older man relented and agreed to loan Rob his Chevy 2500 Elegant Carpet Cleaning Service van.

After they had eaten Leroy went into his bedroom and came out dangling the keys in front of his body. He pulled them back when Rob reached to take them. Anger boiled in Rob's belly. Hold it down, he told himself.

"You'd better not mess it up." Leroy snarled. "And I want the gas tank full. Bring it back Friday morning, you hear?"

Rob yanked the keys from his hand and mumbled, "I will." He had the keys now and Leroy wasn't getting them back until he was finished with them. *Just let him try.* A part of Rob wished the man would try to wrest them from his hand. Then he'd have a reason to hit him. His knuckles ached with the desire to crack Leroy's jaw. He yearned to feel his fist sinking into his soft, overblown belly. Instead he calmly walked away and looking back at his sister he added, "Thanks." Leroy could think what he wanted, but Rob and Myrna knew who deserved the gratitude.

Twenty-four hours later, in the coolness of the Oklahoma night air, Rob shivered and pulled the collar of his jacket tightly around his neck. He fought back the hatred he felt for himself and for what he was about to do.

Rob waited until two o'clock before moving toward the deck again. He was relatively sure the door would be locked, but it wasn't the first time he'd broken in through a patio door. He had been in many houses while the occupants slept.

His focus was on the coins. He'd find them, take them and whatever else he could find and it would be over.

He was only in the den a few minutes when he heard a low-pitched snarl from the stairs. Shining his penlight in the direction of the sound, he faced the same pair of yellow eyes. This time they were coming toward him.

*I should have known that animal would be in the house. After all, I saw him go inside last night.* He cursed himself for his stupidity.

The cat yowled again, louder, so loud Rob was sure whoever was in the house would be awakened. Rob backed toward the door as the cat continued to advance. He jerked the drape away and slid the door open. He tried to close it but the black menace came out with him.

Rob raced to the van. He looked back, but if the cat was behind him, its black coat was hidden in the darkness.

He started his car's engine and drove without headlights out of the neighborhood. When he passed the house at 253 Mission Lane, he looked at it and muttered, "I'll be back."

# TWO

The clock's alarm roused Paige. Still groggy from the short night, she rolled to her side, eyes slits as she reached for the off switch and wished for a few more minutes of sleep. In the dorm she could have slept an hour longer but she wasn't in the dorm. She berated herself for allowing her brother to talk her into house sitting for him. She groaned and sat up expecting to see a ball of black fur at the end of the bed but only saw the indentation in the blanket where the cat had been.

A half hour later, dressed in jeans and sweater, dusky skin shining from a hot shower and ebony curls pinned into a loose knot on the back of her head, Paige headed downstairs.

"Pepper. Kitty-kitty. Where are you, buddy?" No mewing answered her call. Paige went to the utility room, and seeing food in Pepper's bowl, assumed the cat hadn't been up for an early morning snack. "Pepper, I don't have time for this. I have to go. Where are you, Kitty?"

Grabbing a banana to eat on the thirty-minute drive to the university, Paige picked up her open book bag and realized her novel was still in the den.

Can't forget that, she thought. I have to get it read before Monday.

She hurried into the den. Her book lay on the sofa cushion where she'd left it the night before. Sun streaming into the room from the direction of the patio doors captured her attention. The drapes were open, pulled loose from the rod at the open edge and the door was ajar. Patiently washing himself on the deck was Pepper. Paige stopped, her mind not comprehending what her eyes were seeing.

*How did Pepper get outside? Why are the drapes open?*

Without conscious effort, she retraced last night's movements. She saw herself letting Pepper in, re-locking the door and closing the drape. A sickening fear began in her stomach and traveled to her throat, ending in an involuntary cry. She looked around expecting to find another person in the room. She was alone.

Pepper's paw softly patted the glass door. The sound wasn't the same one she had heard last night before she let him in. Fighting fear, she gasped in short breaths of air. Pepper patted the glass again. Someone had been out there and that someone had been in the house last night!

Paige slid the door open and tentatively looked around the yard as Pepper raced by her. The October morning was clear and cool, the sun shining through the trees from the direction of the greenbelt. Nothing appeared to be disturbed on the deck. A chaise and two chairs still held the bright pads of summer. She knew her brother and his wife always packed them away for the winter, but it was fall, two months before they would have to be stored in the garage. She contemplated whether or not she should do it, but just thinking about going outside where she'd heard the noises the night before convinced her to let them be. Stepping back into the room, Paige closed the door behind her and locked it. She tried to open it, but the lock held it shut.

"Now what do I do?" she said aloud to the room. *Should I call the police?* Her mind raced. *If I call the police, they'll want to know if anything was stolen. If I don't find anything, they'll think I just forgot to lock the door myself. But what if I don't call them? What if the person is hiding in the house?* With that thought, she dialed the emergency number.

---

Sleep deprived but hopeful, Rob drove the white van back to the neighborhood where he'd been the night before. He had slept fitfully for five hours after last night's debacle, but today was the beginning of his new life. Fate had intervened, given him the information about the coins and the owners leaving town, and now Leroy's truck. Things were finally beginning to go his way.

He drove slowly down the shady street past million dollar homes nestled away from the road behind large bushes and trees in an attempt at seclusion. Passing 253 Mission Lane he pulled into the driveway beside the empty house next door. He knew this place well. He'd parked here last night and many times before while watching the movements at 253.

The house at 255 sat on an acre of land just before the cul-de-sac's curve and was hidden from the view of the street by a thick hedge between the two properties. The houses across from 253 and 255 were almost hidden from view, and it was their isolation that kept them from seeing the man who had come and gone across the street for several weeks.

Rob wanted to make up for the blunders of the night before and was careful to close the van's door quietly although no one at 253 could possibly hear it. Confidently crossing in front of the house at 255, he thumped the "For Sale" sign in the yard and was nearing the hedge when he heard a vehicle pulling into 253's driveway.

A towering burning bush hedge formed a fiery red barrier between the two houses and easily masked Rob's six-foot-one presence. Through a break in the hedge, the window he'd used to watch the house for several weeks, he saw a dark-haired girl meet a uniformed police officer at the front door. The two of them talked a few minutes then the cop walked around the house out of his sight.

Beads of sweat dotted Rob's forehead. He considered leaving but was afraid of being seen driving away. He wiped his sweaty palms on his pants and rubbed the back of his neck. It was safer to stay where he was. With any luck the cop wouldn't find him.

From behind the bushes Rob saw the policeman return to the front porch, then he and the girl entered the house. A half hour later they emerged. The patrolman opened his car door and called back to the girl, "Don't forget to set the alarm." She waved and answered something Rob couldn't hear. In her arms she held a black cat.

Rob cursed the cat under his breath and watched the patrol car leave. By the time he looked back at 253, the front door had closed. He hurried to the van and paused before getting in. *What do I do now?* He rubbed his hand over the back of his neck again, ran his fingers through his shaggy mane of hair, then got into the van and started the engine.

He had to get into that house, find the coins, and if there was anything else of value, he'd load it in the van and take it to his fence.

Those coins. He had to have them.

Maybe there was another way.

---

Paige watched the police vehicle leave. She turned the lock, tapped in the alarm code and stood in the entry hall wondering what to do next. The policeman had spent almost an hour with her, and it was too late to make her two morning classes. She contemplated attending her afternoon class but was uneasy leaving the safety of the locked house.

*I can't believe I didn't set the alarm.* She brushed a loose curl behind her ear and walked down the hall into the kitchen. *But, if I did, why didn't it go off when the door was opened? There just isn't any other explanation except that I forgot.* Paige ran water into a tea kettle and sat it on the stove. She kicked off her shoes and shoved them against the cabinet with one stocking foot. *I'm usually a detail person. I was scared last night. Wouldn't that have been the very reason to set the alarm?*

Being a sound sleeper was beneficial in a noisy dorm but not when someone is breaking into your house.

Maybe she had imagined everything, but, then again...

Rob pulled the van into a nearby Wal-Mart parking lot and shut off the engine. Heart pounding from the policeman-sighting, he shivered and kneaded the back of his neck in an effort to erase his growing apprehension. He slumped in the seat, closed his eyes and was immediately transported back into the god-awful coldness of his jail cell. Before him loomed the cold gray cell of Davidson Correctional Center. The smell of the open toilet assailed his senses as though it sat in the van's seat beside him. He pictured the hard bunks jutting out from the walls, the thin cotton mattress, and the rough blanket that had covered him but never given him warmth.

Night and day the memories of those years behind bars haunted him. This burglary was his way to erase them, to get out of town, his chance to get away from the people who knew him and what he'd done. They were constantly bugging him. "This is a good job, McGruder. You'll make enough off this one you can retire." They'd laugh and jab him like it was a joke but they would never leave him alone and he knew it. So far he'd been able to put them off with excuses of having to work or his sister needed him; weak excuses, he knew, and they knew. The time would come when he'd have to give in just to save his own life. The only retirement in this occupation was death or running away. He chose running to dying but it had to be soon. After this, he'd never break the law again. It was the only chance he had for a life. Twenty-five years old and nothing to show for it. All he wanted now was a chance to start over, to make his life worth something.

As clear as the pictures in his mind were of the jail cell, so were the red and blue strobe lights of the cop's car as it came up behind him over two years ago. When he saw them, he contemplated running but knew he would get busted sooner or later, so he stopped. So many times he wished he'd taken his chances and kept going.

It was hell being locked up, being told what to do and what not to do all the time, and he couldn't stand that again. A man couldn't think for himself or he was a target of the guards or of an inmate. The biggest and the meanest ruled with fear in those places. He was big but certainly not the meanest although, because of his size, some of the inmates gave him a wide berth. He put on a big show of being a tough guy and was probably as afraid as any of the others but no one ever let it show. He remembered the nights he couldn't sleep for fear of being killed by someone he had looked at wrong. Anything would set some of those guys off. Rob struggled to block out the thoughts but with the memories came bile, burning the back of his throat.

Abruptly he sat up and clutched the van's steering wheel. The fear always began in the pit of his stomach. If he hadn't been delivering a stolen car, and they hadn't been able to tie him in with the burglary gang, he might not have had to serve so much time. No probation for him. He served it all, the full two years and learned more in those two years than he ever wanted to know. One bit of information that had paid off was how to deactivate a house alarm without alerting the alarm company or the homeowner. But the only way that information could ever help him make a better life was in a situation like this, burglarizing and stealing something that didn't belong to him.

Rob shook the thoughts away. He had made a blunder or two on this job but he was smarter than he was before prison. This time he wouldn't get caught. After it was over he would go to LA or San Francisco, someplace on the west coast. This job would give him enough money to make a new start. He'd buy himself a new identity. Something else he'd found out in prison--how easy it is to change identities. It was time to make it happen. The house, the coins--the girl awaited him. He wouldn't screw it up. The cat might be in the house and might be a nuisance but it was only a cat after all. This time it wouldn't surprise him and he could deal with it.

An hour later Rob crouched behind a row of azalea bushes next door to 253 Mission Lane. When he began his vigil, the overcast October sky was as solidly gray as gunmetal. A few hours later the afternoon sun broke through and warmed the day to a pleasant 73 degrees. He spread out a newspaper to sit on in order to keep his jeans from picking up the dead grass. A stone path led from the front of 253 to the deck and he planned to walk through the grass and onto the stones. Then he would stomp the grass off his shoes and wipe the stones with the newspaper. Footprints on the grass would be impossible to see and nothing on the stones would be visible. If the cops looked they'd find nothing. He drank from a large bottle of Aquafina. Around four o'clock he opened a Quik Trip sack, took out a ham and cheese sandwich, and waited patiently for evening and the perfect time. It would happen. He was sure of that. It was his last chance.

# THREE

Unnerved by the events of the night before, Paige stayed in all day. She kept the house locked, the alarm on, and decided she wouldn't even answer the door if someone came. Thoughts whirled through her mind. She had classes tomorrow. She couldn't quit going to school for three weeks. She thought she might move back to the dorm but she knew she couldn't leave Pepper, and she couldn't take him with her. Maybe she could ask Katy to come and stay with her. She decided she would talk to her roommate when she saw her on Friday.

Around six o'clock Pepper wanted out. Loathe to open the door, Paige carefully turned off the alarm system and slid the door open just enough for Pepper to escape. Loneliness crept over her as she watched the shiny black Siamese head for the green belt. Quickly re-locking the door, she punched in the alarm code, closed the drapes then walked across the hall and into the kitchen.

Light oak cabinets with black opaque appliances formed the back of the kitchen to her left. An island separated the working space from the morning room. A round oak table and chairs and a few pieces of furniture filled the area near the oriel-style bay window and Dutch door that looked out onto the deck and greenbelt. The door and bay windows were covered with sage rod pocket shades that allowed in light but gave privacy when pulled down. On this evening, the shades were closed. A television set next to the fireplace was tuned to the news, the sound turned low.

Paige half watched, half listened to the program while she prepared herself a sandwich. She poured Pepsi from a can into a glass, took some chips from a bag and placed them on the plate with her sandwich.

A movement in the hallway caught her eye. A tall man stepped into her view, a small pistol pointed in her direction.

Paige screamed and began backing away.

"Stop!" he commanded, his cold gray eyes holding her in place.

"How did you get in the house?"

"Shut up!" he commanded again. "Get yourself over here *now!*"

Gripped by fear Paige took a step toward him. The man motioned for her to go into the den. Woodenly she obeyed. He followed her, the gun pressed into her back. He pushed her toward the sofa.

"Face down," he directed. Roughly pulling her hands behind her back, he began to wind silver tape around her wrists. He worked quickly, carefully covering her fingers then wound the tape around her feet and ankles.

She lay motionless, fearful of his next move. The intruder demanded, "Where are the coins?" Paige didn't answer immediately. "Listen, lady, I don't want to hurt you, but I will if you don't help me."

"I don't know," Paige stuttered. "I -- I really don't know."

She winced as the man grabbed a handful of her hair and jerked her head backward. He looked into her face, so close she felt his hot breath. "Don't lie to me. Where are the coins?"

Struggling against the pain, Paige gasped. "Honest. I don't know."

He took her slender body in his hands and easily sat her upright on the sofa. He held her chin roughly in one of his gloved hands and pressed the gun to her forehead. "You will die," he growled, "if I don't get what

I want!" His voice lowered his tone ominous. "Now, tell me where he keeps them."

Trying not to panic but frightened to her core, she told him part of the truth. "They aren't here. He took them with him."

"You're lying!" The gun barrel bit into her flesh. "Tell me. Now!"

Paige began to cry. "I think he keeps them in his desk, but...." The man loosened his hold on her and went quickly to the desk. "Where are they?" He frantically opened drawers, rifling through each one strewing papers onto the floor.

Paige whimpered her scalp and face stinging from his assault. "I think he keeps them in the bottom right drawer in a notebook. It's a big one. It's black."

The noise stopped abruptly. Paige closed her eyes and breathed a prayer. The coins weren't there. He wouldn't find them. Opening her eyes, she looked into the man's face looming over her.

"I've waited my whole life for this chance," he said, suddenly quieter, controlled. "Nobody's gonna stop me now. You had better think carefully." He spoke the next words slowly, emphasizing each one, his hand on the back of her neck. "Is there anywhere else he might keep them?"

Paige's breath quickened, her heart pounded. She tried to pull away from his grasp. "They might be in -- in –" she hesitated. Think, Paige, she thought. *You have to get yourself out of this. You can do it.* "I don't know where they are but I can help you look for them. It would be easier to help you than to try to tell you all the places to look!" Her voice sounded desperate in her own ears.

The man laughed. "You think you can out hustle me? It can't be done, so don't even try."

He gripped the back of her neck turning her head upward. Pain shot through her upper back. "Now tell me some places to look!"

"Upstairs – uh – uh…" she stuttered, grasping for a thought, anything that would appease him. "A cabinet… I think there's a cabinet – or -- a – dresser in the bedroom." She remembered the antique wardrobe Ashley had purchased recently. "In the bedroom, the one on the left at the top of the stairs." Her words came in a flood. "It's old. They just bought it. Maybe they keep them there." If she could get him out of the room, she hoped she could free her hands and escape.

"And if they don't?"

A tired stillness washed over Paige. She relaxed, her face still in his grasp. Her voice a whisper, she answered, "Then I don't know."

The man released her and stepped back. He looked at her for a long moment before turning and striding out of the room. She could hear his footsteps on the tiled hallway then the heavy tread of his steps as he ran up the stairs.

Gathering strength, she attempted to move her hands and loosen the tape, but it held tight. Her hands and feet tingled as the flow of blood slowed in them and the movement shot pain through her wrists, her fingers and feet. She could no longer hear the thief but knew he was upstairs opening drawers and doors looking for coins he wouldn't find. Most were safely with Brad on his way to the Harrow Coin Club meeting and auction in London, the remainder in a safe in the closet under the staircase, the doorway hidden from casual view. Even if she told him where they were, she didn't know the combination.

Thoughts whirled through Paige's mind like a feather caught in a violent maelstrom. She fought to take control, to be calm and think of her options. The man wanted something she couldn't give him. One option was to talk him into stealing something else. Maybe, if she promised not to tell, but how many victims had promised that?

*I'm a psychology major. Surely I can outsmart and out-talk a crook.* She remembered a case in Atlanta where a young woman was taken hostage.

This lady just talked to the murderer from her heart, and he let her turn him in. In discussing the case in class the professor had said that if you make yourself human to the criminal, not just someone standing in the way of what he wants, they aren't as apt to hurt you. She began to rehearse what she could say to him and hoped it would sound like it was coming from her heart. This man was evidently desperate and all desperation stemmed from some unmet need. Although she didn't know what that need was and knew she couldn't fill it, she hoped she could convey her concern for him enough that it would keep him from hurting her.

The man burst into the room. "Okay, lady. They aren't upstairs. You have one more chance." He stepped toward her. "Where are the coins?"

Paige took a tremulous breath to calm herself. "You're right. They aren't. I shouldn't have lied to you. I'm trying to get you to leave me alone and not hurt me. I was afraid to tell you the truth." She lowered her eyes and looked at the floor where he stood.

He stopped his advance. "And that is?" he asked.

She hesitated, hoping he'd understand and not become angrier, "They're on the plane with him to London. My brother took them with him to a coin show."

For a long moment the man was quiet, and then Paige heard a whispered curse. She raised her head and saw his face blanch, his expression change from one of anger to hopelessness and then, despair. The smoky gray eyes quickly faded into dull slate pools.

"I'm sorry. I was scared," she went on. Her words had changed him, changed him from a mad, raving killer to a man without hope. She was still frightened, but she saw he was, after all, human and had feelings. Neither of them spoke, his eyes staring into her face yet unseeing. "I'm supposed to be protecting my brother's house, and that's what I was trying to do." Paige spoke softly. A few tears of relief pooled in her eyes. To her surprise, she saw his shoulders droop and in the place of anger rose a terrible sadness.

--------

Rob's energy drained away and his legs melted under him. With a groan, he fell into the nearest chair and stared into the young girl's face. Shame flooded him. She meant it, he thought. He realized she was scared, saw how he was terrorizing her and for what? The coins weren't even here. And even if they were, they didn't belong to him. How was he to start a new life if he began it by hurting someone else? That wasn't the new Rob McGruder. That was the guy he'd always been.

Before him the girl's face transformed into that of his sister's. Years ago, he'd seen this same expression on Myrna's face when their dad had asked her if she was pregnant; panic mixed with sorrow. Panic because of what he might do to her, and sorrow because of what she saw coming. Rob realized he didn't want to hurt this girl, but he was caught in a hurricane with his whole life in its path. He couldn't stop now.

"How much money do you have?" His absently rubbed at the tension in his neck and spoke with effort, his voice passive.

The girl hesitated. He knew she was surprised to see the change in him but he wasn't surprised. It took too much effort to be the tough guy. All those years on the street, in crime, in prison. Too hard. It has to end.

"Not much," she said. "About twenty dollars in my backpack. It's in the kitchen."

He'd asked her a question. What was it? The money. He'd asked about the money. "Okay." Now what? She has twenty dollars. That won't even buy me a tank of gas. He looked around the room. "So what's here I can sell?"

"What kind of things do you want?" she asked quietly, her eyes never leaving his face.

"Stuff I can sell," he repeated, "jewelry, cameras, computers." He gestured toward the unit on the desk.

Paige watched him, and when he turned back to her, she answered, her voice almost a whisper, "Ashley has some good jewelry, but I honestly don't know if it's here, or if she took it with her. Did you see her jewel case in the bedroom?"

"Yeah, I saw it. There's nothing but junk in there. Anything else? Golf clubs? Rob clasped his gloved hands in his lap.

"In the garage, I think." The girl appeared to be helping him. She no longer looked scared, just small and helpless.

He put his head in his hands. Hot tears of regret seared his eyes as he saw his future dissolving before him. *It's happening again. I hated every minute of it when I had to do it before and now I've screwed this up.*

With the thought of imprisonment, bile burned the back of his throat. Bolting from his chair, Rob ran to the toilet in the hall. He slammed the door and leaned over the bowl. Coughing and sputtering he allowed the fire of incarceration to boil out of him and be flushed away.

When his sickness had subsided, Rob yanked off his thin latex gloves and threw them on the floor, took a handful of cold water and splashed it on his face then rinsed the vomit from his mouth. Both hands supported his lean body as he bent over the basin, water dripping from his fingers onto the tiled floor. He took in deep breaths and gripped the cold porcelain sink edge, at the moment his anchor of stability. In the mirror his image swam before his eyes. He didn't see the strong chiseled face of the free man he was, but, rather, a man in an orange jumpsuit behind steel bars. Sweat replaced the water drops on his face and fear rolled in his belly. Rob squeezed his eyes shut. He ran his wet hand across his forehead and the back of his neck. With a deep breath, he stood upright, pulled a towel from the rack and began to dry his face and hands. He retrieved his gloves, pulled them on, and then began to carefully wipe away his prints from the ceramic fixtures. He closed the lid of the toilet seat and sat down. His next move would decide his future.

---

Alone in the den, hands and feet throbbing, numbness seeping into her fingers and toes, Paige thought, if I can reach the phone maybe I can knock it off the hook, push the buttons with my nose or tongue. She struggled to stand, but when she tried, the floor disappeared beneath her. She considered his reaction if he saw her trying to call and decided to remain where she was. So far he hadn't really hurt her. If she cooperated, maybe he'd let her go. She had thought she was so smart, making herself human to this man. Instead, he'd run out of the room. She'd seen his humanity, his frailty and wondered if that made her danger greater. In another situation, her interest in understanding behaviors would have piqued her curiosity about him. She would have wanted to know more, his story, why he was here. But, today, she just wanted him to go away.

---

Steps labored, Rob returned to the den. He stood in the doorway acutely aware of the ache the girl must be experiencing in her hands and feet. A clock somewhere behind him chimed seven. It was time to end this fiasco.

The girl's eyes questioned him and he loathed what he was doing to her. "What's your name?" Rob asked.

"Paige," she answered, her eyes never leaving his face.

"Look, Paige, I told you I didn't want to hurt you, and I don't, but I'm not stupid. I know you'll go straight to the cops if I let you go." She shook her head. "Don't bull…," he stopped. His voice quiet, he continued, "Don't lie to me." Myrna didn't like him to cuss, but this wasn't Myrna. He had to keep remembering that. *Careful, Rob-boy, don't lose it. You still have to get away from all this without going back to prison.*

Rob took a deep breath and slumped against the doorjamb. "This is what's going down. I'm going to load up all the stuff I can sell then I'm going to leave you here."

"You're going to just leave me here – *alone* – tied up?"

Rob recognized the terror in her eyes, heard the panic in her voice.

"They won't be back for three weeks. I'll die! Please…" As quickly as her fear had come, it ebbed. Rob recognized the "fight or flight" impulse rising up in its place.

He straightened. "Yeah, all alone," his voice was stronger now, no longer tired or gentle. He had to fight, too.

Looking into the panicked girl's face, Rob's mind took him to a place he never liked to go. He was doing just what his father had done. Terrorizing people was Mac McGruder's way of life. His wife. His daughter. Even his own son.

His dad's raspy voice echoed in his mind, "You gotta make yourself tough. You're just lucky I didn't name you what I wanted to, Marion, like me. That would have made you tough."

*I've tried all my life to be tough and all it got me was grief,* Rob thought. *This has to be the end of it even if someone dies. It's either me or the girl, and it isn't going to be me.*

"I do what I gotta do!" Even as the words spewed from his mouth, Rob saw his father towering over a frightened Myrna, forcing her to admit her wrongdoing. The words belonged to Mac McGruder, not to his son. But the son couldn't stop.

At 9:30 Rob pulled the van into the garage. He had all he wanted from the house plus the garage door opener he'd taken from Paige's car. After loading the stolen goods, he came back into the den. For a moment he stood quietly beside the sofa where the girl lay whimpering.

"Please. Please," she begged, her voice muffled by the soft cushion.

He whispered, "I'm sorry. I'm really sorry." Then he was gone.

# FOUR

An hour later Rob wheeled the van into the alley behind his small garage apartment and parked out of sight of the street.

Inside the one room efficiency, he ripped off his gloves and took off his jacket. He stuffed the gloves in his pocket and tossed the jacket on the lone chair then sprawled on the single bed. Every muscle in his body ached. He longed to take the time to stand under a hot shower and let the water wash away the filth. It wasn't only his body that was dirty. It was his soul. Exhaustion overwhelmed him and kept him on his back. At the moment he didn't think he would have the energy to get up and meet his fence at the time they'd planned.

Had he covered his tracks? He went over it again in his mind. No finger prints. Miles from his apartment, a dumpster held the water bottle, newspaper, sandwich wrapper, toy gun and tape he'd bought at Wal-Mart, all in the Quik Trip bag. In the bottom of that bag was the garage door opener he'd taken from the girl's car.

Paige. Her name was Paige. She had a name, a life. When he took the money from her backpack, he realized she was a college student. He had seen some books. One was about psychology. A notebook had her name and another name, Dr. Winslow, and a title, "Clinical Evaluations." He'd never been to college. It hadn't ever entered his mind to go back to school. She must be smart, he thought. Paige must be smart. He wished he hadn't asked her to tell him her name. Then she'd be less of a person, just a girl in the way of what he had to do.

Images of this girl refused to go away. They played on his mind, filled his thoughts. He pictured her lying on the sofa in the dark, bound, and scared. He knew what it felt like to be alone and afraid you are going to die. And he remembered her scent; not sweet but soft, light and fresh. He wasn't sure he'd ever smelled anything like it before. Suddenly restless, Rob sat up and wearily rubbed the back of his neck. The thought of being responsible for a death sickened him.

"What else could I do?" he muttered aloud. "It was either me or her."

He walked across the room, opened the refrigerator and stared at a carton of milk and package of cheese. The odor of the spoiled milk turned his stomach. He closed the door. The clock on the stove told him it was nearing the time he'd set to meet Benny and make the exchange.

Rob returned to the bed, sat down heavily and rubbed his tired eyes with his fists. The girl's face remained before him. He could hear her crying. Nothing could shut out the sight and sound. Would it ever go away?

He spoke aloud to drive out the memory. "What a dope I am. Why did I have to go through with it? I should have just..." What? he asked himself. What should I have done?

He jumped to his feet, and with thoughts reeling, began to pace the small apartment. *I can't wait to get out of Tulsa and start over. No one knows I'm going to leave. The delivery company fired me because I took off too much time scoping out the house. But I had to. Anyway, no one will miss me. I'll take the van back to Leroy in the morning, come back here to get my things and leave.*

Myrna. He stopped. His sister. *Myrna will miss me. I have to leave Myrna but I can't tell her without telling her why. She'll be hurt but I can't help it. I have to go. She has Leroy. She won't be torn between the two of us any longer. Leroy will be glad to see the last of me, but not as happy as I'll be to never see his face again.*

The girl. Rob shook his head. Can't think about the girl.

But he did think about her and, in the end, came to the decision to call nine-one-one as he was leaving town. He would call from a pay phone. He wondered if the cops could trace a pay phone. He thought of fingerprints. His gloves. He dug in his pocket and pulled out the latex gloves. Yes, he thought, I can wear gloves then they won't find fingerprints on the phone if they trace it. His mind raced ahead with the plan. *I-40 will take me to California. The phone will have to be far away from the interstate.* He pictured the highways. There was one that went north. He'd go there first then back to Turner Turnpike and I-40. He traced his journey to Oklahoma City, Amarillo and into New Mexico and Arizona. He had no map so he would have to get one somewhere along the way; a highway map of the United States. Would he go to Los Angeles or north to San Francisco?

But his schemes couldn't chase out the vision of the girl. He had to take care of her first. After he called, someone would find her. He went to the sink and began washing his hands. She'll be all right, he told himself. I'll be gone by then and I won't be a murderer.

Rob massaged his aching temples. A pit, he thought. Another stinkin' pit and I'm not sure how I'll ever climb out of it. He shook the thought away. I have to. I can't stay down here much longer.

Rob left his apartment and drove to a deserted warehouse complex on the outskirts of town. He wound through darkened passageways and finally emerged in the back of the area. As he neared the metal building, one of three large doors slowly slid open. Rob cut off the headlights and directed the van into the black interior. He heard the door closing behind him. He waited in the silence.

It was no surprise when a bright light shone through the side window. The passenger door opened and a voice called out, "It's all right." Immediately, light illuminated the interior of the warehouse.

A stocky man chewing on a cigar looked at him over the front seat. "Hey, Rob." The man smiled around crooked yellow teeth. Although his mouth smiled it didn't reach his eyes.

"Benny." Rob pulled the handle on the driver's door and climbed out of the van. The two men met at the front and shook hands.

"Whatcha got?"

Rob looked around the building before answering. "Where's Rudy?"

"Right here." A pale thin man stepped from behind the van and walked toward them.

Rob nodded to him. The man made no response as he shoved a black pistol into the back of his belt.

Benny took his cigar from his mouth and spit a piece of it onto the floor. "Well?"

Rob motioned to the back of the van. "Let's do it."

Benny poked the cigar butt back in his mouth and grinned. "You got the goods. I got the money."

# FIVE

Leroy waited for him on the small front porch and approached the driveway as Rob parked the van. Before his brother-in-law could speak, Rob tossed him the keys and strode to his Toyota parked on the curb.

"Hey!" Leroy called.

Rob ignored him. He slammed into his car, started the engine and, tires squealing sped away leaving behind a suspicious Leroy examining the exterior of his vehicle for damages.

"Jerk!" Rob muttered, thinking of his sister's husband.

His tired eyes burned with tears as he thought of Myrna. *I wish I could say good-bye. It has to be this way, Sis. I'm sorry. I have to do it.*

Rob glanced at the clock on the dashboard. Eight thirty. He turned toward his apartment thinking about how good a hot shower and change of clothes would feel before picking up the clothes he'd packed after meeting Benny. He was anxious to get out of town but his body screamed to climb back into the crumpled bed and sleep.

Rob shrugged his shoulders to relieve the tension and rubbed at the stiffness in the back of his neck. Freedom. It had been years since he'd felt any kind of freedom. His whole life had been filled with emptiness and failure. Things were changing for him. A new town. A new life. Rob stopped for a traffic light.

Later, when the memory of this moment returned to him, it came back in the same slow motion as the moment he caught the flash of red. Slowly he turned his head, his gaze falling on a woman waiting for a city bus. She was short. Her red coat reached the tops of her shoes. On her arm, a large green shopping bag. Time stood still, and then realization slapped him in the face.

*The housekeeper!* He had left a loose end after all. How could he have forgotten?

For weeks he'd watched the house and knew the occupants' schedules. During the week they left every morning at seven and were home every evening by six. The only other person he had ever seen was a woman who came every Friday morning at nine o'clock and let herself in with a key. The same red coat! The same green bag! A city bus stopped at the corner hiding her from his view. It drove away, and she was gone. She was on her way to 253 Mission Lane. She would find the girl.

Rob's head dropped to the steering wheel, all the pain of his twenty-five years pounding in his chest. How could he have forgotten?

The light changed and the car behind him sounded its horn. Grim determination replaced the pain as the young man steered his car toward the highway that would take him out of town.

No time to go back to the apartment. This time, he vowed, if they catch up with me, I won't stop. But he did. He made one stop on his way out of town, at a phone booth and then he drove back to Interstate 40 and away from Tulsa.

He headed west on the Interstate for 192 miles before having to stop to refuel in Clinton, Oklahoma. At the Texaco Mart, he bought a cup of coffee and some Advil hoping the caffeine and drug would take away the headache that still plagued him.

Several hours later the Toyota passed through Tijeras Canyon approaching Albuquerque. Only then did Rob begin to feel hunger and fatigue. His last good night's sleep, too long ago to remember. His last meal, Thursday afternoon while waiting for the girl.

"Paige." He said her name aloud. It would have been better if she had remained nameless to him, but he felt sure the housekeeper had rescued her. If not the housekeeper, then the phone call. He was off the hook. Relieved of guilt for the moment, Rob shook the memory from his mind.

A red and white EconoLodge sign on I-40 promised a bed. Food would be nearby. It was six o'clock and dark in New Mexico, cooler than it had been in Tulsa. Rob got out of the car, pulled on his jacket and entered the motel lobby.

After checking in, he found the Owl Café which had been described to him by the motel clerk as serving the best chile cheeseburgers in the state. He downed two of them along with French fries and coffee. Tiredness threatened to overtake him, but he had something he wanted to do before giving in to it.

In a nearby Target store, he found a pair of jeans, a long-sleeved shirt, and a jacket in his size. He picked up Jockey shorts, socks, deodorant, toothbrush, toothpaste and some razors. Driving away, he noticed a sign in the same strip mall: "Hair Clips." On the window, in large letters, "Walk-in's Welcome, Open 'Til Nine." On impulse, Rob parked and went into the shop. Thirty minutes later he emerged, hair cropped to less than a quarter of inch. He rubbed his hand over his head and smiled to himself. If they're looking for a guy with long hair, they won't find him here. A more confident Rob McGruder drove back to his motel room, showered and fell immediately into bed.

After nine hours of sleep, he shaved off two month's growth of facial hair, packed his old clothes, including his gloves, in the Target sack, and left the room. Driving to the Owl for breakfast, he eyed a dumpster behind the café, pulled beside it and tossed in the sack of clothing. To put his old life behind him, he had to dispose of the clothes he'd worn or they'd forever be a reminder of his unforgivable crime.

Relieved of one more burden, Rob headed for California. Miles after he had left Tulsa, he'd picked up one brief news bulletin about a young woman being found by a house keeper. The announcer said the girl was unconscious and unable to give police any information. The radio signal dissolved into static and Rob heard no more. Although no police cars pursued him, fear had pushed at his back, driving him toward the coast. Today the fear seemed far away and his pace slowed as he continued west.

Too bad about those coins, he said to himself. I could have made a bundle on them. The thought of the coins brought another memory to Rob's mind. He smiled.

Gerri. Good old nosy Gerri, his sort-of girlfriend at the travel agency. He remembered how Gerri's incessant talking had started this whole episode.

Her favorite time for talking, much to his dismay, was right after sex. For some reason sex wound her up, and she wanted to "relate," as she called it. What it amounted to was her talking about whatever came into her mind and Rob trying to shut her out and go to sleep. But one night he heard her.

"I had this rich lady in today," she said, her voice cigarette husky although she had never smoked. "She and her husband are going to England for three weeks. It's some kind of coin show. Doesn't that just take the cake? All the way over there for coins. That's when you have more money than you need."

Rob drifted in and out of a conscious state as she continued. "This lady told me her husband has been collecting coins since he was ten years old and, according to her, he has hundreds of U.S. coins and some from foreign countries. What do you think of that?" Gerri nudged him. Rob grunted to let her know he was listening.

"She told me about a 1924, I think it was, silver dollar worth two hundred bucks and some kind of 1800s coin worth over five thousand dollars."

Now Rob was listening. He turned toward Gerri in the bed. From the street light illuminating her bedroom, Rob could see Gerri's tousled auburn hair fanned out on the pillow. She's a beautiful woman, he thought, but she talks too much. However, right now he was interested in what she had to say.

"You say they have a lot of coins like that?"

She had his undivided attention and took advantage of it. Her hand slipped under the cover and touched him. At the moment he wasn't interested in more sex. He moved away from her and sat up in the bed. "Tell me about these people, Sugar. What else did she say?"

Not to be denied, Gerri moved closer to him. "Well, she said he kept them at home even though she's told him over and over they need to be in a bank vault." She hesitated, "because they're worth a fortune." She began to caress between Rob's thighs, her voice throaty with desire as she continued. "They're going to London in October and will be gone 3 weeks. Did I mention that?" Her fingers began to work their magic.

Rob reached for her. "Where did you say they live?"

After the night with Gerri, his plan began to take shape.

Good ole Gerri, Rob thought. She'll miss me. A familiar yearning began in his groin. And I'll miss her.

---

Rob drove all day. Four hundred and eighty miles from Albuquerque, two signs in Kingman, Arizona, captured his attention. One read "Needles and Los Angeles" and the other, "Las Vegas." On impulse, he turned the Toyota onto Highway 93 to Vegas.

A few hours later, on that Saturday night in October, Rob found himself on Las Vegas Boulevard. The power of the Strip assaulted his senses and at the same time, excited him. Scintillating lights beckoned the tourists to come in to the larger-than-life thematic casinos. Pedestrians filled the sidewalks and crosswalks. Traffic crawled and sometimes came to a standstill but it gave him time to get his fill of the lights and people. At the end of the street the bumper-to-bumper traffic thinned. Rob made a few turns, not knowing where he was in the city, and found himself in front of a building on North 15th Street. Its sign read "Fremont Villa Men's Boarding House."

# SIX

A dark skinned man in a crumpled blue suit entered the hospital room and approached the bed, his black loafers making a soft clicking noise on the tiled floor. "Miss Lewis. Excuse me. I'd like to talk to you again if I may." He took a notepad and pen from his jacket pocket.

The girl's eyes fluttered open. She tried to focus. "Who are you?"

"Detective Gene Adamson. I spoke to you yesterday after you were brought in. Remember?" He ran his hand over his dark, curly hair.

"I'm sorry," she said weakly, "I don't..." She slowly lifted her hand and touched her throbbing forehead.

"That's quite a bump you've got there."

"I think I must have hit my head. It isn't clear." Paige flexed her fingers. "My hands feel funny," she whispered.

The detective cleared his throat. "Miss Lewis, do you think I could ask you some questions about what happened?"

Paige closed her eyes. *What happened?* She attempted to raise her hand to her head again. Her arm flailed and fell heavily to her side. "My head hurts so much. I feel awful." The room spun, drawing her down into a vacuum of pain.

"Sir," a voice boomed from the doorway. A middle-aged blond man dressed in scrubs strode into the room. "May I ask what you're doing here?"

Detective Adamson offered his hand. "I'm from the Tulsa Detective Division. I'm investigating the robbery and assault on Miss Lewis. I just need to ask her a few questions."

"I'm Dr. Thomas and Miss Lewis is my patient." He reached for the detective's hand and began to guide him from the room. "I'll have to ask you to leave. She's in no shape to be answering any questions. She's had a severe shock and concussion. I'm sure she'll be able to talk to you when she's feeling better." When Detective Adamson was in the hall, the doctor released his hand. In a whisper, he added, "I have your card. You'll be notified as soon as she's able to talk."

The doctor stepped back into the room and shut the door. He approached Paige's bed, leaned toward her, and spoke softly. "Paige, can you hear me? It's Dr. Thomas."

The girl didn't open her eyes. "My head," she began.

"I know, Paige. Right now I need to look in your eyes." The doctor pulled a pen light from his shirt pocket, held her eyelids open and flashed the light into each one several times. When he had finished, he patted her shoulder. "You're going to be just fine."

He left the girl sleeping.

---

The door opened and a pink-uniformed woman entered with a tray of food.

"You awake, hon?" the woman asked. Without waiting for an answer she set the tray on the bed table and rolled it next to the bed. "Your breakfast's here." She pushed a button on the side of the bed that raised the head. "Enough?" she asked and pushed the table across the bed so Paige could reach it. "Looks like a beautiful day," she said and opened the blinds. Sunlight streamed into the room and Paige grimaced. "Too much?" The woman turned the slats upward to diffuse the light. "Enjoy your breakfast," she said and left the room.

Dizzy and nauseated, Paige pushed the food table away. It was obvious she was in the hospital although she had no memory of how she got there. Her head still ached but not as much as it had and her body was stiff and sore. With difficulty she pressed the same button the pink lady had pushed. The head of her bed lowered. She wondered why she was here and why she was in pain and why her hands didn't work the way she wanted them to.

Paige closed her eyes. Something bad had happened to her; she could feel it. But what was it? It hurt too much to think.

It seemed only a few minutes when Paige heard someone in the room. A woman in pink scrubs picked up the full food tray. "Not hungry," she said when she saw Paige looking at her. It wasn't a question that needed an answer.

The nurse carried the tray into the hall then returned. "Paige," she said and pulled away the bedcovers. "Let's get up for a little bit so we can change your bed."

As soon as she was sitting up the dizziness returned, her stomach churned and white lights blurred her vision. "I can't," Paige said.

"Okay, honey, lie down for a little while. We'll try it again later."

True to her word, she came back within the hour and this time Paige was able to sit up and even to take a few steps to a recliner where she sat while the nurse changed her bed.

She was grateful when she was allowed to lie down again and dozed until late morning when Dr. Thomas entered her hospital room.

Paige smiled at him. He had first been her brother's doctor, and when she moved to Tulsa, she, too, had gone to him for her medical care. He was more like a friend than just their physician.

He pulled a chair closer to the bed. "I'm on my way home from church, and thought I'd check on you. Do you know what day it is?"

Paige thought about it. "I don't think I do. Church? Is it Sunday? What happened to..."

"Friday and Saturday?" He finished for her. "You slept through them." Propping a foot on the chair, he opened her chart and balanced it on his knee. "You're doing much better today. Looks like you've been up."

"With help," she said, voice almost a whisper. "My feet feel strange."

"Right." He set the chart on the bedside table and removed an ophthalmoscope from his white coat pocket. "Let's see how you're doing." He held her eyelids open and shined light into them. "How's the headache?" he asked.

"Better. So much better. I remember waking up a few times with a lot of pain."

Dr. Thomas nodded. "Any nausea?" He returned the instrument to his pocket and took out another one.

Paige shook her head. "Only when I tried to sit up the first time."

The doctor rolled a pin wheel over the skin around her wrists and ankles. "Sharp or dull?" he asked. Paige's responses indicated the feeling was returning.

The doctor picked up the chart and wrote a few notes in it. "Paige, do you remember why you are here?"

"I've tried but I can't quite think—it was bad, I know that much, but..."

"You fell. Do you know why?"

Paige closed her eyes. "A man. It was a man." Tears formed. "He hurt me and left me. I don't remember."

"I'm not surprised," he answered. "It's natural to have some amnesia with a head injury."

Paige's memory was shrouded but she recalled feeling suffocated, wanting to get up, trying to turn over. "I remember hearing Pepper crying outside the door." Her voice shook. "I was helpless. It was hard to breathe. My hands and feet hurt." She touched her hand to her head. "After that it was all blackness and a blur." She looked up at the doctor through tears. "What happened to me? Do you know?"

The doctor took her hand in his. "All I know is that you fell, probably trying to get to the phone. You were wedged between a chair and a sofa and a desk, I think the police said. When they brought you here you had a concussion. We kept you for observation and to allow your brain to heal. Do you recall anything about the person who did this?"

Paige closed her eyes again. A face loomed before her and she gasped. "I remember him now. Oh, God, I was so scared." She put her hands over her face and wept.

The doctor gently touched a wrist and counted her pulse. "It's all right, Paige. It's over." He waited until his patient had quieted. "Do you want the police to catch this guy?" he asked.

"They haven't got him yet?" Fear rose in her. "What if he comes back?"

"He won't. He's gone, Paige. You're safe, but the detective is here and really needs to talk to you so they can get his description and find him. Do you feel like talking to him?"

Several seconds passed before Paige said. "I'm remembering. It was so awful." She turned her face away from him. "I'd like to forget it."

"I know. It must have been terrible, but he has to have some information to begin looking for the person who did this."

"It's a lot to ask, Dr. Thomas, but do you have time to stay with me while I talk to him?"

The doctor looked at his watch. "Sure," he said softly. "I've finished rounds and have some time. I'd be glad to be here with you."

Dr. Thomas went to the doorway and motioned for the detective to come in.

"Miss Lewis would like for me to be present while you question her." Dr. Thomas walked to the far side of the bed, crossed his arms across his chest and leaned against the window sill.

The detective greeted Paige and pulled his pad and pen from his pocket. "Let's start at the beginning, Miss Lewis."

Forty-five minutes later the detective left the room. Paige's face was beaded with perspiration. The doctor wiped it with a damp cloth. "Tough, wasn't it?" he said.

Paige began to cry. "Will I ever be the same?" she asked. "When I think about it..." She looked at the purple bruises around her wrists.

Dr. Thomas touched her arm. "Paige," he said softly. "I think you should see a psychiatrist. I'm going to set you up with one when you go home."

The girl's eyes widened. "Home? I have to leave?"

"Yes, I'm releasing you tomorrow."

"But I have no place to go." Paige pushed herself to a sitting position in the bed

The doctor crossed to the foot of the bed. He rested the chart on it and smiled. "It's all right. I spoke to your roommate a few minutes ago."

"Katy? How did you know to call her?"

"The police found your book bag and called the university. They gave them Katy's name. She called the hospital and wanted to come right then but we told her to wait until you were better. She's coming to see you later and will take you to the dorm tomorrow." He pulled the chair closer and sat down. "We got in touch with your family, too."

Paige sighed. She hadn't even thought about her brother and her parents. "Mom and Dad. They're probably worried. They're in Hawaii. It's a special trip for their anniversary."

Dr. Thomas crossed his arms, tucked the chart under one arm and nodded. "They're on their way. So are your brother and his wife."

Panic filled Paige. Where would she go when they came? "I can't go back to their house, doctor." Quick tears filled her eyes.

The physician patted her arm. "Don't worry about that now, Paige. We'll see to it your parents know and they'll make arrangements for your comfort.

Knowing her parents, she relaxed, sure they would do just that.

Dr. Thomas looked at his watch. "I have to go now. You're doing all right physically but the emotional part is going to take time. You know that, don't you?"

When Paige nodded, he said, "I'll be back tomorrow. I'll bring the psychiatrist to meet you then." He stood up. "Is there anything else I can get you?" With Paige's negative response, he left the room.

The young girl lay back on her pillow and felt the warm, salty tears beginning again. "I hate this," she thought. "And whoever you are who did this to me. I hate you, too!"

In that moment of emotional pain, Paige vowed she'd never again allow anyone to hurt her or take advantage of her as this man had done. She would survive and show him and everyone else just how strong she could be.

# SEVEN

Geraldine Harper sang "Can't you feel the love tonight?" as the hot water streamed over her curly auburn hair and ran down her shapely body. She giggled, sure Rob would be as happy as she was when she told him.

"I love you, Robbie," she called out to the tile wall. "Just wait. You're gonna be so excited." She poured shampoo into her hand and began working in the suds. "Mrs. Robert McGruder. Gerri McGruder."

She stepped out of the shower, toweled herself dry and stood naked before the mirror. She smiled at her reflection then pulled her thick auburn hair away from her face and pinned it behind her ears. She zipped open a makeup bag and placed it on the counter top.

She smiled at her happy reflection and thought, you are one lucky woman. A slight twinge of nausea stopped her. "My, my," she said aloud. "So soon." She stood still for a moment allowing the feeling to pass, then began patting liquid base to her lightly freckled face. Her expression darkened and her brow furrowed. Where are you, my sweet man?

Rob should have called her sometime during the week or over the weekend. It had been days since she last saw him. "I need you, Honey," she whispered aloud. Gerri's eyes closed as she remembered the last time the two of them had made love. Her arms ached to hold him, to feel his touch. She loved this man more than she had ever loved anyone.

All day Sunday she'd expected him to appear at her door. He had no phone and would show up when he wanted to see her and she always welcomed him. About ten o'clock that night, knowing he wasn't coming, she'd gotten into her Chevy and driven to his apartment. She found no lights on and no sign of his Toyota.

*If I didn't have to go to work today, I'd come find you. You'll call. I know you will. You'll call when you can.*

An hour later, Gerri hurried through the door of Corbin's Travel Agency, waved to the other agent seated at a desk across the room. She slid into the chair at her own desk and picked up her headset. The door behind her opened, a man leaned around it and called to her, "Gerri, can you come in here for a minute?"

She had no idea what Bill Corbin wanted, but, at this moment, she could only think of the baby she and Rob had made and of her concern over his whereabouts.

"Sit down, please." Bill's seriousness alarmed her. "Have you seen the paper?" She shook her head. "You need to hear this. It concerns one of our clients." He picked up a newspaper and read, " 'When Lillian Carter, housekeeper for Brad and Ashley Lewis, went to her job on Friday morning, she discovered Mr. Lewis' sister, Paige Lewis, bound with duct tape and unconscious on the floor of the den.'"

Ashley Lewis was my client, she thought. Her husband's the one with the coins. A nausea that wasn't morning sickness rolled in her stomach. Bill continued to read.

" 'Miss Lewis was unconscious. It appeared she had fallen and hit her head in an attempt to reach a phone. Police investigating the scene reported an intruder had broken into the house on Thursday evening and stolen various items. He then bound Miss Lewis and left her. Mr. and Mrs. Lewis are out of the country and not expected to return for three weeks. "If it hadn't been for the housekeeper, Miss Lewis would have died," police investigators said. Because of the woman's injuries the police weren't able to get a description of the intruder until Sunday. The man is in his early twenties, had long blond hair, a mustache and facial hair and was wearing blue jeans, a white tee shirt and a light tan jacket bearing the insignia of an eagle on the pocket.' "

*Eagle on the pocket.* The room whirled, blackness closed in. Gerri reeled in her chair and didn't hear Bill Corbin call her name. Nor did she feel him catch her before she hit the floor.

It is said to be darkest before the dawn but Gerri Harper had seen no dawn. With a baby growing inside her, and the man she loved gone from her life, she sank into despair.

"Gerri. Gerri." A hand touched her arm. Startled, she looked into the concerned eyes of her fellow employee and friend, Lynn Abbott. "Honey, you're a million miles away. Have been all week. What's going on?"

Gerri shook her head, took off her headset and stood up. "I need to go home."

"Why don't you come home with me?" Lynn asked. "I'll fix us something to eat and maybe we can talk. Okay?" Too weak to argue, Gerri nodded.

Lynn guided the red-haired woman into her car after assuring her she'd bring her back later to pick up her Chevy and then drove the few miles to her apartment. Gerri said little on the way and sat in silence in her friend's living room while Lynn prepared their food.

"It isn't much," Lynn apologized. "Just a sandwich. That's all I have here."

"Doesn't matter," Gerri mumbled. "I can't eat."

Lynn put the plate on the coffee table. "Tell me, Gerri, what's happened?"

Gerri sobbed then rushed into the bathroom and vomited. Lynn followed her, rinsed a washrag in cold water and handed it to her friend.

After the retching subsided Gerri sat on the floor. "I can't do this," the red-haired woman cried, her face in her hands. "I can't."

Lynn knelt on the tile floor beside her. "Are you sick?"

Gerri shook her head and held the washcloth to her forehead. "I'm pregnant and Rob's gone. He won't be coming back. What am I going to do?" Gerri rested her head against the wall and closed her eyes, tears streaming down her cheeks.

"Oh, my," was all Lynn could say as she watched her friend weep.

They sat together for a long time, Gerri crying and Lynn comforting her.

Gerri's tears slowed and she sighed. "What am I going to do?"

"You have some choices, you know." Lynn moved to sit on the side of the tub.

Gerri looked into her friend's eyes. "I know. I've been thinking about it. Should I have the baby and allow someone to adopt it or should I keep it myself and try to raise it alone?"

"There is another option," Lynn said.

Gerri shook her head. "Not for me. I couldn't do that."

Lynn took her hands. "I promise you this. Whatever you decide, I'm with you. I'll be here for you all the way."

Gerri was grateful for her friend's support, but, in her heart, she knew the ultimate decision was hers alone and whatever she decided would change her life forever.

# EIGHT

As soon as Leroy pulled out of the driveway on Monday morning Myrna turned on the television. She flipped from one local channel to another and stopped when she saw a newswoman standing in front of a large house. The woman spoke into a hand-held microphone.

"We're in front of a home in south Tulsa where a young woman was left last Thursday night by an intruder who broke into the house and stole valuables. Then he taped the woman's hands and feet and left her. The young woman, Paige Lewis, a student at Tulsa University, was house sitting for her brother, Brad Lewis, and his wife. They were not supposed to return for three weeks. If the house keeper, Mrs. Lillian Carter, who came every Friday morning, had not found her, this story would have a very different ending. Police tell us the young woman was only able to speak to detectives yesterday because of her injuries. She described the man as in his early twenties with long, bushy blond hair."

Myrna gasped.

The newsperson looked at a paper in her hand. "Miss Lewis is cooperating with police and when we have a composite drawing, we'll show it to you. When last seen the man was wearing blue jeans, a white tee shirt and a tan jacket with the insignia of an eagle on the pocket. If anyone has seen this man, please call your local police or Crime stoppers. He's believed to be armed....."

Myrna switched off the television and carefully replaced the channel changer on the table beside her husband's recliner.

When Rob had returned the van on Friday, he'd left without a word to her. She recalled her shock when Leroy had burst into the bedroom where she was making the bed.

"He's *your* worthless brother!" her husband yelled, pushing her against the wall.

"What?" Myrna asked, confused. "What did he do?"

"He didn't say a word. Just threw the keys at me and dug out." Leroy gave her another push. "He's up to no good. I know it. He's done something and you better find out what!" With those words he'd given her a final shove and left her, mind reeling, in the bedroom.

And now she knew Rob had done something bad. All weekend she'd feared Leroy would find out what it was. Tears ran down her cheeks. It's beginning again, she thought. I don't know how much more of this I can take. She wiped at the tears with her fingers and reached for the telephone beside Leroy's chair. She knew the number by heart although she'd never called it. She punched in the digits and held her breath as the phone rang on the other end. Voice mail answered her call. She hesitated then left a short message. "Mr. Castleberry, this is Rob McGruder sister, Myrna Watson. I think my brother has left town. Would you mind checking his apartment and calling me back?" She left her number, although she knew he had it as Rob's next of kin. She put her head in her hands and began to sob. "Rob. Rob. Why have you done this to me again?"

A few hours later Myrna answered the phone on the second ring. Her heart stilled when Rob's landlord identified himself.

"Mrs. Watson, I think you're right. No one's in the apartment, and I haven't seen Rob's car since last Thursday. It doesn't look like he took much. There's still clothing and linens." He paused. When Myrna didn't respond, he continued, "What would you like for me to do with them?"

"I—I-- don't know," she stammered, trying to focus. Now she knew he was gone, that he was in trouble again. "I guess, if he doesn't come back, just …." Anger fomented in her stomach. Her voice rose. "Just throw them out. I don't want them and I guess he doesn't either." Before the landlord could respond, she added. "Does he owe you any money?"

"No, he's paid up until the end of the month. He does have a security deposit coming. What do you want me to do with that?"

"Keep it," she said. "Thanks for calling." She pressed the "off" button and slammed the phone onto its cradle.

"How could you do this?" She cried aloud to the empty room. "What kind of a monster are you? Do you have any idea what kind of trouble you're in, and how much trouble I'll be in when Leroy hears this?" She could only pray her husband would never find out.

# NINE

## TWO WEEKS LATER, LAS VEGAS, NEVADA

"Hey, Roberto. Mi amigo!" A dark haired man hailed Rob from the stairs. "Wait up."

Rob paused at the door of his room. The man trotted up the steps, his muscular legs taking them two at a time. "I tried to catch you at breakfast. I got a job for you."

"A job? What doing, Rico?" Rob looked down at the man who stood a foot shorter than him.

"With me, man." Rico gave him a playful jab on his left bicep. "Doin' construction." His wide smile revealed straight white teeth.

"I'm no carpenter. You know that."

Rico's coffee colored eyes twinkled. "You know and I know but John Henry don't know. Besides, you're a smart man. You can learn. You need a job, don't you?"

Rob nodded.

Rico started for the stairs. "Come on, man. The van's leavin' pronto."

"Wait," Rob called after him. "What do I need to take?"

"Nothin' but ID, and I know you got that." With a wink, the brown-skinned man paused at the top of the steps. "And I even know where you got it."

Rob hesitated, surprised by Rico's statement, then he patted his back pocket to be sure he had his wallet and descended the stairs behind Rico Calderon.

A quarter hour later seven men climbed into a Ford Excursion and drove away from the boarding house. Heavy traffic slowed the vehicle going south on the freeway giving the two men time to talk about what Rob could expect when they reached the site. An hour later, the SUV passed through a tall wire fence and parked near dozens of other vans and trucks.

When the men climbed from the vehicle, Rob smelled the exhaust fumes he saw billowing from the noisy engines of huge yellow machines on the site. Beeping sounds could be heard all around him as the equipment moved. Amazed by the massive steel girders rising from a deep pit in the desert floor he asked, "What's this going to be?"

"Another casino."

"Way out here?" Unfinished stucco houses and wide roadways rose from the flat desert surrounding them.

"Sure, man. They're all over the place. You don't have to be on the Strip to gamble. They bring it to you." Rico turned and gestured for Rob to follow him.

The two men approached a man with a cell phone at his ear. As they neared, he closed the phone and straightened the Dallas Cowboys baseball cap he wore. His muscles rippled under the sleeves of a white tee shirt. Rob estimated this man was in his thirties and was surprised when Rico introduced him as the foreman.

"This is John Henry Taylor. He's the boss." He motioned to Rob and said, "This is the guy I told you about, John Henry. Rob Martin. He just moved in the boarding house. A crack-jack worker."

The man stood almost three inches taller than Rob. The two shook hands and Rob felt the foreman's blue-gray eyes studying him then relaxed when the man smiled. "Just call me John. We can use a good man." He turned to Rico. "Take him to Dan and get him signed up, then show him around." The cell phone in his hand rang. He rolled his eyes. "Technology," he said and called over his shoulder as he walked away, "Talk to you later."

Rob followed Rico across the site to a nearby trailer. It had been so easy.

The day went quickly for Rob and he found he liked working outside. Since his arrival in Las Vegas he had walked the streets near the Strip taking in the sights and the people, trying to decide what to do with his life. The rows and rows of noisy machines in the casinos fascinated him. Old and young, men and women, sitting for hours pushing buttons and pulling levers. Rob held on to his money. He had no desire to throw it away gambling after what he had risked to get it.

He'd briefly considered looking for work in one of the hotels, but he couldn't imagine being inside all the time, never knowing whether it was night or day, smelling the smoke, hearing the jangling of the slot machines. He wanted the freedom of seeing the sky, of breathing fresh air. Those years in a cell with three smokers had been almost more than he could stand. With this new job came the freedom he craved. It paid good money, he liked what they had him doing, and all the guys he met were friendly. Yes, this just might be the new life he'd been looking for.

Around six o'clock the Excursion deposited the seven men in front of the Fremont Villa. Most headed for a nearby bar and grill.

"I'm hungry." Rico stretched and scratched his flat belly. "How does some good chorizo and Chile rellenos sound to you?"

Rob laughed. "I'm not sure what that is, but I like Taco Hut."

"Gringo food." Rico frowned. "Stick with me and I'll teach you how to eat the real thing. Mama Serena has been cooking many years for her ten children and fifteen grandchildren. She'll be happy to feed two more muchachos." He hitched up his jeans. "Follow me."

"I've been doing that all day." Rob liked this man.

The two of them headed in the opposite direction of the bar and grill. They walked a few blocks then turned a corner into a shabby neighborhood. Several dusky-skinned youths watched them from in front of a boarded up building. Rob's steps slowed. Rico noticed and grinned. "It's all right, man. You're safe with Rico. These are mi compadres."

Rob realized these men weren't the gangs he'd tried to avoid in prison and was ashamed of his discomfort. He knew Rico had seen it but couldn't tell his new friend why his sudden hesitation.

A few blocks later the two men stopped before a small adobe home. A chile reistra hung on one end of the narrow porch. Rico rapped on the blue door and called out, "Mama Serena, donde esta? Su favoito aqui."

Hurried footsteps, the door swung open and a Latino woman's chubby arms embraced Rico. "Mi favorito! She exclaimed. Seeing the man with him, she switched to English. "You're in time for some posole and frijoles."

Rico returned her hug and turned her toward Rob. "Mi amigo, Roberto, Mama Serena. I brought him to eat some of your delicious food."

The woman's warm smile welcomed Rob. A yellow blouse and full, flowered skirt flowed over her ample body. Loose dark hair framed her round face.

Serena's wide smile welcomed Rob. "I'm happy you came. Rico's friends find a home with the Aragons. Come." She led them across the immaculate living room. "The food is on the table. No one here except Carlos and me tonight."

In the kitchen the man called Carlos sat on one side of a long wooden table. Wrinkled, leathery skin covered his thin body. A halo of lustrous silver hair crowned his head. In contrast his wife's dark eyes and smooth brown skin made her appear much younger than her husband.

Carlos rose unsteadily and shook Rob's hand his smile lighting up his deep brown eyes. Rico circled the table and gently hugged the man. Serena set two plates across from the guests and served them from aromatic dishes simmering on the stove.

Rico had been right. The food was new to Rob but he ate the pork and hominy dish and refried beans like a famished man until he felt he could hold no more.

"Magnifico, Mama." Rico kissed his fingertips and tossed an imaginary kiss across the table. Serena pretended to catch it and planted it on her lips.

The gesture brought his own mother to Rob's mind. To be able to throw her a kiss as Rico had done and have her return it in such a loving manner. What he wouldn't give to be able to experience that kind of relationship with her today.

"Eh, Roberto?" Rico snapped his fingers across the table.

Startled, Rob looked around. All eyes were on him. "I'm sorry. Did I miss something?"

"Si." Rico winked at Serena. "I asked you what you thought of Mama's dinner. You didn't like?"

Rob's face reddened. "Oh, no. I liked it." He pointed to his empty plate and bowl. "I liked it a lot."

The two Hispanic men laughed. Serena patted Rob's arm. "Stop it, Rico. You're being mean to my new friend." She looked at Rob, her hand still on his arm. "You were in thought, yes?"

Her eyes held Rob's. "Yes." He paused. "I was thinking of my mother. I haven't had a meal with a family in years and ... " His voice faltered. He cleared his throat.

Serena pressed his arm, her touch warm and gentle. "I understand, Roberto. Your mother. She's not with us?"

Rob shook his head.

"How long?" Her eyes moistened in sympathy.

A long moment passed before Rob could speak. "Thirteen years. She died when I was twelve."

After leaving the Aragon's home, the two men walked in silence for a few blocks before Rico spoke. "I'm sorry about your mama."

Rob nodded emotion still near the surface.

"I, too, miss Mamacita."

It hadn't occurred to Rob to ask about Rico's family, his life. They'd only known each other a week, and become close friends after this one day. Rob shivered in the fall air and wished he'd worn a jacket. "Where is she, Rico? Does she live in Vegas?"

"Oh, no. She's in Hermosillo."

Rob glanced at Rico. "Where? I've never heard of that."

Rico chuckled. "I guess not. It's in Sonora, below Arizona and Nogales. In Mexico." When Rob didn't respond, Rico added, "You don't know much about my country, do you?"

Rob shook his head. "I quit school when I was sixteen. Didn't do well when I was in it." He crossed his arms in an attempt at warmth. "How did you get here?"

"*Ay*, a long story." Rico looked up at Rob, a question in his eyes. "You want me to tell?"

Rob nodded.

The men stopped to allow cars to pass before crossing the street. Rico took in a deep breath. "My family is large. Seven brothers and six sisters. Two of my brothers are no longer with us. Moises and Diego."

"No longer..." Rob began, and then remembered the way Mama Serena had spoken of his mother's death.

Rico continued, lost in his own thoughts. "We all wanted more for our family. I am the oldest, named after my father, my grandfather and his father. Federico Eliseo Secundino Calderon."

"That's a lot of names for a kid." Uncomfortable with his friend's melancholy, Rob tried to lighten the mood.

Rico smiled up at him. "Si. That's why I'm Rico, the rich one. My papa had hopes for his first born."

Rob laughed.

Rico's smile faded and he looked away. He heaved a sigh. "Ay, Papasito. He loved his children. Never got to see the youngest girl born, Adora. He got very sick--the pneumonia and--died."

"How old were you, Rico?" Rob felt a new bond with his friend, having lost both of his own parents.

"Fifteen. I, too, had to stop my schooling and help Mama support our family. My brother, Raul, and I worked at many jobs. My oldest sister, Estrella, worked as a maid for a wealthy family in Hermosillo. She was thirteen. Very difficult. For all of us, but most of all for Mamacita." Rico stopped and turned to Rob. "Roberto, I had to leave my home as you did to come here to make a better living for myself and my family."

Rob didn't know how Rico could know so much about him when he hadn't told anyone about his own life. He turned the conversation away from himself. "Are they all still in Mexico?"

"Si, all but Diego and Moises," Rico answered, a faraway look shrouded his eyes.

He began walking faster. "It's cold. Vamonos."

Inside the front hallway of the boarding house, the smell of freshly brewed coffee filled the air. Rico started up the stairs, but Rob took his arm. "The rest of the story, my friend. Let's have some coffee. I want to know about your family."

Rico hesitated and smiled, not his usual wide grin, but with warmth. He followed Rob into the dining room. They found a table away from four men playing dominoes.

"How did you get here, Rico? Why did you come?" Rob asked.

"Mama wanted her boys to stay at home, but she knew we could make money in America. Raul and I applied for a green card so we could come here and work. It took a long time, but we waited. I was twenty years old and Raul, nineteen. Finally I came here. Raul is in Phoenix." He paused and sighed. "We waited and waited. Moises and Diego didn't want to wait. They were young, fifteen and thirteen. They found some people who said they could bring them across the border. We tried to talk them out of it, but they ran away in the night."

When Rico said no more, Rob gently prodded him. "What happened to them?"

Rico studied his empty coffee mug. "They were found in the back of a truck dead--with many other people. There was no air."

Shocked into silence, Rob pictured the scene in his mind and shuddered.

"Si. Que mala suerte. Muy triste." Rico slipped into his native tongue, and then added English, "Bad luck. Very sad."

He raised his eyes and looked into Rob's. "Rico learned a hard lesson when my brothers left us." He pointed his finger at his friend. "Never take the easy way out. It is never easy. It is always hard, and it gives pain to someone."

Rico's words, like an arrow, struck Rob's heart.

# TEN

As Tulsa receded into the background, Rob's life in Las Vegas became the norm. A year went by and Rico and Rob moved out of the boarding house. They shared a two bedroom apartment farther from the middle of the Strip. Rob traded in his old Toyota and bought a used Dodge truck. They drove to work together every day and had dinner with the Aragons two or three times a month. He looked on Mama Serena and Papa Carlos as his adoptive parents and they treated him like one of their children. He was at peace. For the first time in years, Rob was truly a happy man.

John Taylor came to Rob and Rico after work a few weeks after their move and offered both men the opportunity to take classes at a local technical school to become welder's assistants. Rob jumped at the chance. Rico's reason for taking the offer was the money.

"Ay carrumba!" he said. "Muchos pesos para mi familia." He rubbed his fingers and thumb together, his dark eyes twinkling and teased, "When I return to Mexico, Rico will be wealthy. And we change your name to Rico, too. We both be rich. Si?" Rob had laughed with him. Then, more seriously, the Hispanic man added, "Some day I will go back to my country and I will be able to help my people."

Rob hated the day his friend would leave, but in his heart, he knew that day would come. Rico loved his country, loved his family and was only in Nevada to help them. He would go back and Rob knew he would miss this man who had become the brother he never had.

John Taylor mentored both men and soon they became the promised welder's assistants. He encouraged them to join the Union and, when they did, he promoted both of them to chief welders.

And one day Rob told Rico about his past. They'd been out with guys from the job doing a little drinking and gambling. Rob felt particularly close to his friend and that night when they came back to their apartment, he told Rico about his life, about prison, and finally, about Paige Lewis and the robbery.

Rico just shook his head. "I know you are not Rob Martin and you have much to hide. When we meet, I know."

"How did you know, Rico? How did I give it away?"

"The sadness in your eyes. Such sadness, like a scared …" he searched for the word. "Conejo," he said and made a gesture of long ears.

"A rabbit?" Rob asked. "I was like a scared rabbit?"

"Si, scared. Sad. Roberto needed a friend." Rico shook his friend's shoulder. "And Rico came. Rico will be his friend."

Rob shook his head. "You are an unusual man, my friend. Most men would have run away from me. In fact, you were the only one who spoke to me that first week at the Freemont."

"A man does not run from sadness. Only a boy runs away. A man stays and becomes a friend."

Rico was his friend. Of that he was sure but Rob had to ask. "So, Rico, now that you know, do you think you should turn me in?"

Rico paused a long time before answering. Rob was used to this because his friend never answered quickly if it was a question that needed pondering. "I do not say what you did was a good thing, but Rico cannot decide for you." His dark eyes were somber, the same look he had when he spoke of his brothers' deaths. "Some day you will have to say what you did. It will be what you decide."

Rob couldn't imagine ever telling what he did to anyone else and hoped that time never came. He just wanted to stay here in Las Vegas and live out his new life in peace and never have to think about the criminal he'd been before he came to this town.

---

Two years passed, good years where the two men worked and spent time together. Many times during the first year Rob wanted to call Myrna, had even tried once but Leroy answered. In his heart he knew it was guilt that kept him from trying again. He had left so quickly without saying good bye, and it wasn't the first time he'd done it to her. He told himself she was all right but it didn't free him from the guilt he felt when he thought of her.

Then came the day he dreaded. Rico received word his mother was ill and he went back to Mexico to take care of her and his family. Rob drove his friend to the airport where he would fly to Tucson, meet his brother and from there the two of them would take a bus into Mexico.

"Is there some way I can call you?" Rob asked as they unloaded the one bag Rico carried.

"No telefono," he answered. "But, I will call when I can. There are phones in the town. I will call."

"Call me collect, if you have to," Rob said. "I don't want to lose track of you." The two men shook hands. "Do you think you will ever come back?"

Rico shook his head. "No se, mi amigo. I do not know."

He was gone leaving Rob with the familiar emptiness he had experienced many times before in his life and with each time, the pain intensified.

Rob remained friends with Mama and Papa Aragon, but it wasn't the same without Rico. They understood his loneliness and insisted he come for dinner every week. It filled a void but he missed Rico more than he thought he would. He and John Taylor began meeting once a week for a beer after work. Rob liked the man who had mentored him and gave him credit for setting him on a career path that fit his skills. Without John's help, he would never have discovered what he enjoyed doing, and he enjoyed welding. It was satisfying to be able to put scraps of metal together and see the finished product, something that could withstand thousands of pounds of weight and force. He finally believed he was giving to the world instead of taking from it.

In July, the summer after Rico left, John invited Rob to join his family and some friends at his home for an Independence Day cook out. He was nervous about being with people he didn't know but he went. At the last minute he remembered something his mother had taught him. He could hear her soft voice instructing him, "When you go to someone's house to dinner, always take a gift for the hostess." He stopped on the way and bought a bouquet of flowers.

Shanna Taylor met him at the door. She had a baby on her hip and introduced her as Gracie Lea, their year-old daughter. John had shown him pictures of the girl and Rob was taken with her hazel eyes and raven curls. "She's a beauty," he told Shanna.

"And a handful," John's wife had responded. Shanna had her chestnut colored hair pulled into a pony tail. Over her bathing suit she wore a purple cover-up. Rob wanted to say she, too, was a beauty but decided that wouldn't be good manners since it was the first time he had ever met her. He gave her the flowers and she "oohed" over them, thanked him and then led him through the house to a covered patio in the back yard. Four couples milled around a pool where several children swam.

John shook his hand and introduced him to the others. Rob immediately felt at ease and fell into conversation with the men. The afternoon was hot but mist sprayers on the patio made it bearable. Rob hadn't brought a swim suit, didn't own one, but none of the other men swam either.

Rob loved being there. He loved the family atmosphere and conversation. This is my kind of life, he thought. This is the way I want to live.

A dripping boy padded up to the men and Rob knew immediately this was John's son. Tall for an eight-year-old, thin with a thatch of blond hair, he was a carbon copy of his father.

"Hey, Buddy, what do you need?" John asked.

The boy leaned in close to his dad and spoke a few words Rob couldn't hear. John shook his head and said, "Not this time. Maybe when there aren't so many people here." Then he turned to Rob. "Have you met our son, Bobby?"

The boy faced Rob and said quickly, politely, "Bob. My name is Bob."

John grinned. "Right. Sorry about that. We're trying to remember. He wants to be called Bob."

Rob extended his hand and the boy shook it. "You know, Bob, my mother always called me Bobby when I was young." From where he sat he could look right into the boy's eyes. "She would have called me anything I asked her to." He motioned toward John. "Just like your dad is doing."

"Sometimes they forget," Bob said. "Did you want your mom to call you Bobby?"

"I guess I didn't care if she called me Bobby, but..." he paused, remembering. If his father heard her, Mac McGruder would rail, "Bobby

65

Mac. The kid's name is Robert. Call him that, not that sissy name Bobby." His father's voice would change into a high-pitched falsetto when he'd say "Bobby." It was Rob who would feel ashamed, for himself, as well as for his mother.

He shook away the images. "But my dad didn't call me Bobby. He thought I should be called by my given name, Robert."

"That's my real name, too, but I don't really like it. I like Bob."

"Well, I'm sure your parents will call you whatever you want. Just give them some slack because grown-ups can forget." Rob reached out and smoothed Bob's wet hair. He realized it was a fatherly gesture and wondered at the boy's calm response.

Another boy joined them and Rob's gaze followed the two back to the pool. When he turned to the men at the table, he found John watching him.

"You've never said much about yourself, Rob. Do you have any children?"

Rob shook his head. "No, I've never been married."

"Well, some men haven't been married and still have children."

Rob agreed. "True, but not me. No kids."

John tossed his empty bottle into a trash container near the table. "You should. You'd be great with a son."

Rob's heart filled. A son. What would it be like to have a son of his own? Maybe some day it would happen to him.

---

Two more years passed. It had been five years since he had been to Tulsa, since he had seen his sister, but the time had not dulled the knowledge of the robbery. Many nights he awoke with a start, the girl's face before him, accusing him. Always in the background of his dream were the sirens, sirens coming to get him. On those nights he especially wished he could talk to Rico, but the calls from his friend had been few. Rob wished Rico would be able to return to Las Vegas but knew it would never happen. His mother had died and Rico felt he had to stay and take care of his brothers and sisters. Rob was saddened but Rico, ever the optimist, had encouraged his friend, "It is where Rico belongs," he told him. "Some day you will find where you belong, too."

But Rob believed he was where he belonged, right here in Las Vegas and that's where he planned to stay the rest of his life until a telephone call changed everything.

# ELEVEN

The silver aircraft taxiing to gate 23 sparkled in the blinding July sun. That's my flight, Rob thought. Do I really want to take it?

His right hand brushed across short-cropped hair, once the color of wet sand now almost bleached white from the relentless desert sun. With his left hand he absently fingered the gold stud in his ear lobe. Acutely aware of the contrast between his present appearance and the way he looked five years ago, he wondered if he had changed enough to be unrecognizable to those who knew him in Tulsa. He pulled an airline folder from the hip pocket of his chinos and read the name on the ticket: Robert Martin.

Robert McGruder, a.k.a. Rob Martin, was on his way back to Oklahoma.

Once a thin man, he now had muscles that bulged beneath a light blue cotton shirt as he leaned over to unzip the canvas bag at his feet. With one hand he put the boarding pass in his hip pocket and with the other stuffed the return ticket into the carry-on. His hand lingered on the soft material of his new bag. It was a nice one, expensive, better than anything he'd ever had. Five years ago he'd arrived in Las Vegas with all he owned in a plastic Target sack. His thoughts returned to the last five years and how much his life had changed.

The most important change was his friendship with Rico Calderon. Through his friend, he'd been included in a real family, the Aragons, been to their home and met most of their children and grandchildren at one time or another. The words Rico spoke to him the first night they'd gone out together made a deep impression on him.

"Never take the easy way out. It is never easy. It is always hard, and it gives pain to someone."

From the time he first heard those words they had continued to echo in his heart.

The call for flight 1032 interrupted Rob's reverie. He shouldered the new bag and moved with the crowd toward the jet way.

Rob fastened his seat belt and looked out the small window as the aircraft pushed off. I don't want to leave Vegas, he thought. Tulsa held nothing for him but he would do what he could for Myrna then he would come back home.

The flight attendant came through the cabin taking drink orders and Rob ordered an orange juice then settled back into his seat. The day was clear with no clouds to shade the desert from the blazing sun. He watched the Arizona landscape pass below the aircraft and marveled at the Grand Canyon, remembering how close he'd come to it five years before.

He pictured his sister's delicate face. Until two days ago she hadn't known where he was. Those eyes that had held such sadness since she'd been forced to give up her only child were probably sadder still with the loss of her brother.

Rob shifted in the cramped seat and attempted to stretch his long legs. For a week he'd been thinking about his sister more than usual. Finally, three days ago, he took a chance and placed the call. It was late in Tulsa but she said she hadn't been asleep. She told him she had just gotten home from the hospital. He remembered the sound of her voice when she asked if it was really him. Monotone, robotic, not like the old Myrna. "Rob, Leroy's been in an accident. He may die. I wish you were here."

Without hesitation he answered. "I'll be there." He had no problem arranging to leave his job for a short time because he'd taken very little time off in the time he'd worked for John.

Today, five years later, here he was, flying for the first time in his life and on his way back to Tulsa. What lay ahead for him wasn't clear.

---

Myrna was waiting outside security. He could tell she didn't recognize him. She looked smaller and thinner than he remembered. Her eyes were bloodshot, the skin around them dark and sunken. He said her name and her eyes widened.

"Rob?" She cocked her head to one side and stared at him.

He put his arms around her but she didn't return his hug.

"You look different. Where have you been?"

Expecting the question but puzzled at by her lack of response, he asked, "Is there somewhere around here we can sit and talk?"

She nodded and directed him to the airport café where they got mugs of coffee and sat at a table. Dismayed by her appearance he studied his almost unrecognizable sister. Her hollow eyes once a deep sky blue were now the color of faded denim and her oily brown hair hung in uncombed strings around her face. A lump of fear rose in his throat.

"I'm sorry, Sis. I should have called sooner."

She nodded.

Rob searched for words. He needed to say more, to make it up to her in some way. He began to tell her about Las Vegas, his job, his new career.

Myrna simply listened, her untouched coffee growing cold.

Confused by her demeanor and silence after he finished talking, he asked about Leroy.

Voice emotionless, she related the facts. "He was coming from a job in Sand Springs. Traffic was slow. A semi was stopped in front of him. Another car--a big car came from behind and pushed his van into the rear of the truck." She took a shallow breath. "He has a head injury, his neck is broken and he's in Intensive Care and probably won't live."

Rob reached across the table and took her hand. Her bones felt as delicate as a bird's, and her skin's coldness startled him. "Sis, I'm so sorry."

Her hand remained limp. "Don't be. It's hard, but I'll get through it." Without looking at him she said through gritted teeth, "I've gotten through everything else in my life."

Her words struck like a slap in Rob's face, and he instinctively recoiled. Myrna's eyes met his, and he had to look away.

They sat in silence for a few moments, Rob groping for something to say. There was one question uppermost in his mind, and although it probably wasn't the time to ask it, he had to know. "Has anyone been looking for me?"

His sister shook her head and her eyes narrowed into slits. A faint, mirthless smile touched her lips. "You did something wrong, didn't you?"

Rob considered telling her the truth. Taking a deep breath, he answered, "I did do something, but I can't tell you. I think it's all right since no one has ever asked you about me. There's just one thing. I have a different name now. I'm Robert Martin. Can you handle that?"

Myrna emitted a short "ha" and looked away. "I've handled more than that in my life."

She'd been left before, too many times, and she would be abandoned again if Leroy died, and he went back to Las Vegas. In that moment he feared his life was changing again, and this time he had no control over the direction it would take.

# TWELVE

From a window in the third floor counseling office of St. Elizabeth's hospital, Paige Lewis watched traffic move at a snail's pace along Yale Avenue. The psychologist pulled back the sleeve of her black and white stripped blouse and checked the time on her watch. She had an appointment in ten minutes with Myrna Watson, a woman whom she had counseled every afternoon since Leroy Watson was admitted to ICU. Today's visit was different. According to Myrna, she would have her brother with her, the brother she hadn't seen in five years. She didn't tell Paige why they hadn't seen each other, only that he was coming now when she needed him. Paige believed Leroy would probably die, and if he didn't, he faced a long recovery. His wife was definitely going to need someone.

Paige unfastened the gold clip that held her dark hair, smoothed the curls that had escaped around her face and refastened the clip at the base of her neck. Smoothing her palms around the waistband of white summer slacks and re-tucking the blouse where it had loosened in the back, she turned from the window, retrieved a black blazer from a brass coat tree and slipped it on. Anchored on the jacket's breast pocket was a name badge identifying the wearer as a Patient Counselor.

The slim woman glanced around the room and appraised the furniture she had selected. She brushed her hand over the back of one of the mauve chairs that blended with the muted floral of the sofa. After straightening a vase of flowers on the low coffee table, she picked up a stack of papers and moved it to a small desk sitting almost unnoticed in the back corner of the room.

If she'd had her way in the beginning, she would have chosen bright colors that spoke of joy instead of sadness, but the hospital administration wanted those who faced death to see this room as a peaceful haven. They had been right. There was very little joy in what she had seen in this room over the last two years

Two years. Wonderful fulfilling years. It amazed her to realize the good that had come from a harrowing experience. She still keenly remembered the robbery five years ago, the man, and the way he'd left her to die. She would never forget the terror that had gripped her.

Paige returned to the window.

For months after that experience she had been afraid the man would come back.

Frightened of the darkness, vulnerable and mistrusting of situations and strangers, she found out first hand what violence and trauma, even the threat of death can do to a person. She frowned, remembering the dream that had plagued her since the experience. The Xanax helped and the nightmare came less and less. As much as she didn't want to take the drug, she realized its benefit in her life.

Immediately after the experience the features of the man were vivid in her mind, but the years had faded the memory, and as she became more and more engrossed in her career, the less she wanted to remember that time in her life. Periodically, at odd moments during the day, in the early waking hours of the morning or in her dreams, the man's gray eyes were before her. Most times they were menacing. Sometimes they were filled with despair. But she was no longer afraid of them. Over the years her imagination had misled her a few times into thinking some gray-eyed, blond bushy-haired man she'd seen somewhere was "the one." That, too, had ceased and she resigned herself to the knowledge that she would probably never know who was responsible.

Paige recalled how much she had wanted to graduate with her class but the experience stole a full year from her life. Her parents had cut their Hawaiian trip short, and knowing she didn't want to return to her brother's house, had immediately rented a condominium near the hospital. The three of them lived there until Paige was able to return to classes, and then they returned to Atlanta, sold their home and moved to Tulsa to be near their children and live out their retirement. She felt her parents had given up so much for her. Brad and Ashley had, too. They came back from England, put their house on the market and moved out of the neighborhood. No one wanted to keep any ties with the terrible thing that had happened in their family. She recalled how proud all of them were when she graduated with a degree in psychology. She'd stayed in that condo and liked living there because it was filled with memories of the love she'd received from her parents during her recovery.

After a year of doing clinicals in Tulsa, she landed her dream job.

Paige smiled. She turned and surveyed the room. As terrible as the experience had been, from it had come the passion of her life; to help others face death, just as she had, and to survive it.

A light tapping brought the psychologist to the door. Standing on the other side was Myrna and a tall, blond, good-looking man in a blue Polo shirt and khaki trousers. Before she could invite them in, she noticed the man flinch. He drew in a breath and his face flushed.

Myrna broke into the moment by announcing, "Paige, I want you to meet my brother, Rob...Martin."

# THIRTEEN

*The girl!*

Cold fear struck Rob like an icy wind blowing down his collar. Instinctively his hand went to the back of his neck to rub away the chill.

The woman was smiling. His sister's mouth moved. Blood pounded in Rob's ears blocking out all sound. What were they saying?

In his silence he was aware of the woman's smile fading slightly, of her confused expression, then, finally, his hearing returned.

"Mr. Martin."

Rob saw her hand extended toward him and remembered the last time he had touched her. Taking her hand in his, he was acutely aware of her smallness and her smooth, soft skin. At the same time he caught her delicate fragrance.

Shame reddened his face. *How could I have done that to her?* The cold fingers of fear and guilt crawled up the back of his neck. In that moment Rob was transported back in time to the despicable felon he had been. The man he hated and had tried to forget. He thought that man had ceased to exist-- until today.

"I'm happy you can be here with your sister." Paige's voice was kind. "May I call you Rob?"

At his nod, she continued. "Please call me Paige." She gestured and stepped back into the room. "Come, sit down. We'll talk awhile before we see Leroy."

*See Leroy? No way am I going to see him. When he sees me, he'll give me away.*

Rob attempted to calm himself. He noticed nothing in the girl's demeanor that revealed she suspected him of being anyone other than Myrna's brother. For the next few minutes the two women talked. Rob's thoughts swirled keeping him from being able to concentrate on the conversation. His mind was on Paige and any sign of recognition on her part.

"Has Myrna explained Leroy's condition to you, Rob?"

He couldn't find his voice and shook his head.

"It's a wonder he survived the crash at all," she faced the sofa where he and his sister sat. "He has multiple internal injuries. His neck's broken in three places and he has severe chest trauma. The doctor had to do a tracheotomy in the emergency room to facilitate breathing and to suction out his lungs."

Rob looked at his sister who sat passively at his side.

Paige continued. "The doctor attached tongs to his skull to stabilize his neck. So far he hasn't been stable enough for any surgery."

"He can't talk, Rob." Myrna said not looking at him. "They have a …." She searched for the word.

"A ventilator in the trach." She motioned to the front of her throat. "He's in and out of consciousness."

Myrna looked at Rob but her eyes were unfocused and distant. "They say he might be able to hear us talking to him, but so far he hasn't seemed to hear me."

"You never know." Paige said. "Many times patients have come back from deep comas and been able to relate everything that went on in the room. Don't give up talking to him, Myrna."

Myrna sighed and twisted the thin gold band on her left hand. "I won't," she said.

"Are you ready to see him now?" Paige asked.

Rob helped his sister to her feet and followed the two women to the ICU. Leroy couldn't talk so there was no fear that his brother-in-law would give him away.

Even with what Paige had told him about Leroy's condition, Rob wasn't prepared for the starkness of the room and gravity of the situation. Plastic lines snaked from Leroy's motionless body attaching him to blinking monitors. Two bags of clear liquid dripped into a single tube taped to one of his arms. A blood pressure cuff wrapped around the bicep of his free arm tightened and clicked and hissed until Leroy's numbers appeared on a screen. Metal tongs clamped on either side of his skull and connected to ropes and weights at the head of the bed reminded Rob of Frankenstein in the lab of the mad scientist. A tube attached to the front of Leroy's throat played a rhythmical hissing tune as it pumped life-giving oxygen into his lungs. This was hardly the chunky, barrel-chested, gruff creature that had tormented Rob for six years and whose memory had kept him from his sister for five more.

The two women entered the room leaving Rob standing alone in the doorway. Myrna approached the side of the bed and without emotion said, "Leroy, Rob's come home."

There was no response and none had been expected.

Paige turned to Rob and motioned for him to join his sister. "You can come in and talk to him."

He took a few tentative steps toward Paige. "What do I say?"

"Anything you'd say to him if you knew he could hear you."

*What would I say if he could hear me? We never had a conversation that wasn't about how stupid and bad I was.* Rob shifted his weight from foot to foot anxious to escape. He was as uncomfortable in Leroy's comatose presence now as he had ever been.

As he looked down at the man a memory flashed across his mind.

A few months after Rico had left Vegas John Taylor pulled Rob aside. "What's this I hear about you and Carl?"

Rob didn't want to tell him about his supervisor's conduct but at John's insistence, he said, "He hassles me about my work then gives me menial jobs. It's no big deal."

"It is," John said. "I'm sure you've heard that one bad apple can spoil the whole bunch." "I heard he bad mouths you to the others. You heard any of that?"

Rob nodded but said nothing.

"I'll take care of it," John said. The tall man lifted his cap and wiped his hand over his short hair. "You know I had a boss who hassled me, too. A long time ago." Rob could still hear John's Texas drawl.

"I was so stressed out by this guy that I thought I might have to quit my job. Finally I realized that he really couldn't do any more to me than what I allowed. I have the power over my life, not anyone else. I can let someone bother me or not let it bother me. It's my choice." John started to go then turned so all Rob could see was his profile with the bright sun behind him. "You know, I've always believed people come into our lives for a reason and when I figured out why my boss was in mine, we got along better. Maybe you need to figure out why Carl's in yours."

Rob had thought about John's words for a long time and finally made the decision to talk to his supervisor. Rob asked Carl if he felt he wasn't doing a good job and asked him to show him how to do it better. It had so taken the man aback that he apologized for talking about him to the other men, and in the end, the two of them had become good friends.

79

Standing in the stark closeness of the intensive care room, Rob thought about John's words. Why had Leroy been in his life, and why had he let this man rule his life with anger for so long? Was it Leroy he hated or himself? Maybe what he saw in his brother-in-law was something he saw in Robert McGruder and had always wanted to run from. The memory only took moments but the change they made in Rob was profound. He realized his brother-in-law's actions brought back memories of his own father and how much like the man Rob himself was.

It's me I hate, he thought. *But even when Leroy was at his worst he had no more power over me than he does now.* He turned to his sister, "Do you mind if I talk to him alone?"

Myrna's eyes registered astonishment. "Why?"

"It's all right, Sis." He moved nearer the bed. "I need to say some things to Leroy."

Still not sure if she should leave the two men alone, Myrna stammered, "Rob—Rob--please don't...."

"I won't. It'll be all right." A strange calmness filled Rob.

Tentatively, Myrna followed Paige from the room.

Rob looked down at the still frame of his brother-in-law. "I'm not sure you will hear this but I need to say it anyway." He cleared his throat, moved closer to the bed and looked into Leroy's ashen face. "Leroy, I want you to know I don't hold anything against you any more. I hope you don't hold anything against me either even though you probably should. I just want you to know I'm here with Myrna and I promise to take good care of her."

Relief washed over Rob. It was over. There was peace between them and an end to years of hurt and misunderstanding. His decision to come to Tulsa had been the right one.

Rob and Myrna left the hospital that evening at nine o'clock. As they walked across the parking lot and neared the white Chevy Corsica she'd driven from the airport, Myrna reached into her purse and handed Rob the keys. "You drive."

"I can't, Myrna. The only person who can drive a rental is the person who rented it." He extended the keys toward her.

"A rental? What makes you think it's a rental?" She walked to the passenger side of the vehicle.

Rob followed her and asked, "It's not? Whose car is it?"

"It's mine. Now unlock the door and drive us home." Her voice was tired, her eyes dark and sullen.

Once inside the automobile Myrna asked. "You want to tell me what you said to Leroy?"

Rob sighed. "I just made it right between us."

Myrna didn't respond.

Rob maneuvered the Corsica out of the lot. "Can I ask you a question?"

When Myrna didn't respond, he glanced over at her. Her eyes were closed.

They drove in silence for several blocks before she spoke. "I guess you want to know what changed and why Leroy gave me a car."

Rob knew his brother-in-law had forbidden Myrna from driving, and even though she had begged him for her own transportation, he'd always refused. "I sure do," he said.

Myrna rubbed her eyes. "Over a year ago I had all I could take. I was so tired of being treated like a child, like someone who was just a burden." Her voice hardened. "A useless weight, as Leroy always reminded me." She sighed. "I couldn't work, couldn't leave the house, and had to be at home to answer job calls for him. If I needed to go to the grocery store or do any other shopping, it had to be at his convenience, when he could take me, even when your car was available."

When he was in prison, Rob had left his Toyota with Myrna hoping she could use it to come see him but Leroy wouldn't let her drive around Tulsa, much less to visit him in Holdenville. She had been able to write him letters but could never accept the collect calls from the prison so for two years they hadn't spoken.

"Finally, I got up the nerve to tell him I had to have one day to myself," Myrna continued. "I took Sundays off. I'd walk away on Sunday morning and not come back until dinner time." She shifted in her seat. "If the weather was bad I'd take a bus but most of the time I just walked, to the library or to the shopping center."

"You walked?" Rob asked, incredulous because he knew the distances from their east-side home. "How did you do it?"

Myrna paused and answered dully. "Desperation. You can do anything if you're desperate enough."

Rob knew how true this was.

"One morning I passed a church and heard singing. I decided to go in. I'd never been in a church before. You know we weren't raised that way. Even when Daddy died the funeral home had to supply a preacher for us." Her voice took on a sharpness. "You don't remember that because you weren't there."

"I know," he said, staring straight ahead, recalling that he'd learned of his father's death from an acquaintance, and how he'd searched for his sister. "I've told you how sorry I am about that." He paused, wondering if he should say what was in his mind. "If I'd been there--"

She finished it for him. "I wouldn't have had to marry Leroy."

Rob sighed. "Why did you, Sis? I never understood why you married a man twenty-two years older than you."

Myrna sat forward straining against the seat belt, her words clipped, anger boiling in her throat. "I was eighteen, cleaning apartments, and he was cleaning carpets and he was the only person who seemed to care that I had no place to go when Daddy died. You certainly didn't. You left me at home with that man when I was only fourteen, when I was pregnant, when you knew it was going to be hard for me."

Surprised at the venom in her tone, Rob reached toward her. She pulled away from his touch. "Sis—" he began.

"Don't *Sis* me. You have no idea what it was like knowing I was going to have to give up the baby I was carrying. The baby I loved, by the way." Myrna clasped her hands together, her voice shrill. "I wanted that baby so much. And where were you? Not there like you'd promised Mama."

Rob had never seen his sister angry. She'd been the quiet peacemaker, always calm, even passive. Not knowing how to respond, he drove in silence.

By the time they pulled into the driveway Myrna appeared to relax. Neither moved to leave the vehicle.

"About the car." Myrna said, her voice monotone.

Rob cast a sideways glance at his sister. The old Myrna was back.

"That Sunday I went into the church. After the service they invited me to a dinner they were having. They called it a potluck. I stayed all afternoon and went back to the evening service that night. I didn't call Leroy all day."

Rob saw a slight smile on her lips. He waited, afraid his speaking would set her off again.

"It was about ten o'clock when I finally got home. Leroy was so worried. I thought he'd be mad, but he wasn't." Her voice slowed. "He was just worried." She was quiet for several seconds. "He asked me where I'd been and I told him. I said I was going back the next Sunday. The next week he bought me this car. He never said another word about whether

I could drive it or not." Myrna touched her forehead with her fingertips. "It was so strange. Things changed a little between us. He wasn't as mean to me." She opened her door and looked at Rob. "It was nice."

# FOURTEEN

Another death.

Paige had been up all night with the parents of a four-year-old who had been struck by an automobile. His condition began to worsen around midnight when she was called in to be with the family. He died a few hours later.

Paige entered the cafeteria but had no appetite. She headed for the coffee pot and was reaching for a Styrofoam cup when she heard her name.

She turned and looked into the face of Rob Martin. Startled by his grave expression, she asked, "Is it Leroy? Has there been a change?"

"No, nothing's changed." Rob, obviously uncomfortable, cleared his throat. "I'd like to talk to you if you're free. If not, it can wait."

"I'm free. Can we have some coffee while we talk?" Her body ached to sit down, to rest, but helping people was her life and that always came before her fatigue.

Paige found a table away from the few people in the cafeteria. When they were seated with their coffee, she asked, "What is it? Is something wrong?"

His eyes finally met hers. It's my sister."

"Myrna? Is she all right?"

Rob shook his head. "I don't know. She seems so different--and then last night..." He paused again, looked away from her.

"Last night? Here at the hospital?" Paige wondered why he was so reluctant to continue when he was the one who had approached her.

"Not here. On the way home." He took a drink of his coffee and made a face. "Is this coffee or motor oil?"

Paige laughed. "You aren't the only one who wonders that. We all do but we've learned to drink it." A smile curled Rob's lips and she noticed his eyes. They were familiar to her in some way. The man was what her sister-in-law would call drop-dead handsome. Tall, muscular, tanned with sun bleached hair and his eyes... She shuddered and a brief unease surprised her. *I must really be tired.*

"Just tell me, Rob. What happened yesterday?"

Rob touched the stud in his ear, cleared his throat again before continuing. "She was tired when we started home and was answering a question I had asked her about how she got her car. All of a sudden she was angry and screaming at me. Then, just as quickly, she was quiet again." He pushed his cup away, clasped his hands together and leaned forward on the table.

Paige had been concerned about Myrna, too. She'd noticed her malaise, her lack of emotion and contemplated how much she should share with the brother. But Myrna needed help and Rob had come to her for that help. She drained her coffee and asked, "Do you want to come to my office and talk about this? It will be more private."

She sensed Rob's hesitation then he pushed back his chair. "Sure," he said.

Walking to Paige's office, Rob said, "I don't want Myrna to know I'm talking to you about her. I think she'd be upset."

Paige assured him their conversation would be confidential.

In the office they settled into the chair and sofa where they'd sat the day before. Paige began, "Rob, I think your sister is probably still in shock. I don't know what her relationship was with her husband but I've been concerned about her reactions this entire time. I've spoken to her about seeing one of the doctors on staff but she's refused. Perhaps you could suggest the same thing."

"What kind of doctor? Do you think she's sick?"

"Not physically. She may be having some kind of emotional response and I think she needs to see a psychiatrist."

Rob's look told her he was unsure of what she said.

She quickly added, "Or I can talk to her again in your presence so it'll look like my idea." Relief shown on his face.

"I'll do that when she comes this afternoon for our appointment. Come with her."

Rob nodded.

Paige, thinking their conversation had ended, stood up, but Rob remained seated. "Is there something else?" she asked.

"I was wondering about Leroy. Do you think he could hear me?"

"That's something we don't know for sure. What do you think?"

Rob shrugged. "It didn't seem like he heard me."

Paige went to his side. When she touched his shoulder she felt it tremble. "I'm sure he did." She removed her hand and quietly asked, "Is there anything else?"

Rob stood and extended his hand. She took it in hers and was surprised by the warmth she felt when they touched. "Thanks, Miss Lewis."

"Paige. Please call me Paige."

"Paige."

Taking her hand away she said, "Please feel free to talk to me any time."

Paige watched the man walk away.

Wearily she stepped back into the office and closed the door. She leaned against it for a moment, moved slowly to the sofa and sat down heavily. So much pain. Everywhere. People hurting. Her clients. Myrna. She stared at her limp hands resting in her lap then she raised them to her face and wept.

---

Leroy died at noon that day.

The nurses removed all the tubes and lines from his body, turned off the machines and left his wife with him in his room.

Myrna stared through dull eyes at the body of her husband. She wasn't surprised by her lack of feeling. She approached Leroy's lifeless body but didn't touch him.

"A woman is supposed to be upset when her husband dies," she said, "but that's if they love each other. We didn't love each other, did we? The only nice thing you ever did for me was to buy me the car." She smoothed a few strands of hair across his head. "That's not true. You did marry me when I was alone."

She looked up when Rob came into the room. "He looks better now than when he was alive," she said.

Rob stood beside her and circled her waist with his arm. "You mean since he's been sick?"

Myrna shook her head. "No, I mean...." She paused. "I mean ever. He always had an unhappy look on his face. Now, for the first time since I've known him, he looks peaceful."

She pulled away from Rob and walked to the other side of the bed, smoothed the few strands of Leroy's hair again. "I'm sorry, Leroy. I wish I could have made you happy."

"Myrna," Rob said impatiently. "You didn't have anything to do with Leroy's unhappiness. You can't blame yourself. He wasn't a very nice man most of the time you knew him."

Myrna's head snapped up. Eyes blazing, she glared at her brother. "How dare you say anything about him. You didn't know him. All you knew was how he was when you were around."

She saw the confusion on her brother's face.

"After all, who was it gave you his truck so you could..." she paused, cocked her head to the side and her voice changed to a mock, "help your friend move?"

She saw her brother recoil and was glad. Was now the time to let everything out? Everything she'd wanted to say for so long?

At that moment, Paige entered the room and Myrna held her tongue. Leroy wasn't here to monitor her any longer, and she didn't care what her brother thought about her. She could never forget the loneliness and abandonment she felt every time Rob left her.

---

Rob drove his sister home and when they were in the house, he asked if there was anyone to be contacted about Leroy, Myrna said, "No. No one."

He asked her if he could call the preacher from the church she'd attended.

She screamed, "I said no."

Rob kept his voice quiet but he was fearful because of his sister's strange behavior since he had been back in Tulsa. "Myrna, we have to do something about a funeral."

She looked at him with vacant eyes then went into her bedroom muttering, "Just leave me alone and do whatever you want."

Not knowing where to turn, he went to Paige. She suggested her father, a retired minister, might be able to help them, and set up a meeting between Jim Lewis and Rob in her office.

The tall black man stood when Rob entered. "This is my dad, Rob. He was a minister for thirty years." Somewhat surprised that her father was African American, Rob shook his hand.

Rev. Lewis was dressed casually in khaki pants and an open collared white shirt. His smile was friendly. "I'm very sorry about your loss," he said, his voice a deep baritone. "How can I be of help to you?"

Rob explained how Myrna didn't want any funeral. "We can't just put him in the grave with no one there. I think we need to do something."

Rev. Lewis sat forward on the sofa beside Paige, forearms resting on his knees. "Do you expect many people to attend the ceremony?" he asked.

Rob shook his head. "Not that I know of. It might just be the two of us."

"And me," Paige said.

"And you, if you want to come." It pleased him to think Paige would be there.

Rev. Lewis leaned back into the cushions. "I hope you don't mind, but my daughter and I have talked about this. What do you think about a brief graveside ceremony? If you like, I could say a few words about your brother-in-law and have a prayer." He looked at Paige then back at Rob. "Would that be something your sister would like?"

"I'm sure whatever you think is best will be all right with both of us."

Rev. Lewis leaned forward again and picked up a pad and pen from the table in front of him. "Can you tell me something about this man? Leroy Watson, is that correct?"

Rob nodded.

"When was he born? Where?"

"I don't know." Rob spread his hands. "Look. I don't know much about Leroy. He and I didn't get along very well most of the time and I haven't seen him in five years." Rob rose from his chair and walked to the back of it. "I don't think Myrna is in any shape to tell you anything but you're welcome to come over to the house and talk to her, or..." he paused and rubbed his eyes. Tiredness washed over him. He hadn't slept well since being in Tulsa. Too much to deal with, Myrna's strange behavior, Leroy's death and the woman he'd robbed. He wanted to escape this place. "Or, just say whatever it is preacher's say and let it go at that."

Paige and her father stood. Rev. Lewis walked to his side and put a hand on his shoulder. "I understand, son. Don't worry about it. I'll be there and I'll take care of everything."

Relieved, but embarrassed about his behavior, Rob left the matter of the funeral in the Rev. Lewis' hands.

It rained during the night and a light mist still fell as the five people huddled under a canopy beside the grave. With Rev. Lewis was a small white woman he introduced as his wife. At first Rob thought the woman was his second wife but when he looked into her eyes, he knew she was Paige's mother. They were sea-dark purple just like her daughter's. Their union explained Paige's tanned skin and dark hair.

Mrs. Lewis greeted him, her hand small in his, and he remembered how Paige's hand had felt in his when they had met a few days ago. When her fragrance reached him, he recognized it as the same as Paige's. He quickly turned to his sister and put his arm around her shoulders. She made no movement that let him know she was aware of his presence.

The preacher did as he promised. He said a few words about Leroy and God and dying, read from the Bible then prayed a short prayer. Rob didn't hear much of what was said because his mind was still on Paige and the way her hand had felt in his, and the way she always smelled.

Myrna insisted on staying to watch the casket lowered into the ground. She didn't want to leave until the workers had filled the grave with soil. So Rob, Paige and the Lewises stayed with her.

When the men had finished, the Lewises approached her. Ignoring them, she went to her car and got into the passenger seat.

Rob shook hands with the couple. "I apologize for Myrna," he said.

"Grief affects people in different ways, Mr. Martin," the reverend said, his voice kind, his expression gentle. "We understand."

Rob thanked them for coming, and as he walked away Paige came to his side. "Have you been able to talk to Myrna about seeing a doctor?"

"She hasn't said two words to me since we left the hospital the day Leroy died. She wouldn't even go to the funeral home to make the arrangements. I did that. She just stays in her room with the door shut." They neared the Lewis' vehicle. "What should I do?"

"Let me check on some things. Call me tomorrow at the hospital." She pulled a card from her purse. "I'll talk to Dr. Fairchild, a psychiatrist. She helped me a few years ago. Maybe she'll have a suggestion. Call around one."

He walked slowly to the Corsica where Myrna was leaning back in her seat with her eyes closed. He didn't disturb her but his heart ached for his sister. Before he had the car in Park gear at her home, Myrna opened the door and, without looking at him or speaking, went into the house.

Rob watched her from the car and thought. What am I going to do? I want to go back to Las Vegas, back to my job, my quiet life but I can't leave now. He rested his forehead on the steering wheel and sighed. He knew that inside the house Myrna was already in her room closed away from the world and him.

Maybe Paige will be able to help.

As requested, he made the call at one o'clock the next day. Paige answered on the first ring and asked if there had been any changes. Rob stepped into the kitchen and spoke quietly even though he was sure Myrna couldn't hear him had he yelled. "None. She's come out of her room a few times but she hasn't said anything to me, hasn't eaten."

"Typical," was all Paige said. Before he could respond, she continued, "I spoke to Dr. Fairchild this morning. She suggested you and I talk to her together, have an intervention. Are you willing to do that?"

"An intervention. You mean, like tell her something's wrong with her? I'm not sure she'll listen to us."

Paige assured him, "No, we won't tell her something's wrong with her. Just that we're here to help her. I think we have to do this if you want to save her."

"Save her? What do you mean?" Rob's alarm grew.

"She's depressed. She may go so deeply into depression we can't help her out."

Rob's heart sank. "Will it work?"

"We can only try."

"Okay. How do we do it?" Anything for Myrna whom he had neglected for too long.

"I have three families I need to see tomorrow. I'll see them in the morning then clear my calendar for the rest of the day. I can probably be there around eleven."

"Fine. But how do we do this? What am I supposed to say?"

"Don't worry," Paige assured him. "I'll do most of the talking and you can follow my lead."

Rob agreed and hung up the phone. Myrna's bedroom door remained closed. *What is she doing in there?*

Fear pressed into his chest. Fear for his sister and fear of what she might say when he and Paige confronted her. He had seen her anger toward him and worried she would give his secret away. He liked Paige, was sorry about what he'd done to her, and he didn't want her to ever find out the truth about the past they shared.

# FIFTEEN

Rob was waiting at the front door when Paige arrived.

"Has she come out since we talked?" she asked.

"Not that I've heard." Paige's scent brought back the memory of the robbery.

"Show me where she is," Paige said.

"Sure," Rob pushed his thoughts away and led her to the bedroom.

Paige tapped on the door and called Myrna's name. Silence. She knocked again. "Myrna. It's Paige. May I come in?" When there was still no answer, she opened the door and entered the darkened room. Rob waited in the doorway.

Rumpled bed linens covered Myrna's head and body. Paige approached the bed and knelt on the floor speaking quietly. After a few moments Myrna uncovered her head. Rob couldn't make out the words but could hear the counselor's soothing tone. Finally, Myrna crawled out of the bed.

Rob and Paige exchanged looks when they saw that Myrna had on the clothes she'd worn to the funeral. Black dress wrinkled, hair disheveled, shoes still on her feet.

Paige led the woman to the living room where she and Rob seated themselves on each side of her. The pungent odor of sweat and unwashed hair wafted from Myrna as she slumped against the back of the sofa, hands lying limply in her lap, palms upward.

Paige began by telling Myrna of their concern for her. Rob, mesmerized by the psychologist's gentle words and calming tone, winced when he heard her say, "I want to tell you about something terrible that happened to me five years ago. I felt like you do now. Nothing to live for, wanting to hide and escape from my feelings."

Rob's mouth went dry. Fear crept into his gut. He wiped his sweaty palms on his pant legs. He didn't want to hear what Paige was going to say. Didn't want to hear because he knew what it would be. He wanted to stop Paige, but how? How to stop her without giving himself away?

She continued, "I was in my senior year at the university, twenty-two years old, had my life ahead of me. I was house-sitting for my brother and his wife and a man with a gun broke in. He stole some things, taped my hands and feet and left me to die."

A spasm shook Myrna. She straightened slightly and Paige continued.

"I remember trying to get to the phone but I fell and knocked myself out."

When Rob heard this, the skin on his face burned. He wiped his hand across his brow.

Paige's attention was on Myrna and not his discomfort. "All night I was in and out of consciousness." She paused and looked away from the two of them. Her voice deepened. "But I can remember the fear and the pain." She looked into Myrna's eyes. "The next morning the housekeeper found me. I spent three days in the hospital."

Rob waited, fearing Myrna's response. When she spoke, she looked at Paige, not at her brother. "Did they find the person who did it?"

Rob shuddered and wiped away the dots of sweat gathering around his hairline.

Paige shook her head. "I wasn't able to talk to the police for a couple of days. I gave them a description but they didn't find anything, never even found the stolen goods. He'd worn gloves so there were no fingerprints. I'd heard a vehicle in the garage but I never saw it." She sighed and leaned back onto the sofa cushion. "No, they never found him."

Myrna's eyes didn't leave Paige's face. "Didn't that make you mad? I mean, that he got away with it?"

Rob struggled to control his breath, to keep from running out of the room, away from this story, away from the woman he'd harmed and the sister he'd left behind.

"At first, it did. I had nightmares, awful nightmares." A look came into her eyes that told Rob she was back at that time. He knew because he, too, would go back to the day he chose his own life over hers. She said she had nightmares, and he wondered if he was in those dreams. Was she remembering what he looked like? Had he changed enough to keep her from recognizing him?

Paige returned her gaze to Myrna. "I didn't want to get out of bed, was terrified he'd come back. I wasted a lot of time hating him and being afraid." She smiled. "But thank goodness for my parents and my doctor. They insisted I see a psychiatrist." She looked up at Rob. "It took me close to a year before I could go back to school and graduate and finally give up wondering who had done this to me."

"You gave up? Don't you want to know?" Myrna's eyes darted toward Rob.

He held his breath, waiting for her answer.

"I did but only because I wanted him caught so he'd never be able to do that to anyone else. But ...." Paige slowly shook her head. "What would it accomplish? I admit that in the beginning it seemed like the end of the road, and I had to fight the constant terror that something else was going to happen to me. It took a long time to trust again but my family

97

and my psychiatrist helped me see that fear or pain can move you forward if you let it. It's a wall until you embrace it. Then it becomes a door and on the other side can be great reward." Paige smiled. "As bad as it was, it changed my life for the better."

"Changed your life? How?" Myrna asked. Rob wondered, too, and was glad Myrna had asked the question.

"If it hadn't been for that experience, I'd never have known what it's like to face death and fear and to overcome it." She regarded both of them. "I found my passion, my purpose in life. Helping people, particularly people who are going through something that threatens to steal their lives." She took Myrna's hand. "Like this depression is trying to steal yours." Paige reached for Rob's hand and placed it into hers and Myrna's. "Rob and I aren't going to let that happen to you. You're too valuable to us."

At Paige's insistence Rob rode with her and his sister and promised to take him home after they had Myrna settled into the hospital. He assumed she was afraid Myrna might not go with her if he wasn't along. When he was in the back seat of her Mustang and Myrna belted into the passenger seat, he wished he had been more forceful and told her he would drive Myrna to the hospital and she could follow him. Instead of staying away from Paige he was in her car, and she was becoming more and more involved in his life.

The psychiatrist had left word at the admitting desk to have them brought up to the psychiatric floor where she met them. Almost as tall as Rob and rail-thin in her white lab coat, Dr. Fairchild introduced herself. She straightened her bifocals and brushed a wiry gray hair out of her eyes. Turning to Myrna she extended both of her hands and gently took one of Myrna's. "Let's go into my office. We'll leave your brother out here for a few minutes while we talk. Paige will be with us." She turned to Rob and signaled for him to wait in a nearby chair.

Left alone in the empty hall, Rob rubbed his hand over the back of his neck. What would they ask Myrna? Did she realize he was the man who had robbed Paige? He remembered her tone when she'd reminded him he'd borrowed Leroy's van to help a guy move. He had seen the way she glanced at him when she'd asked Paige if she'd like to know who had done that to her. It all pointed to him. *She knew.* Besides that she was angry at him for leaving her.

Rob paced to the end of the hallway and looked out the window onto the roof of lower hospital floors. *If she knew why I'd left her,* he said to himself, *maybe she wouldn't be so mad. But I might not get the chance to tell her before she gives me away.* He looked back at the doctor's office as the door opened and Paige stepped out into the hall.

Hurrying toward her, he asked, "Is Myrna all right? Did she say anything?"

Paige held her palm toward him. "Slow down. She's all right. Dr. Fairchild is doing an evaluation to determine if they have enough to keep her here." Before Rob could respond, she took his arm and began directing him toward another closed door. "Let's go into this conference room where we can talk."

Her attitude toward him didn't appear to have changed. Maybe Myrna hadn't said anything yet. Rob followed Paige into the room. A walnut table with several leather chairs surrounding it filled the small room. Paige pulled out a chair for herself and motioned for Rob to sit down, too.

As soon as he was seated he leaned forward, his forearms on the table. "What do you mean about deciding if she can stay here? I thought that's why we came?"

"Don't worry, Rob." Paige patted his clenched fists. "In order for the hospital to be able to accept her as an in-patient, she has to meet certain criteria. The main one is whether or not she has a diagnosis of some form of mental illness." Rob's mouth opened to speak. Paige quickly continued. "Depression is a form of mental illness and Myrna is definitely depressed. But she needs to meet other criteria, too. However, she can be admitted on this one diagnosis while they do a complete psychiatric assessment."

Rob saw Paige look down at her hand on his then suddenly release him. An expression passed over her face then quickly faded and she continued, "If they keep her, and I'm sure they will, it will only be from three to seven days while they regulate medication and do some very cursory therapy, which will probably include talking to you. Then they'll assign her to a therapist so she can go home."

It all sounded so easy, the way she explained it, but, in his heart, Rob knew it wasn't. So many secrets that might come out. His life hanging in the balance and some of it in the hands of a mentally ill woman.

Rob stood up. He walked to the windows and noticed the grating covering them. Eight floors up, he thought, and they're worried someone might jump out. The situation alarmed him, for himself and for his sister. He returned to his chair. "Paige, why do you think Myrna is depressed?"

He saw a flicker of hesitation in her eyes before looking away. Then she raised her head and looked into his eyes. "Depression is called frozen rage. I think Myrna's very angry about something. Probably something that happened a long time ago."

"Oh, no." He moaned, leaned his elbows on the table and dropped his head onto his hands.

A lifetime of pain was in the sound. Paige touched his bowed head. "What is it? Tell me."

Rob rubbed his hand across his eyes. She had to lean closer to hear him.

"It's my fault. She's mad at me.

When several moments passed and Rob didn't continue, Paige said, "It's all right. It's important for Myrna."

He sat back in his chair, his eyes shut. "Myrna was my little sister and most of the time I didn't give her much thought. I guess I ignored her. I had things to deal with at home." He cleared his throat and sat forward, his head again in his hands. "She was so quiet, played by herself most of the time."

His voice broke. He rubbed his eyes with the heels of his palms. "My mom..." His voice broke. He took a deep breath and continued. "My mom and I--she read to me." A sad smile tipped his mouth as he reminisced. "We played games and she read stories. Wonderful stories."

He shifted in his chair, the smile gone. "Myrna wasn't always with us. Sometimes she stayed in her room just playing with her dolls." He looked away. "Sometimes I'd hear her in her room talking to them. She carried them around the house, rocked them." His voice softened. "Now that I think of it, sometimes she'd sit with one of her dolls in the rocking chair when Mom read." He shook his head. "I don't know why I'd forgotten that. She was just so quiet. Like she wasn't with us, was in her own world."

"What kinds of stories did your mother read to you?"

"Kings and princes and faraway places, nursery rhymes. My favorite was about Jack and the Beanstalk. I liked to think I could do something like that-- grow a plant and climb away from the world, but my giant wasn't at the top of the beanstalk. My giant was..." He stopped, looked away.

When he didn't go on, Paige asked, "Who was the giant you wanted to get away from?"

"My dad." Rob said. "Sometimes, late at night, I'd hear them arguing but most of the time he wasn't there. He never said anything to me that wasn't some type of put-down, some kind of criticism. I couldn't do anything to please him and gave up trying." Rob took another deep breath. "He hated it when he'd see me with Mom playing a game or reading. He had a special name for me then." Rob looked back at her. "Butt-face, Bobby, Bobby the boob-head. Dumb names." He shook his head. "I hated those names. The one I hated the most was Bobby Mac."

"Why that one?" Paige asked softly.

"My mom called me Bobby and he hated it for some reason. He could turn anything good into something bad. That's why I wanted to be Robert--Rob. I think he really hated me because my mother loved me."

Paige's expression didn't betray her revulsion for Rob's father.

Rob cleared his throat. "When I was twelve, my mother got sick. It was right after Christmas." He looked away again, eyes slightly out of focus. "I was twelve. Myrna was ten. We were just kids. Every day I'd come home and go into Mom's room and sit with her. I'd bathe her face with a washcloth and give her water. I'd heat a can of soup and feed it to her." More quietly, he added, "Every day after school. That's all I did."

"Your father?"

"I don't know." Rob exhaled. "I don't remember him being there much. I know he didn't sleep in her bed after she got sick. As far as I know he never went into her room. I'm not even sure what we ate or how we ever had clean clothes. Those things have just gone from my memory."

"Didn't you have any other family?"

Rob shook his head.

"What about a doctor?"

Rob shrugged his shoulders. "I don't remember a doctor."

"What was her sickness?"

"I'm not sure of that either. Maybe some kind of cancer." The look in Rob's eyes told Paige he was back in that room. "Our house smelled of her illness in a way I can't describe." He brought one of his hands to his eyes. "One day I came home from school and went in to her like I always did." His voice deepened and pain infused every word. "The bed was unmade but she wasn't in it. It looked like she'd just gotten up and walked away. I was so happy because I thought she was well. I went all over the house calling to her." A sad smile tipped his mouth. "My dad met me in the kitchen." He looked at Paige, his hands gripped together on the table in front of him. "You know what he said?" His smile faded. "He said, 'She's dead.' That's all. Just-- 'She's dead.'" Rob's eyes were dry, glazed. "That's all I ever knew. If he had a funeral for her, I never knew about it. I don't know if she was buried or cremated and…." He rubbed his hand across his forehead. "…and I never asked." His last words rang hard and cold.

"Is that why Myrna is mad? Because your mother died?"

Rob didn't meet her eyes. "No. She isn't mad at anyone but me."

Confused, Paige asked, "Why would she be mad at you? Did she think you'd taken her mother?"

Rob shook his head. "No, I don't think she missed our mother like I did. The one thing I remember about Myrna after Mom died was when she came to me and asked me if I had told the truth. Was I going to take care of her? I told her I would, and, as far as I know, she went back to her room. We never talked about it again." He slumped in his chair. "No, it wasn't about Mom." He shook his head sadly. "She's mad because I left home when she was only fourteen—and--pregnant."

Rob leaned forward. "One day, not long before she died, Mom asked me to bring Myrna into the room, something she'd never done before. She told us she loved us and then she asked me to take care of my little sister. Of course, I said I would. Then Mom told Myrna that she would be all right because her big brother would always be there for her."

"And you weren't."

Rob's voice rose. "No, I wasn't, particularly the day Myrna found out she was pregnant--or maybe I should say, the day our father found out she was pregnant." Rob faced her in his chair, his voice hardened. "I walked into the room and heard him call her a slut. She was *fourteen.* How can you call a fourteen-year-old a slut? How can you?" His chair scraped against the tile floor as he pushed it with his legs and stood up. "I won't ever forget the look on her face. She cried and said she wasn't bad, that she was in love. He laughed and said something about her not knowing what love was--like he did." Rob's breath came in gasps. "Then-- then he--he slapped her. Slapped her so hard I thought it would break her neck. I ran up behind him and told him to leave her alone, and he turned on me and hit me with his fist. Knocked me on the floor. He came toward me and I thought he was going to kill me. I've never seen anyone look at me with such hatred, even...." His eyes darted to Paige's before he stopped himself.

Rob paced the small space. "Myrna was crying and screaming, crawling toward me. Then he went back to her and told her he was going to show her just what she'd done. She would have the baby and then she'd give it away." Rob walked around the table, leaned forward on it, arms outstretched, his voice a whisper. "I'll never forget the look on her face. She cried and begged him to let her keep it. She promised to be good." He sat down heavily. "I hope I never have to see anything like that again in my life."

"But why would that make her mad at you, Rob?"

"Because..." He covered his eyes with his hands. "That night I left home. I left her."

"Why?"

"I've never told Myrna before. After she married Leroy, well, it just never came up--until that night in the car, and that didn't seem like the

104

time to say anything." Rob rubbed his hand across his brow. "After all this happened, our dad left the house. I did what I could for Myrna. She had a cut lip. My eye was swelling. I asked her who the father was, if there was a chance he would marry her. She wouldn't tell me, said he was too young. I don't know how we did it, but we just went to bed like we always did, like nothing happened."

Paige knew that was typical behavior for abused families. When the abuse ended, they went on as usual. She guessed this wasn't the first time Rob's father had been violent.

Rob's voice changed, lower pitched, etched with a sixteen-year-old's fear. "My dad came into my room that night and woke me up. He had a knife, and I really thought I was dead. I could feel it--here." He touched his hand to his throat. "He said he'd kill me if he found me in his house the next day." Rob eyes glazed over, clouded with the memory of being a child alone in his room that night. "When he closed my door, I got dressed, put some clothes in a bag and climbed out the window." He took a deep breath and stood up. "I was sixteen."

"What did you do?"

He began to pace again, hands in his pockets. He spoke quickly, words clipped. "I stayed in Tulsa. We didn't have a phone at the house so I couldn't call Myrna. I didn't try to go back there. I was too scared." He strode back to the table and slammed his fist on it. "I was a coward."

"No," Paige said. "No, Rob. You were a child. You did the only thing you knew to do. How did you live?"

Rob shrugged. "It wasn't easy." He sat down, clasped his fingers on the table in front of him, knuckles white. "I slept on the street for awhile. Then I made some friends and moved in with them. Got a job bagging groceries. Never went back to school. Pretty nasty way to live, I can tell you that." He stood up and faced the window.

"When did you see Myrna again?" She saw his shoulders droop, his head bowed to his chest.

"Four years later. I ran into an old neighbor a few months after our dad died and he told me about it. I went looking for her, finally tracked her down to an apartment complex where she'd been working. They told me she was married. She'd married Leroy." He turned, searched her face, spread his hands, palms up. "And that's the story. That's why she's mad at me."

Paige sat quietly for a few minutes looking at the sadness in Rob's eyes. She rose and stood beside him. "And you, Rob. What about you?"

"Me?" He choked out the word, cleared his throat and began to work his mouth in an effort to hold back the emotion. He squeezed his eyes shut.

Tentative at first, Paige put her hand lightly on his shoulder and felt that same tremor when she had touched him before. "I'm so sorry, Rob. No one should ever have to endure what the two of you have." She dropped her hand to her side. "I can only imagine how much hurt both of you have suffered. I know it was difficult to talk about it but it will help us know how to treat Myrna." When he didn't answer or look up, she knew he didn't want her to see the tears filling his eyes. "I'll give you a few minutes while I check with the doctor to see how she's doing." Then she left him alone in the room.

# SIXTEEN

Rob helped his sister sign the necessary papers. He talked with the doctor and four hours after bringing Myrna to the hospital, he and Paige left her resting in a private room on the eighth floor.

Paige pressed the automatic unlock on her key chain and the two of them climbed into her Mustang. Rob rubbed his hand along the back of his neck and looked across the front seat at her.

"Are you all right?" she asked. "I know it's emotionally draining having to deal with something like this."

Rob nodded. "You're sure she'll be okay?"

"I'm sure."

Her nearness excited him. Their eyes met and held. His face flushed, and at the same time, he noticed the color heighten on her cheeks.

They drove in silence until they neared the freeway exit that would take them to Myrna's house. "Are you hungry?" Paige asked.

Exhausted from the ordeal of the last five days, Rob felt all he wanted to do was go home and sleep, but her question awakened his hunger. He simply nodded.

"When was the last time you ate?"

"I'm not sure. I've been so worried about Myrna, and she hasn't been eating. I guess I haven't had a real meal since I got here. There's not much food at the house-- some peanut butter and crackers, what I've picked up at the hospital cafeteria. I really haven't thought too much about it."

"There's a little bistro on Garnett Road near Myrna's." He saw her eyes dart in his direction. She hesitated then said, "They have pretty good food. Would you like to stop there?"

Rob knew it was dangerous being with Paige. Any minute she might realize who he was. But, he thought, if I have to spend time with her and she sees me as a nice guy, maybe she won't ever suspect I'm the one who... Even in his private thoughts he had trouble admitting his crime against her. "Sure," he said. "I'd like that."

The cafe was small and quiet, not many patrons yet on this early Friday evening. After the waiter took their orders and left them water and coffee, Paige asked, "Are you all right with what happened today?" Paige held her cup between her palms. "About Myrna?"

Rob was all right with Myrna's hospitalization. What he wasn't sure he was all right with was telling her so much about himself.

Rob took a drink of his coffee and nodded, avoiding her question. "Dr. Fairchild seems to be concerned about Myrna."

"She'll do what's best for your sister. She's probably one of the best in her field. St. Elizabeth's is lucky to have her."

His confession on his mind, he asked, "Paige, did you have a good family? Was it anything like mine?"

Her expression softened. "Rob, your home life was not as unusual as you think. I hear about families like yours all the time and it breaks my heart. I don't know how you and Myrna survived it."

Rob smiled wryly. "I'm not sure Myrna has."

"She will, just as you have."

Rob shook his head. "I'm not sure I'm there yet." He shifted in his chair. "Your parents seem nice."

"My parents are wonderful, loving people." She paused. "You remember what I told you happened to me five years ago?"

Rob flinched. Of course, he thought. I remember. I was responsible. He nodded.

"Well, they sold their home in Atlanta and moved here. They wanted to live out their retirement near my brother and me, particularly after what I'd been through. It was a sacrifice for them because they'd always lived in Georgia and had many friends there." She reached for her coffee and took a sip. "It was my brother Brad's house where I was attacked. He and Ashley even sold their home so I wouldn't ever have to go there again. That's the kind of family we have."

Rob had nothing to say. He remembered the house as though it was yesterday. He couldn't imagine his own father ever sacrificing for anyone. He wished he hadn't asked her the question because her answer had caused a slow ache to cut its way into his heart. But Paige wasn't finished.

"We see each other every Sunday for church and lunch and any other time we can. Talk a lot on the phone during the week. My brother has a child, a beautiful little boy, Landon. He's almost a year old. He looks a lot like Brad and my dad. I'm just crazy about the kid."

Rob nodded and nervously spun his cup between his hands. Enough! He wanted to scream then realized she'd seen how her words affected him.

"I'm sorry," she said. "I didn't mean to go on about them."

Sorry that she'd read him so easily and fearing he'd upset her, he said, "It's all right. I'm glad you have a good family." He remembered being curious about something Paige had said earlier, and recalling it gave him a way to change the subject.

"Paige, I have another question." He saw the interest on her face. "It's about what you said this morning--about your purpose, your passion. What exactly does that mean?"

She thought a moment, finished her coffee and placed the cup on the table. "Do you have anything you love to do?"

He shook his head. "I don't think so."

"Well..." He could see her searching for a way to explain. "It's like there's something you have to do and aren't happy or satisfied unless you're doing it. For instance, what kind of work do you do?"

"I'm a welder."

"When you're doing that, are you completely satisfied?"

Rob smiled. "Only when I think about how much money I'm making."

"Then you can take it or leave it?" Paige's expression was serious.

Could he take it or leave it? "Yes. If I found something better, I'd do it."

"Let's look at this from another angle." She laughed. "What do you want more than anything in the world?"

Rob hesitated. When he was in prison he'd wanted to be free more than anything in the world. Then he'd wanted to start over. That's when he'd robbed and left Paige. None of this could he voice. He remembered how he'd felt at Mama Serena's and wasn't sure he wanted it more than anything in the world, but it was the only answer that came to him. "I don't know. Maybe to be a part of a real family."

Paige's voice softened. "Then, that may be your passion -- your purpose, because whatever's in your heart will eventually find a way into your life."

"Even if it comes from something as bad as what happened to you?"

She nodded. "Even then."

He had heard how she answered Myrna but he wanted to hear it again. "And you aren't mad at the person who did this; don't want to find out who he is?"

110

She shook her head. "Sometimes I still wonder, but what good would it do for me to be mad at someone I don't even know? It wouldn't hurt him but it would hurt me. I had to accept what happened or forever let it dominate me. I refuse to be dominated by something I can't change, past, present or future."

A lump filled Rob's throat. He looked away, fought to regain his composure. *What's the matter with me?* He heard the concern in her voice. "Are you all right, Rob?"

He wasn't. Something about this woman troubled him and threatened to shatter his world. He wanted to run away, escape his feelings, go back to the life he'd left less than a week ago, but somewhere deep inside, he knew he couldn't leave. Fate had changed his destiny and this woman was a part of it.

# SEVENTEEN

As Dr. Fairchild requested, Rob didn't visit his sister, giving the weekend staff time for evaluation and for Myrna to rest without any interruptions. He spent Saturday and Sunday wandering around the house and thinking about what he needed to do. By Monday morning he'd decided two things. He had to stay in Tulsa for awhile and take care of Myrna. That would mean going back to Vegas to get his clothes and his truck.

Monday morning he entered the hospital and turned at the sound of his name. His heart began to pound at the sight of Paige hurrying toward him. She wore an electric blue pantsuit and as she neared he noticed the deep purple of her eyes. He didn't think he'd ever seen anyone lovelier in his life. He took the hand she extended and smiled down at her.

"I knew you'd be here early," she said.

Reluctantly releasing her hand they got into the elevator.

"My meeting with Dr. Fairchild is at nine," he explained. "I wanted to be on time. Are you going to be there?"

"No." She shook her loose black curls. "I have some other appointments."

Surprised by his own disappointment, Rob mumbled, "Oh."

"But," she continued, "I'd like to hear how it goes. If you're still around about eleven-thirty, I should be finished. We can grab a bite to eat in the cafeteria and you can tell me about your visit." She looked up at him. "That is if you're still here."

I'll be here, he thought, no matter what time we finish. "Sure. I'll come to your office."

Paige's expression confused him. It was at first friendly then, for a split second, it had darkened but she smiled again as she walked away. Questions and doubts tumbled around in his mind as he wondered if she was remembering. Rob rubbed the back of his neck and took a deep breath as the elevator reached the eighth floor.

The meeting with Dr. Fairchild began promptly and lasted over an hour. She asked him to tell her anything he thought would be of help to his sister. He told her the same story he'd told Paige on Friday, but she made no comment about it when he finished.

She leafed through a chart on her desk before speaking. "Mr. Martin," she said and pushed her glasses back up on the bridge of her nose. "We had to have two diagnoses to be able to keep your sister as an in-house patient. First," she read from the papers, "we're sure she's clinically depressed. Secondly, based on the Body Mass Index, she's lost 15% or more of her ideal body weight."

Rob nodded. The doctor continued, "Our plan is to continue with some assessments the next day or two, prescribe anti-depressants and then we'll set up some private and family therapy sessions. We need to get to the root of her illness." The doctor stopped, removed her glasses and rubbed her eyes. "We want to find out why she's depressed and not eating. You understand, don't you?"

"Of course." Rob thought he knew the root of the problem and wondered why Dr. Fairchild didn't after what he'd told her.

As though reading his thoughts, she said, "You've given me some valuable information, and I know it must not have been easy for you to talk about it. The time will come when you need to share some of that with your sister. Until then, I'd rather you didn't say anything to her about the past. When you see her, keep it light. If she asks questions, be evasive. Tell her you don't know what's going to happen."

"That part will be true."

"I know." Dr. Fairchild agreed. She replaced her glasses and looked back at the papers before closing the chart. "If you'd like, you can go see Myrna for a few minutes this morning." She leaned back in her chair. "Do you have any questions?"

"I do." Rob said. "I've been living in Las Vegas. Since Myrna needs me right now I need to go back there and pack my things, get my truck." He spread his hands. "I'll have to give up my apartment and I need to do it before the end of the month"

The doctor nodded and placed her hands behind her head, her thin arms making a wing-like extension above her shoulders. When she made no comment, Rob continued.

"Should I go now while Myrna's in the hospital or wait until she gets out and take her with me?"

Dr. Fairchild dropped her arms and sat forward abruptly. "Go now if you need to. Alone. It will be quite awhile before Myrna's ready to travel. She needs to be in therapy for at least six months, maybe longer."

Rob was surprised it would take so long and realized he would need to find a job during that time. He said, "I guess I can leave this week, if that would be all right?"

The doctor nodded. "I suggest you make a decision about the date you're leaving and when you'll be back before you tell her. Don't leave her in the dark, make her feel you're abandoning her again. You understand?"

Rob hoped Dr. Fairchild didn't notice him cringe when her words struck him. "I understand."

"I want to warn you that Myrna is on medication, and we're attempting to determine the amount she needs. Please don't show her you have any concerns about her condition even though she'll seem different to you. Am I making myself clear?" At Rob's nod, she continued. "I assure you she's all right."

The doctor rose from her chair and walked around her desk. Rob stood and shook her cool bony hand. He wondered if Dr. Fairchild thawed with patients. He felt no warmth from her and feared she judged him for abandoning his sister. If she found out what he'd done to Paige, he was certain she would turn him in to the police. His only hope was that Myrna didn't ever voice her suspicions about him to anyone.

Myrna sat in a chair quietly staring out the grated window. It appeared an effort for her to turn her head and look at him. She wore a terry cloth robe and Rob wondered where it came from. She'd had a bath and her hair was washed. She looked normal except for her eyes which were unfocused when she looked at him.

He pulled a straight chair from near the door and sat down beside her. Rob reached for her hand and felt its limpness in his own. "How are you, Sis?"

Slowly Myrna answered, "Okay. How are you?"

"I'm all right." His voice caught in his throat. She looked so small and vulnerable.

He squeezed his sister's hand. "Myrna, I'm going to move to Tulsa for a while, until you're well." She made no movement, no action to show she understood. "I have to go back to Las Vegas and bring my things here." Still no sign of comprehension from her. "I'll fly there and drive my truck back."

"A truck."

He smiled. "Yeah. I traded in my old car for it a few years ago."

"Truck," she repeated.

Rob felt an absence of breath for a second and panic spread out of his chest. *Oh, no. She's thinking of Leroy's truck and the day I borrowed it.*

Again she spoke. "Leroy died in his truck."

Rob realized he was wrong about her thoughts. "Yes, he did." He remembered the doctor had told him to keep it light, to talk about nothing that wouldn't upset her. Quickly he changed the subject from her husband's death. "It's a beautiful day. Pretty hot, though."

Myrna smiled slowly. "Go. Get your things. Move back here. We can live together."

A wave of love for his sister swept over him. "I will, Sis. I'll go …" He counted the days and made his decision. "I'll go tomorrow. I'll be back by the weekend."

---

Myrna sat alone in her room staring at the window. It was the first time in many months she was at peace. Rob was moving back to town. Was that a good thing? Her mind wouldn't allow her to explore what that meant. And Leroy was dead. She tried to touch the feelings in her heart but everything was so fuzzy. She didn't care. Maybe she was glad he was gone? But that seemed unkind and if there was one thing Myrna hoped she wasn't, it was unkind.

There was something else, too. Rob. It was about Rob. What was it? Was it something he'd done? She couldn't remember no matter how hard she tried. Maybe it would come back to her. It was important. Whatever it was saddened her when she tried to think about it.

She stroked her face with a fingertip. Am I alive or dead? Maybe I'm the one who_died. She wanted to laugh but it took so much effort. She closed her eyes and wished she could lie down on the bed she saw beside her chair. Could she walk over to it? Her legs didn't want to move, and she was so tired.

Her hand rested on something in her lap. She dropped her head to look at it. An oblong black object, rubber, lay there. A long black tube reached from one end of it to the bed. A red piece stuck out the unattached end. What was it? Something tried to come into her mind, but it was so hard to think. Still, if she pushed it. Maybe that's what she was supposed to do. It took so much strength, but she held it in both hands and pressed the button. It only took a few minutes before someone came into the room.

Thank God, Myrna thought.

# EIGHTEEN

It was eleven o'clock when Rob went to Paige's office. The door was closed so he waited a few steps down the hall. Eleven thirty came but the door remained shut. He thought about knocking but decided that wouldn't be the right thing to do if she was with a client.

Quarter to twelve. Noon. Still no sign of movement from the office. He wondered if she had changed her mind.

A nurse walked by and smiled at him. She went to the door, rapped softly and went inside. A few minutes later she emerged carrying some papers. Rob stopped her as she passed him. "Excuse me. Can you tell me if Paige-- if Miss Lewis will be out soon?" A question crossed her face. "I was supposed to meet her at eleven thirty. I just wondered if I should wait."

"Are you a client?"

He shook his head. "My sister is."

"I wouldn't wait if I were you. She's had an emergency and will probably be tied up for a long time. If you want to leave her a message, I'll be sure she gets it when she's finished."

Rob followed the nurse to the desk where she gave him some paper and a pen. He wrote, 'I need to talk to you about Myrna and my plans. Call me at home when you can.' He jotted down his number and signed it then folded the paper, wrote her name on the front and handed it to the nurse. Thanking her he looked once more at the closed office door, and left the hospital.

Driving home Rob realized how disappointed he was at not being able to see Paige when they'd planned to meet. Something crazy's going on with me, he thought. He'd had short relationships with a few women in the past, usually sexual in nature, but had never felt strongly about any of them. It was confusing to think of what he'd done to Paige and today being drawn to her.

The last woman he'd had a relationship with had been Gerri. He liked her as well as any woman he'd ever been with, but he had hardly given her a thought since leaving Tulsa. After changing his name and his life in Las Vegas, he made a pact with himself, an imposed celibacy, a penance for all his past wrongs. Many times he'd been presented with opportunities and might have taken advantage of one of them had it not been for Rico's presence in his life. The two spent most of their free time together and Rico never went out with women. Rob remembered asking him about it. He could still see the twinkle in the Hispanic's chocolate colored eyes.

"Sex? Does my friend think I am not a man with hungers?"

Rob teased him. "Of course, you are. You're a man, aren't you?"

The two men laughed. Then Rico became serious. "Answer, mi amigo, would you want your woman to be used by men before you?"

Rob had never thought about it in those terms. He remembered the way he had treated Gerri. He liked her and knew she loved him because she had told him all the time. He knew she was waiting for him to tell her he felt the same way, but he'd never said those words to her or to anyone. Shame filled him as he realized how he'd used her.

"But you don't even go out with women." Rob wanted to move the guilt away from himself.

"Ay. What would Rico do if he fell in love with an American senorita? Someday Rico must go back to Hermosillo and she would not like to leave her family." He wagged his finger and smiled. "Mi amante will be found in the place I live."

And now Rob was in the place he was going to live. Was that the reason he'd never allowed himself to find a woman in Vegas? Did something in him know he wouldn't live there forever? Was it ridiculous to think that by some strange twist of fate, Paige was supposed to be the woman for him? His amante-- his love?

How he wished he could talk to Rico now, but there was no way for Rico to call him. He had not heard from his friend before knowing he was leaving Las Vegas and had not been able to leave him the Tulsa phone number. He told the Aragons he was leaving but had planned to be back much sooner. Even they didn't have his number. Rico's address was back at his apartment in Las Vegas. How he wished he had brought it with him. At least he could have written him a letter.

Rob hurried home to wait for Paige's call. Walking through the house he was suddenly aware of Myrna's rumpled bed and went into her room intending to straighten it. He was appalled by the disarray. Piles of clothing lay on the floor where she had stepped out of them, clothing he hadn't seen Myrna wear since he'd been with her. The foul odor of unwashed bed linens and her clothes filled his nostrils. Quickly stripping the bed he carried the dirty sheets to the washing machine and began the cycle. Going back to gather the clothing he became aware of dust covered surfaces in the living room and bedroom.

He had no idea how long it had been since Myrna had cleaned house. It was Rico who had taught him about neatness and Rob had come to appreciate a clean place to live. Since he had come to Tulsa, his life had been so confusing he hadn't noticed the filth until today. From his friend he learned how to use a washing machine, mop, dust cloth and vacuum sweeper and he used that knowledge on Myrna's house while he waited for Paige's call.

By the time she called after four o'clock, the small house had been thoroughly cleaned and Rob was just finishing up in the bathroom.

"Sorry about lunch," she began. Rob heard the tiredness in her voice.

"No problem. Hard day?"

He heard her sigh. "Sad. Traumatic. Devastating. But I think it's going to be all right."

How could sad, traumatic and devastating be all right? This woman was a mystery.

"About Myrna--" she began.

"If you're too tired, we can talk another time."

"We can do it now, if you want." He did want. "It'll help me unwind after what I've been through today. In fact, how about your coming up to my office? We can get something to eat in the hospital cafeteria."

Rob laughed. "No thanks. How about I stop and get something?"

He heard her hesitation before she agreed.

"You like pizza or Chinese?" he asked, wondering at her hesitation.

"You choose. Come on when you're ready. I have some paper work to finish but it'll be done by the time you get here."

True to her word, she was putting away the last of the paper work when he knocked on the open office door. She greeted him and took the sack he carried. "Ah. Chinese. Just what I wanted." When she smiled, he noticed the faint hint of a dimple in her right cheek. Her make up had faded leaving only creamy tan skin. They sat together on the sofa and ate from the cartons. They talked about how hot the weather was, how it was the hottest summer on record in the entire country and how good the food tasted.

"What did you do this afternoon?" Paige asked as the two of them cleared away the empty containers.

He told her about the dirty state of the house and Myrna's clothing. She nodded knowingly. "That's normal for a depressed person. You're a special guy if you can clean a house. I'd like to come see how well you did and maybe hire you for my place."

"Any time."

They settled into the sofa and Paige rested her stocking feet on the coffee table. It seemed strange to Rob to be so relaxed with her, to feel he was miles and years away from the man who had tortured and robbed her. It was hard to admit, but he finally could accept that he had tortured her. Abruptly he sat up and leaned forward, his arms on his knees.

"Are you all right?" Paige sat forward, too.

Rob nodded and attempted to shake his thoughts away. He wanted to make it right. He'd taken the easy way out five years ago just as Rico had said. If he and Paige got together and became anything besides friends, could he keep his secret from her? And why was he even thinking in those terms?

He felt her soft touch on his arm. She misunderstood his discomfort, thought it had to do with Myrna. "Tell me, Rob. What happened today?"

He wanted to cover her hand resting on his arm. Instead he moved away from her touch and said, "Myrna was drugged. We couldn't talk much because she just wasn't there, but she was relaxed, seemed to be all right."

Paige lifted her hand and smoothed loose curls away from her face. "Didn't you talk to the doctor about that?"

Rob related his conversation with Dr. Fairchild and his sister, leaving out the part about going back to Las Vegas. When he'd finished, Paige looked puzzled. "Then, why -- what seems to be...."

"I'm going to have to move back here for awhile, until Myrna's well." Rob turned to face her. "I've made a decision."

Paige nodded, waiting.

"I need to go back to Vegas and move out of my apartment, get my things. I need to do it while Myrna's in the hospital and so..." He raked his hand across his short hair. "So, I'm going tomorrow."

Paige's face remained expressionless. He hoped she'd be happy he was going to be in Tulsa longer or disappointed he would be gone awhile, some kind of response. As his feelings for Paige grew so did his confusion about those feelings. Silently berating himself for thinking she might care one way or the other, he stood up. "I guess I'd better be going. I need to pack and go see Myrna before my flight leaves tomorrow afternoon."

"You don't have to go yet." Paige stood, her hand reaching toward him. "I mean-- I mean..." She stammered. "It's still early." She drew her hand back. "Rob." He turned at his name. "It's just that-- we haven't really talked about Myrna."

"I know. It's all right."

Then she said something that startled him. "Your eyes. I don't think I've ever seen anyone with eyes like yours."

He stiffened. "What do you mean?"

"I just mean they're so different. Most people have blue or green or brown, but yours are grey and blue. I've just never...." She stopped, stumbled on her words. "Rob, I didn't mean anything except that your eyes are very nice." She stepped back. "I like what I see in them."

"What do you see?" His hands came out of his pockets, his fists clenched at his side. Fear gripped him, the fear that she was remembering.

Paige thought a moment. "I see gentleness and--longing." Their eyes met and held. After a long embarrassing moment, Rob mumbled "See you later," and walked out the door.

# NINETEEN

Rob looked at his watch as the plane banked and circled for its landing at McCarran International Airport. Nine fifteen. He leaned toward the window admiring the neon city springing from the Nevada desert. He recognized the stunning green of the MGM Grand, the gold-striped Mandalay Bay, and the red lights of the Stratosphere. Below him shown the radiant fingers of the Rio, the New York New York skyline, the pyramidal Luxor's white beacon light, all summoning the pleasure-seekers from below. Excited passengers squirmed within the confines of their seat belts murmuring in the expectation of sudden riches at the gaming tables and machines.

Rob felt it, the same sensation he had five years earlier. From all corners of the world Las Vegas draws its participants with its flashy promises, its self-gratifying hedonism. Even those who didn't gamble, like Rob, felt its pull from the ordinary, the natural into the belly of its debauchery.

This was the Strip, the heart of the Las Vegas economy, but far removed from those who lived and worked and raised families in this western town. Yet, it touched them all. Its greedy tentacles constantly stretched toward them. Still, in the midst of all this, Rob had found a new life and become a new man.

A few times he and Rico had gone with men from the boarding house to casinos off the Strip. Sometimes the other men pooled their money, played Video Poker, Black Jack or Roulette then they would divide the winnings, if there were any. Rob and Rico never gambled; Rico saving what he earned and sending every spare dollar he had to his family in Mexico. Rob felt his money had been too hard to come by to throw it away on games of chance. He'd already gambled -- with lawlessness. To an outsider who knew his story, it would appear he'd won, but Rob knew he'd lost his self-respect, his conscience and his past. He hoped the old life was truly behind him and that he could live out the rest of his life as Robert Martin and forget he had ever been the felon, Rob McGruder.

Seat belt sign off, the passengers hurriedly gathered their belongings and stood up, impatient to get to the tables and machines. Rob waited until the aisle was clear before rising from his seat. Reluctantly he walked down the jet way and into the bustling gate area. He was already saying good-bye to this place that had been both a place of refuge and his redemption. Leaving Las Vegas would be leaving a life where he'd felt safe, been independent and respectable. But it wouldn't be for good. His future was here and he'd return when Myrna was better.

The next evening Rob turned his Dodge pickup into the Summerside addition of northwest Las Vegas. Few trees adorned the small areas in front of the gray stucco homes lining Orchard Street. River rock and cactus filled some of the yards while others had minute areas of wide-bladed, deep green grass. Men and women visited in the yards of some of the homes, children rode skateboards, tricycles and bikes on the sidewalks of the lively neighborhood. Rob recognized Bob Taylor in the front yard of a house near the home of John and Shanna. He waved but the boy was involved in a game and didn't see him.

The tanned, lanky John Taylor was waiting for Rob when he pulled into the driveway. After their greeting John took Rob through the house into the backyard where his wife, Shanna, was in the pool with their daughter. Shanna's hair was pulled back in a pony tail under a wide-brimmed straw hat that shaded her face from the brutal Nevada sun. She called out, "Welcome home, Stranger." Gracie waved and mimicked her mother saying something that sounded like, "Come home, Gwangeh."

Rob laughed, returned her wave and squatted beside the pool. "I have a question to ask you, Miss Gracie."

She pushed her wet raven curls off her face and flashed him a wide grin. "What, Misteh Wob?"

"How old are you?"

The girl raised three pudgy fingers in the air and shouted, "Fwee!"

Shanna and Rob laughed aloud. John joined them and knelt beside Rob.

"Well, I just want to know this. How did you get so pretty in just three years?"

Gracie cocked her head to one side. She looked at her mother, "Tell him, Mom."

Quickly, John answered, "She takes after her mother."

A look passed between the man and wife. For a moment in time they were cocooned in a world that existed for only the two of them, and Rob felt like an intruder in their presence. Their tenderness struck him like a hard fist landing on his gut and it took his breath away.

Shanna's voice broke into his thoughts. "Are you ready to get out, Gracie?"

"No, swim moh." The little girl wiggled to free herself from her mother's grasp.

"Then it's time for more suntan lotion." She handed the child to her husband who easily lifted the dripping girl from the pool and carried her to a table under the patio cover where he rubbed lotion on the child's face and body. As Rob stood alone, Shanna joined her husband and daughter. He watched as John lotioned his wife's arms and neck. When he'd finished, he leaned down and kissed her lightly on the lips.

"My tuhn! My tuhn!" Gracie raised her hands to her dad. He lifted her, wet body against his, and hugged her ending with a noisy kiss on her nose. She giggled and jumped down.

"Walk," her mother reminded her when she started toward the water. As Shanna lowered herself into the pool, she smiled at Rob, "It's good to see you again, Rob."

He returned her smile and basked in the warmth that had settled over his heart. This is what a family is about, the way life is supposed to be. The image of his father flashed across his mind and a block of ice dropped over the warm place causing it to ache with an icy emptiness.

John pulled two beers out of a cooler, extending one toward Rob, "You back to stay?"

Rob shook his head and walked to the table. "Sorry to say, I'm not." He saw the disappointment on his friend's face. "My sister needs me for awhile now that her husband died."

The two men sat down and Rob took a drink of his beer. The feel of the bubbles on his tongue reminded him he hadn't had anything like this to drink since he left Vegas. He and Rico hadn't been big drinkers but they did enjoy their occasional brew.

John asked about Rob's plans.

"I plan to get a job welding in Tulsa if possible," Rob told him. "Of course, it'll be temporary."

John gave him advice about finding a job when he got back then the two talked about what the company was working on. Rob asked about some of the men and enjoyed the easy conversation with his friend. He liked being back in Vegas and knew without a doubt that this was where he belonged. He respected John Taylor as he had respected no other man in his life except Rico.

"John, have you heard anything from Rico?" Rob asked.

The man took a drink of his beer. "No, haven't heard a thing, but then he never did call me, always called you."

"I know." Rob leaned back in his chair and crossed his leg over one knee. "There isn't any way to get hold of him in Mexico. I guess, if he doesn't call while I'm here, I can write him."

John nodded. "Is everything all right with you, Rob? You seem kind of troubled."

Rob thought about telling him, but how much did he really want to share about what was happening in his life? If he explained, then he'd have to tell the story of Paige and the robbery, and he wasn't ready for that. Instead of answering that question, he asked one of his own. "John, is your job your purpose in life?"

It was clear from his expression that the question surprised him. "Where did that come from, Rob?"

I met someone who talked about having a passion and who asked me if I had one. If I do, I don't know what it is. I just wondered if you feel you have a purpose in life or something you feel strongly about. I wonder if it's important to a person to have one."

John leaned forward holding his cold bottle between his hands, his voice low. "I had one when I was younger. It was a real passion and I thought it was my purpose."

Rob waited for him to continue.

"I grew up in Plano, Texas, went to Plano West High School. My dad took me to every Dallas Cowboy home game. That was the time of Tom Landry. My dad says I saw Don Meredith play but I was only seven when he retired and really don't remember him. I remember Roger Staubach and Chuck Howley and Bob Lilly and my personal hero, Drew Pearson." John leaned back, enjoyment lighting his face.

All this was out of Rob's domain. He'd never been allowed to play football nor watch it on television. He'd heard of the Cowboys but didn't know much about any football team.

John smiled and took a drink of his beer. "In 1971 when I was nine years old, I saw Duane Thomas score the first touchdown in the new stadium and beat the Patriots forty-four to twenty-two. That year my dad took me to New Orleans to watch Dallas play Miami and win Super Bowl Six. It was great."

Rob wondered what this had to do with the question he'd asked. Before he could comment John continued. "It was my passion to play for the Cowboys."

"What happened?"

"I was tall, not heavy, but I could catch that ball. At Plano West I was all- conference receiver. I got scholarship offers to Tech and UTEP and a few smaller colleges but I wanted to stay in Dallas so the Cowboys would notice me. So, I went to SMU without a scholarship."

Gracie's high-pitched voice interrupted him. "Daddy, Daddy, watch me!"

"I'm watching, Baby." The three-year-old swam away from her mother and then swam back, her water wings holding her above the water.

The patio door slid open and Bob Taylor and a friend came out in the yard. When John's son saw Rob, he smiled. "Hi, Mister Rob," the name coined by his sister.

Rob extended his hand and the boy shook it. "I think you've gotten taller since I last saw you."

"Growing like a weed. I think he'll be taller than his dad," John said, clearly proud of his ten-year-old son.

"Won't be long before he's driving," Rob teased.

Bob's head bobbed in agreement.

129

"Slow down there, Friend. No driving yet," and he laughed. "What's up, Son?"

"Zane and I want to go swimming." He looked toward the pool.

"It's your sister's time but I think she's almost through. You can get in your suits and wait until Mom takes her out." He looked toward Rob. "The boys are a little rambunctious for Gracie." He asked Zane, "Do you have permission from your mom?"

"Yes, sir," the boy said.

Bob headed for the door, "We'll play Game Boy until Gracie's out."

The two boys slid the door closed and John sighed, "They grow up so fast."

Rob wanted to get back to his question and was thinking of a way to steer the conversation back when John gestured toward the departing boy and the girl in the pool.

"That's Shanna's passion." John returned his wife's smile.

As though on cue, Shanna Taylor took off her hat and loosed her chestnut hair. Golden highlights shown under the late evening sun. He understood how children could be a passion and wondered if he'd ever know what it meant to have a child of his own. She helped Gracie out of the pool and the two of them dried with beach towels before going into the house.

John continued. "You want to know passion. I had it. It was all about football and the Cowboys. Those NFL guys are big." John motioned to Rob's empty beer and asked if he wanted another. At Rob's refusal, he pulled a bottle from the cooler for himself, unscrewed the cap and took a long drink. He wiped his mouth with the back of his hand and settled back in his chair. "I figured I needed to be heavier and that I couldn't get there on my own so at the end of the college season, I started taking Equipoise."

At Rob's questioning look, John explained. "A steroid to help me beef up."

"How did you get it?"

"Easy. Those kinds of things are readily available to athletes. I got it from a friend who got it from a friend--you know, something like that."

"Did it help?"

"Yeah, it did. I worked out every day, ate a lot of protein and carbs and got a lot heavier and stronger but I started having bad side effects. My skin broke out. I had headaches and was really irritable with everyone. Wanted to fight all the time. I stopped taking it when my breasts began to develop." He chuckled.

"That must have scared you."

"Scared the hell out of me! But, when I went off it, I felt worse. I was tired, couldn't eat or sleep. Depressed." He shook his head remembering. "I'd made a name for myself at SMU but I wasn't in the draft. Still, the Cowboys accepted me in training camp and put me on the practice squad. If they liked what they saw they'd give me a spot on the roster. But they noticed the steroid signs. Acne, how I'd suddenly gotten bigger than when I was in college." Sadness etched his expression. "This was before THG and the undetectable drugs." He cleared his throat. "They tested me."

Rob watched as John's gaze shifted and his eyes looked back on the years with sadness. "You didn't make it?"

John shook his head. "They found it in my system. I'd stopped it about a month before but I didn't know the detection time is around four to five months. So, I was out."

"Out of the Cowboys?"

"Out of football-- forever."

"Whoa. That's heavy." Rob knew what it meant to lose a dream.

"Damn right it was." John sat his bottle on the table with a bang. "And my passion died. Suddenly I had no reason for living."

"What did you do?"

131

"I tried to kill myself with booze for awhile then my dad got hold of me." John smiled bitterly and shook his head. "Boy, was he sore at me for doing the steroids and then turning to booze. Shanna almost didn't marry me. We'd been going together since we were seventeen. She was so pissed." He laughed.

Rob didn't see the humor in what had happened to his friend.

"Between her and my dad they let me know they weren't going to allow me to throw my life away."

"What did you do?"

"I learned a valuable lesson. You can't take a short cut--ever. You have to do things right. Short cuts end up hurting you and the ones you love. Then came the hardest part." He leaned forward and rested his arms on the table. "Forgiving myself. It's easier to forgive others than it is to forgive ourselves when we mess up. But that's what really set me free and I could go on and marry Shanna and make a life for myself."

Rob had his answer, and more than that, he had words that struck at his heart. Taking short cuts, as he had when he robbed Paige, hurt so many people. Most of all it had hurt him. In robbing Paige he had stolen his own self respect. Something he would have to live with the rest of his life.

---

Mama Serena wrapped her pudgy arms around Rob. She called into the house, "Papa, it's Roberto. He's home."

*Home.*

Rob followed the plump woman through the front of the house and into the kitchen where Carlos Aragon sat in his usual place at the wooden table. Beside him a young man stood up when they entered. Rob walked around to the elder man and shook his hand. A wide smile lit Carlos' craggy face. "Roberto, this is our first son, home from Iraq." He turned to his son. "Manolito, Roberto es el amigo de Rico."

The younger man's smile welcomed Rob as they shook hands. "Ah, Rico's friend. He told me about you. I saw him last week." Manolito's speech was without any accent.

"He's here?" Rob hoped his friend was in Vegas and he would be able to see him.

"In Mexico. I was in Hermosillo visiting the family of one of my army buddies. He'd been injured and sent home before me." He smiled at his parents. "Mama and Papa told me I had to see Rico so I did."

Anxious to hear more, Rob asked, "How is he?"

Manolito's eyes twinkled. "He's married."

Had it been that long since he'd heard from Rico? "Married? How long?"

"Just a few months," Manolito said. "They're expecting their first child."

Rob remembered the last time he'd talked to Rico. It had been right after Christmas. He hadn't mentioned anyone so it must have happened very quickly. Rico had found his amante, his love. Envious of his friend but, at the same time, happy for him, Rob asked, "What's she like--his wife?"

"Rosa's tall, taller than Rico, graduated from Mexico University, a schoolteacher. They live with his sisters and brothers." He looked at his mother. "She's pretty and smart but she can't cook like Mama, but who can?" The three men laughed when Serena blushed and waved them away.

"What's he doing?" Rob asked.

"He's working for an American contractor. The town has become a place for tourists and they're building hotels and restaurants." He smiled at Rob. "He has a good job. He's happy."

Rob touched the gold stud in his ear. Manolito smiled again and motioned toward it. "Rico still has his, too." The Spanish man laughed aloud at Rob's surprised expression. "He told me."

"What?" Mama Serena raised her hands in consternation. "Tell me what you talk about. Do not keep secrets from the mama or you no eat."

Both men laughed and sat down at the table. Rob liked this man as well as all the other Aragons he'd met. If only he'd come here before robbing Paige. If only he'd taken a chance and just left Tulsa without thinking stealing from someone was the best way to go.

Mama Serena held a plate over the table. "Begin or you will not have a tamale, Roberto."

"It's no big deal. Not a very interesting story." Rob took one of the tamales and bit into it. "It was a spur-of-the-moment thing." Mama Serena's look questioned his term. "I mean, we didn't plan to do it. Rico and I went out with some of the guys from work one night and everyone had a little too much to drink." The three listeners nodded knowingly. "Some of the guys decided to get tattoos. Rico and I didn't want to but they kept pressuring us. Finally we told them we'd get an ear pierced instead."

Mama Serena said, "And no more story?"

"No more story." Rob chewed his tamale. "But every time I touch it I think of my friend, Rico, and how much he changed my life."

"He said the same thing about you." Manolito nodded. "He said he touches his ear and mi amigo is near." He said the last words with an accent. "He misses you, too."

Rob was sad to have to leave his friends but knowing he would see them again made it easier. From them he had learned about family, about caring for another person and, more important, that Robert McGruder Martin was capable of love.

The trip home gave Rob time to think about his life and his plans. He knew it wouldn't be difficult to avoid the people who had wanted him to break the law for the short time he would be in Tulsa. Staying away from the old hang outs would be simple. Those people didn't come into his sister's neighborhood and he wouldn't go into theirs, and none of them knew he was back in town. Anyway, he had changed. No more crime for him. As soon as Myrna got out of the hospital he'd be able to stay away from Paige Lewis, too. As much as he was drawn to her, he had to keep his distance until he left Tulsa. She had noticed his eyes. What would she notice next? She could never find out who he was.

He got back to Tulsa early Sunday morning. He slept a few hours and in the afternoon visited his sister for over an hour. She appeared relaxed, asked him about his trip and told him she thought she would be going home soon. He wished he had someone to talk to about her but Dr. Fairchild wasn't at work and when he spoke to one of the nurses, he was told to come back Monday.

Before going to the hospital the next morning Rob went to the union office. In Vegas he'd talked with the business agent and pulled his travel card from the local there. He wanted to deposit it in Tulsa and sign up on the work list.

When he got there, he found that no other welder had signed the list, and a construction company working on a downtown building renovation was looking for someone with his qualifications. He drove to the construction office and was hired to begin working the next morning. Buoyed by his good luck, he went to the hospital. Paige was waiting with Myrna in Dr. Fairchild's office. The four of them exchanged greetings.

He was embarrassed about the way he had left Paige before he went to Vegas and avoided eye contact with her as much as possible. After today he would bring his sister to see Dr. Fairchild but he would make it a point to get Paige out of their lives.

The psychiatrist handed written instructions to Myrna. "These will tell you exactly when and how you should take your medication. If you have any problems, any questions, please call. I don't expect any and believe you'll do very well."

Myrna nodded.

"I would rather you not drive for a few weeks," the doctor continued. "We don't want you to have stress of any kind and sometimes driving can be stressful." She looked at Rob. "Is there any way you can bring her for her appointments, Mr. Martin?"

Rob explained the job he had gotten that morning was from six until three in the afternoon and bringing her after that wouldn't be a problem. A twice weekly four o'clock therapy session was set.

Before leaving the office Myrna went to Paige and hugged her. "Rob and I thank you so much for all you've done." She smiled and gestured to include her brother. "I think the two of you saved my life."

Rob nodded and mumbled a thank you in Paige's direction. He looked up and found her eyes on him. He could see she was curious about his attitude and forced a smile as he turned away. He was excited by this woman but she could recognize him at any time. Being in her presence made him remember the past. That's it, he thought. She reminds me of who I used to be. It's nothing more than that.

When Rob turned the car into the drive way, Myrna reached across the seat and touched him. "It'll be all right, Rob. I'm getting better and won't cause you any more trouble."

"Trouble? You haven't caused me any trouble."

"Of course, I have. You had to leave your home and job and move here." Tears glistened in her eyes. "You have no idea how much it means to me. I'll make it up to you some way."

Rob took her hand. "You have nothing to make up to me. I'm right where I want to be, with you, and I plan to stay as long as you need me. I'm just glad I can be here." He squeezed her hand and opened his door. "Now come in and see what a great housekeeper I am."

Myrna laughed, a sound Rob hadn't heard from her since he'd returned to Tulsa. It felt good to have his sister on her way back.

They walked through the house, Rob showing off his cleaning skills and Myrna exclaiming that her house hadn't been this clean in months, which was probably true. When they got to the kitchen, she opened the refrigerator. "Uh oh." She winked at her brother. "Old mother Hubbard's cupboard is bare. What will she feed her poor dog?"

They laughed remembering the nursery rhyme they'd learned from their mother. "You make me a list and I'll go to the grocery store and get us something for that poor dog." He left her, still smiling, in the kitchen.

Happier than he'd been in a long time, Rob thought he might be coming out of that ditch he'd been in most of his life. It was exhilarating knowing he was where he was supposed to be, but when his thoughts returned to Paige and their relationship, the darkness returned.

He shook the thoughts from his mind. Today was for Myrna and for the first time in his life he was determined to think of someone besides himself.

# TWENTY

Summer turned into a colorful, wet fall in Oklahoma. Rob had written to Rico and given him Myrna's number, telling him the hours he would be at home. One night, early in September, Rico called.

"Why didn't you tell me about Rosa when we talked last January?" he asked.

He heard Rico's rich laughter over the wires. "I did not know *mi amante* when we spoke. I met her soon after."

"And you got married right away?"

"Mi amigo, when you find your own love, you will not want to wait either. You haven't found her yet, have you?" he teased.

Rob hesitated before answering. "No, I haven't met mine yet." But with Rico's question, his thoughts had immediately gone to Paige. No way could she be his true love, he thought. When he found his love, it would be in Las Vegas.

The two men talked only a few minutes because of the expense of long distance from Mexico. Before they hung up, Rob told his friend again to call him collect when the baby came in February and Rico promised he would.

Rob had wanted to tell Rico about his time in Tulsa, about Paige and his sister, but this conversation was for Rico, not him. He'd told him very little in the letter he'd written and hoped the time would come when they would have the chance to talk more.

Rob liked his job and the men he worked with. Every week he drove Myrna to the hospital for her therapy session and waited in the car. He told her it was because he had just come from work, wasn't cleaned up and was tired. In truth, he didn't want to run the chance of seeing Paige. Sometimes his sister would come back after the session and tell him she'd seen the psychologist who had asked about Rob. He imagined Paige was just being polite. Every time it happened he was even surer he didn't want to go into the hospital. That changed the first week of October. Although his sister had been driving herself for the past few weeks, Rob was asked to attend a session with her.

"Why?" he asked. "Why do they want me?"

"Because you're a part of my life and Dr. Fairchild feels it's time we do this together." She touched the sleeve of his denim jacket. "It's all right. It will help us, Rob. It will help both of us."

Rob thought about her words. "It will help both of us." What kind of help did he need? His main concern was that his sister would say something about what he did. Still he agreed to accompany her the following week.

Rain fell the day of the therapy session, and because of the weather, Rob was able to leave work early. He had time to shower and change clothes before they left for the hospital.

"Please don't be nervous," she told him. "It isn't so bad. You don't have to say anything you don't want to. There are a few things we need to talk about together with the doctor."

"You know I talked to her while you were in the hospital, don't you?" They hadn't ever spoken of this, and he wanted to tell her in private before they were with Dr. Fairchild.

Myrna shook her head. "No, I didn't know. She never said anything. What about?"

Rob took in a deep breath. "Well, I told her about our childhood, our mother…" He looked over at her. "I told her about our father and how he treated you when you were…"

Pain filled Myrna's eyes. She looked away and nodded. "I told her, too."

"I told her I left that night."

She nodded again.

"And I told her why."

Myrna's eyes darted to his face. "You never told *me*."

I know," he said, remembering her reaction that first night in the car and in Leroy's room after he'd died. "Do you want me to tell you now or when we're in the session?"

She looked away and finally answered, "Maybe we'd better wait."

"One more thing, Sis," he said. "I need to know what you've told the doctor about when I left five years ago."

"Scared?" She laughed with disdain.

Rob winced. He waited a second then looked at his sister.

Her expression was cold. "That's something we'll need to talk about some time, but not today. You don't need to worry. I haven't said anything about that--yet." She smiled with no humor. "My dear brother, you may have been able to fool everyone else but you've never fooled me."

"Myrna…" he stammered, "you don't understand."

"Of course, I do. I understand more than you think." She sighed and placed her hand over her eyes. When she spoke again, her voice was softer, the coldness gone. "Let's don't get into this now. The time will come." She raised her eyes to his. "I'll keep your secret."

Neither of them had spoken again after this exchange. They were ushered into the doctor's office by a receptionist and waited in silence until

Dr. Fairchild entered. She exchanged a sheaf of papers she was carrying with a folder from her desk while apologizing for keeping them waiting. After shaking their hands, she took a seat in a straight back chair across from where they sat on a leather couch. She began by asking Myrna how her week had been then turned to Rob.

"You understand, Mr. Martin, that whatever you say here is confidential. You may say whatever you wish or not say anything. However, for your sister's sake, I hope you'll feel free to talk about some things. "

He nodded.

"Your sister has something to say to you." She turned to the woman. "Go ahead, dear. It's time."

Myrna shifted in her seat and faced her brother. She looked down at her hands, fingers laced together in her lap. She spoke softly. "Rob." She raised her eyes to his. "I've been so mad at you and so hurt because you left me with Daddy that night after..." She looked at the doctor who nodded. Turning back at her brother, she continued, her voice rising, full of choked emotion. "Why, Rob? I just have to know why you lied to me." She began to cry. "You promised Mama. You promised me. But you left me with him. You don't know how awful it was." Tears streamed down her cheeks. Her fists clenched, she raised them toward him. "I hate you for doing that to me. Tell me. You have to tell me now. Why did you leave me?"

Her anger took his breath away. She waited. The doctor waited. He cleared his throat and blurted out the words he had wanted to say to her for so long. "He threatened to kill me."

Questions replaced the anger on Myrna's face. "What?" she asked. Her fists unclenched and fell into her lap. "What are you saying? Who threatened to kill you?"

Rob told her all of it. Some of it was the same story he'd related to Paige a few months before, but he told her more, why he'd left, how he'd

141

lived on the streets as a sixteen year old and why he hadn't been there when their father died. He told her of his life of crime and the horrible years he'd spent in prison and of his desire to have a new life. Her expression changed from questions to incredulousness to understanding. "I'm so sorry, Sis. Please, forgive me." Years of stored-up tears surfaced and ran down his face. His sister leaned across the couch, buried her face in his shoulder and wept with him.

Finally understanding what had driven them apart, the two children grieved for their lost parents and their lost youth.

At the end of the session Dr. Fairchild told them about a hospital program available for people who had suffered losses in their lives.

"A small group meets together one evening a week for ten weeks," she explained. "They complete activities designed to help them talk about their grief." She suggested they attend together

Rob hesitated. He had hoped he could leave Tulsa now that Myrna seemed to be getting better, and he certainly wasn't interested in staying and sharing his thoughts with strangers.

"Mr. Martin." The doctor smiled at him for the first time since they'd met. "I assure you it is handled discreetly. I've known others who have been reluctant to attend but by the time the program was completed, they all benefited greatly, and to a man, were grateful for the experience."

He looked at his sister. She nodded. "I think we should. You'll do it with me, won't you?" Seeing his reticence, she added, "Please do this for me."

Not waiting for his answer, Dr. Fairchild handed Myrna a sheet of paper with the information. "The first meeting is week after next on Tuesday evening. It will be held in the conference room on this floor, and," she added, "the facilitator is Paige Lewis."

Myrna gasped, her hand at her throat. "Maybe we shouldn't."

"She's very good at this." Dr. Fairchild touched Myrna's shoulder. "I don't like to insist, but I feel this is an important part of your healing."

Since Myrna was finally rational, Rob knew his sister had realized the danger of being with Paige. He could refuse to attend but a part of him liked having an excuse to be around Paige again even though it meant putting off his return to Vegas. He kept his voice neutral and said, "Myrna, it will be fine. I think the doctor's right. This is something we need to do." He saw the questions in her eyes and smiled. "It'll be all right."

"Okay. I do like Paige," she said. "I know she'll be helpful." She thanked the doctor and took her brother's arm as the two of them left the office.

Rob knew he should have said he wouldn't do it, maybe said he was leaving town but the opportunity to see Paige every week was too strong. At the same time, he was fearful she would remember him one day and if that happened, he would rather die than go back to prison. He told himself he would be careful.

# TWENTY-ONE

The following Tuesday Rob found himself dreading the evening. He'd had too long to think about it and now he was sure it wasn't a good idea after all. As much as he anticipated seeing her, he feared the outcome even more. He finally decided he'd go and do whatever was required of him but he would avoid Paige as much as possible.

Rob stalled getting dressed and he and Myrna were the last to arrive at the session. Three other people sat with Paige at the table, two men and one woman. One man and woman were obviously a couple. The other man's olive skin, dark eyes and broad cheekbones hinted at his Italian heritage. He was slightly overweight, and he wore his black hair slicked back behind his ears. Paige shook hands with Myrna and Rob and when they were seated she looked around the table and asked if everyone was comfortable. Quietly each member of the group nodded. Rob shifted in his seat, rubbed his hand over the back of his neck then touched the stud in his ear to quiet himself. *Rico, buddy, sure wish you were here. You'd lighten this group up.*

"I'd like for each of you to introduce yourself and tell us about the loss you have experienced." Paige motioned to the couple on her left.

The man looked at the woman and nodded. She spoke. "We're Kay and Mike Granger. We lost..." She shook her head and lifted a tissue to her mouth.

When her husband spoke, Rob had to strain to hear him across the table. "Our little boy, Mickey, was hit by a car in July and --we--lost him. He was only four."

Paige thanked them and motioned to the slicked-back hair man. Rob noticed his eyes were different colors; one was brown and the other green and decided he didn't like the man very much.

"I'm Paul De Luca. My wife, Elizabeth, died six months ago. She had breast cancer and was sick for two years. I have three kids, twins six and a son who is eight. My kids have been having a hard time with her death, and I don't know how to help them. I figured I needed to get help myself before I can do them any good."

Rob saw Myrna nod and smile at the man. Then it was his turn. He realized he had no idea what to say.

"Uh--I'm not sure why I'm here. I came with my sister," he stuttered. "Oh, my name is Rob Martin." He felt foolish and wished he was some place else.

"It's all right, Rob," Paige assured him. "Many times a person discovers why they're here after being in the program a few weeks." She gestured for Myrna to take her turn.

"I'm Myrna Watson. My husband died in July. He was in a wreck."

Paige talked about grief and loss but Rob's mind wasn't on her words. He pretended to be interested in what she said but instead watched the movement of her lips and fantasized about how it would feel to have them pressed against his own. He watched for the periodic dimpling of her cheek when she smiled and wished he could touch the smoothness of her skin with his fingertips. When she looked at him, he was struck by the vivid color of her eyes and had to turn his gaze away. He didn't let his mind explore the possibility of her discovering the truth about him, but rather enjoyed being able to drink in her nearness without thoughts of risk.

The Grangers opened up and talked about their son sharing through tears the deep loss they felt.

Paul De Luca revealed he was an attorney. "I think I've gotten through my grief pretty well," he said. "I prepared myself for it from the beginning but it was still hard. But it's my kids that I worry about. They cry for their mother sometimes and I don't know what to say that will comfort them."

That's real pain, Rob thought and his judgment of the man changed.

Myrna shared a little about her life with Leroy, leaving out much of the abuse and sadness she'd experienced. Rob didn't offer to say anything and was grateful Paige didn't try to draw him out.

After two hours the session ended. Paige gave them each a sheet of paper with the instructions to write down some thoughts about how people handle grief, what had been said to them when their loved one died, and their own thoughts after the death of the person. Rob had no idea what he'd write but took a sheet. Paige had cards with their names and phone numbers written on them and suggested they take one and call that person during the week. She explained it didn't have to be a long call, just a call to let the person know you're thinking of them. The card he chose was Mike Granger. He doubted he'd call him and wondered who had his name.

When everyone stood to leave, he hurried out the door expecting Myrna to be close behind. When she wasn't, he waited in the hall. The Grangers walked passed him and said "Good night."

Where is Myrna? He didn't want to go back into the room and chance having to talk to Paige. Myrna and the lawyer walked into the hall talking. Rob heard him say, "I'll call you this week." His sister smiled. He didn't hear her response.

Now what's going on? He told himself Paul must have drawn her name and that was the reason for their conversation.

Kay Granger called him on Saturday. He thought she was probably uncomfortable making the call but when she spoke she didn't sound uncomfortable. She said she'd been thinking about him and hoped he would find out why he was there. Remembering he was supposed to call her husband, he asked if he could speak with Mike. When he took the phone, Rob said the same things he'd heard Paige say at the meeting. "I've been thinking about you and hope you're doing all right."

Mike thanked him and said they'd see him on Tuesday.

What a crock! Rob thought. *This is ridiculous. I'm going to tell Myrna I can't go any more. I have no reason to be there and don't want to be.* But he knew in his heart he'd go back, not only on Tuesday but every week until the end. He would do it for Myrna, and for himself. He wanted to see Paige.

The Monday night before the meeting, Rob had a dream. He was often aware of dreaming when he slept but seldom remembered any contents. In this dream he saw his mother and father. They were standing on the front porch of their old house, and they were holding hands and smiling. He didn't recall ever seeing his dad smile, but his mother looked more beautiful than he remembered. Neither spoke to him but when he awoke, a deep longing settled in his heart. Mom, he thought, I miss you so much. Rob wondered why he would dream about his father. The more he thought about the dream the more he was sure what he would talk about at the meeting that night.

After the Grangers and Paul had shared their answers to the assignment, it was Rob's turn. "I didn't do my homework from last week..." He waited but no one commented. "...mainly because I didn't know why I was here, like I told you, so I couldn't say anything about what people said to me or any of the other things we were supposed to write about." He looked at his hands clasped together on the table in front of him. "No one talked about my mother after she died." He looked over at Myrna. Her eyes were downcast, her expression unreadable. "And I didn't know when my father died. I didn't..." he paused and cleared his throat. "I didn't live at home and didn't hear about it for a long time." He couldn't meet the eyes of the others at the table and kept his own focused between Paul and Kay Granger. "And that's why I couldn't do it."

No one spoke. Then he felt Myrna's hand on his arm, a slight squeeze. "I can tell you about that," she said. All eyes shifted to her. Rob heard Myrna inhale deeply before she began, her hand still resting on his arm. "I was only ten when my mother died. Rob's right. We didn't talk about it much, but my teacher found out and she talked to me."

Rob's eyes darted toward her. This was news to him. If his teacher knew about it, she had never said anything to him. Myrna continued, "She told me I could talk to her or cry with her anytime I wanted to. I did--many times. When I did, she'd hold me like a mother would, and tell me my mama wasn't really gone because she'd always live in my heart."

Rob stifled a gasp. *Live in my heart.* Hadn't that been true for him all these years?

"She told me about Heaven." Myrna smiled at her brother, holding him in her gaze. "We never heard about Heaven, did we, Rob?" He shook his head in answer and couldn't look away.

"I asked her to tell me about it and she told me such wonderful things about how it was there; trees and flowers, animals and birds, wonderful fruit, and she said that if we wanted candy, then we'd have that, too. But the best part was that all the people we loved were there waiting for us, and they were happy all the time." She looked at each person at the table. The Grangers held hands, smiling through their tears. Paul wiped at his eyes. "And I was glad for my mama..." Her voice broke and tears streamed down her face, too, "because she wasn't ever happy on earth."

A cleansing warmth flowed through Rob's heart. If this was true, his mother was in a good place, a better place than when she'd lived with them. He remembered his dream and the smile on her face, but his dad was there, too. Was it possible that horrible man was in Heaven? How could that be fair?

Myrna squeezed his arm again. "And our dad," she spoke directly to him. "When he died," she had to pause to get control. "When he died, I didn't even care." She sobbed. "God help me, but I didn't even care." Her hands covered her face and she repeated. "Even though I was alone, I didn't care."

Rob put his arm around her, awkwardly at first, then he leaned closer to her and she rested her head on his shoulder. What could he say? He knew why she didn't care, knew why she was probably happy he was gone. But she had said she was alone.

He was supposed to be there for her and even though she knew why he left, it still wasn't right. Couldn't he have come back? Couldn't he have stood up to his father and come back sooner? He accused himself of his cowardice. Did everyone at the table see that he was a coward? Even if no one else condemned him, he condemned himself.

The evening ended with another assignment from Paige. This time they were to draw a Life Graph. They were to begin at their birth and on one side of the line draw in the positive events of their lives and on the other side, draw in the negatives. Rob practically raced to the car and waited for Myrna there. He didn't want to have to face any of the other participants, didn't want to hear words of sympathy, if there were any. Or maybe, he told himself, he was afraid they'd ask him why he wasn't there for his sister and would see just how weak he really was.

He and Myrna spoke little on the way home, both lost in their own thoughts. When they walked in the front door, his sister hugged him. She touched his face and said, "I love you, Rob."

He nodded. Had either of them ever said those words to each other, ever in their lives? He couldn't speak over the emotion that closed his throat.

"It's all right, Rob. I understand." Then she went to her bedroom and shut the door.

For a long time Rob stood where she'd left him. Why couldn't he tell her he loved her, too? Why were those words so hard to say? And she said she understood. Did she? How could she when he didn't understand himself?

---

The next few days moved quickly. Rob's thoughts were on the assignment. Could he do it? Would he do it? It would certainly be easier to cop out again but was that fair to the others, and especially to Myrna? She had spoken so freely at the last meeting, had spoken from her heart. Could he do that with complete strangers? Could he draw a line and talk about the negative things in his life? The positives were so few, that wouldn't be a problem, but the negatives, prison, the robbery, changing his identity. How could he talk about his life and leave those big events out?

He left the house Saturday morning and drove around for a couple of hours thinking about the assignment. Maybe it was time for him to drop out, go back to Vegas. Myrna seemed to be doing pretty well. She could probably get along without him now. But wouldn't that be abandoning her again? He had to stay for her. And there was Paige. What would she think of him if he ran away from this? And why did he care what Paige thought?

When he returned home, he found Myrna seated at one end of the dining room table, paper and pencil in hand. Her line was drawn and she was writing. She looked up when he came in. No words, just sat there looking at him.

"All right, all right," he said, tossing his jacket on the sofa. "I'm going to do it."

She smiled and handed him a blank piece of paper and a pencil. "Do you need a ruler to make the line?" she asked, holding it toward him.

He wanted to say, "Hell, no!" Instead, he calmly took the ruler and sat down across from her. They worked quietly for several minutes. He wrote in all the positives, which mostly had to do with his mother and things he remembered about her. He drew in a few happy times at school and then skipped a long period and wrote "Las Vegas." Most of what he wrote for those five years was above the line, positives.

A muffled sob from Myrna broke into his concentration. When he looked up, her head was on the table and her shoulders shook.

"Sis, are you all right?"

No answer, just harder sobs. He went to her and put his hand on her back. "Sis, what's the matter?"

Slowly, she raised her head, her eyes filled with anguish. Unable to speak, she sobbed harder.

Now frightened, Rob knelt beside her. "Tell me, Sis, what is it?"

She shook her head and tried to speak, her words inaudible. Then he heard them. "My baby. My baby."

And Rob knew what she meant. The baby she'd given up. He looked at her graph, sodden with tears, and there it was written, "Age 15, Gave my baby away."

He held her until her crying subsided and she could speak.

When she turned fifteen a month after he left, she had dropped out of school and hidden in the house, cutting off all ties with school friends. At home alone all day she tried to think of ways to escape, some way she could leave and keep her baby. But she was so young, and she had no where to go.

"I thought about finding my elementary teacher who had helped me when our mother died, but I was too ashamed and afraid she would be mad at me."

She told Rob about the weeks and months of her father's torments. "He never called me by my name again. He just called me slut," she said. "When I started showing, he told me every day how ugly I was."

As Rob heard her story, he cursed himself. It was his fault. All of it. If he'd been the kind of brother he should have, she wouldn't have had to go through all that.

"You always wondered why I married Leroy."

He nodded, fearing what other guilt would be thrown on him.

"After I had..." she stopped, tears forming again. "After I had my baby and gave her up..."

A girl. She had a girl.

Myrna's face softened. "I got to see her, Rob. She was so small and so beautiful." Her eyes focused on an unseen realm and Rob didn't break into the silence of her memory. Finally she looked at him and smiled. "I named her. When I held her that one time, I told her she was named Sally. She was finally real but I was going to have to let her go." Tears flowed from her eyes as she remembered. "I told her I loved her and that I'd never forget her and hoped she'd remember me, too." She looked at Rob. "Do you think she does?"

He didn't know. He didn't think so but he couldn't tell her what he thought. "I'm sure she does," he said.

Satisfied, she said, "I never went back to school. I got a job at an apartment complex near the house and cleaned the apartments when the people moved out. That's where I met Leroy. Sometimes he was there cleaning carpets and we would talk. He seemed nice, too. He was my only friend, like a real father to me at first."

Rob saw her smile and was ashamed. Her only friend, taking the place of the father she needed. Where was her brother? Both he and their father had left her vulnerable to an older man.

The two of them were sitting on the sofa by this time. She sat sideways, her head resting on the sofa back. "At first Leroy was really good to me, but he always treated me like a child."

"Did he ever hit you, Myrna?" Rob hoped the answer was no but feared it wasn't.

She looked away. "Once or twice. Mostly it was his words that hurt, but I was used to that."

"Oh, God, Myrna, I'm so sorry I wasn't there for you."

She reached out and touched him. "Leroy found me crying one day after Daddy died and asked me to marry him. I didn't have anywhere to go, so I was glad to. I thought he'd take care of me and love me like I'd always wanted. And he told me we could have a child, but we never did. He wouldn't go to the doctor and wouldn't let me go to see why we couldn't get pregnant. I think he was afraid it would be his fault and he was too proud to admit it. It was after that when he began to be mean."

What was there to say? As bad as Leroy was, he was there when she needed him. What would have happened to her if he hadn't been? Silently he thanked Leroy and said aloud. "I'm glad he was there for you when you needed someone."

Myrna's eyes widened. "You're glad? I thought you hated him."

"I did but I think I really hated myself more because I left you."

"You talked to Leroy in the hospital and said you made it right. What did you mean?" she asked.

153

Rob took one of his sister's hands in his. "I guess you might say I told him I was sorry for all the years we hated each other and told him I'd take care of you now."

"Do you think he heard you?"

Rob shrugged. "I don't know but I felt better afterwards." He squeezed her hand and stood up. "It's like Paige said. Hating him would hurt me more than it would him." And he thought of his father.

# Twenty-Two

Rob finished his graph and did it honestly, knowing that if he had to talk about it, he would leave out the worst parts. Paige had told the group that people usually found their greatest loss when they made their graph. So far he hadn't found his. Was it his mother? Did he feel her loss more than anyone else? Although he did miss her, his memories of her had been good. He did realize he had spent much of his boyhood trying to shield her from Mac McGruder and was relieved that her death had made possible her escape from him. Selfishly, he also realized it had set him free from the burden of protecting her. He had to admit, when he was given that liberty, he'd taken it too far and let his sister down. He had left her to the mercy of her father and she'd found no mercy there. She was the one who needed his protection when Ann McGruder was gone, and he had failed. Rob decided his failures began and ended with Mac McGruder.

The following Tuesday, the group sat around the table again. Each one of the others shared their graphs. Every person shed tears when they reached the one loss that had never been healed. For the Grangers it was their son. For Paul it was the death of the mother of his children. Although he seemed to have been able to work through it, he grieved for his children's loss.

Then it was Rob's turn. He began to share from his graph. When he reached his mother's death, he stopped. It wasn't necessary to go on. He knew his greatest loss. To speak of it he would have to bare his heart and he wasn't sure that was possible. He'd told Paige about his life, some of his life, but this he had never spoken before. He touched the stud in his ear and the words Rico had spoken almost five years ago again echoed in mind, "Never take the easy way out." And John Taylor's words, "You have to do things right."

I'm here, he thought. For some reason I'm here. Can I do it? Can I let these people see into me? He knew it would be easier to keep the pain to himself as he'd always done. *Step up, Rob McGruder. For once in your life be a man.*

He took a deep breath, cleared his throat and looked into the eyes of each member of the group. He touched the stud again. *Okay, Rico. Here I go.* "I hated my father because he was cruel and didn't care about me." From the corner of his eye he saw Myrna flinch and lower her head. He reached for her hand and took it in his. "I wish I'd had a father who loved me," and his voice broke. But the chasm had been crossed. He had opened his heart to three strangers, his sister and a woman who had played a greater role in his life than she would ever know.

After that night he looked forward to Tuesdays. But after every session he hurried out of the room, not staying for the small talk like the others did. He'd wait in the car for Myrna. When she asked him why he left so quickly, he gave her the excuse that he was tired, needed to get to bed early.

One Tuesday a few weeks later, she told him she'd drive her own car and he could take his truck. He assured her he didn't mind waiting for her but she insisted. She told him she was going to go to Paul's house after the meeting and stay with his kids while he took the sitter home.

"You and Paul got something going on?" he asked.

Suddenly shy, she said, "Rob, Paul and I have become," she paused, "friends. We talk on the phone and he's come over a few times during the day and taken me to lunch."

"Why didn't you tell me?"

She shrugged. "I guess I was kind of embarrassed. I didn't want anyone in the group to know. It just seems strange for us since we're both there working through our grief even though it isn't about our husband or wife." She turned her back to him. "I don't know why I felt I had to hide it, Rob." When she faced him, she spoke more strongly. "I guess it was too special to me to share it with someone. I was afraid..." Again she paused and Rob saw realization in her expression. "I think I was afraid that if it's something good, somehow it will be taken away from me."

Rob looked at her for a long time before he spoke. Myriads of thoughts raced through his mind. Thoughts he couldn't put into words, but he understood. Everything good in her life had been stolen from her. She didn't want to lose this, too. He reached toward her, put his arms around her. It wasn't something he'd done many times. Then he spoke. "I understand, and Myrna..." He took a step back. "I love you."

She smiled, tears pooling in her eyes. "You said it. Was it so hard after all?"

Rob shook his head. "No, it wasn't. It just came from how I feel."

"And you weren't afraid to say it." Myrna hugged him. "Thank you, Rob. I love you, too."

After that, Myrna and Paul were open with their relationship. The attorney came to the house a few times, he took Myrna to dinner, and the two of them spent time with his children.

The grief sessions ended Christmas week. Paige told them she wanted them to go through the holidays then to meet again the first Tuesday after the new year so they could talk about how they'd fared. "Holidays are typically the most difficult for us when we've lost someone. I want to see how you're all doing."

"I have an idea," Myrna said. "If it's all right with you, Paige, could we all come to our house that night? I'll fix some snacks and we can kind of have an ending party."

The psychologist hesitated. "We've never done that before." She looked around the table. "What do you think?"

Everyone agreed it was a good idea. Even though Rob had grown attached to this small group and, just as Dr. Fairchild predicted, had benefited from the experience and was grateful for the changes he saw in his sister and felt in himself, he looked forward to the time when he wouldn't have to be around Paige and the subtle constant fear she would recognize him and, with the recognition, his new life would end. At the same time he knew he'd miss seeing her. Soon he'd be going home and it would be over.

---

After the death of Rob's mother Christmas had been just another day for him. The first holiday after her death no tree was purchased and Mac McGruder bought nothing for his children. When Rob realized the holiday would pass without celebration, he decided he wanted to try to do something for his sister. Since he had no money of his own he felt his only recourse was to steal a couple of dollars out of his father's wallet. He couldn't remember what he bought and wondered if she did. He didn't even have a memory of giving it to her. The biggest part of the memory was the fear he felt when he stole the money and his dread for several weeks afterward that his father would find out. Even though his theft wasn't discovered, he was so frightened he never tried it again.

That was the last thought Rob had given the holiday until he spent it with Rico and the Aragons the first Christmas in Las Vegas. When Rico left Nevada, Rob had still gone to Mama and Papa Aragon's for Christmas Day. Although he wasn't blood family, their children and grandchildren welcomed him, and he loved being a part of their festivities. As Christmas approached his thoughts went back to the five happy holidays he had spent with his Hispanic family and dreaded the loneliness of the small celebration he assumed he and Myrna would have.

A week before Christmas he was surprised when Myrna suggested he join her at Paul's house for Christmas dinner. "Are you sure? I don't want to horn in on your time with them."

"Don't be silly, Rob. You're family. We want you there."

Family. Hearing that word always made his heart ache. He was never sure if it was because of the lack of his past family that brought the ache or the desire for a real family of his own. His spirits lifted when he realized he wouldn't be alone on that special day. In truth, he liked Paul and was anxious to meet his three children.

Christmas Day dawned cool and crisp, the winter sky the color of pre-washed denim. Rob drove to Tulsa's west side where Paul and his children lived in a renovated Victorian wood frame house. The entire area had once been a part of the Arkansas River bed and was now home to some of the city's most beautiful landscaping. Paul employed a part-time gardener to keep the greenery from overtaking his yard, and even in December, although the trees, bushes and grass were dormant, there was a lovely symmetry about the place.

Rob had only seen houses like Paul's in pictures. Besides the beauty of his yard, Myrna had helped Paul and his children decorate the outside of the home and the effect was extraordinary. They had laced Christmas lights and holly through the Jenny Lind spandrels that gave the porch a light airy feeling. Large stone pots sat around the porch filled with poinsettias and greenery. A teakwood swing hung on one end of the porch and white wicker furniture sat on the other. Sparkling white lights hung from the roof and circled every window. Bushes and hedges shined with the same white lights. As Rob walked up on the porch he admired a tall Douglas fir filled with silver ornaments and colored lights that could be seen through the picture window.

It was no less decorated inside. To the right of the entry hall was the living room that held the Christmas tree. The floor around the tree was filled with multicolored wrapped presents and every table had some kind of evergreen decoration on it.

Paul and Myrna met him at the door. She wore an apron with a large Santa Claus on the front over her black pants and green sweater. Paul was dressed in dark pants, a white shirt and a red and green vest. His dark hair was slicked back on the sides as it had been when they first met. It looked to Rob like he had put on a little more weight around his middle and gave Myrna the credit for that since she was cooking for the family most of the time.

Myrna hugged him when he came in. Paul took his jacket and asked if he would like a glass of egg nog. Not sure what it was and embarrassed to admit his ignorance, he declined.

"It's good, Rob," Myrna assured him. "I think you'll like it."

"I can put a little whiskey in it, if you'd like," Paul grinned and held his fingers up to show about a quarter of an inch space between them.

Egg and whiskey? Sounded pretty bad to Rob but to be courteous he agreed. He followed Paul and Myrna into the kitchen and Paul fixed him a cup of the nog and whiskey. To his surprise, he liked it.

Before coming today, Myrna had given him advice about bringing presents for the kids and intimated that there would be gifts for him under the tree. He had told her he had no idea what to buy for all of them and, at his insistence, she had taken his money and bought the gifts

160

herself. However, he had brought one gift that was still in the pocket of his jacket.

Paul's children came into the kitchen and Rob was introduced to Kristen and Kim, six year old twin girls and Josh, the eight year old son. All three of the children looked like Paul, dark hair, brown eyes. One of the girls was slightly taller than the other but, other than that, they looked identical to Rob.

He remembered some of the things Paul had spoken about during the grief recovery meetings, how the children had been subdued and depressed since losing their mother. Today the twins were animated, excited about the holiday. Josh was quiet and disappeared after the introductions.

When Josh left the group, Rob stepped back into the dining room and saw him go into the living room. Something about the boy tugged at Rob's heart. He excused himself and left the girls, Paul and Myrna in the kitchen preparing the dinner. When he entered the living room, Josh was sitting on the floor looking up at the tree. He was sure the boy was thinking about his mother. When he walked into the room, Josh didn't look up and Rob hesitated to speak. He remembered a few Christmases before his mother became ill and those memories were happy ones, but they had almost been obliterated by the grey, empty years since her death.

"Do you mind if I come in?" he asked Josh.

The boy spoke in a whisper. "Sure." He stayed in his place on the floor.

Rob knelt down beside him. "The tree is beautiful, isn't it?"

Josh nodded.

"Did your mom decorate it like this when she was here?"

At first Rob thought Josh would get up and run away from him. Instead tears glistened in the boy's eyes and he nodded again.

"My mom used to decorate a tree for us, too, for Myrna and me."

"My mom used to decorate it better than—than…" Josh stopped and wiped his nose with the back of his hand.

"Better than Myrna?"

"Yeah. Better than her." He gestured toward the kitchen and his tone hardened when he said "her."

Rob's heart sank. *He doesn't like Myrna. Maybe he sees how much his father likes her.*

"I bet she did," he said. "There's no one who can do things like our mothers." Josh kept his eyes on the tree. "Our mother died, too."

Josh's head swung around and he looked into Rob's face for the first time. "When?"

"I was twelve and Myrna," he made the same gesture toward the kitchen, "was ten."

Josh's expression softened. "So you haven't had a mother for a long time."

Rob sat on the floor. "I sure haven't. And not a day goes by that I don't miss her."

Josh nodded. "Me, too."

"But," Rob sat his empty cup on the floor beside him, "it did get a little better as I got older. After awhile it didn't hurt so much. I think Myrna feels the same way."

Josh looked away but his expression conveyed thought. They sat in silence for a few minutes before Josh whispered, "Do you think my dad wants your sister to be my new mom?"

Rob contemplated his answer. It had to be the right one, the one that would put the child at ease and give him peace with the new woman in his life. "No, I'm sure your dad doesn't want to ever replace your mother. I think maybe he just wants to give you someone else to love you." He placed his hand on the boy's head and slightly tousled his dark hair. "We can't ever have too many people to love us, Josh. I know for sure that

Myrna will never try to take the place of your mother and you don't have to worry about that."

Josh nodded, his eyes held a trust as they looked into Rob's. "She seems nice."

Breakthrough. "She is," Rob said. "She's real nice."

Paul called from the dining room. "Time to eat, you two."

The dining room was no less decorated than the rest of the house. Red candles and a holly centerpiece on a lacy green tablecloth graced the dark cherry wood dining room table. A small crystal chandelier hung over the table. If his sister had done all this, Rob decided she had talents he had never seen before.

After dinner and the kitchen clean up, the whole family gathered to open presents. The girls, on their knees in front of the tree looked at every gift, calling out who they were for until Paul told them to begin giving them out. Wrapping paper was quickly removed and toys and clothing were revealed for them. Rob watched Josh and saw a little bit of excitement as he made his discoveries.

When Josh opened one of the presents, he held it before him and said nothing. Rob could see it was a picture frame and the boy's eyes were glued to what it held. Finally the boy looked up at his dad and in a hushed voice said, "It's Mom and me."

The girls came over to him and looked over his shoulder. "We got one, too, only ours is us and Mom." One of them quickly picked up a frame and showed it to him.

Paul smiled and took Myrna's hand. "Myrna and I thought you would like to have your own special picture of you and your mother." He looked at Myrna, his eyes soft. "In fact, it was her idea."

Rob laughed and all the others in the room turned toward him. He went to the closet and took a small package from his jacket pocket and handed it to his sister. "You won't believe this," he said.

Myrna opened it, careful not to rip the paper. A smile lit her face and tears formed in her eyes. She showed the picture to Paul. "It's Mom with us," she said.

All three children crowded around her and looked over her shoulder. The picture was a snapshot but the three people in it were clear. Josh was the first to speak. "Wow. That's your mom?" he asked.

Myrna nodded. "That's me," she pointed. "And that's Rob, and that's our mother." She looked at her brother. "Where did you get it?"

For a minute he couldn't speak. He cleared his throat. "When I left, I took it with me. I've had it all this time. I got a copy of mine so you could have one, too."

Myrna got up and came to him. She put her arms around him. "You have no idea how much this means to me. I don't have any pictures of her and have always wanted one. Thank you, Rob. Thank you."

Over her shoulder he saw Josh smiling.

# Twenty-Three

The weekend before the final grief recovery session, Rob helped Myrna clean the house. She spent all day Tuesday baking and when Rob got home, he commented on the smell. "This reminds me of when Mom baked." He closed his eyes and took a deep breath." he said. "If I didn't know better, I'd think she was standing right beside you."

"Maybe she is," Myrna said. She, too, closed her eyes and breathed in. "It feels good being whole again."

"Whole?"

"I mean," she opened her eyes. "I mean that for so long I felt like I was a fragment of a person. Even when we were little, I always felt something was missing with me. I never knew what it was until now."

"And that is?" Rob asked.

Myrna lowered her eyes. When their eyes met again he saw the happiness in them. "Someone who really loves me. Rob, when I was a little girl, I had an imaginary friend. I don't think you knew that." He shook his head. "She was my baby and my friend. Her name was Sally."

"Like your baby?"

She nodded and brushed a honey colored strand of hair behind her ear. "I talked to her all the time"

"I heard you talking when you were in your room. You always had a doll with you. Was that her?"

She shook her head. "No, Sally wasn't real. She couldn't be because if she was, then she might get thrown away by Daddy."

"He did that?"

Myrna nodded. "Many times. Usually when he'd see me with Mama and I'd have a doll, he'd take it from me and look at it and say it was ugly. Then he'd tell me dolls and children who are ugly didn't deserve to live and sometime while I wasn't at home, he would come in my room and get it and throw it away. Even Mama couldn't stop him but she'd try. Mama would hold me while I cried then she'd get me another one." She straightened the sweatshirt she wore and smoothed it around her waist. "But he couldn't touch Sally."

Her story saddened Rob but didn't surprise him.

"Oh, I knew she wasn't real, but somehow she was." Her look asked for his understanding. "You know what I mean?"

Although he didn't, he said he did. He probably would have invented someone or something, too, if he had thought about it. "Nothing was safe from our father."

Myrna agreed. "I know. I guess I hated him as much as I loved Sally. Then he took my real baby away, just like he'd taken my dolls, but Mama wasn't there to get me another one." A wistful smile spread across her face. "Not until now."

"What does that mean? You're pregnant?"

"No," she laughed. "It's Paul. New Year's Eve he asked me to marry him. Rob, we love each other so much." Excitement lit her face. "You saw how it was with us and the kids."

He had seen how it was with her and the girls, and how he hoped it was now with Josh. "Do his kids know?"

"He talked to them first, even before he asked me. He said at first Josh was a little reluctant but the girls are happy about it.

"And Josh, now?" He remembered sitting in front of the Christmas tree with the sad little boy.

"He told his dad that as long as I didn't think I was his mother, it would be all right with him if we got married." She smiled. "I know, Rob. I know you talked to him. He told Paul what you said." She took his hand and squeezed it. "That was so sweet of you."

Rob leaned against the counter and put his hands in his pockets. "I knew how he was feeling is all. It wasn't much."

"It was more than you think, and the picture. That was like a miracle. I think maybe the pictures did it with Josh more than anything else." She wiped her hands on a paper towel and threw it away. "And, Rob, you know, I'm not too old to have a child of my own. I'm only twenty-nine. Lots of women are having their first baby at my age."

"What does Paul say?" As if it was any of his business but this was his sister and he wanted to protect her.

"He wants more kids, too. We wouldn't have any right away, but you know how much I've always wanted a baby."

What could he say? "Are you sure this is what you want?"

Myrna nodded, the excitement in her voice growing. "I'm sure. We're going to get married in June. He wants to give me an engagement ring but I told him I had to talk to you first."

"Have you told anyone else?"

She smiled. "Yes. We've told Paige. We thought we needed to talk to her about it."

"And?"

"She was a little concerned because of what I've been through, the depression and everything, and she wants to be sure it isn't too soon for Paul and me, after the deaths."

Rob agreed.

"Both of us are going to have sessions with her, together and separately." She took Rob's hand. "Please be happy for me, Rob. I know this is right and we want it so much. We're both sure it isn't too soon. It's so wonderful to feel this way and have a future to look forward to."

"If you're sure, Sis. I am happy for you." Then a slow ache clutched his heart and settled in his stomach. It was wonderful. His sister had found someone who loved her and felt whole because of it. But would it ever happen to him?

---

The food was good, the guests happy. Rob left Paige, Myrna, Paul and the Grangers talking together in the dining room and wandered back into the living room. For the last ten weeks he had stayed away from Paige. He always avoided her eyes when he was talking but when she wasn't looking at him, he watched her. Tonight would be the last time he'd have to be with her and he felt safer just knowing it. Still, he was drawn to her and often found her face swimming to the surface of his mind.

He hadn't said anything to Myrna yet but he planned to leave by the end of the week and come back in June for the wedding. She had Paul now and was doing well. She didn't need him any longer.

Brought back from his thoughts, he looked up to see Paige taking a seat on the sofa beside him. Her fragrance wafted toward him and excited his senses. At the same time, his feelings scared him. Before he could move away, she leaned toward him and whispered, "Myrna told you, didn't she?" When he nodded, she continued, "I hope you understand we'll do everything we can to be sure she and Paul aren't making a mistake."

He turned toward her, their faces close. He licked his lips, realizing how much he wanted to kiss hers. He simply nodded again, stood up and walked away. In a moment she was at his side. "Did I say something wrong, Rob?" Her hand was on his arm. He shook his head, took in a deep breath and faced her.

"No, you didn't say anything wrong. I'm sure you'll help them. I guess it's just a surprise." She dropped her hand leaving the place she had touched growing cold. He missed the warmth.

Paige said no more. He saw the questions in her eyes before she rejoined the group in the dining room.

What was it about her that drew him? He decided he'd leave and let them finish the night without him but before he could make his escape Paige announced, "It's time for us to sit down and have our session."

Myrna gestured for him to join her and Paul on the sofa. Angry at himself for staying he sat down.

"You all right?" Myrna asked.

Rob pushed his discomfort down and tried to relax into the sofa cushion. "Great," he lied and patted his sister's hand. "Just great."

After the sharing, it was finally over. Amidst the farewells Kay Granger wrapped her arms around him, her head just level with his chest. "Thank you, Rob, for having us. The things you've said in the group have really helped all of us."

Mike was right behind her and put his arms around him, too. He had never hugged another man. Even as close as he was with Rico, the two always shook hands and this closeness with virtual strangers, especially men, made him uncomfortable. He moved away from the door before anyone else could trap him into another hug.

The Grangers left with coats and scarves pulled up around their necks to shield them from the fresh snow swirling in the cold north wind. Paige buttoned her coat, pulled on leather gloves and hugged Myrna again, thanking her for opening her house. Rob escaped into the bedroom, away from their good-byes. He heard the front door close. His sister called to him and he stuck his head into the room, grateful to see she was alone.

"I'm going to Paul's. I'll stay with the kids while he drives the sitter home. I'm taking my car." She blew him a kiss and stepped out into the wintry night.

Car doors slammed. Engines started and Rob breathed a sigh of relief. Gone. They were all gone. No more Paige. He could put that part of his life behind him without the constant fear of being discovered, and, hopefully, she would disappear from his thoughts, too.

Only a few minutes had passed before he heard a light tapping on the door and Paige's voice. "Rob."

"Oh, no," he groaned. "What now?"

When he opened the door, Paige came in quickly, shoulders hunched against the cold. "I'm sorry to bother you, Rob," she said. "Something's wrong with my car, wouldn't start, not a sound." She unbuttoned her coat but left it on. "I hope you don't care if I wait in here. It's just too cold outside."

"Sure," he muttered.

"I called Triple A and they said it could be awhile, maybe thirty or forty five minutes before they can get here."

Rob gathered himself. "Do you want me to look at it?"

She smiled. "I have a feeling it's something hopeless, the starter or something like that. They'll be here soon and can tow it to my mechanic. May I sit down?" Paige asked.

Rob nodded.

"If you have other plans I can wait outside."

"No, I don't have any plans. Sure, sit down."

Paige shook off her coat and sat on the sofa.

Will you...," he hesitated. "Uh...will you need a ride home after they take your car?"

"Oh, no, I'll call a taxi."

Involuntarily the words came out of his mouth. "I'll take you."

"I don't want to put you out. Really, I can call a cab." She sat forward with her hands in her lap, her legs together like a child perched on the edge of the couch.

He sat down in the recliner. "It's no trouble. I'll take you." No trouble but a stupid idea, he thought.

Neither spoke. The wind howled. Rob could hear a muffled banging in the backyard. He remembered noticing that the gate latch needed to be replaced and promised himself he would do it on the week end.

Paige pushed herself back into the sofa, her hands still clasped in her lap. Rob thought about turning on the television. What was there for them to talk about? Were they going to sit this way for forty-five minutes?

It was Paige who finally broke the silence. "I hope you're all right with what I said earlier, about Paul and Myrna."

He nodded without looking at her.

"Dr. Fairchild and I will do everything we can to be sure they're ready for this new relationship. I was a little worried it was too soon for both of them, and it wouldn't be the right thing for them to do."

He bristled. "How can you decide what's good for another person?"

Paige hesitated before answering. "I don't guess I can."

"Then why don't you let them make their own decisions?" Anger surfaced, and he fought to hold it back. "How can you decide what's best for someone else?" Clear memories of guards telling him what to do for two years fed his anger.

Surprised, she answered, "No, of course not. We just want to be sure she's healthy enough to …"

"Get married? Maybe that's exactly what she needs to get healthy."

Paige recognized the strain in his voice. "You may be right." They sat in silence for several minutes before she spoke again. "I noticed this is a new sofa." She ran her hand over the brushed velvet fabric. "I like this color. Sage. My brother had a sofa like this." She paused. Rob sensed a tension, then, as quickly as he saw it, she relaxed and gave a soft laugh. "Maybe it's not the same."

Rob tried to remember the Lewis' sofa. He couldn't. All he could remember was the small, dark-haired girl lying face down, her wrists and ankles taped together, crying, begging him not to leave her.

In the silence that followed, their eyes met and held. Rob feared she too, was remembering that night and groped to change the subject. "Myrna bought that with the insurance money."

Paige nodded. "Did she buy anything else for the house?"

"No, just that. She's being careful with the money. She doesn't want to run out." These are just words to fill the time, he thought.

"She told me," Paige said. "I think she said she had to be at home to take calls for Leroy's work."

Rob nodded. Unable to think of anything else to say, he looked at his watch.

"Are you sure you don't have something else to do? I can wait in the car if you do."

Embarrassed for appearing to want her to leave, he answered, "No, I don't have any plans. I was just going to stay here and wait for Myrna. Besides you can't wait in the car. You'd freeze."

Paige sat forward. "Rob, I need to ask you a question. Have I done something to you, offended you in some way?"

"Offended me? No, why do you think you have?"

"Well, you seem to be so distant. Before, when Leroy was still alive and when we talked about Myrna--even when we had dinner together that night, and during the class, you were more relaxed even though you left so quickly after every session. But, tonight -- I don't know. Maybe I'm wrong but I feel you aren't comfortable with me or something. I hope I haven't done anything..."

Rob stood abruptly. "No, you haven't done anything." He walked across the floor, started to look out the window then thought better of it. "It's just me. I'm sorry." Dampness from the snow curled her hair around her face. He wanted to push it away from her cheeks, to feel her skin on his fingertips. Every fiber in him wanted to sit beside her, take her hand and tell her how he felt. But it wasn't possible. As drawn to her as he was, he was equally drawn away from her.

She'd remembered the sofa, the place he'd left her to die. She had mentioned his eyes that evening at the hospital. It was only a matter of time before she remembered more and recognized him.

Deep in his heart, Rob wanted to be able to tell Paige the truth. He hated having to keep this lie, wanted to get it out in the open, see what she'd do. But he feared the repercussions of a confession. He had a new life and couldn't bear to think about losing it or about going back to prison. His hand went to the back of his neck, then, as quickly, he dropped it. Instead he touched the stud in his ear. *Rico, friend, help me.*

A knock on the door broke the silence. They said in unison, "That was quick." He hurried to open it while Paige pulled on her coat. She followed the driver outside while Rob got his fleece-lined jacket from the closet. Checking to be sure he had his keys, he locked the door behind him.

He had the truck warmed up by the time the two of them climbed into it. As soon as the tow truck had Paige's car on the trailer and was on its way, she gave Rob directions to her condo and they pulled out of the driveway.

"I appreciate this, Rob."

It felt good to have her in the seat beside him. "No problem. Glad to do it."

"If you had been gone, and I'd have had to stay in the car…"

"You would have frozen."

They both laughed.

"Right. Probably. When you and Myrna got home, you'd have found an icicle out in front of your house."

Rob looked over at her. "I'm just glad I was home and could help you."

She met his gaze, reached across the seat and patted his arm. "It seems you help a lot of people."

"What do you mean?" Fear clutched his heart. Was she serious or was she being sarcastic?

"Well, you were there for Myrna when she needed you." She saw the look on his face. "I know, you weren't when you were younger, but you were when it counted. And you were there for your mother when she was ill. You were even there for me the evening you brought dinner to the hospital."

"That wasn't anything." He relaxed.

"Yes, it was. It meant more than you know. I'd had a rough day and you came to the hospital, brought me my favorite food, Chinese, and let me talk. That gave me a break, showed me there was still normalcy somewhere in my world." She rested her head on the seat back. "My job can be hard with all the tragedies I see every day. People dying, the ones they love dying. I think the ones who don't die but will never be the same physically are the hardest." She sighed. "And they are all trying to make sense out of it and go on with their lives. Sometimes it seems that's all that's out there. That's why I like leading the grief recovery group. I get to see people come to grips with their losses and discover that their lives still have meaning."

"Your purpose."

She looked at him. "You remember. Yes, my purpose."

"Are you really satisfied with never knowing who did…" Rob began.

"Who robbed me?" Paige smiled. "Is it so hard to understand that knowing wouldn't solve anything? If I knew, nothing could be changed." She gestured with her hand in an upward direction. "So, I let it go. He never came back and hopefully, he never did it again. But it doesn't matter to me. Can't matter to me. It's over and I have to make the most of my life."

Rob let it drop.

He turned onto her street and she pointed out her house. He wondered if he should walk her to the door, but before he could make a decision, he heard himself speak. "Paige, would you have dinner with me sometime?"

*What have I done?*

In the semi-darkness he could see her smile. "You know, I'd really like that."

"How about Saturday night?" He couldn't stop now.

"Sounds good to me. Around six?"

He nodded. "I'll pick you up at six."

She scooted out of the seat, told him good night and thanked him again, then she was gone. He watched her run up to her door and when she had it open, she turned and waved to him.

Excited with the prospect of seeing her again but cursing himself for not ending their relationship, he drove home. He would stay in Tulsa a week more, just for the date, and then he'd go back to Vegas.

***

The rest of the week passed too quickly for Rob. He was sure he wasn't ready for this date, his first in many years. Maybe the first in his life.

All his other encounters with women had been different, spontaneous, unplanned. This was a real date; a pick-her-up-at-her-house-and-go-to-dinner date. Every time he thought of it his stomach churned. When Myrna asked what his plans were for the weekend, he thought about keeping it from her, and then realized she might find out from Paige. His sister's expression changed. Myrna took his hands in hers, looked him in the eyes and asked, "Are you really sure about this?"

He'd nodded. "I think so." He squeezed her hands. "Sis, I know what you're thinking."

"Do you?" she asked.

He looked away from her then back into her eyes. "You know what I did, don't you?"

She nodded. "Of course, I do. I've known from the beginning."

"The beginning?"

"When you left. I knew then."

Rob's head dropped to his chest. "I'm so sorry. I wish I could take it all back."

Myrna moved away from him. "I'm sure you do, but you can't. We have to make the best of the decisions we've made in the past."

"What do you think I should do?" he asked honestly.

She shook her head. "That's not my call. I made up my mind a long time ago to let you work this thing out on your own." She went back to his side. "I know you'll do the right thing."

"I've changed, Myrna. You know that."

"I do know. I can see it," she said.

"This is going to be a one time date, Sis. Don't worry."

"You like her, Rob?" He simply nodded. A few moments passed, and then quietly she asked, "What are you going to wear?"

He hadn't even considered clothes but realized all he had were the khakis he'd bought last July, the same pants he'd worn to Leroy's funeral and to every Tuesday night session. "I hadn't thought of that. I guess I need to buy something, don't I?"

She hugged him. "Where are you taking her?"

Relieved everything was out in the open with his sister; Rob realized he hadn't thought about that either. His sister told him about the Polo Club, an upscale restaurant across town in Utica Square. Paul had taken her there when he proposed. Myrna assured him it was quiet and had good food. He called for a reservation Friday afternoon and the next morning went to the mall.

An older well-dressed man in the men's department of Penney's helped him choose gray slacks, a navy sport coat and a long-sleeved shirt in blue and gray with a touch of gold. He realized he only owned two pairs of shoes, his heavy work boots and a pair of walking shoes. A few minutes later he came away from the shoe department with black leather loafers.

When he got home, he tried on his new clothes for Myrna. She pressed his shirt and told him he looked handsome. He thanked her and assured her once more that everything would be all right, then he told her how the date had come about and finished by saying, "I doubt if I'll see her again after this."

She took a deep breath and said, "It might be better."

It would be better if this was the only time, and he made up his mind that it wouldn't happen again. He reminded himself of the danger of being with Paige, but his excitement knowing he would be seeing her far outweighed his sense of peril.

Although the weather had warmed on Saturday, snow still covered the ground with the streets and walkways clear and dry. Rob straightened his jacket and ran his hand over his freshly cut hair. He picked up the keys to his sister's car, thanked her for letting him borrow it and left for his date.

A few miles away, Paige applied the finishing touches to her make up and critically eyed herself in a full length mirror. She sprayed Lavender perfume behind her ears and on her wrists, then clipped a pearl lariat necklace around the neck of her wine jewel neck sweater and, dropping her arms, straightened the hem back down over her black wool dress pants. Akoya saltwater pearl drops danced below the curls that always escaped when she clipped her hair back. She turned full circle in front of the mirror, looking back over her shoulder and smoothed the pants over her buttocks then stepped into black ankle high leather boots. The stacked heel would keep her steady in case she had to walk into any snow or ice. Satisfied with what she saw, she went to a coat closet and took out her heather grey Merino walker and a fringed scarf the color of wild raspberries. On her way to the living room she passed the mirror above the mahogany buffet in the dining room and stopped long enough to attempt to capture stray curls and push them back into the clip. She gave herself another cursory appraisal then shook her head and wondered at her nervousness.

Of course, this was the first date she'd had in over a year, but hadn't she planned it this way? Hadn't she turned down every offer after her break up with Daniel? He'd been a great guy, a radiologist she'd met at the hospital. He was the first man she'd ever felt she was in love with, but he wanted to get married and have kids right away. She told him she wasn't ready for all that yet, but he didn't understand and had broken it off with her. After their split, he'd transferred to Oklahoma City. Four months later when one of the nurses told her he'd gotten married, she was hurt and questioned whether she'd made a mistake then told herself he must have just wanted a wife, any wife, and assured herself she'd made the right decision.

She'd been surprised at how quickly she'd agreed to dinner with Rob but was sure this date wouldn't lead to anything serious. She had to admit she liked this man and had been drawn to him from the moment they'd met seven months ago. Besides being handsome, he was quiet and gentle on the outside, but she sensed something deeper, some ember within that threatened to burst into flame, and she wasn't sure what its ignition would bring. She just knew that, whatever it was drew her to him every time she was in his presence. It was frightening and, at the same time, exciting.

A cold shiver ran up her spine and into her scalp. She shuddered. There was something about Rob that had always caused her slight discomfort. What was it? It was as though she should know something, but she couldn't place what it was. Could it be her imagination?

He asked her if she wanted to know who had robbed her. She assured him she no longer cared, but was that true? When she had the dream, she always strained to see the man's face. But if she saw it and it was someone she knew...

She shook off the thoughts. It was just because he had brought up the robbery to her. That had to be the reason she felt uncomfortable. But she, also, knew she didn't want to get serious with him. She wasn't sure if it was because he was white like Daniel had been or if there was another reason.

It was just a date—a one time thing. Pushing down her apprehension, Paige was certain she could control whatever happened between them.

---

When Paige opened the door, both she and Rob stood in the doorway for several seconds, neither speaking.

"Oh, my. Please come in out of the cold." She stepped back and he came in just enough for her to close the door behind him.

Her scent accosted his senses. He breathed it in then broke the uncomfortable silence of his arrival. "You look pretty," he said. "That's a pretty color." He motioned to her sweater.

Paige laughed nervously. "Thanks. You look nice, too."

"Thanks," he mumbled. He looked around the room and saw her coat draped on the back of the sofa. He reached for it. "I guess we can go."

Paige reached for the coat at the same time then let him help her into it. When she turned to face him, she drew in a deep breath. "Rob, are you as nervous as I am?"

He smiled. "I really am. You feel the same way?

"Boy, do I. I have to be honest. I haven't had a date in a long time and it isn't the most natural feeling."

"Well, what can we do?" he asked. "I think we need to get over it before we go, don't you?"

"Absolutely. Let's start over only you don't have to go back outside." She pretended she was opening the door in front of him. "Rob," she said, this time her voice held a sincere greeting. "It's so good to see you. You look nice and I'm really looking forward to having dinner with you."

He responded in kind. "Paige, you look beautiful. I've been looking forward to our dinner, too."

They laughed together.

"Now, isn't that better?" she asked.

Rob agreed. What they had just done reminded him of pleasant childhood memories of his mother.

The restaurant was crowded with well-dressed diners. The maitre-d seated them near a table of eight and apologized that none of the private booths were available, but Rob and Paige were both secretly glad to be at an open table. The booths looked more intimate than either of them desired at this point. When asked if they'd like something to drink, Paige asked for something that sounded like "pinogreasio" wine and Rob decided he'd try some with her. When he drank at all, it was usually beer because the only wine he'd ever tasted was sharp and acrid and he hadn't liked it at all.

The two glasses held a clear substance Rob assumed was what Paige had ordered although he thought all wine was red. She held her goblet toward him and said, "What shall we drink to?" He touched his glass to hers and nodded for her to decide. She thought a moment then said, "To our friendship."

"To our friendship," Rob repeated and sipped the liquid at the same time she did. To his surprise he liked it. He didn't recognize some of the words on the menu and opted for something he knew, a steak. Paige ordered seafood. When they finished their wine, they ordered another. Neither had eaten much during the day in anticipation of their meeting and they both began to feel slightly light-headed before the food arrived. They made jokes about needing a designated driver to take them home if they drank any more and vowed this was the last glass.

They talked about Paige's work, about Rob's job and how he had become a welder. He told her about Rico, the Aragons and John Taylor. She admitted she'd never been to Las Vegas so he described it to her, and she said she'd like to go there some day. Rob told her he'd love to show her the Strip, and as people do when they are comfortable and caught up in the moment, they thought it would be fun for the four of them, Paige, Rob, Myrna and Paul to all go out there together some day. But deep in both their hearts they knew it wasn't likely to happen. It was just something to dream about for one night.

Rob's steak was one of the best he'd ever eaten and Paige declared her seafood delicious. For dessert she suggested something Rob had never heard of called Crème Brule. It turned out he liked the creamy custard topped with a sugary glaze and congratulated her choice.

"You remember the family I told you about in Las Vegas?" he asked.

Paige nodded. "The Hispanic family?"

"Right." He spooned some custard and held it before him. "This reminds me of something Mama Serena called flan."

"I don't think I've ever had flan although I've heard of it." She took another bite. "Is it as good as this?"

Rob licked his lips and pretended to be thinking. "You know, I think it is, but as much as I like the Aragons, I do believe the company is better tonight."

Paige laughed. "You really know how to make a woman feel good."

Rob laughed with her but didn't say what he was thinking. He had not said it to make her feel good. He meant it. He liked being with her more than he was willing to admit.

They drank coffee and talked longer, both unwilling to bring the evening to an end. When the waiter brought the check, Rob hid his surprise at the price of the meal and was glad he had a newly-acquired credit card to use.

In the car, Paige sighed and said, "I've enjoyed this so much. Thank you for the wonderful meal."

"Thank you for coming with me. I've had a good time, too." He started the engine but didn't immediately put the car into gear. "Is there anything else you'd like to do, someplace you'd like to go?"

She looked at her watch. "My goodness, we spent almost three hours in the restaurant. It's ten o'clock."

Rob smiled. "Is that your bedtime?"

"No," she laughed, "but I do turn into a pumpkin."

"And you lose your shoe or something like that."

"Yes, Prince Charming, I'll lose my shoe and my clothes will become rags—"

"And I'll find the shoe and come looking for you but the wicked stepmother will...what will she do?" Rob's smile turned into laughter.

"You will overcome her evil and return my shoe and we'll live happily...." Their laughter died followed by an uneasy silence. Paige cleared her throat. "May I ask you a personal question?"

Rob sobered, anxiety fluttered in his belly. He nodded.

"You have wonderful manners. You've told me about your life and I just wondered who taught you?"

He exhaled in relief. "Mom. She taught me."

"But you were so young when she died," Paige said.

Rob shifted in his seat and turned toward her. "I think she must have known my dad wouldn't show me how to act and she would say, 'Bobby, you have to know how to treat a woman,' and we'd practice."

"Practice?"

"Yeah. She'd set two chairs side by side and pretend it was a car. Then she'd show me how to open the door and help the woman in. Then I'd get in and we'd pretend we were going somewhere and I was driving, which I really liked, of course. Then we'd stop and I'd get out and go open the door for her and help her out." He chuckled. "She showed me how to pull out the chair for her and open a door and let her go in first. What was worse, she made me practice with my sister, too." He shook his head, smiling. "She would tell me that some day I'd have a son and I'd need to teach him good manners. She was some kind of mom to teach me all that."

"And you remembered."

He nodded. "I did. But I have to tell you, I haven't had much practice doing it in my life."

She reached across the seat and patted his arm. "Well, Bobby, you do a great job of it now." When she saw his expression change, she added, "I'm sorry. I shouldn't have called you by that name."

Rob smiled, "No, it's all right. It's just that no one's called me Bobby in a long time. Takes me back." He covered her hand with his. "Thanks."

They sat this way for a time with his hand on hers. Rob knew this wouldn't be the last time he saw her. He was sure she felt the same way.

# TWENTY-FOUR

Since the engagement Myrna's life was consumed with Paul, the kids and wedding plans. At her suggestion Paul took the children out of after-school day care and Myrna stayed with them until he came home from work. She cooked for them every day. Sometimes she came home in the evenings before Rob went to bed but since his work day started at six every morning, he was in bed before nine and up at five so they seldom saw each other during the week. But the two of them had Saturday mornings together. Myrna usually fixed a big breakfast for him then they spent a few hours doing their laundry and cleaning house together. But, by Saturday afternoon, she was gone again, back to her new family. She attended Paul's church and was with him all day Sunday.

Rob encouraged his sister to go ahead and get married, not wait until June. She was doing all the things, or most of the things she'd be doing as Paul's wife now. But she wanted the wedding she'd never had. Also, she wanted her brother to walk her down the aisle and give her away. He agreed but still thought the waiting was silly.

Rob didn't like being alone when he came home from work every day, nor did he like the long weekends in an empty house, but he had adjusted. After his date with Paige, he found himself pacing around the apartment, turning the television on and flipping channels then turning it off and pacing some more. He knew he should be thinking about going back to

Vegas but kept putting it off. He reached for the phone a number of times, but wasn't sure what he would say if he called her. He wanted to see her again but his budget had to recover from the Polo Club, and he wasn't sure where he would ask her to go with him. So he waited a couple of weeks and didn't call until a Friday afternoon when he dialed the hospital and asked for her office. She answered on the first ring.

Then he was tongue-tied. "Hello," she said for the second time.

"Paige," he croaked.

She hesitated. "Rob, is that you?"

"It's me. I just wanted to call you."

"Okay."

"Well." He could have kicked himself for not having anything in his mind. Finally, he blurted, "I want to see you again. I know it's late, but is there any way we can get together tonight?"

He heard her soft laugh on the other end of the line. "I was wondering what happened to you. I thought maybe you were just my imagination."

He realized she was teasing him and relaxed. "I'm sorry I didn't call sooner. I guess my mom didn't teach me that one."

She laughed again. "If she did, you forgot."

"That's possible. Well, what do you think? Is there something we can do tonight?" He realized she might have other plans. Surely she had many men wanting to take her out. "That is, if you aren't busy."

"I should be coy and tell you I need to look at my calendar, but I'll skip the coy and tell you I have no plans and I'd love to see you."

*Love to see me.* No words formed in his mind after her admission.

"So, what do you suggest?" she asked into his silence.

"I guess we have to eat. Would you like to go somewhere?"

"Someplace a little less 'Polo Club'?"

It was his turn to laugh. "Right. Someplace we don't have to dress up or you'll have to see me in the same pants and jacket only this time my shirt's wrinkled. Myrna didn't iron it for me and that's something else Mom didn't teach me."

She laughed again. "Well, ironing can be learned. Even I can teach you how to do that. Maybe you should bring your shirt over and we'll have a lesson tonight." She paused. "Actually, that isn't a bad idea. Do you want to just bring something to my house and we'll eat there. We don't have to dress up and go out."

"More Chinese?"

"My favorite. Come around six but leave the shirt at home. We'll save it for another time."

And the date was made.

An hour later Paige let him in the front door. She was in stocking feet and wearing a sapphire ribbed turtleneck and jeans. Her damp sable curls were pulled away from her face and held in a disorderly stack on the back of her head. She smiled broadly and he noticed the dimple again. He wanted to touch it, to run his finger across her lips.

"Ah. Just what I wanted." She reached for the sack. Mistaking the gesture, Rob took her hand and did something he had never thought of doing. He kissed it.

Surprise, then delight shone on her face. "Well," she said. "A gentleman calls." She bowed her head slightly and laughed. "Mom?"

Embarrassed, he said, "No, not Mom. I did that on my own."

"You do it well." She cocked her head, her expression serious. "I think there's more to the man than meets the eye."

"Probably." There was more than she knew, more than he wanted her to know but still, he wanted her to know everything about him and not change toward him. Would that be possible? He handed her the sack and she carried it to the kitchen.

The living room was furnished much like the hospital counseling office. Overstuffed chair and sofa, a wooden rocker, gleaming cherry wood tables, geometrically designed area rug. Rob studied the picture hanging over the fireplace. A barefoot woman in a red dress danced with a tuxedo-clad man. A maid and a butler held umbrellas against the apparent rain on a gray, stormy day.

"That's called 'The Dancing Butler' by Jack Vettriano." Paige came up behind him "I love that picture. I found it at a local auction and had to have it. I don't know what it is about it, but it does something for me." She folded her arms across her chest and asked, "What do you see?"

Rob didn't know much about art but he liked this one. "Well, I see that it's stormy and they're on the beach. She must have taken off her shoes so they wouldn't get wet." He stepped back beside Paige and crossed his arms. "And they must be rich to have a maid and butler to be out there holding umbrellas for them. There's a basket. Picnic? I think I'd rather have my picnic inside."

Paige laughed softly. She tapped him on the chest, "Ah, such a romantic." As she went back to the kitchen she called over her shoulder, "Come on in. We'll eat in here."

He followed her through the dining room and into a bright yellow and red kitchen, much different than the muted shades of the living room. "Red refrigerator and stove, red Mustang, red dress," he said gesturing toward the picture in the living room. "I think I'm seeing a pattern here."

Paige grinned, her cheek dimpling, and took plates from the yellow cabinets.

"I don't think I've ever seen red appliances before."

"Special order," she said, handing him the plates while she poured two glasses of water." I like bright colors but had to go mellower at the hospital. The living room is my mom's taste. She decorated it when we lived here together, and I've never gotten around to changing it. I finally did the kitchen about a year ago. They say red makes you hungry. Guess that's why I always want to eat when I come in here." They both laughed as she pulled cartons from the sack.

They ate at the small round yellow table, talking about their week, about Myrna, about Paige's family. When they finished, every container was empty.

"How about coffee?" she asked.

"Sounds great."

He gathered the remnants of their meal and put the plates in the sink while she filled the coffee maker.

"You can go into the living room and get comfortable. I'll bring the coffee. I seem to remember you drink yours black."

He nodded. "Just like you."

Momentary surprise flowed into another smile. "Ah, yes. The hospital cafeteria."

He made a face, gave an exaggerated shudder and left the room.

In the living room, they both settled into opposite ends of the sofa, Paige with her feet tucked under her.

To Rob, Paige was stunningly beautiful. He remembered how she looked Saturday in the wine sweater against her olive skin, and tonight, the sapphire complimented her eyes. He thought about what it would be like to reach out and put his arms around her. Instead he sat forward and held his hot mug of coffee between his hands.

"Rob," Paige turned to face him, legs still under her body. "I've had a great time tonight."

"Me, too."

Actually, I'm surprised at how well we've gotten along."

"Why?" Concern played across his brow.

"Well," Paige sat her mug on the coffee table. "The way you were acting--you know, you practically ignored me during the sessions. I thought you didn't like me."

He sat his mug down and turned on the sofa to face her. "Oh, no, Paige. It's not like that at all."

"I thought I'd done something--" she began.

He moved across the sofa and took her hands in his. "No, Paige. I like you very much."

She pulled away and stood up, walked across the room.

Had he done too much too soon? And, after all, what did he think he was doing? He stood and took a step toward her. "I'm sorry; I didn't mean to scare you. I won't hurt you."

Paige looked into his eyes. "I didn't think you would. Why would you even say something like that?"

"Well, the way you got up--" he began.

"I'm sorry, Rob. It was a--just a reaction." She crossed her arms. "I like being with you. I just don't want you to get the wrong idea."

At a loss for words, Rob went toward the door. "Maybe I'd better leave."

"No, don't leave yet." Paige moved toward him. "I mean -- I mean..." she stammered. Her face reddened. "You don't have to go. It's still early."

Without thinking about the consequences, Rob reached for her and pulled her into his arms. He could feel the beat of her heart against his chest. Gently he placed his hand on the back of her neck and turned her face to his. A light touch of their lips sent electric shocks through his body. He wanted to devour her but held back. Another light kiss then she backed away, her hands on his arms.

"Rob." Her voice breathy. "We can't do this?"

"Do what? Why not?" He asked, his voice husky with desire.

He didn't move. Her eyes searched his. In her touch he felt her need for him as great as his for her. "You're a client."

He shook his head. "Not any more. We're friends. Remember?" He pulled her to him again and she didn't resist. This time his mouth hungrily covered hers.

When the kiss ended, she stepped back away from him, held her arms in front of her, palms facing him.

Rob saw the fear on her face and reached toward her. She moved backwards too quickly and lost her balance. As she started to fall Rob caught her and pulled her into his arms again. He breathed her name and felt her stiffen.

Rob, don't." She pushed him away. "Please, don't."

He stepped back still holding her arms, her hands against his chest.

Paige shook her head and looked down. "You don't understand. This can't happen."

Rob released her, remorse filling him. "What is it, then? Don't you feel it? I do. I really like you."

"That's just it, Rob. I like you, too. But it can't happen." Paige sat in a chair and leaned heavily against its back.

Rob faced her. He could see it in her eyes. Her feelings for him were as real as his for her but there was something that kept her from him. Did she know who he was? That he was the man who...

"Are you afraid of me?"

She sighed. "Of course not. It's not about that, Rob." Her voice softened. The tears pooled in her eyes. "It's about us." She stretched her arms toward him and rubbed her skin. "Don't you see it? We're different."

Then he understood.

With Rob's understanding the tension between them melted. Energy drained from him. Emotion filled his throat. An ache began in his stomach and surrounded his heart. After all these years of waiting, of wanting. Here, in front of me, but--

Paige's eyes were on him. Compassionate. Gentle.

"What can we do?"

She shook her head. "There's nothing to do. It is what it is."

I never thought--" he began.

"Oh, Rob. You had to have thought about it."

"No. I didn't. I never even noticed." He hadn't. All he'd seen was her beauty, her heart, never the color of her skin.

Paige sighed and leaned forward. "And you didn't notice my mother and father were of different races, too? Come on, Rob. Be honest."

He remembered Reverend and Mrs. Lewis, remembered the petite light-skinned woman and the large dark-skinned man. He remembered Mrs. Lewis' eyes. The same vivid purple as Paige's.

Rob went to her chair, knelt before it and took her hands in his. She didn't pull away from his touch. "Yes," he said. "I noticed. I see it now." He held his hand next to hers. "Look, Paige. See for yourself."

Their skin color was nearly the same. His, tanned by sun. Hers, tanned by birth.

Paige laughed.

"I don't care what color you are or what color I am."

"Rob," she breathed his name.

He cared for her. She knew it and he knew she had feelings for him.

He still held her hands. He brought them to his face and kissed them, moved toward her and reached to take her in his arms. She didn't resist and allowed him to bring her to her feet and be held. She rested her head against his chest.

Rob stroked her cheeks with his thumbs. His fingers tangled in her hair. Aroused by the sensation, Paige relaxed. He pulled her toward him. Their mouths touched. First a gentle brushing together. His lips parted against hers. She leaned into him and responded, opening her lips and seeking his tongue with her own. She allowed herself to forget the barriers, the hurdles that seemed to loom so large just moments ago and sank into his kiss, not wanting it to end.

They held each other, breathless from the passion, neither speaking.

Paige stepped back and looked into Rob's face. The desire she read there strengthened the resolve she felt. Before he could move toward her again, she said, "Rob, there are some things we have to talk about."

The analytical Paige took over. Surprise and questioning filled Rob's eyes. She knew it was an abrupt departure from the moment they'd just shared. He released her.

"Let's sit down," she said, and motioned toward the sofa.

Paige sat at the opposite end of the sofa from him. "Rob." Her voice broke. She looked away, struggling to gain control.

Rob moved toward her. Before he could touch her, she held her hands toward him and said, "No, please. I have to tell you."

He waited, not touching her.

"Tell me," he said.

Paige took in another breath. She looked away then back at him, cleared her throat.

"I don't want to get involved right now."

"What?" Rob didn't understand.

"At least not with a white man."

"What in the hell are you talking about?" His anger silenced her. "This isn't fifty years ago, Paige. Not get involved with a white man. That's just an excuse. It's bullshit, Paige. What's the real reason?"

Shocked, she could only shake her head.

"I've never met anyone who is more open to everyone than you." He paced toward the door, thinking he'd leave, then turned back to face her. "It isn't about race at all. It's about something else. Is it me? Is there something about me that turns you off?"

She stood. "Rob…"

"Be honest with me, Paige. What's the real reason?" Who was he to demand honesty? The thought flitted across his mind and he dismissed it. It was hard enough opening his heart to this woman and being rejected, but to be lied to on top of it. "You're the one who has the passion, who has found her purpose in life. You're the one who made me see I was drifting; made me question what my purpose is. You're the one who helps people who don't have any hope." Rob paced across the floor. "Don't give me that crap that you don't want to have a relationship with a white man. That's bullshit, Paige, and you know it!"

Paige's eyes narrowed; she dropped her head into her hands. "I'm sorry you don't understand, Rob."

"Oh, I understand, all right. You're afraid to fall in love, aren't you? Maybe just afraid to fall in love with me."

Paige shook her head. "Of course not. What ever gave you that idea?"

"Because I think there's a lot more to it. It's not about our color at all, is it?"

Paige stood up and walked to the fireplace then turned and faced him, her voice low. "What did you tell me you wanted more than anything in the world?"

Anger spent, he sank into the sofa.

She sat beside him. When had he told her what he wanted?

"That night, after we took Myrna to the hospital," she reminded him.

He remembered. "To be a dad."

Surprised, she added, "You didn't say that. You wanted to be a part of a real family, and I guess that means you want to have children."

"I do. I want to have children."

Her expression sobered. "Most people want that." She looked down at her hands folded in her lap. "I don't, Rob. I don't want to have kids. I want to keep doing what I'm doing and children would interfere with that." She took a deep breath, her voice shaky but she didn't look at him. "I really like being with you but our being together would preclude marriage and children, and I know that's not what you want."

Stunned into silence, his heart aching in his chest, he weighed his options. Paige and no children or no Paige. "I'd have to think about that."

She touched his face. "No, Rob, it wouldn't work no matter how hard we'd try. You'd have to give up too much. I couldn't ask you to do that."

He had to admit she was right but it still sounded like an excuse to him and he told her once more before he left her. "It's bullshit, Paige. Your excuses are bullshit.

# TWENTY-FIVE

What was going on with Paige? Was it about color, or kids or something else? Maybe he had been too harsh with her and it really was about not wanting children. If that was the case, could he give up his desire for a family? Even for Paige? And what about Vegas? Wasn't he going back there? He had to work it all out in his mind, and he told himself it was best to do it now. The thought of being with Paige was ludicrous. He should be running back to Nevada as fast as he could. The questions swirled around in his mind but no answer surfaced.

He wrestled with it all week and after thinking about it all day Saturday, Rob called her. The phone rang a long time before she answered. "Rob?"

"Yes, it's me. How did you know?"

"Caller I.D. I started not to answer."

"I'm glad you did," he said. "I think we need to talk."

He was met by silence on her end.

"I know it's late but can I come over now?"

He heard her sigh. "Of course you can come."

Thirty minutes later she answered his knock. As soon as she closed the door behind him, he reached for her, took her into his arms and held her. Neither spoke.

She stepped back. "Does this mean what I think it does?" she asked.

Without speaking he lowered his lips to hers. First a light kiss, like their first. He drew back looking into her eyes. He wanted to say it, wanted to say the words he felt in his heart but had never said to a woman.

A smile teased her mouth. "Well, are you going to kiss me or not?" This time the kiss wasn't light. It was deep, filled with his desire for her. Emotions he'd kept buried for too long threatened to overwhelm him. His tongue found hers and she met his intensity. He kissed her eyes, her forehead, her neck. His hand found her breast and she gasped.

"Rob. No." She pulled away from him.

*What have I done?* "I'm sorry, Paige." He tried to hold her. "I shouldn't have done that," he said as she turned away from him. He put his hands on her shoulders. Expecting her to move away again, he was surprised when she leaned back into him.

"You're right. You came on a little strong. I'm not ready for anything like that, Rob." She faced him and touched his face. "Please give me some time. Can you handle that?"

Anything. He could handle anything as long as she didn't make him leave. "I can. I'm really sorry."

Her expression changed. Brow knit, she had a faraway look in her eyes.

"Paige."

Her eyes focused on him again.

Then he said the words he had only said to his mother and his sister. "I love you."

She smiled and wrapped her arms around his neck bringing his lips to hers; a gentle touch. "I know what that took for you to say, Rob." Her fingertips traced his mouth. "I wish I could say it to you, but I can't. Not yet." Then she raised herself on her tiptoes and pulled his face close to hers. "I guess you came to talk, didn't you?"

He laughed. "Well, yes, but I like this better than talking."

"Me, too," she said and kissed him again.

They sat on the sofa. Paige tucked her feet under her and curled into his arms.

"I've thought about you all week," he began. "I know I want to be with you, even if it means no children yet."

"Maybe never, Rob." She leaned away from him, her expression serious. "You have to understand that."

"I know," he said, forcing the ache in his heart away. "But, I love you. I've wanted you for a long time and I can't give you up."

Paige ran her hand over his cheek. "Oh, Rob. You are so honest. I do believe you are the most honest man I've ever known."

Rob paled. *If you only knew.*

She continued. "I'd like for my family to meet you."

"I've met your mom and dad," he reminded her. "At the funeral."

"I know, but you didn't really get to talk to them. Maybe tomorrow. Could you come to church with me tomorrow and to lunch with them?"

"Church? I don't think so. Let's give it some time." He decided he'd better tell her the truth up front. Well, some of the truth.

"I've never been to church. You know that. I'm just not sure it's something I want to do."

She didn't speak.

"Does that make a difference?" he asked, suddenly nervous about his honesty.

"Well…"

Her pause worried him. He could see that she was troubled and he hoped he hadn't completely messed things up already.

Serious again, she looked away. "Rob, my family and church are important to me. I don't know if it does make a difference. I guess it's something we'll have to talk about. Something we'll both have to think about."

Rob's heart skipped a beat. Were there too many barriers between them? Maybe this relationship was doomed before it could get off the ground.

Rob and Paige talked on the phone daily. They spent Friday nights and some part of Saturday together every weekend. He didn't have to worry about telling Myrna about their relationship. She had asked him about Paige after their first date but he had been noncommittal, like it wasn't anything important. She hadn't asked him again. He guessed she assumed he wasn't seeing the psychologist any more or she was so involved in her own life, she hadn't given it another thought.

But he wanted to talk to someone, to ask if he was being foolish. It was definitely unwise to get involved with the woman who could send him back to prison but he couldn't give her up now.

Children. That was one of the big differences that stood between them, and her family and church. If only Rico would call. But he was involved in his own life, too. The baby was due any time, he had his family to take care of. No, this was Rob's problem. He had to figure it out himself. But the longer he stayed in Tulsa, the farther his life in Las Vegas receded into the background.

Paige tried to concentrate on the sermon but her mind kept returning to Rob. She was falling in love with him and it bothered her. They were so different. He still wouldn't go to church with her, and he kept putting off meeting her family. It wasn't natural for her to keep something this important from them. A few times she'd had to give them excuses when they wanted to get together on the weekend and she had plans with Rob.

Her mother had questioned her a few times about why she seemed preoccupied. She told her it was because of her work. But she didn't think her mother believed her. However, she didn't pry, and for that, Paige was grateful.

At lunch this Sunday the talk was about the trip the whole family was taking in May. Her brother, Brad, a media specialist who had his own company, had a job taping a conference on a cruise ship to Hawaii.

"Your favorite speakers are going to be there, Paige. Deepak Chopra and Wayne Dyer. Come on. Go with us." Brad said.

Her parents and Brad's wife, Ashley, chimed in.

She shook her head. "I can't. Really. I can't get away from the hospital."

"How long have you worked there, Paige?" Brad asked. "Three years?"

She nodded.

"And how much time have you taken off?"

"Not much." She hadn't had any reason to take time off.

Brad continued, "I believe you had a week off after the first year when we all went to Tahoe." He looked at his wife and parents for their agreement. Ashley gave an almost imperceptible negative shake of her head. But her husband didn't notice and went on. "This will be Mom and Dad's chance to see Hawaii since they didn't get a chance the last time."

Paige covered a gasp. Their last trip had been cut short because of her.

"Honey," Paige's father gave his son a warning look and reached across the table to take her hand, his dark skin in contrast with the lighter brown of her own. "I know how it is. Remember when I was a pastor and had a problem getting away, too."

She remembered how many years the family went to visit relatives without their father because he felt he couldn't leave his flock. "I do remember, Dad," she said. "And I understand now why you felt that way. There's so much to do, so many people who need you." Guilt struck at her heart. It was true that it was hard for her to leave, but the main reason wasn't her job. It was Rob. She didn't want to leave him right now.

Jim Lewis squeezed her hand. "Honey, if there's any way we can change your mind..."

His wife stopped him. "Jim," Beverly Lewis said, "she's a grown woman. She can make her own decisions and doesn't need us putting pressure on her." She looked at her daughter, kindness in her eyes. "You know we'd love to have you come along, but if you feel you can't, we understand."

Relieved, Paige still felt the guilt of her deceit. "This is to make up for your other trip," she said. "The one you had to cut short because of me."

No one spoke. Ashley wiped food from her son's face with a napkin then turned to Paige. "That wasn't your fault, Paige, and don't you think for one minute that it was." She raised her head, daring the others to speak. "If you feel you need to stay home, then do. It's not our business to try to get you to go, nor," she gave her husband a look and this time he read it, "should we try to make you feel badly because you choose not to go."

Brad shrugged. "It's your call, Paige. I just think it would do you good to get out of the hospital for awhile."

Quick tears threatened Paige and she had to look away from their faces. They were her life; the people she loved the most and she was lying to them. And for what? A man who didn't share her love for all the things she held dear. *Oh, God, am I making a mistake?*

# Twenty-Six

"Me llamo Papa Rico," he exclaimed. "Mi hijo se llama Manuel Frederico Eliseo Secundino Calderon. Manuel, mi hijo."

Rob had to laugh. "Speak English, Rico. You know I don't understand Spanish."

Rico exploded in laughter. "My son is here."

"It's March. Wasn't he supposed to be here in February?" Rob rubbed his hand over his neck. Rico a father. He tried to picture a little baby Rico.

"He came just one week ago." Rico was laughing.

"And you're just now calling me?" Rob's irritation came through the line.

Rico was silent. "What is it, mi amigo?"

Chagrined, he apologized. "I guess you have other things to do now besides baby sit me." He laughed, a stiff sound in his own ears.

"Never too much for my friend. Tell me."

"I'm sorry, Rico. This is a wonderful time in you life and I shouldn't be messing it up for you. It's nothing I can't handle. Tell me about little Manuel."

"Beautiful baby, like his mother." He paused. "And like his papa." Rico's laugh was infectious and Rob had to join in.

"Nothing humble about you, friend."

203

"Now you know about Manuel. What about my friend?"

Rob told him about the woman he had fallen in love with. He told Rico that she didn't want to have children and how hard it was for him to make a choice between his love for her and his desire for his own child.

"That is a hard choice for you," Rico said.

"Yes, it is and there's another problem. There's one thing I haven't told you." He hesitated.

"Tell me now, my friend." Rico said gently.

"She's the one--the one…"

"The one?" Rico repeated.

"She's the one in the robbery."

Silence.

"Are you there?" Rob asked.

Rico spoke several words in Spanish very quickly and Rob didn't catch any of them. In English his words were measured, "Mi amigo is in trouble, no?"

"Yes, I guess you can call it trouble." He pictured Rico shaking his head.

"I cannot help you. This is a problem only you can make right."

"But how do I do that, Rico? I love her."

"Ay carrumba! Love? Be sure before you find yourself where you don't want to be."

Where he doesn't want to be? He well knew Rico's meaning. Prison. The place he doesn't want to be. And was he not in prison now? A prison made by lies?

# TWENTY-SEVEN

Rob walked out onto the sidewalk with three other men from the building they were renovating.

"How about some lagers at Nathan's?" one of the men addressed the group.

"Not me," Rob said. "Got something I have to do. Maybe another time."

The others waved at him and started in the opposite direction.

Rob hurried toward the parking lot, anxious to get home, shower and see Paige. For a month he had thought about Rico's phone call but nothing could stop him from continuing the relationship with this woman. As dangerous as it was for him he was falling more and more in love with her and pushing thoughts of a family farther and farther away.

He heard his name, "MacGruder. Hey, Mac!" He turned and looked into two blood shot eyes. The skin on the man's thin sharp boned face was covered with pock-marks and Rob knew immediately who it was. He thought about ignoring him, but before he could walk away, the wizened creature called out to him again, "You don't remember your old cell mate?"

Rob looked around quickly to see if any of the other men he'd come out with had heard, but they were down the street heading toward the tavern. "Spud Smith," he said. Rob stood head and shoulders above the little man's balding head. "I'd know you anywhere."

The man grinned exposing crooked yellow teeth. "What're you doing back in Tulsa? I thought you planned to get out of town when you got out."

At Rob's surprised look, Spud laughed, "I talked to Benny. He told me you left town after you pulled that robbery over in Southern Acres."

He hadn't told Benny where the stuff came from, but Rob knew the man had a criminal mind and it wasn't hard to figure it out when he heard about it on the news.

"I did, but I came back." Rob kept his voice nonchalant. "Why are you here? Didn't you live in Wichita?"

Spud cackled. "Got too hot for me there. Had to get out of Dodge, just like you."

The man lit a cigarette, blue smoke rising between them. A burst of April wind whipped a loose newspaper up the sidewalk, twisting and turning it until its rising and falling came to rest wrapped around Spud's grimy jeans' leg. He shook it loose and it fell to the sidewalk beside him, suddenly dead, the wind gone. Both men watched it, waiting for it to rise up again like a living thing and make its way down the street.

"What's up with you? Done any jobs lately?" Spud took another long drag on his cigarette and blew the smoke toward Rob.

Rob stepped away from the haze and shook his head.

"Well," Spud stepped closer to Rob, "you up for somethin'?"

"No. I don't do that any more." Rob turned to leave.

"People know who you are, MacGruder?"

Rob faced the little man and waited.

"Well, do they?" Spud dropped his cigarette butt on the sidewalk and ground it out with the toe of his shoe. When he smiled his crooked teeth grin it brought a broken down picket fence to mind. "Didn't think so." He kicked at the newspaper.

Impatient with the game, Rob asked, "What do you want?"

Spud stepped into the gap between them and whispered, "I got my eye on some convenience stores around town. I've been casin' 'em and think they'll be easy scores. I'll do all the work. All's I need's a driver." He looked around again. "You in?"

"No, Spud, I'm not in. Like I told you I don't do that any more." He waved his hand in dismissal and turned to leave. "Find someone else."

"You want your boss to know you're an ex-con?"

Rob stopped, his back to the man, anger mixed with fear, fists clenched. He pictured his hands around the scrawny chicken neck squeezing the life out of him.

"Tell anyone whatever you want, Spud. I'm not doing it." And he walked away.

Spud called after him. "See you later, Mac."

No one called him Mac. That was his father's name. He had beat up more than one guy that had put that name on him.

Rob slept badly the next few nights. Every time he saw his boss, he expected to be pulled aside and asked about his past. But nothing happened. He didn't see Spud and hoped it was over.

⋯⋯⋯⋯⋯⋯⋯⋯⋯⋯⋯⋯⋯⋯⋯⋯⋯⋯⋯⋯⋯⋯

Paige and Rob sat together on her sofa, a movie played on the television in front of them but neither appeared to be following it. A bowl of popcorn sat untouched on the coffee table.

Paige's mind was on her family and on the secret she was keeping from them. Rob's mind was on Spud Smith and the secret he had been keeping for the last few years. What was he going to do about Spud? He couldn't go back into crime but would telling Spud 'no' be enough to make him leave him alone? He doubted it. And what if his boss found out the truth? More important than losing his job was Paige finding out the truth.

The movie ended, the credits ran and neither moved to turn off the set. A blank screen finally got Paige's attention. She picked up the remote. The screen went black. She turned to Rob and saw his eyes were downcast, looking at his hands. He laced his fingers together then pulled them apart then repeated the lacing.

"Rob." She had to say his name a second time before he looked up. "Is there something wrong?"

He shook his head and put his arm around her. She leaned into him. His hand caressed her face then tipped her head up and he kissed her. Her lips parted and desire coursed through his body. He wanted her now. Wanted to feel her naked body next to his. An explosion of need erupted in his body, his kiss a fervent hunger.

Paige groaned and spoke his name.

His hand moved between her legs.

She pushed him away. "No, Rob. Stop."

Nothing in him wanted to stop. He knew he could take her if he wanted but if it wasn't what she wanted, he couldn't do it. His breath came in gulps.

Paige moved away from him.

"I just can't." Her voice broke. "I'm sorry."

Her words shot him back to the day he left her tied up. Now they were both sorry. Is that what this is all about, he thought, two people who are always sorry for something? But he was the one who should be sorry again. He knew where she stood. She had told him often enough.

"No, I shouldn't have gone that far."

She touched his face. "Rob, I wanted to." She stopped. "But I couldn't. I can't. I've told you I'm just not ready."

"Will you ever be ready?"

Paige's eyes held a sorrow he hadn't seen in them before. "You remember I told you I hadn't had a date in a long time when we went out?"

He remembered.

"Last year I had been with a man, a man I thought I was in love with." She hesitated, and when she spoke again he had to strain to hear her words. "He was my first and I thought we had a future together." She ran her hand lightly over the skin on his arm but not meeting his eyes. "But he wanted to get married right away, wanted to have children, and wanted me to stop working." The movement of her hand ceased and she touched her forehead with the tips of her fingers. "I wasn't ready for that and we broke up."

She wasn't over him. Rob could see that she had loved this man and she probably still did. That's why she wasn't ready to commit to him. He had to know. "Do you still love him?"

"Of course not." Then, "I don't think so." She didn't meet his eyes. "There's more to it than that."

Rob was afraid to ask so he waited for her to continue.

"He was white."

"So now you don't trust white men?" Rob shook his head and stood up. "It's like I said before, Paige, that's bull shit. I guess I'd better go."

She didn't stop him but she followed him to the door. The words he wanted to speak stuck in his throat so he just leaned down and kissed her lightly on her lips.

"Call me, Rob." He nodded and was gone.

Rob had nothing to say to Paige so he didn't call. Hope for a future with her had begun to die with their last conversation. She was still in love with someone else even though she might not admit it. Rob couldn't imagine his life without her, but his need for a family of his own hadn't left him. He wanted his own son, wanted more than one child and that was the very reason Paige had broken up with the man she still loved. Rob didn't believe color had anything to do with why she couldn't commit to him.

He wasn't sure he would ever find someone who wanted a family the way he did, or even if he wanted to try. It was difficult to imagine opening his heart to someone again. What he really wanted to do was to reveal who he was to her, but what would be the point now? She had said she wouldn't ask him to give up his desires for her, but in reality, it was she who wasn't willing to give anything up

But he couldn't stay away and he knew it. He planned to call her after work the same day Spud Smith caught him again in the parking lot.

"Just giving you some time to think over my offer. I think we can make a good haul on this one."

Rob waved him away. "I don't want to hear about it. Leave me out and stay away from me."

"Well, you know, old buddy, I'll just have to find that boss of yours and…"

"Do it, then. Do what you have to do. Just stay away from me." He pushed him aside and got into his truck, spraying gravel as he drove away.

He didn't call Paige that night. Fortunately Myrna didn't come home until late and by then he had stopped pacing the floor and had made a decision. After a sleepless night, he approached his boss on the job.

Bull McCasland was a head shorter than Rob, a stocky, solidly built Irishman who had spent twelve years in the Navy. His rusty hair was fading but not the tattoos that covered his freckled arms. Rob had no idea what his real name was. All he had been told was to call him Bull and that's what he looked like. His head jutted out over a short neck a man's hands couldn't reach around. He was a man you would expect to have a gruff voice but it wasn't. He was quiet, fair and Rob felt he had to take a chance on this man's understanding.

Rob waited until the other workers had left before approaching his boss. "Do you have a minute, Bull?" he asked.

The man nodded. "Sure. Something on your mind?"

Rob told him about being in prison, about his years in Las Vegas and about his changed life. "There's a guy who's been catching me after work and threatening to tell you about me, a guy I was in prison with."

Bull's brown eyes searched Rob's face. "What does he want you to do?"

"How did you know he wanted me to do something?" Rob asked, surprised at his boss' insight.

"I've known guys like him," Bull said. "In the Navy, on jobs. They're scum, living off other people. Stands to reason he's one of them."

"He wants to pull some robberies of some convenience stores. Wants me to help him."

"Are you going to?"

"No." The word came out louder than Rob intended. "Absolutely not."

"Have you been to the police?"

Police? Rob had never considered going to the police. He shook his head.

"Don't you think you need to do that?" Bull's arms were across his chest. He watched while Rob considered his words. "You think you'll be in trouble?"

Rob nodded. "I'm not sure. How could I tell the police the truth about changing my name and everything?"

Bull shook his head. "Well, you want to let this weasel get away with these hold ups?"

The thought of going to the police, the fear of being discovered as the one who had robbed the Lewis' paralyzed his thinking. But he didn't want Spud to get away with anything.

"I'd sure be disappointed if you don't." Bull shifted his weight in apparent readiness to walk away.

Rob stopped him. "Wait. I'm not sure how to do it. Do I just go to the police station? Won't they think I'm some kind of a crazy?"

Bull smiled showing teeth surprisingly straight and white. "I think I can help with that if you're willing. I have a neighbor who's a detective for the TPD. How about I talk to him, tell him about you and what you've told me? If he needs more information, then he can talk to you. What do you say?"

What could he say? Rob took a deep breath and agreed. Maybe he should have been going to church with Paige. It might make him look less like what a policeman would think he was.

On the way home Rob mulled over the conversation. The blood in his veins chilled with the thought of talking to anyone in law enforcement. If he got out of this, he'd leave for sure, go back to Vegas and work for John Taylor. There was nothing keeping him in Tulsa now that Myrna was getting married and he had no future with Paige. Yes, leaving Tulsa was his best option and he planned to do it as soon as this was over.

---

But thoughts of Paige still trickled through Rob's waking mind. As quickly as he was aware of them he'd push them away. But sometimes they'd clamp hold of his heart, squeezing it until he wanted to cry out with pain. In those times it took longer to dispose of them and, when they were gone, for a time the ache remained.

Finally he called her. It had been a week. That was as long as he could stand it. During that week he had nervously waited every day to hear if Bull's cop friend wanted to talk to him. His boss hadn't mentioned anything about their conversation again and Spud hadn't shown up. The suspense drove him back to Paige. Again he wished he had someone else to talk to but only Rico would understand. Only Rico knew about his past.

When Paige answered the phone that Saturday morning, Rob half wished he hadn't called. What was he going to say? The first words out of his mouth were, "I tried to stay away, but I can't. I'm hopeless."

Hearing her laughter over the phone tranquilized his stress. "Not any more hopeless than I am. I was afraid you would give up and never see me again."

Softly. "You know I can't do that." *As much as I wish I could.*

"Thank goodness," she said, as softly as he had spoken. "Can you come over now? I want to see you."

As quickly as his truck would take him, he was there. She drew him into her house and clung to him. His passion aroused again, he had to step back from her. Didn't she understand what she was doing to him?

"It's all right, Rob," she said. "I want you to make love to me."

Surprised, he held her away from him and looked into her eyes. "Don't do this unless it's real." He thought about women he had had sex with, Gerri in particular. He hadn't loved any of them, and when it was over, he remembered how he felt about them. In some cases it was revulsion. With Gerri, he knew she loved him, but he had little respect for her. It had to be different with the woman he loved.

Paige moved in closer to him, her body pressed against his. Her arms went around his neck, and she pulled his head down to hers. Her mouth moved against his, her tongue opening his lips with its urgency. She pulled the tail of his shirt loose and slipped her hand under it, pressing her fingers into his back.

Rob held her away from him. "Do you love me, Paige?" He could see the desire in her eyes but she didn't speak. "Can you say it?"

She tried to pull him closer to her. "Rob. I want you. I want to make love to you."

He stepped back. "But do you love me?" As much as he wanted her in this way, he wanted her love more.

She shook her head. "I can't say it, Rob." She released him and turned her back to him.

Frustrated and angry he wanted to strike out at her, wanted to hurt her the way she had just hurt him. She'd led him on and he had stopped her. What kind of fool was he? Wasn't sex enough for him now? Did there have to be love, too? He started to speak, started to spit out his disappointment, throw it in her face. In that moment he saw her, a scared young girl bound, lying on her face begging him not to leave her to die.

He had already hurt her as much as he ever would. He couldn't do it again. "I'm sorry, Paige." Sorry again. "As much as I want to make love to you, I know that if we do, you will wish you hadn't." He turned her toward him and took both her hands in his. "Then I'd lose you for sure and I couldn't stand that. You asked me for time. I'll give it to you. Maybe you will love me some day. Maybe there's hope for us. Until we know for sure, I can wait."

# TWENTY-EIGHT

Monday afternoon Bull McCasland stopped Rob after work. "My detective friend wants to talk to you."

Fear roiled in Rob's stomach and he thought he might be sick again, like in the old days. His hand went to the back of his neck in an attempt to erase the chill crawling up it. His first response was to run, to get in his truck and drive away, leave Tulsa, escape. Instead he took a deep breath and asked, "When?"

"He can be here tomorrow after work if that's okay with you."

A reprieve. He could still escape, start over somewhere else, and get a new name. And spend the rest of his life running? "I'm okay with that." He turned to leave then called back, "And thanks. Thanks for setting it up for me."

That evening, Rico called. He wasn't the old up-beat friend Rob knew. This time Rob asked the question, "What's wrong, friend?"

Rico sighed. "Sadness." Rob heard a strangled cry. "Mi hijo esta..."

"Your son? What, Rico?"

Rico spoke one word. "Muerte."

Rob knew what this Spanish word meant. Rico had lost his son. His heart sank. "No. Not Manuel."

"Si, mi hijo."

"What happened?" Rob whispered.

"Sickness. My heart, it breaks."

What does a person say to someone who has lost his first child, a person who has a broken heart? "Oh, friend, I am so sorry. I'm sad, too, and my heart breaks for you."

Rico's silence scared Rob.

"Are you going to be all right, Rico?"

Another deep sigh. "Si, I will be all right but *mi amante*, she is more sad."

"Rosa." Rob spoke her name. How hard it must be for her. "Will she be all right?" A silly question, one he was told not to ask during the grief recovery sessions. Of course, they would never be the same again. Death has a way of changing everything for people.

"We will go on, Roberto. It is hard but we will go on."

"I'm so glad you called me, Rico. I wish there was something I could do for you."

"You do much for me. You are my friend. You understand. One thing you can do."

"Anything."

"Say a prayer to the Blessed Mother for your friend."

Rob wanted to help Rico and didn't voice the thoughts running through his mind. Say a prayer? How do you do that? The blessed Mother?

As far as Rob could remember he had never said a prayer to anyone or anything. But from the conversation with Rico had come two thoughts. Maybe it was time to go to church with Paige and also, perhaps it was better to never have a child. To have a son and for the son to die; it was impossible to imagine the pain that would cause. He didn't think he would be able to live through something like that. Yes, maybe Paige was right. No children.

As soon as he got this Spud thing out of the way he'd tell Paige what he had decided.

-------

The next afternoon he met the detective in Bull's office.

"This is Rob Martin," Bull said to the officer.

The black man extended his hand and Rob shook it. "And this is Detective Gene Adamson, Rob. He'll help you with your problem." Then he left them alone.

Uneasy, Rob sat across from the man. "How long have you been with the TPD?" he asked, hoping the man would tell him it had only been a few months. Someone who wasn't familiar with the old Rob McGruder would be better than a long time employee.

"Twelve years," he said.

*Uh-oh.*

The detective pulled a pen and notebook from his jacket. "You want to tell me about all this?"

*Not really. What I'd like to do is get out of here.* "How much did Bull tell you?"

"Why don't you tell me?" the man said.

Cagey, Rob thought. Just like all cops. Don't give anything away. Make you do it.

Rob considered what he should tell and finally decided the truth would either set him free or kill him. "I was in prison a few years back. When I got out, I wanted to get away from the reason I had gone there in the first place so I left town."

"When was that?" Detective Adamson wrote on his pad.

*Almost six years.* He stretched the truth. "Seven years or so."

217

"Um. And where did you go?" He wrote again then looked back at Rob, waiting.

"I went to Las Vegas."

"Nevada?" At Rob's nod, he wrote some more. "And?"

Rob took a deep breath. "I changed my name. I wanted to get completely away from who I had been in case they, the guys who wanted me to keep breaking the law, tried to catch up with me." He knew he was speaking too fast.

"And what was your name before?"

Here it comes, Rob thought. "Robert McGruder."

Detective Adamson wrote.

He needed to steer the cop away from this part of his life. "I know Bull told you a guy from prison has been trying to get me to help him hold up some convenience stores." The detective nodded. "When I told him I didn't do that any more, he threatened to tell Bull that I'm an ex-con. So I told him myself. He thought I needed to tell the police, tell you so Spud can get caught."

"Spud? Spud Smith?" The detective straightened, his expression changing from passivity to genuine interest.

"Yeah, that's him. You know him?"

"Are you kidding? We've been trying to catch him for a long time." He rested his pen and pad on the table. "You think he'll try to talk to you again?"

Slightly confused but encouraged by the change, Rob said, "Probably. Last time I saw him he said he'd see me later."

"Are you up to working with us to catch this guy?" The man's intense interest removed the suspicion Rob had felt from him in the beginning of their conversation.

*Work with the cops? That's something new.* "How?"

"The next time he catches you, tell him you'll do it. Be sure he knows you are only doing it to get him off your back. Maybe tell him it will be the only time you'll help him if he'll leave you alone after this. Then you let us know where and when and we'll be there."

It sounded good except for one thing. When they caught Spud, he'd tell everything he knew about Rob. But what else could he do? He had to agree.

---

It had been almost a week since Paige had heard from Rob. Their last meeting had been a disaster. She had put herself out there, almost begging him to have sex with her and he refused. Refused because she couldn't tell him she loved him. What had been the matter with her? Over and over since that day she had kicked herself for her stupidity and was embarrassed about her behavior. Maybe he didn't want to see her again.

Her family would be leaving in a month on the cruise. It might be a good idea for her to go with them, just get away from Tulsa and from Rob. But would she be getting away from Rob? It looked to her like he wasn't going to call her. She thought about calling him but what would she say? I'm sorry I was so--slutty. That was the way she saw it. Slutty.

By mid week, she had almost decided to make reservations on the cruise when he called her.

"I'm sorry I haven't called sooner," he said. "I've really had a lot going on lately."

"It's all right," she lied. "I've been pretty busy, too."

"Paige, do you think we might be able to get together this weekend?"

A strange way to ask, she thought. "I imagine we can. What do you have in mind?"

"I was wondering if maybe we could set up a time when I can meet your family."

"Are you kidding?"

"No, I'm serious. I think I'm ready to meet them if you want me to."

"Well, sure," she said. "What changed your mind?"

"Haven't you wanted me to meet them?" She was aware he hadn't answered her question.

"Of course, but I thought..."

"I know. I haven't been ready. But I'm ready now if you want me to."

"Do you mean go to church first or what?"

"Not yet. Maybe later. Maybe we could just have a little meeting at your house. Nothing big."

"I'll talk to them." An apprehensive excitement settled over her. How would she tell her family about Rob? What would she say about how long they'd been seeing each other and why she hadn't told them sooner? Still, this was a big step for him and she knew it.

"And there's one more thing, Paige." Rob said. "I don't know anything about church or God or anything like that, but do you pray to the Blessed Mother?"

Paige laughed. "What? Where did you hear that?"

"Do you pray to the Blessed Mother?" Rob repeated.

"No, we don't. I'm not Catholic. Why?"

"You know my friend, Rico?" She remembered Rob's friend from Las Vegas. He had said Rico changed his life although he hadn't told her in what way. "He had a baby in February and it died."

"Oh, no. I'm so sorry."

"He asked me to say a prayer to the Blessed Mother, and I don't know how to do that. Actually, I don't even know who the Blessed Mother is."

Paige thought for a minute. "Catholics call the mother of Jesus the Blessed Mother. They believe that she will go to God to answer your prayer. You can pray to her or you can pray to God, but I believe that whatever you do, if it's a prayer, God will hear it and that's all that counts." She knew he was confused by her answer. It was like speaking a foreign language to him. That same uneasiness about Rob hit her. Were their differences too much to overcome?

Rob's voice broke into her thoughts. "Paige. I've come to another conclusion."

"What's that?"

"I've decided it's better not to have children."

Surprised, Paige asked, "That's not something I ever expected to hear from you."

"I know, but after talking to Rico, I don't think I could stand it to have a child and have him die."

The child might not die, she thought. Probably wouldn't. But she didn't say it. He finally wanted what she wanted. The rest would come soon enough.

The conversation ended with Paige saying she'd talk to her parents about a time to get together, and she would get back to him. She immediately dialed her parents' number. When her mother answered, she was at a loss for a way to tell them about Rob. They talked generally for a few minutes, then Bev Lewis, ever the perceptive mother asked, "Honey, what's the real reason you called?"

She started to protest but instead said, "You always know, don't you, Mom?" She took a deep breath. "There's someone I want you and Dad to meet, and Brad and Ashley, too."

"And?" Typical of her mother. Wait until she hears it all before she comments.

"He's someone I've been seeing for a while and I'd like you all to meet him."

"Do you want to tell me about him?"

*Not really.* Her own reluctance confused her. Why wouldn't she want to tell her mother all about him? "He's nice." She exhaled the breath she had been holding. "He's just a guy who likes me a lot, Mom, and I like him, too. But I'm not ready to fall in love again, if that's what you want to know."

Paige heard her mother's *hmmm* before she spoke. "So this may or may not be serious in the future and you want an opinion from someone not so close to the situation. Is that what you're saying?"

"Kind of. You have always been good at seeing things I don't. Sometimes my imagination gets in the way."

"It happens to all of us, Paige. We see what we want to see and that can blind us to the truth." She laughed a small tinkling sound. "Just let us know where and when and we'll be there with our Sherlock Holmes clothes on."

It was Paige's turn to laugh. "I knew I could count on you."

Her next call was to her sister-in-law, Ashley. She, too, was happy to meet this new man in Paige's life, but her reason was much different.

"Great, Paige. It's time you found someone and settled down."

"Oh, Ashley. Like I'm some kind of a party girl. This is just someone I'd like for all of you to meet. It may not be serious at all."

"You always say that."

"Always? When have I ever said that before?" Paige asked.

Ashley's voice softened. "Daniel. Don't you remember?"

Yes, she remembered, remembered more than she wanted to. That had been a mistake but her family hadn't seen it. They had loved him, thought the two of them were meant for each other, and, at the time, she'd thought so, too. But this was different. Rob didn't want children.

"I remember and I was right, wasn't I? It turned out it wasn't serious."

For the beat of a second, Ashley was quiet. "How about everyone coming out to our house Saturday afternoon? We can have a cook out in the evening and…"

Paige interrupted. "How about we don't eat? Just come for a short visit, maybe some coffee and cookies. Let's don't drag this out the first time."

It was agreed. The next Saturday afternoon they'd all meet at Brad and Ashley's new home overlooking the Arkansas River.

Relieved the plans were out of the way and having Rob's agreement after she called him back, discomfort still plagued Paige. She couldn't put her finger on the reason and finally decided it was, as usual, just her imagination.

Rob and Paige drove toward the southwest part of Tulsa. Rob's thoughts were only half present. Every day he expected Spud to meet him after work. He hadn't heard from the detective but kept his card in his wallet in readiness to call him as soon as Spud showed up again. He had looked at the card a dozen times and every time he did, fear threatened to send him running out of town again.

Rob drove Paige's Mustang down a paved road alongside the river. The road curved and began a slight upward climb through cottonwoods, ash and maples. A final turn brought them to a stop in front of a gate.

"You have to put in the code," Paige said. She gave him four numbers. "That's the year Brad was born."

Rob punched in the four numbers and the gate slid open.

"They moved out here after the robbery. They felt it was safer," she explained.

Safer from most crooks, he thought. I'm sure anyone bent on a burglary could find a way to get in and now he knew the code. He stopped himself. *What am I thinking?*

"They have twenty-four hour camera surveillance all over the neighborhood and security people who patrol day and night, too." She pointed to a black object almost hidden in a tree near the gate. "There are cameras like that one taking pictures of cars and license plates. Before you can get in, Brad has to tell security what license plates and cars and names of people he's expecting."

A guard stepped out of a log building beneath the camera, clipboard in hand. He made a note on it and waved to Paige as they passed him.

"Sounds like they've got it covered," he murmured. All that security would make it harder. Just knowing the gate code wouldn't be much help, and he understood why she had wanted to bring her own car.

They followed a winding blacktop road that rose through thick plant overgrowth. Driveways and glimpses of houses were visible through the trees along the way. "This is it," she pointed to an entrance on her right. They followed the graveled drive and after a sharp turn entered an open space. The dwelling sat to the left of the circular driveway that curved in front of what looked to Rob like a house made of glass.

"Did you notice the driveway is gravel and makes a lot of noise?" Paige asked. She pointed to the blacktopped drive way. "But this part isn't gravel?"

Rob said he saw the difference.

"You can hear someone coming up the road, a warning, but Brad didn't want people to have to walk on the rocks." Her voice carried a hysterical quality. "He's really been paranoid since the robbery. Scared someone will try to get in and kidnap Landon."

Rob cringed. The reality of what he was about to do slapped him in the face. The desire to escape flooded over him. It took all his energy and will to calmly climb out of the red car and follow Paige to the front door where a walnut skinned man awaited them.

Her brother held a brown-eyed child in one arm, and with his free arm, hugged his sister to him all the while never taking his eyes off Rob. Paige stepped back and introduced the two men. Brad's mouth smiled but his eyes didn't.

Rob wanted to look away but forced himself to meet Brad's eyes. *Can he tell who I am just by looking at me?*

Brad was shorter than Rob by a few inches, stocky but not fat and wore rimless glasses. He was dressed in sharply pressed jeans with a dark purple polo shirt. His hair was cropped close to his head and Rob saw no resemblance between the brother and sister. Brad forced a bleak smile as the two men shook hands. A tall slim woman joined them. She had a wide expressive mouth and her face radiated friendliness.

"This is Ashley, my sister-in-law," Paige said. The woman stood almost the height of her husband. Her black hair was in plaits with beaded ends and she wore a loose multicolored blouse and crop pants. She invited them into a foyer that was lit by the sun shining in through tall windows above the wood hewn front door. Paige's mother and father entered from another light-filled room on the left. Rob remembered the small silver-haired Bev Lewis with her daughter's stunning eyes. She shook his hand warmly. Both of them were casually dressed but still in a fashion that made Rob realize was far nicer than his jeans and uncollared tee. Paige had said she was wearing jeans but he now saw that even hers were of a better quality than his.

Jim Lewis, larger than any of the others in the room, gripped Rob's hand tightly. His dark eyes held a smile. "It's good to see you again, my boy," Jim boomed. "We're happy to have Paige bring you here."

Bev Lewis looked toward her daughter. "When Paige told us about you, she forgot to mention who it was we were meeting."

Paige blushed. "I've said I'm sorry about that." She looked up at Rob. "After I set up this meeting, I remembered you had met my mom and dad and called them to tell them who I was bringing."

"We were delighted," Bev assured him.

Brad Lewis' voice held a trace of irritation. "Let's go into the great room," he said and walked away. The others followed. The women and Jim Lewis chatted animatedly about something Rob didn't follow. His concern was with the brother and if he suspected something?

Bev took the little boy from Brad and sat in an ivory rocking chair near the tall windows that looked out onto a scene of astounding beauty; trees already near full bloom in grassy meadows that rolled down to the Arkansas River below. The other furniture in the room had straight clean lines in colors of ivory, blues and greens. Glass tables and silver lamps filled spaces beside love seats, couches and chairs. A rock fireplace cut into one square of the floor to ceiling windows. Several eclectic area rugs covered some of the rich hardwood floor.

"This is beautiful," Rob said when they all had been seated. He and Paige sat on a loveseat to one side of the fireplace.

They talked for a few minutes about the beauty of the setting then Ashley and Paige excused themselves to get coffee for the gathering. Bev said she was going to take Landon to his room for a nap and Rob was left alone with the men.

Jim Lewis' question was the first and expected. "What do you do for a living, Rob?"

Rob told him about his job and added that he had learned it when he lived in Las Vegas.

"Las Vegas?" Brad asked. "When did you move here?"

"I think I told you," his father interjected, "about Rob's sister and her husband's death." Rob noted the narrowing of his eyes toward his son when he said it.

"Right. You did." Brad looked from his father to Rob. "So you weren't raised in Vegas."

Rob felt the grilling coming. He measured his words. "No, I was raised here. Went to school at Hale." Not quite a lie. He had attended Hale High School before dropping out. "I left and went to Vegas after that." He didn't have to say how long after that, did he?

Brad nodded. "I grew up in Atlanta. Came here before Paige did."

"What do you do, Brad?" Anything to get the subject off of himself.

"I worked for the Williams Company in their media department for a long time. I have a business of my own now." Brad's tone was level, tight.

"Media? Television, movies?"

"I film events and put them on CDs and DVDs. Used to put them on tape," he answered with obvious scorn for Rob's ignorance. "We have the ability to air them direct as they happen or sell them to air later."

"Sounds interesting." What else could he say? He knew nothing about this kind of life. Fortunately the women came in with coffee and a plate of cookies. Paige handed him a cup and sat beside him again.

The conversation turned to other subjects with Rob saying as little as possible. Then Brad asked one of the questions Rob had expected and dreaded. "Where do you go to church, Rob?"

Paige shot her brother a warning look and answered for him. "He doesn't go to church, Brad. I thought I told you that."

Brad's mouth turned up in a forced smile. "I guess I forgot," he said with evident sarcasm. He looked at Rob and widened his eyes in an effort of innocence. "I sure hope you'll come with Paige some time. We'd love to have you join us for our usual Sunday get-together." His open look failed and came off as rude and calculating.

"Maybe some day," Rob said.

Rob was the first to see the black cat appear in the doorway. It regarded the room then ran toward the group. Rob's shoulders jerked involuntarily and he started to stand. He relaxed when the cat jumped into Ashley's lap and curled into a ball.

Paige touched his arm. She had seen the flash of fear in his eyes.

Relieved the cat didn't appear to recognize him, he heaved an audible sigh and covered her hand with his.

Brad had witnessed his discomfort, too. He leaned back in his chair and steepled his fingers together. "Got a problem with cats, Martin?" he said, unsuccessfully smothering a laugh.

Both Paige and Rob's heads turned toward him. "Brad!" Paige said.

Ashley reached toward her husband, "Brad, please." Her plaits made a soft chorus when she shook her head.

Mr. Lewis' face betrayed his embarrassment, "Son," he said.

Brad leaned forward and spread his hands, "Just asking. He looked like he had seen a ghost," he retorted with a smile. "I thought maybe he was afraid or something." Then he laughed openly, no humor in his voice. "You'd think Pepper was an attack cat or something."

Paige stood. "I think we need to go," she said. They all stood in unison, everyone eager to be free of the discomfort.

Their leave was quick, Paige leading the way out. She followed Rob to the driver's side of the car and when he opened the door, she climbed in. He walked around to the passenger side of the Mustang and looked back at the four people watching them from the porch. Mrs. Lewis and Ashley gave weak waves. Reverend Lewis, his hands in his pockets, smiled at him and Brad stood with his arms crossed over his chest, a scowl on his face.

Paige took off fast, her wheels spinning as they hit the gravel. "Damn Brad," she muttered. "He can be such a …" she searched for the word.

"Jerk?"

"You saw it, too."

"I've known some in my life," Rob said and laughed.

She faced him. "What's so damned funny?"

"You," he said, still laughing. "I've never seen you like this. Mad and cussing. I didn't know you knew how." It became funnier the more he thought of it.

Then she smiled. She listened to his laughter for a few seconds before she burst out laughing, too.

The tension broken, she said, "I'm so sorry about how they acted, Rob."

"It wasn't everyone, Paige. It's obvious your brother doesn't like me."

"I think he's just protective. He'll like you when he gets to know you." Was she assuring him or herself?

But Rob wasn't sure he wanted Brad to get to know him. "Do you think it's because of the robbery that's he's so suspicious?"

Paige looked at him. "I hadn't thought of that. But why would he be suspicious of you?"

Why, he thought. Because I'm the guy who did it and something in him knows.

He didn't answer her.

"You know, you may be right," she admitted. "It may have something to do with his being suspicious of everyone since the robbery. I've always felt it was partly his own fault it happened."

His fault? "How so?"

"Well, he kept the coins at home instead of in a bank vault. He had a pretty good safe under the stairs, but still they shouldn't have been there."

*Under the stairs.* That's where they were all the time and she didn't tell him. For an instant he thought about being angry at her then, as quickly, let it go. What else could she have done?

"And he and Ashley were always talking about them to everyone. I think they probably told someone about them and somehow some crook got hold of the information and decided to try to get them." Her mind seemed to be working it out and away from him. "If it was someone who knew him, then they knew he'd be out of town, too." She shook her head. "He can be such a -- such a..."

"Jerk?" Rob said.

Paige laughed and nodded.

They enjoyed the rest of the afternoon and evening together. He took her to dinner at a small café where they ate Mexican food. At her condo they drank an after-dinner liqueur and talked about inconsequential things. He promised to call her Sunday afternoon and left after only one passionate kiss. He didn't tell her he loved her this time. He knew he was falling more and more in love with her, and he wished with all his heart it could work, but after the meeting with her family, he was sure it wouldn't.

# Twenty-Nine

Rob was surprised when Myrna came home after church on Sunday instead of spending the day with Paul and his kids.

"Have you eaten?" she asked as soon as she came through the door.

He put down the Sunday paper and started to get up from the recliner. "Not yet. What are you doing home?"

"I live here, remember?" Her voice broke. She hurried past him and into her bedroom.

Rob followed her into her bedroom where he found her trying to unzip the back of her dress. She turned away from him when he came in and said, "Can you get this for me?"

"Something the matter?" he asked as he pulled the zipper down.

"Nothing I can't handle." She faced him. "I'll be out as soon as I change and I'll fix us some lunch."

Following her cue to leave the room, he shut the door behind him. He wondered what had happened between Myrna and Paul, or was it one of the kids? Josh, maybe, although from the few things she had said since Christmas, everyone was getting along well.

Myrna avoided looking at him when she came out of her bedroom and went right to the kitchen. He heard the cabinet doors opening and slamming then heard a deep sob. "There's no food in this house. Where's the food?"

By then he was at her side. Her hands covered her face but she wouldn't drop them when he tried to turn her toward him. "No," she said. "Leave me alone." But when the sobs took over, she finally let him hold her.

He let her cry awhile before asking, "What is it, Myrna? You and Paul have a fight?"

She nodded her head. "He can be so bull headed. Everything has to always go his way. Sometimes I get so mad at him…" her voice broke into more sobbing.

"Do you want to tell me about it?" He rubbed his hand lightly over her back.

She wiped her tears on the tail of her shirt. "It's always about the kids. He doesn't think I know what to do for them and sometimes when I try to do something I think will help, then he tells me to let him handle it. It makes me so mad."

"What kinds of things?" Maybe if he knew what she was talking about, he could smooth it out.

She looked up at him, her eyes red-rimmed. "Like this morning. I went over to help the girls get dressed for church like I always do. He had their clothes picked out, like he always does, and they told me they didn't want to wear those dresses. They wanted to wear some nice pants like some of the other girls wear to church. They looked nice in them, too. But, oh no," her voice went high and mocking, "Paul thinks girls are supposed to wear dresses to church." She stomped her foot. "That's old fashioned." By now her voice was strident. "That's the dark ages." She pulled away from him and began to pace as she talked. "He said I wear a dress and I told him that was because I wanted to, but that I could wear pants if I wanted. That's when he said all females should wear dresses to church just like all men have to wear suits and ties." She slammed her fist on the counter. "Isn't that the dumbest thing you've ever heard?"

It was the dumbest thing Rob had ever heard but he wanted to try to stay neutral. "So, what happened?"

"So the girls had to change into dresses and they cried, of course, and while they were changing he told me that it was his place to decide how his--get this *his* daughters should dress." Her voice quietened. "I didn't say anything else, just got into my car and drove to church and didn't even talk to him. Afterwards, I kissed all the kids and told them I had to come home and see you and I'd see them tomorrow. The girls were crying again." She stopped in front of him, her eyes sadder than Rob had ever seen them. "Oh, Rob, it broke my heart."

He put his hand on her shoulder. "Myrna. They are his kids."

"I know, but I feel like they're mine, too. Maybe I've been expecting too much. I thought we had talked about this and had agreed that I was to be the mother-part of their lives. We even talked about how they might want to call me Mom some day." She shook her head, the tears gathering again. "I've seen him be stubborn about some things with them but he's never been that way with me before, not like this morning. Usually we're able to work things out."

"You didn't give him the chance this morning, Sis. You left." Rob wanted to strangle this guy who had made his sister so unhappy but he kept his tone passive. "Maybe he'll think about it and you can still work it out."

Myrna shook her head. "He'll have to do a lot of talking to convince me it won't happen again."

At that moment the phone rang. They looked at each other. It rang a second time. "You answer it, Rob," she said.

It was Paul and he wanted to talk to Myrna. Rob held his hand over the receiver when he told her.

"How does he sound?" she asked.

He thought for a minute. "Not angry."

She took the cordless phone from him and walked into her bedroom. Rob heard her door click shut. He breathed a sigh of relief. His life was messed up enough. He didn't need to be trying to fix anyone else's mess.

As it turned out, Myrna was on the phone over an hour. He finally left and went to get something to eat at a fast food restaurant. He drove around a while, thought about going by Paige's but knew she and her family were probably having their weekly lunch-after-church. He had told her he would call her in the afternoon but had no idea what he would say to her. He recognized there was a gulf standing between them, her family and his returning desire for children.

When he thought of not having children, the slow ache of his heart told him something different. Yes, he had a fear of losing a child, but never having one? He had told Paige he didn't want children any longer. That had been from fear after talking to a heart-sore Rico, and that was a lie. He didn't mean it to be a lie at the time, but it was. Everything in him still wanted his own son.

And the church and family thing. Even if he agreed to go to church with her, he knew he would never be comfortable with her brother. So, instead of going home and facing Myrna, if she were still there, or finding a phone and calling Paige, he went to a movie and lost himself in a Clint Eastwood adventure.

# THIRTY

For a change Brad was quiet at the family lunch. Paige let her father and mother and Ashley carry the conversation about the cruise while she took over Landon's feeding, insisting she sit beside the boy and help him eat mashed up vegetables and fruit. She periodically sneaked a look at her brooding brother. Knowing him, he would speak his mind soon enough without anyone's help.

"Too bad your boyfriend couldn't make it today," Brad finally said into a conversational lull. The others looked at him, then at Paige and quickly back at their own plates of food.

Cowards, she thought. She tried to catch the eyes of her parents and Ashley but none of them looked her way. Only Brad's eyes burned into hers. Never one to back down to her big brother, she tossed her head. "Yeah, too bad." That should have been enough but she had to insert the knife. "Not that you aren't happy about it." She was used to years of having to meet Brad's digs head on. She turned back to feeding her nephew.

"Okay, you two," Jim Lewis held up his hand toward them. "Not here. Not now."

Ashley shook her head and touched her husband's arm. He moved it from under her touch, his eyes still on Paige. Bev Lewis wiped her lips with her napkin.

Brad dragged his eyes from his sister and looked at his dad. "I'm not going to say anything the rest of you aren't thinking." Before anyone could respond, he continued, his eyes back on her. "This guy isn't for you, Paige. You two are totally different. You're too good for him anyway."

Paige looked up from Landon, her eyes blazing at her brother. "You don't even know him. He's a better man than you are, Brad Lewis. I can say that with certainty because I've known you all my life."

"No more!" their father warned. "We're in a public place. If you two have any more to say to each other, take it outside." He turned to his son. "And, young man, you have no business speaking for the rest of us. You don't know what we think."

Brad said no more but it was evident he fumed at the way his father had addressed him.

It was a stand off. Paige waited a few minutes then excused herself. Her mother and Ashley tried to apologize but she didn't allow them. Evidently her family wasn't as perceptive as she had thought. She needed to get away from everyone. She hoped Rob didn't call and if he did, she wasn't sure she would even answer the phone.

---

When Rob came home Sunday evening, Myrna's bedroom door was still closed. He could hear her talking and knew she was on the phone with Paul. He went into his room and fell exhausted into bed. He hadn't called Paige, but what was there to say anyway? Sleep came on him quickly. Restless, uneasy dreams teased him all night and he arose with a feeling of misgiving the next morning.

He hadn't heard from Spud in too long. Maybe he had changed his mind and planned to carry out his robberies alone. Rob hoped so because he dreaded having to get involved in this sting operation that just might end up with him being stung as well.

At the end of the work day, Rob's reserves were depleted. The stress of Paige's family, Myrna's situation with Paul and his own fears left him drained. When he neared the parking lot he noticed a rusted gray Crown Victoria parked so close to his truck he would have to get in on the passenger side. It irritated him that someone would park that way in a lot with so many empty spaces. As he approached, the driver's door of the Crown Vic opened and he heard a voice he immediately recognized.

"Hey, Mac, what's up?" Spud closed the door with his hip.

Rob's fatigue fled and he stopped at the front fender, his senses heightened. He caught the name Spud had called him, knowing the little man knew just what he was doing. A mocking smile played across the man's lips.

Rob knew Spud was testing him. He didn't answer and kept his expression bland.

"Given my offer any thought?" Spud asked, leaning against the dusty side of the car.

*Now's the time. I can play it like the cops want or I can walk away again.* He waited for Spud's next move.

"What if I told you I know something you don't know? Something you'd probably like to know?" He pulled a cigarette from the pocket of his shirt.

Rob put one hand on the hood of the Ford, not for support but for something to hold onto to keep himself from throttling Spud right in the parking lot. "And that would be?"

Spud took a lighter from his pocket and held it to his cigarette. He took his time lighting it and replacing the lighter then pulled in a long of smoke and blew it skyward.

Rob watched him. He knew what Spud was doing, trying to get one-up on him. It was a prison game and he knew better than this little weasel how to play it. His expression imperceptible, he waited.

"What if I tell you your old lady's steppin' out on you?"

*My old lady? Paige?* Rob felt a twinge of fear but kept his face stony. "I'd say you are as dumb as you look."

Spud bristled. He straightened up, his voice louder, "Oh, yeah. Well, what if I tell you that every day after you leave for work she goes to some rich guy's house and spends the day with him."

*Myrna. He's talking about Myrna and Paul.*

"I see them kissing on the porch before he leaves in a really nice BMW." Spud spit out the words. Satisfied he was one-up, he leaned again against the car and dragged a lungful of smoke from the cigarette.

Rob realized Spud knew where he lived, had probably followed him home and had watched his house. Fury washed over him. He could take this little guy out right here. No one was around. He'd kill him with his bare hands. The only thing stopping him was the cops. Detective Adamson would know it was him and he would go back to prison for killing a slime-ball who needed to be dead. He wasn't worth that no matter how much he wanted to do it.

In a split second he was upon Spud. He caught his cigarette hand with his left one and twisted it on top of the car. The cigarette rolled out of his fingers and onto the ground. With his right hand he grabbed Spud's left one and rammed it across the man's throat. He stomped on both of Spud's feet with his heavy work boots causing the man to cry out in pain. Immobilized the man gasped, his own arm cutting off his breath, panic in his eyes.

"Okay, let me tell you what I want to do to you. I want to put my hands around your neck and squeeze the life out of you." His face almost touched Spud's. It felt good to press him against the car, to hear him croaking "no," to feel the bones of his scrawny wrists beneath his hands. "I could break every bone in your body with one move," he growled into Spud's face.

Spud eyes darted around frantically. No one was in sight.

"No one's going to help you," Rob said. "I can kill you right here and throw you in the bed of my truck and drive you to the river. No tellin' when you'd come up."

Spud's eyes held real terror, more than Rob had ever seen when the two of them were cell mates.

"Now let me tell you how it's going to be."

Rob stepped off Spud's feet and propelled him into the small space between the two vehicles. He pushed the man against the side of his car, holding him there with both hands against his chest. "This is how it's going to be, Scum-bag. You are never," he stressed the word, "*never* to go near my house again or my old lady. You got that?"

Spud's head bobbed up and down in agreement.

"And you and me are going to hit whatever it is you have planned and we're going to split the take sixty-forty with me getting sixty. Got that?"

Spud started to speak. Rob pressed his chest harder. "Answer me."

"Yes, Mac," he began and eyes wide thought better of it and finished with "Gruder."

Rob didn't lessen the pressure. "Where is it and what do you have planned?"

Spud didn't answer immediately. Rob raised one hand and grasped his throat.

"Now's the time to talk if you want to live one more minute."

"Okay," Spud said quickly. "It's a Fast Cash place. They have a lot of money on the fifteenth of the month for people who want to cash their checks. We hit 'em early, right after they open and before anybody's come in."

That's probably one of the dumbest things I've every heard, Rob thought. "And you don't think they have surveillance cameras?" He moved his hand from the throat but still pressed his chest with one hand.

"Sure they do. I've thought of that, too." He spoke quickly, obviously eager to get it out and change the subject from his death. "I'm going to wear a mask, a Sylvester Stallone mask." He choked a giggle. "It'll be so quick. In and out. Unless you want to be the one to go in."

"Hell, no. I'm not that dumb."

"Not dumb, McGruder. It'll work. I've got it all figured out. There's only one guy or girl who works there. It'll be quick. They'll give me the money and I'm gone."

"You have a gun?" Rob asked, his mind working to get information and get away from this filth.

Spud grinned showing his stained teeth and the thought that the picket fence needed painting almost gagged Rob.

"Of course, don't you?"

"No," Rob said. "I'm a felon, remember?"

The little man grinned again. "I can get you one. Easy."

"I don't need one. Just use yours." He released Spud. "Where is this place?"

"On the north side." He gave Rob the street names. "We can go in your truck if you want to."

"No way," Rob said. "I'll drive your hunk of junk. That way if the cops chase us they can shoot holes in it instead of mine."

Spud laughed at this. "No cops, Buddy. There won't be no cops. It'll go down too fast. They'll never catch us. I'll ditch this rig right after so be sure you wear gloves so they don't find no fingerprints."

Rob knew about gloves and fingerprints. He told Spud where they'd meet the following Thursday morning and where he'd leave his truck while he drove the rusty Crown Vic. Then he picked the man up by the armpits and slapped him against his car. "You play me and you'll be dead. If I ever see your scrawny butt anywhere near my house again, I'll put your eyes out. And after this, never again. You'll stay away from me. Got that?"

Spud's head bounced up and down like a yo-yo, his mouth gaped open and spittle drooled down his chin. Rob released him and pushed him toward the back of his car. "Now get that hunk of crap out of here and don't ever park that close to my truck again."

Spud turned to leave and Rob gave him push with the flat of his boot that sent him sprawling on the ground. He looked back, real fear in his eyes. In his haste to stand, he slipped and fell again. Almost on hands and knees he crawled until he was out of reach then scrambled to his car and got in. Rob stepped back and watched him speed away.

Rob calmly unlocked his truck. Once he was seated he took a deep breath. His legs were jelly. His hands shook. He was at one time hot and cold. Bile rose in his throat. He couldn't think clearly. *I may die right here,* he thought and part of him wished he would.

When he got home the house was empty and for that he was thankful. He didn't want his sister to see him in this state. Still weak from the experience he went into his bedroom and lay on his unmade bed for what seemed to him only minutes but when he looked at the clock, it was after five. He must have fallen asleep or passed out. He knew he had met Spud a little after three and hadn't spent over fifteen minutes with him.

Spud's memory flashed into his mind. *Filth. The man is filth, scum.* Rob sat up. He wished for something to wash away the feel of the man; beer, whiskey, anything that would burn the image and smell of Spud Smith out of him. Knowing there was nothing like that in the house, he stood and peeled off his grimy work clothes. He balled them up and threw them into the floor of his closet then went into the bathroom and turned on the shower. It was still cold when he stood under it but he didn't care. If he couldn't drink away the feel of the vermin, he'd wash it off. He soaped over and over and stayed until he emptied the hot water tank.

Words, phrases, actions from the Spud encounter continued to rise in pencil sketches in his mind. This is the time to get drunk, he thought, to forget. He went to the kitchen, still naked from his shower, knowing he would find no alcohol there. As Myrna had pointed out, there was no food either. He slammed the cabinet doors. He thought about leaving and what that would mean. Go somewhere else, not Vegas. Change his name again. Start over.

He took a deep breath. And run forever. Never have a home. Never have a life.

He'd come too far and wasn't going to start over. He had to go back to his bedroom for his wallet. He took out the detective's card and threw the billfold on top of his dresser.

This may kill me, he thought, but I'm not going to let that little rat get away.

Detective Adamson answered his cell phone on the first ring. Rob told him about his meeting with Spud and about the plan. The detective said he'd call him back and within thirty minutes was back on the phone with Rob.

"You drive to the place and sit in the car. When Smith comes in, we'll be in there. It won't be the clerk, it'll be one of us. You stay in the car and don't go anywhere. Any questions?"

Rob had none and hung up the phone. Anxious to get it over with, he wished he didn't have to wait two more days. Tomorrow he'd tell Bull why he wouldn't be in Thursday morning. He knew his boss would be all right with him missing part of that day. He could picture himself saying, "I'm sorry I won't be in Thursday morning. I have to go rob a store." He tried to laugh but it wasn't funny. It was dead-on serious.

# THIRTY-ONE

Monday afternoon Paul and Myrna sat across the kitchen table from Kristen, Kim and Josh. The girls kept their eyes downcast, pouts on their faces. Josh twirled a coin on the table top until his father asked him to stop. He obediently let the coin drop to the table, folded his hands in front of him and looked at his father with indifference.

"I have something I need to say to all of you," Paul began. Josh's expression changed to suspicion. The girls didn't look up. "I made a mistake yesterday." Both girls raised their eyes, looked at one another then at Myrna and finally at their father. Paul took Myrna's hand in his. Josh looked down at his own hands. "Kris, Kim, I guess I forget you are getting older. You're six now, almost seven, and you probably know what you like to wear." They nodded.

Paul looked at Myrna. "Myrna helped me see this." Both girls looked at Myrna with obvious appreciation. "I know times have changed. I want you to know I prefer you wear dresses to church but I will let you choose what you wear as long as it is clean and nice looking." He looked from one to another. "Is that all right?

The girls shouted "yes" at the same time and ran around the table kissing their father and smothering Myrna with kisses and thank yous. They skipped out of the room leaving Josh sitting at the table, a pensive look on his face. "Dad," he said. "What about me?"

"What about you, Josh?"

The boy straightened in his chair and leaned forward. "I'm the only kid in my class that has to wear a tie. What about that?"

Myrna laughed, and when she did, Paul smiled. He looked at her, his expression soft and he squeezed her hand before turning back to his son. "You decide, son," he said. "It's up to you."

Josh nodded and got up. "Thanks," he said looking at his father. He picked up the coin from the table then raised his eyes to Myrna's. "Thank you, too," he said and gestured toward his father. "You're a good influence on him." He left the room smiling.

Paul put his arm around Myrna and pulled her to him. "Thank you." He kissed her. "You are the best thing that's happened to this family in a long time. I don't ever want to fight with you again. I can't stand it."

She touched his face. "I can't either." She poked his nose with her finger. "You did good, Dad. Now let me get dinner on the table. I want to get home and tell Rob everything's all right before he goes to bed.

---

After talking to the detective Rob dressed and decided he'd go to Burger King for his dinner but as he headed for the door, he heard a knock. When he opened the door he was surprised to see Paige on the other side.

Without a word, she came in and stood in the middle of the room. "Are you all right?"

"Sure, why?" He closed the door.

"Well, you didn't call me yesterday," she said. "That isn't like you. I tried to call here about an hour ago and no one answered. I was worried."

*You should be. I'm about to pull a robbery with a small time crook.*

"I must have been in the shower. I took a shower when I got home from work, and I took a short nap. I didn't hear the phone." Rob approached her, put his arms around her.

"You don't look like everything's all right."

*Is she a mind reader, too?* He pulled her close. "I'm all right. Just tired."

She relaxed against him and raised her face for him to kiss her. He hesitated then lightly touched her lips with his. Her hand behind his head, she pulled his face to her and kissed him. The passion rose in him. Not again, he thought. I won't fall into that again. He released her, held her at arms length. "Sweetheart," he said. "I'm sorry I worried you." He made his expression as sincere as he could. "I'm really all right. I couldn't call yesterday because of Myrna."

"Myrna?"

"She came home in the afternoon all upset because she and Paul had a fight. We talked about it for awhile then he called. They got on the phone and were on it the rest of the evening."

She wasn't buying it. "They have pay phones, you know."

He nodded and smiled at her. "I'm sorry. It won't happen again." He tipped her head with his fingers under her chin and kissed her again.

She sighed and rested against his chest. "Do you have anything to drink? I could use something?"

He released her and went into the kitchen. "I'm afraid it will have to be coffee or water. That's about all we have here."

"You know you really should get a cell phone," Paige said.

"I know. I will." He filled the coffeemaker with water.

She tapped the phone on the counter with her finger. "And an answering machine."

"Some day," Rob said and took a can of coffee from the cabinet.

"Rob, what's this?" Paige asked.

He looked over at her. She held the detective's card in her hand. "Um..."he stammered. "It's just someone I know."

"I know him, too," she said.

An icy finger slipped across the base of his neck. He measured coffee into the basket. "How's that?" He kept his voice calm.

"Detective Gene Adamson. He's the one who investigated the robbery."

Rob wished he could slowly dissolve into the floor. The one who investigated the robbery he had committed and now he was working with the man. He seemed to be sliding deeper into the dark pit instead of climbing out of it. What else could go wrong?

"He came to the hospital on Sunday after it happened and took my statement." She shook her head. "It had been two days and they didn't have a description of the guy. I guess that's why he got away." She looked up from the card. "How do you know him?"

How could he answer that? Before he had a chance the front door burst open and he heard Myrna call his name. She came into the kitchen and stopped at the door when she saw Paige. "Paige." Her eyes went from the woman to her brother. "Rob?"

Paige greeted her. "Myrna, I've been meaning to call you. I had a fitting for the maid-of-honor dress and it should be ready in plenty of time."

Myrna nodded. "Good," she said. "Is that what you came to tell me?"

"No." Paige smiled. "I was here to see Rob, wondered why he hadn't called yesterday like he said he would." She moved to his side and tucked her arm in his.

Myrna didn't hide the shock on her face. "Rob?" She looked at her brother.

Paige's expression changed and she, too, looked up at Rob.

*Now's the time to disappear.* He just shook his head, wordless. *I wondered what else could go wrong and now I know.* He knew what Myrna was thinking. They were here together and he hadn't told her he was still seeing Paige.

"Rob?" Myrna asked again.

"Rob?" Paige echoed.

He took a deep breath. I guess I can't dig a hole any deeper than I'm in right now, he thought. "Myrna, Paige and I have been seeing each other."

Paige cocked her head to one side. "Seeing each other?"

Myrna's eyes widened. "You can't be serious."

Paige looked at Myrna. "Can't be serious? Why would you say that? You didn't know?"

"Rob?" Myrna repeated.

"Shit." That seemed to be the only word to express what he was feeling.

"Well, that helps a lot," Myrna said, her tone dripping with sarcasm.

Paige looked from one to the other. "I don't understand. What's this about?

Is there a problem?"

Rob held up his hands. "Okay, okay. I'll explain everything. Can we go in the other room and sit down?"

The three of them walked single file into the living room. The women sat next to each other on the sofa. Rob stood in front of them. "Myrna, I didn't tell you because I never see you to talk about things like this."

"We see each other every Saturday morning. You could have told me then."

"I know, but you're usually talking about Paul and I just didn't think to say anything."

"Didn't think to say anything?" Paige asked.

"I mean…" he paused. There was no way out. He would rather be between the cops and Spud Smith than these two women. "I don't know why I didn't say anything." An idea came to him. "I guess I wanted to wait until I knew Paige was into it as much I am."

Paige's eyebrows went up. "Into it as much… You have got to be kidding. You don't think I'm into it as much as you?"

"You know what I mean, Paige. I love you but you…"

Myrna interrupted. "You love her? And you never said anything? I can't believe it!"

Paige turned to Myrna. "You can't believe it? Neither can I." She looked back at Rob and stood up, eyes flashing.

"Paige." He tried to take her hands. "Please, I can explain if you'll let me."

She wouldn't meet his gaze and pulled away from his touch. "I think maybe I'd better go now and let you talk to your sister."

He called to her as she opened the door. "I'll call you later."

With a withering look, she said, "Sure, if you have time." And walked out.

Myrna sat back in the sofa. "Okay, Rob, tell me what's going on with you two."

He sat down beside her, the cushion where Paige sat still warm. "I know I told you I probably wouldn't see her after that one date, but I have been ever since then. Myrna, I have fallen in love with her. I can't help that, can I?" His eyes begged for her understanding.

"No, I can't blame you for that, but you know what will happen if she finds out who you are."

He nodded. "Don't you think I've thought of that a million times?"

"Obviously it didn't do much good." She didn't smile.

Rob leaned back heavily into the sofa cushions. "Some day I'll tell her." He heard a derisive sniff. "I will," he said and saw the disdain on her face.

"And what will she do, Brother?"

He shrugged his shoulders. "My life is such a bag of you-know-what right now it can't get any worse. You want some coffee?"

# THIRTY-TWO

*What's the matter with you, Paige Lewis? Why did you go chasing after him? Don't you have any self-respect? Mortified. That's what I feel. Mortified. Myrna didn't even know about us and we've talked several times about the wedding. How is it I didn't realize that?*

Paige drove home, alternating between anger at herself and anger at Rob. *And Myrna's attitude. She acted like she was unhappy with our relationship. Why?*

After a strained Sunday lunch with her family the day before, Paige had gone home to think, not wanting to talk to anyone, especially Rob. But when he didn't call, it had upset her, upset her so much she hadn't slept well. All day Monday she'd expected to hear from him even though she was aware he had no cell phone and no way to call during his work day. But when three-thirty had come and he still hadn't called, she fumed. She was unable to get to a phone herself until after five. His number rang several times with no answer.

No cell phone. No answering machine. "You people need to move into the twenty-first century," she exclaimed, and that's when she decided to drive to his house. She'd rushed in acting like she owned him. *I must be going crazy. I don't even love him...do I?*

On top of everything else, he had never mentioned to his sister that they were seeing each other. That really fried her. He had said he would call her. Did she even want him to call now? Maybe she didn't want to talk to him. Maybe it would be better if they never saw each other again.

Paige pulled into her garage and shut off the engine. The idea that she might never see Rob again played in her mind. Sadness rose up in her and tears came to her eyes. I'm just mad, she told herself. I'll be all right in a little while. What she didn't want to admit was how much Rob had hurt her by not telling Myrna about them. It didn't matter that she had taken so long before telling her family about him. She had a good reason. She wasn't sure she loved him, wasn't sure where the relationship was going. But with Rob it was different or should have been different. He loved her. He should have wanted to tell the one person he was the closest to about them. And he hadn't. Why?

Paige took a tremulous breath. Aloud, she said, "I'll get over this just as I've gotten over other things in my life."

Detective Adamson's card. Why did Rob have his card? It seemed strange that he would have his card, and he hadn't answered her question about it. Well, if he called like he said he would, she'd ask him again. And if he didn't? She climbed out of the car and slammed the door. "Then who cares anyway?"

The next evening Rob knocked on Paige's door, flowers in hand. Resigned to facing a big fight with her, he had decided the flowers might soften the blow. He had called her office as soon as he got home from work and asked if he could see her. After a hesitation, she had agreed. He dressed in some of his best chinos and planned to offer to take her to dinner somewhere nice. With what he was facing Thursday morning, he feared it just might be the last time he would get to take her anywhere.

Paige wore jeans and a baggy shirt and was barefooted. Obviously she wasn't planning anything special. She didn't smile when she let him in.

He handed her the flowers and asked her to forgive him.

"Thanks," she said without conviction and said nothing about forgiveness. She took the flowers into the kitchen and shoved them into a vase, not taking the time to arrange them.

He followed her into the kitchen and when she turned around, he tried to take her in his arms. She pulled away. "Let's go sit down," she said.

In the living room she sat in a chair across the room from him. "You said you wanted to explain, Rob. Let's hear it."

Her words made him think of what it would be like to have a bullet shot at him. Where to start? He hadn't practiced what he would say because he didn't know how to explain his actions. "I don't know what you want me to explain."

She harrumphed, her face pinched.

"I guess you want to know why I didn't tell Myrna about us." When she nodded, he said, "Well, I told you last night. She was so wrapped up in her life that I just didn't say anything. That's really all there is to it."

Paige sat forward. "I don't buy it, Rob. I think there's more to it than that. I think I know why you didn't say anything."

Tell me, he thought. Maybe you have a better explanation than the one I can give you.

"I think it's because you aren't sure about us. You've told me you love me but I'm not sure you really do. You've said you are all right with me being black and with not having kids but I don't think that's true either. I think you are just leading me on."

"Leading you on?" Angry, he stood. "If anyone's leading anyone on, it would be you. I've been honest with you." *Like hell you have, McGruder.* He stopped, got control and said more quietly. "I love you, Paige. I've told you I don't care about color, and I've told you I would give up having kids because I love you too much to let you go."

When he snapped at her, Paige sat back in her chair, surprised by his anger. She spread her hands. "I shouldn't have said that. I know you haven't been leading me on. It's just that--that I was hurt last night. I thought maybe you were ashamed of our relationship or something."

He knelt before her again. It seemed to him he was always on his knees in front of her. She let him take her hands. "I'm sorry. That's all I can say about last night." He pulled her to her feet and held her. Her arms went around his waist.

"Rob, I want to love you. I'm trying."

He held her away from him so he could look into her eyes. "Honey, love isn't something you have to try to do. You either do it or you don't."

Instead of going out to eat they sat in the kitchen and ate peanut butter and jelly sandwiches. Afterward they sat on the sofa with Paige snuggled into the crook of Rob's arm. They shared long kisses and Rob kept himself under control. No sex, he told himself. *Not until I hear those three words out of her mouth.*

Paige sat up. "Rob, you never told me how you know Detective Adamson."

How was he going to answer that? No way could he tell her the truth but he had to come up with something. His mind went into overdrive. "No big deal," he stalled. "He's my boss' neighbor."

She nodded, waiting for his explanation.

"I—uh--need him to do something for me."

"Some police work?" she asked.

"No--not that." *Think, McGruder, think.* "Remember the gate that was banging that night your car wouldn't start?"

"Not really." Her expression told him she was searching her memory.

"Well, it's broken and I haven't been able to get it fixed. This detective makes iron gates so I've ordered one from him." Pretty good, he thought, but if she knows that a welder can do that with one hand tied behind his back, I'll be in deep trouble again.

"I didn't know that," she said.

"How would you? Is that something the two of you talked about?"

She laughed. "Of course not. We just talked about the robbery. Ask him if he remembers me when you talk to him again."

Not on your life, Rob thought. But he said, "I've never talked to him. My boss is taking care of it for me. We probably won't ever meet." Then he pulled her to him and kissed her again. He had an ulterior motive for the kiss. He wanted to keep her mouth busy doing something besides talking.

---

Rob awoke earlier than usual on Thursday morning. He lay awake for over an hour, his thoughts on what was ahead of him. He planned to leave at the regular time so Myrna wouldn't be suspicious even though he wasn't supposed to meet Spud until 7:30. Last night he had driven by the Fast Cash then to the Wal-Mart lot where he would meet Spud. Seeing the big Wal-Mart sign reminded him of the last lot of this kind he'd parked in. It was there he had bought a box of latex gloves, tape and the toy gun. He had made three trips inside so no one checker could identify him as purchasing the items used in the robbery.

He shook the thoughts away and climbed out of bed. He dressed as usual in heavy jeans and a long sleeved denim shirt because he planned to go to work when the robbery was over. That is, if all went well and the cops got Spud. And if they didn't?

Don't go there, he thought.

At seven fifteen, he pulled into the parking lot and got out of his truck. He walked a few rows over to wait for Spud. At 7:40 Spud's old Ford parked near his Dodge, a full car width between the two vehicles. He watched Spud get out and look inside the truck's window then saw him searching the area with his eyes. Rob walked quickly to where Spud stood and was behind him before the man realized it.

"Hey," Rob said.

Spud wheeled around, his hand in his jacket pocket. "You better be careful, coming up behind a guy carryin'." He showed Rob the black handle of his weapon. He grinned. "I brought one for you, too. It's in the glove compartment."

Rob again pictured what it would be like to choke Spud. It would feel so good to see his eyes bug out, his tongue wave in protest, to hear his last gurgle of life. Instead he pulled a pair of latex gloves from his pocket, shoved his hands into them and got into the driver's seat. Spud crawled into the passenger seat and opened the glove box revealing a metallic pistol.

"Shut that thing!" Rob commanded and slammed it shut. "I told you I didn't need a gun."

Spud held his hands up. "Okay, okay. Just relax. This is in case you need it."

"If you do your job right, I won't." Rob spit out the words.

Spud pulled a gun out of his pocket and held it low in the seat between them. "I'll do my job right. You can count on that."

*A nine millimeter Glock.* Rob said aloud, "Seventeen rounds. You think you'll need that much fire power?"

The little man put the gun back in his pocket. He grinned again, took a cigarette from a pack on the dash board and started to light it. "You never know."

Rob reached across the seat and grabbed the cigarette out of his hand. He tossed it out the open window. "No smoking."

Spud bristled. "Hell, McGruder, I need the nicotine. I'll be all nervous if I don't get it."

"Well, then just be nervous. Maybe it'll give you an edge." Rob pointed to the seat between them where Sylvester Stallone's rubber face stared sightlessly at him. "I don't think Sly smokes." He picked up the mask. "How do you see out of this thing?"

Spud took it from him and poked two fingers through the eye holes. "Right here. Got two holes I can see out of."

Rob started the engine. "This place opens at eight, right?" He looked at his watch. "We better get closer if we want to be there when they open the doors."

"Maybe the girl will be working today. She's a hottie. I wouldn't mind--"

"Shut up!" Rob turned onto the street.

Spud looked hurt but closed his mouth. He reached toward his cigarette package again then pulled his hand back and laced his fingers together in his lap.

Rob had to drive by the Fast Cash a couple of times before his watch said eight. He had told the detective what kind of car he would be in and wanted to give the cops the opportunity to see it before he parked. As far as Rob was concerned, Spud's idea was a bad one. Even if the cops weren't inside, he didn't think it would have worked. He was reasonably sure the business had an alarm and figured the place had outside cameras, too. Before they would have gotten two blocks away an APB would have been out on the car and they'd be on their way to jail. But the cops were inside and he was in the clear. It was Spud who would go down.

Rob pulled the Crown Vic to the right side of the business out of sight of the front door and windows and kept the motor running. Spud gave Rob a thumbs up then pulled the mask over his face and got out. He walked quickly around the car and disappeared through the front door. Rob held his breath. He couldn't see into the establishment but kept his window down. A soft breeze touched his face carrying the smell of rain. Grey clouds moved across the pale sky bringing the threat of early spring storms.

Pop! Rob recognized a gun shot.

Then two, then two more, then Rob lost count. Rob's ears stung from the sound. He reached for the gear shift and started to throw it into reverse. He stopped. There was no need to run. Detective Adamson told him to stay in the car and wait for someone to tell him what to do. Rob shrank in his seat, heart pounding.

Two patrol cars squealed into the lot and two uniformed officers jumped out, guns drawn. They stood behind their open doors, firearms pointed at the front of the business. One patrolman spoke into the device on his shoulder and both looked over at him. One of them headed into the business while the other one came to where Rob waited.

Rob's breathing quickened. The cop held his gun at his side.

"You Robert Martin?" he asked.

Rob didn't trust his voice. He nodded.

"Come with me." The policeman opened his door. "Cut your engine," he said.

Rob turned off the key and followed the officer through the door. The first person he saw was Gene Adamson kneeling over Spud's body. Blood pooled around them. An acrid smell burned his nostrils and filled his lungs. He coughed. Adamson looked up at him. "He drew on us, shot at us. We had to shoot back. He's still alive, barely. Paramedic's on the way."

Everything went white. *I'm going to pass out.* He leaned forward and put his hands on his knees. He felt someone take his arm. "You okay?" a policeman asked.

Rob shook his head. The officer helped him outside and forced him to sit down. "Put your head between your knees," he instructed. He knelt beside Rob. "A lot of people have the same reaction when they see the blood." He left him there.

Rob's head was beginning to clear when EMSA pulled up, sirens blaring. They were followed by paramedics from the fire department. He wanted to get out of this place, wanted to get back to his truck. He looked toward the Crown Vic. A policeman wearing latex gloves was going through the Ford. He saw him open the glove box and take out the gun. He held it carefully and checked the safety then emptied the magazine into a plastic bag and stuck the gun into another bag.

Rob stood up, his legs shaky. Through the window he could see the paramedics working over Spud. Two of the fire department medics were farther in the back of the shop working with the detective that had been shot. Adamson had moved from beside Spud and was with his partner.

Not knowing what to do, Rob stayed near the front door watching. He saw Spud being loaded onto the stretcher. One of them held a bag of fluid over his head, a bag Rob knew was attached under the sheet to Spud Smith. Rob knew he was still alive or they would have covered up his head.

The whole scene was surreal. What was he doing here? Cops everywhere and him a felon and a robber who hadn't been caught--yet. He hated adding the yet to his thoughts.

Why didn't someone tell him what to do?

Detective Adamson came out behind the stretcher and approached him. He stuck out his hand. "Good work, Martin."

He knows my real name, Rob thought, but he called me Martin. He wondered if all the cops knew his name and remembered the other one had called him Martin, too.

"We had to shoot him. We told him to drop his weapon and he started firing. One of the other detectives in the building was grazed."

"There were two of you?" Rob asked.

Adamson nodded and pulled a handkerchief from his back pocket. He wiped it across his forehead and put it back in his pocket. I was acting like the clerk and my partner was behind a door in the back. When Smith saw him, he shot. I had to get him. He was running around waving his weapon, got off about five shots. Crazy guy. I think he took a few bullets in the gut." The siren on the ambulance sounded when the vehicle pulled out of the lot. "I guess you're ready to get out of here, aren't you?"

"Yes," Rob said.

"We have to impound the Ford. One of the officers will take you back to where you parked. Then we need you to come to the station and make a statement. You know where it is?" he asked.

Rob said he did, not reminding the detective when he'd been there and under what circumstances.

Gene Adamson looked toward the street. "Here comes the media." He looked back at Rob. "You don't want to be here for them."

"Right." It wouldn't do to be on television and have Paige and Myrna see this. He might be able to explain it to his sister but there was no way he could tell Paige about it. "Will you keep me out of it?" he asked.

The detective looked at him. "I think it would be better if no one knew who tipped us off. We'll keep it quiet. We won't release your statement either. We need it but it'll be under wraps." He hailed one of the patrolmen. "He needs a ride." He shook Rob's hand again, thanked him and went toward the Channel Eight van that had just pulled in.

Thunder rolled in the distance as the policeman directed Rob to his car and gestured toward the front seat. A man jumped out of the television van carrying a hand held video camera. Behind him a female reporter, mike in hand, looked his way and asked the detective a question. Adamson shook his head. At the same time the paramedics brought the wounded detective outside, his shoulder bleeding through his shirt. The reporter forgot about Rob and rushed toward the detective.

What Rob refused to think about was what would happen if Spud regained consciousness. Would Detective Adamson be able to protect him?

---

Rob pulled his jacket around his neck to protect it from the soft rain that fell. Inside the building he found Bull in his office.

"Hey," Bull said when he walked in. "How'd it go?"

Rob sank into one of the hard backed chairs and told him what had happened, the foiled hold up, the shooting, his trip to the police station to give his statement and his relief that it was over. When he finished, he rubbed his hand across his eyes and started to get up.

"Go home, Martin. You won't be much use here today." Bull came around the desk and clapped him on the shoulder.

He wanted to argue, to insist he stay, but he was dead tired and, with his boss' blessing, he left.

At home he took a long shower then fell asleep in the recliner with the television playing. He woke up a little before five o'clock but couldn't summon the energy to get out of the chair.

The news was full of reports of the attempted robbery and shooting. They reported that the perpetrator was "clinging to life" in a local hospital. Nothing was mentioned about his presence and the reporter only said the police wouldn't say how they happened to be on the scene. An investigation of the incident was pending.

Rob's empty stomach started to cramp. He pushed himself out of the chair and went to the kitchen. He drank two glasses of water then looked through the cupboards. He remembered again what Myrna had said, there was no food in the house; not even cereal or milk. When he and Rico lived together, they had done their own grocery shopping and cooked their own meals.

Tired of eating fast food he determined he would begin to cook again. He had to go to the store, but not tonight. He was too tired; even too tired to get in his truck and find something to eat.

He found two eggs in the refrigerator and had no idea how long they had been in there. When he and Myrna spent Saturday mornings together, she always managed to fix something for them to eat, but he didn't know where she got it. He had accused her of being wrapped up in herself, when, in reality, it was he who was wrapped up in himself. Otherwise he would have known she brought the food with her when she came home on Friday night.

Rob pulled a frying pan from under the stove and scrambled the two eggs. He ate them right from the pan, set it in the sink and filled it with water. Sleep, that's all he wanted to do. No calls to Paige, to anyone. *Too tired*. He turned the ringer down on the phone and fell across his bed.

Rob awoke early Friday morning. Yesterday's events were like a dream, but fortunately, he hadn't done any dreaming during the night, any he could remember. He had slept hard and was refreshed. Getting up early gave him time to wash the pan and brew a pot of coffee before he left for work.

When he got up, Myrna's door was closed as usual. He hadn't heard her come in the night before. Sometime today he'd call Paige but he didn't know what he would say to her. He hadn't seen her since Sunday; not that long but he missed her. What he really missed was just being with her without so many lies between them. He wanted to tell her about Spud, about his part in the hold up, but that would mean she would have to know he was an ex con. How could he carry on a conversation without mentioning what he had been through the day before?

And he would go to the grocery store. He would do it on the way home from work. He would cook something for his supper. His lunch today would be his last fast food meal. He and Rico had packed their lunches in Vegas and he would do it again. Normalcy. That's what he craved.

At six o'clock he slipped out of the house. The sun had risen and the day looked to be sunny and clear. April was almost over. A new month and a new leaf in his life.

At the end of the work day Bull stopped him as he was leaving. He put his hand on Rob's shoulder and gave it a shake. "Good job, Martin. Gene told me you did a good thing. I'm proud of you." The men shook hands and Rob thanked him.

Rob shook his hand. "Thanks for..." he paused.

Bull started to wave him off.

"No. I mean it. Thanks for—for everything." He couldn't put into words how grateful he was for the help his boss had given him.

Bull just nodded, gave a wave and walked back into his office. Rob went out to his truck, glad to know Spud Smith wouldn't be waiting for him.

The construction site was dirty and his welding clothes were always covered with dusty grime, rust and iron shavings so he went home to clean up before his trip to buy groceries. He thought about calling Paige but decided to wait until he knew she would be home from work. He hoped she wouldn't be upset that she hadn't heard from him last night. For the past few days he had other things on his mind, things he couldn't reveal, especially to Paige Lewis.

-----

Albertsons was crowded with shoppers on their way home from work. Rob scanned his list and headed for the far aisle planning to work his way across the store. Choosing dried cereal wasn't difficult because he had eaten only Cheerios all his life. But, today, he stood before the rows of shelves and read the names on the boxes. So many he'd never even tried. Maybe today he'd branch out and....

He heard a familiar voice. "What about this one, Bobby?"

He looked around. Standing near him was a woman with a small boy in the front of her cart. Her back was to him as she and the child looked at the cereal boxes.

"No, not that one, Mommy. I want Cheerios." The child pointed to a yellow box.

The mother moved to replace the box she held in her hand and when she turned, Rob could see her profile. Short auburn hair brushed back behind her ears, light freckles across her nose and cheeks.

Feeling his gaze, she turned toward him then turned away but quickly looked back. Her mouth formed a silent "Oh."

At the same moment Rob breathed her name, "Gerri."

-----

Time stopped for Gerri Harper and at the same time, spiraled backward five years. It was Rob.

She felt, rather than heard, her child pulling on her arm and calling her name. She knew he was saying, "Mommy," but she was unable to move, unable to turn away from the gray eyes that held her.

What do you say to someone you haven't seen in over five years? Someone who broke your heart yet gave you the greatest gift you'd ever had?

Rob spoke her name again. "Gerri." Then, "It's been a long time."

She wanted to laugh or scream or cry. *A long time? You have no idea.*

Instead she forced herself to relax, turned to her child and said quietly. "Honey, this is someone I knew a long time ago. We'll get the cereal in a minute but I need to talk to him now."

The boy looked up at Rob. He quieted and watched his mother and the man.

Gerri spoke. "Yes. It has been a long time." She noticed Rob's short hair and tanned skin. He seemed bigger to her, filled out, not the skinny guy she remembered. Changes in his appearance, but was that all? She motioned toward her son. "This is my son, Rob. His name is Bobby. Bobby, say hello to Mr. McGruder."

"Martin." Rob corrected her.

She didn't understand. "Martin?"

"Yes, my name is Martin now." Rob looked uncomfortable. "I changed it when I moved away."

Gerri exhaled a breath she had drawn in when she'd first seen him. To Bobby she said, "Mr. Martin is his name."

The boy didn't reply. Gerri moved the cart to become a barrier between her and Rob.

"Your son?" Rob asked.

She nodded. *And yours.*

"He looks like you."

*No, he looks like you.*

"Very cute. How old is he?"

"Four. He turned four last June."

Rob nodded. *What a coincidence that his name is Bobby.*

Her son turned in his seat and looked at Rob.

"Hello, Bobby." Rob said.

"Hi." Bobby said then he looked up into his mother's face. She didn't want him to see what she was feeling and smiled down at him.

She looked back at Rob. "How have you been?"

Rob stood behind his cart gripping the handle. "Good. Good. I've moved back here."

She nodded again.

"I guess you know I left town."

She wanted to laugh and couldn't hide the smile. "Of course, I knew." She had to add. "You didn't say good-bye."

The color rose in his face. She liked seeing his discomfort.

"I'm sorry about that, Gerri. It was unexpected. I had to leave quickly."

*I'll say. With the police on your heels!*

"How have you been? I guess you got married?" He gestured toward Bobby.

Gerri relaxed. It was time for him to know. "Actually, I didn't." She waited.

"Oh."

That's all he said.

They stood in silence.

The boy looked at Rob again, holding him in his gaze.

In a sudden motion Rob reached toward the shelf and removed a box of cereal. "I have to go." He maneuvered his cart and began to turn it out of the aisle. "It was good to see you again."

And he was gone. Just like the last time. He was gone.

Gerri leaned toward her son, ruffled his strawberry blond hair then took his head in her hands and kissed his forehead. Oh, Bobby, she thought. You just met your daddy

---

Strange, thought Rob, to meet Gerri and find out she has a child and never married. Their meeting troubled him but he wasn't sure why. She seemed a little frustrated but maybe that was to be expected. After all he had left her without a word and his sudden reappearance must have been as surprising to her as it was to him. Driving with one hand, he touched the stud in his ear and pondered what it all meant. Out of the corner of his eye he glimpsed a flash of silver. A horn honked and brakes squealed.

Momentarily stunned he started to brake then realized he had run a red light and was in the middle of an intersection. Gunning the engine, he steered past the stopped car and left the driver shaking his fist and cursing him. Rob continued two blocks before pulling the truck into a strip mall parking lot. He put the gear into Park and left it running. His pulse pounded, his arms and legs liquid. His head reeled and came to rest on the seat back.

*That was a close one.*

He sat slumped in the seat for a few minutes then slowly began to recover from the scare. *What was I thinking? I don't even remember driving down this street.*

Rob sat up, gripped the steering wheel and put the truck into Drive. Irritated at his carelessness he drove the rest of the way home forcing himself not to think about Gerri or the near accident.

When he stopped the car, it hit him. *The boy.* When Bobby looked him in the eye, there was something so familiar about him. Rob had told Gerri the child looked like her, but now he realized that wasn't true.

Gerri's eyes were green. The boy had darker eyes, more gray and blue. Gerri's hair was auburn. Bobby was a blond.

Rob looked in the rearview mirror at his own reflection.

Time stood still. What he saw in the mirror was the child, the image of his father.

"Oh, God, no." Rob breathed aloud a prayer rather than a curse. He tore his eyes from the vision and went back five years. It couldn't be. He tried to count back in his mind. *It takes nine months. I left in October. June would only be eight months. Maybe it was another man, later, after I left.* He shook away the confusion, rubbed the back of his neck. He and Gerri had been together nearly every weekend for three months after they met at her office. He hadn't been careful, wasn't sure if he even thought about it back then. They'd never talked about it. He'd never asked.

Rob's fist came down on the steering wheel. *Damn you, Robert McGruder! Only thinking of yourself as usual.* He wanted to hit something, hit himself. He struck the seat beside him over and over until he was exhausted from the self-loathing.

For a few minutes he sat still, not moving, mind numb. Slowly the thought began to dawn like the sun creeping out from behind heavy clouds. First a shimmer of light, then a luminescent ray, then a sunburst.

*A son! I have a son!*

# THIRTY-THREE

The phone was ringing as Rob came up the walk, both arms around sacks of groceries. He juggled a sack in one arm and set the other down on the porch. In his haste to dig the house key from his pocket, it dropped out of his hand. He cursed and when he leaned over to pick it up, a package of potatoes rolled out of the bag and bounced down the steps. Keys finally in hand, he unlocked the door and grabbed the phone.

It was Paige. "I was about to hang up."

"I just came in from the store, had my arms full of groceries," he explained, breathless.

"Groceries? You went to the store?"

After what he had been through yesterday and finding out he had a son and Paige's incredulousness at his buying groceries, his first instinct was to hang up on her. His second was to tell her what he had been through. Instead, he held his tongue.

"Rob, are you all right?"

"Yeah," he said.

"You don't sound like yourself."

I'm not, he thought but didn't voice it. In two days I have been responsible for having a guy shot and found out I have a son.

"I guess I shouldn't have called. I'm sorry if this is a bad time." Rob sensed the hurt in her tone.

Ashamed of his attitude, he said, "No, it's all right. I've just had a couple of bad days and then I dropped some groceries outside trying to get to the phone."

"Bad days? Don't we all. What's happened?" She chuckled.

Rob couldn't tell her what had happened and wished he had kept quiet about the bad days. He realized he was going to have to tell her another lie and hated the fact that lately it seemed all he did was lie to her.

"I haven't felt well for the last two days." A lie but maybe a good one.

"You're sick? Have you been to the doctor?" Now she was concerned. He had to assure her or she would be over nursing him back to health.

"Paige, really, I'm all right. I just need to rest. I haven't slept well but still had to go to work." He had an idea that might get him off the hook for a couple of days. He needed time to think about his meeting with Gerri. "I plan to spend the weekend just resting and eating good food. That's why I went to the store."

She didn't say anything for a second. "Is there anything I can do for you?"

"No, but thanks. If I have something contagious, I don't want to give it to you."

"Right. You're probably right, but will you call me if you need anything?"

He assured her he would and added that he loved her. Relieved but sorry he couldn't tell her the truth, he hung up. He hoped the day would come when all his secrets would be out in the open and he could be honest with everyone. He knew it was getting closer to the time when he had to tell Paige who he was and what he had done. But not yet. Not when he had just found out he was a father.

He needed to talk to someone, someone who could help him figure out what to do with this information. Not Myrna, whose mind was filled with her new life and June wedding. Certainly not Paige. Rico. Now wouldn't even be a good time to talk to him. Even if Rico were to call, hitting him with his new fatherhood would be like throwing acid on his grieving heart.

He ran it over in his mind all evening and woke up several times during the night, images of Gerri and the boy swimming to the surface of his consciousness. Sometime during the night his answer came.

Saturday morning he dialed John Taylor in Las Vegas and spilled the story of his relationship with Gerri but omitted the reason he left her in Tulsa.

"Maybe I shouldn't have called you, John, but I don't have anyone here I can talk to." He heard the desperation in his own voice.

"Slow down, Rob," John said, quietly. "Give me time to think about this."

No time, thought Rob. I have to know now. "Do you want me to call you back later?"

"No, just give me a minute." Silence on the line. Finally, "Rob, do you remember when you came out here and asked me if I had a purpose in my life?"

"Yes." Rob's heart slowed to a normal beat.

"Remember I told you that I'd found a new purpose, to love my family?"

Rob remembered and agreed.

"I think I told you I'd learned that you have do things right, that you can't take short cuts because you end up hurting people." John took a deep breath that Rob could hear across the miles. "Well, you took a short cut and it ended up hurting some people, this girl, and her son. Your son, Rob."

Rob's heart began its pounding again. *My son.*

John continued. "Well, you have to make a decision. Do you go on hurting people or do you make it right?"

"Make it right? How can I make it right, John, after all this time?"

"Call her. See if he's your son and then..."

"You mean, call her? What would I say? Is Bobby my son? And then, if he is, what do I do?" Rob's voice shook with renewed emotion.

"It's simple, friend. Just be his dad."

John's words hung in the air. Rob's heart and breathing paused, suspended before him were the words, "just be his dad." It might be simple, but would it be easy? Could he do it? Later, looking back on the hours that followed their talk, Rob saw himself climbing out of the fog and entering the light.

He found a G.A. Harper in the phone book at an address near her old apartment. Rob drove by the small house, noted its well kept lawn and fenced backyard. He took a chance that this was Gerri and went home and tried the number. The voice on the answering machine was automated and said it was the home of the Harpers and the Abbotts and to leave a message. He hung up. Abbott? Who was she living with? Maybe it was the wrong number. He waited another day. Sunday afternoon he punched in the number again and held his breath. She answered on the third ring.

"Gerri." He found his voice. "It's Rob." The silence was so complete, he repeated her name.

"I'm here."

What did he want to say? "I'd like to talk to you."

More silence.

271

"Please, I need to talk to you." His voice rang pathetic in his ears.

"Sure," she said slowly. He heard her exhale a breath. "How about now?"

"On the phone?"

"No" Another silence. "How about we meet someplace for coffee. Maybe in about an hour?"

That soon? "Sure, where?"

"There's a coffee shop about two blocks from me. It shouldn't be too busy this time of the day." She told him the address and hung up.

Fearing what was ahead threw him into a panic. He drank a cold beer hoping the alcohol would relax him. It only gave him heartburn. He chewed two Tums and changed into clean clothes.

An hour later he found the coffee shop and went inside. Of course, she wasn't there. He should have known. She was always late but his fear was that she had changed her mind and wouldn't come after all. He found a booth at the far end of the café and waited. The time that had flown while he made himself ready for the meeting now slowed to a crawl.

Finally the door opened and she came in. Her eyes scanned the room and found him. She didn't move until he stood, then she walked toward him, a tremulous smile on her lips. "Rob." His name from her mouth felt like a caress. He'd expected something else, anger, coldness, not this. Her short auburn hair curled slightly around her face. Dark lashes rimmed her emerald green eyes, eyes he remembered always looking at him with love. Even now they held no reproach. Shame rushed over him and he knew it showed on his face.

They sat across from each other. "Gerri, I'm sorry, so damned sorry."

"Thanks for saying it," she said and sat still for a long time before she spoke again. "I was pretty hurt when you left."

Rob's face flushed.

She continued, "And then I was mad at you."

He nodded in agreement and started to speak.

"But," she stopped him, "you know I was always optimistic about everything." He nodded again. She laughed, a sound he hadn't expected to hear from her. "Some people say I look at the world through rose-colored glasses, and it's true." Her eyes had never left his. "After it was all over—the hurt and the anger at you, I was thankful."

He found his voice. "Thankful?"

Her mouth tipped into a brief smile. "I know it sounds strange but don't you know what a wonderful gift you gave me?" He couldn't answer. "Rob, I have Bobby and I'm so grateful to have him."

"But..." he began.

"I know, you left me, but you didn't know about him, didn't know that I was pregnant." He nodded his head in agreement. "The morning I found out about—everything," she paused and he knew what she was thinking. He looked down, unable to meet her honest gaze. "That's when I was going to tell you."

"I'm sorry," he repeated. He shook his head. "Then you know why I left."

She nodded. "Of course and I, also, know it wouldn't have changed anything. You would have still had to leave."

He had to agree. Rob McGruder would have left anyway.

Their eyes met. "Did you go to the police?"

It was her turn to look away. "I probably should have, but --." She raised her eyes to his. "But, I cared about you, Rob. I knew you well enough to know you didn't do it to hurt anyone. That wasn't you."

Rob sat back in the booth. "Like hell it wasn't. You may think you knew me, Gerri. I was a bastard, the worse kind of--"

She interrupted him. "No, Rob, that's what you thought of yourself, but that wasn't you. At least, that wasn't the man I knew,

273

the real you, the man who wanted a better life. I understood why you did it, and I felt I was partly to blame."

"You? How?"

"Because I told you about the coins and…"

"You would have been in trouble, too, wouldn't you?" Rob regretted the problems he'd caused Gerri, first the robbery, then the baby. There was no way he could ever make up for what he'd done to her.

"Yes, but you know, I really didn't think about that until later. I was pretty cut up because of everything--the baby--you leaving. Honestly, I didn't even think about that for a long time. When I did think about it, I had to consider what would happen if I told. Besides being in trouble and possibly having to go to jail myself for aiding in a crime, I had to think about my baby." She leaned forward and spoke quietly. "I couldn't do that to him."

Rob shifted in his seat. He'd messed up so many people's lives. Would there ever be an end to it? "And your boss. He could have been in trouble, too."

Gerri nodded and sighed. "You see, there was so much at stake and time went by then it seemed too late. Lynn and I talked about it and she agreed that I should just keep quiet."

"Lynn?"

"Lynn Abbott. She's my friend. We worked together. Remember her?"

He did remember another person in the agency but he had never paid much attention to her. His eyes had been on Gerri.

"We share a house. She's keeping Bobby while I'm here."

"Then she knows, too?" Too many people knew the truth.

"She knows." She hesitated, watching him. "But she won't ever say anything either. Besides," she looked into his eyes, "I've kept up with the girl and she's okay."

His heart skipped. "The girl?"

"Yes, Paige Lewis. The one you robbed."

"You know her?" The knot of fear formed once more in his gut.

"No, I don't know her. Lynn's brother is with the police department and that's how she found out about her. Paige Lewis works at St. Elizabeth's." At his pained expression, she added. "Rob, she's all right. She's doing all right."

He simply nodded. The tangles of his life threatened to strangle him and keep him from escaping the dark pit of his past.

"And, no, Lynn didn't say anything about you to her brother. I asked her not to, and being my friend, she agreed to keep my confidence. Besides, by then we would have both been in trouble for not going to the police when it first happened. It might have been wrong, but I had to think of my baby first."

"How did she ask her brother about the girl? About Paige Lewis?" Rob's wiped the sweat from his palms on his pants. "Wasn't he suspicious?"

"We worked for the same agency, remember? He thought she was asking for her boss." She sighed. "It was a mess, Rob, but if the girl was all right and my son was safe, that's what mattered to me."

Rob leaned his elbows on the table and covered his face with his hands. "And I was—am responsible for the mess I put all of you in." He looked up at her and saw clearly the harm his selfish actions had caused, first to Paige, then to Myrna and now to Gerri and their son, and even Gerri's friend had had to lie for him. Although *guilty* screamed in his ears, Gerri's expression carried no condemnation.

He reached across the table and tried to take her hand. She pulled away and dropped her hands into her lap. Embarrassed, he folded his hands on the table in front of him. "I have no excuses, Gerri. How can you ever forgive me?"

She shook her head not meeting his gaze. "I forgave you a long time ago."

"How?" He wasn't sure he believed her.

Gerri smiled. "I remembered something my daddy said a long time ago. 'One man's curse is another man's ladder.' That's how I looked at it; it could become my curse or I could let the situation take me to a better place."

Rob didn't speak. He repeated it to himself. One man's curse is another man's ladder. "You didn't let it become a curse."

"If I hadn't forgiven you, it would have."

The two of them sat in silence; Rob's mind struggling to understand and Gerri giving him time. Rob looked at the mother of his child with a new appreciation for her. He had left her pregnant and alone. She had chosen to have their child and raise him and even now she didn't appear to be accusing him of anything.

Rob spoke softly. "And you named him Bobby."

Gerri nodded. "After his father."

Rob shook his head and looked at her. He'd been so wrong about her. She wasn't the dippy woman he thought she was when they were together. She had substance and stood head and shoulders above him.

His thoughts were interrupted when Gerri spoke, her voice tender. "Rob, do you want to know about Bobby?"

He nodded but couldn't speak over the lump constricting his throat.

"He's in nursery school." She kept her hands folded in her lap. "I quit my job when he was born and moved in with Lynn. Then I got another job working out of our home. Bobby's my first priority and I want to be available for him all the time." She leaned toward him.

"That's why I haven't dated. I didn't want a parade of daddies in his life." She waited for his response.

Rob could only nod. Her life had been unselfish while, in contrast, his had been only about himself. In his mind he didn't deserve to see Bobby and couldn't ask her for the privilege.

"Do you want to see Bobby?" she asked.

Surprised but encouraged, he answered, "you'd let me?"

"Yes, but Rob, you can't come into his life as his father then leave him. Do you understand?

"Of course," he agreed. "Just tell him I'm Rob, the friend from the grocery store until…"

"Until you decide?"

She made it sound wrong, not what he meant to say.

"No, until we see if he likes me." He cleared his throat. "Gerri, I won't hurt him. I promise you that."

She sat in silence, weighing his words. "I know you wouldn't mean to but you have to be very sure this is what you want. Being a father is a long term commitment. I won't allow you to take it lightly with my son. Do you understand?"

He nodded in agreement.

He could see her quandary; do I give my son the father he needs or do I keep this man from him, the man who left him before he was even born? The man who hurt her so deeply.

She sighed, put her hand to her eyes and asked, "When would you want to come over?"

He swallowed. "Soon," he croaked. "Soon."

She started to stand but he had something more to discuss. He reached out and touched her arm. This time she didn't pull away. "Gerri, I want to give you some money. I want to pay child support."

She stood and pushed in her chair. "We'll see. I'm doing all right, have done all right. We'll talk about it later."

He got up and walked around the table. "Whatever you decide and, Gerri…" His voice faltered. "Thank you."

---

They met Monday afternoon. Rob rushed home from work, changed clothes and went to Gerri's. He had wanted to bring a gift, a toy for Bobby, but Gerri objected saying she didn't want the boy to expect presents from him.

Rob rang the door bell and wiped his sweaty hands on the sides of his jeans. He wished he could have brought something, anything to break the ice. He hit his forehead with the palm of his hand. *Dummy! You could have brought something for Gerri, flowers, something.*

Gerri opened the door, her smile putting him at ease. "Come in, Rob." She called down the hall, "Bobby, come in here. We have company."

Running foot steps echoed on the hardwood floor. The boy slipped as he came around the corner and literally scooted into the room. Alarmed that he might be hurt, Rob reached out to him but Gerri held his arm to stop him. "Glad you could drop in," she said, and Bobby giggled. She laughed and looked at Rob then back at her son. "Please, have a seat." With that the little boy rolled on the floor in gales of laughter.

Rob joined in and even had a quip of his own, "Glad to see you again, Bobby. Please don't stand up on my account." This set the boy off once more until the room was filled with their hilarity.

Finally Bobby stood up and walked over to where his mother sat in a wing-backed chair. He and his mother high-fived. Gerri nodded toward Rob who lifted his hand and Bobby slapped it with his palm. "Good job," she said. "You handled that like a pro." The boy giggled again and climbed into her lap.

"Please sit," Gerri said, and Rob sat across from her in a wooden rocker. He looked around the room, a love seat, a small television, a few tables and lamps and soft sheers on the windows. Comfortable, safe, a good place to raise a child.

"So, Bobby, do you remember Mr. Martin from the grocery store?"

Suddenly shy, the boy snuggled into his mother's arms and nodded.

"He's come to see us, to see you especially." Gerri pushed a few strands of his blond hair from his eyes. "Would you like to show him your room?"

The boy hesitated.

Rob asked, "Do you have some toys, Bobby?"

The child nodded.

"Well, I'd really like to see what you have. I used to have some special toys when I was young and I don't have them any more. I don't have anything to play with now."

Bobby sat forward in his mother's lap.

"You think I might be able to play with some of yours? I'd really like to."

Bobby looked at his mother again and at her nod, he climbed down and went to Rob. Taking his hand, he said, "You can play but I need to be in there with you so you'll know what they are."

Goose bumps stood the hair up on his arms. *My son. I'm holding my son's hand.* The boy led him down the hall past a closed bedroom door and into the next room. Rob could see another bedroom beyond this one and at the end of the hallway, a bathroom door stood open.

Bobby's room was a typical boy's room, blue NASCAR bedspread on the single bed, posters of racing cars on the wall, and on the dresser top, two race car replicas. Rob picked up the red and blue one with a yellow number 24 painted on the side.

"That's Jeff Gordon's car. He's my favorite driver."

"It's a good looking car," Rob said.

"It's a Chevrolet," Bobby crossed his arms, serious. "He's a real champion." Bobby picked up the yellow and blue car from the dresser. "This one is a Cheerios car, number forty three. The driver is Jeff Green. I like him, too, but he doesn't win as much." He looked at his mother standing in the doorway. "But Mama says..." he paused.

Gerri smiled. "Don't count..."

"Yeah," he looked back at Rob. "Don't count him out yet."

Rob laughed. "What is it about Jeff Green you like?"

Bobby touched his finger to his lips, thoughtful. "Well, I just like his car." He smiled up at Rob. "And I like Cheerios."

"They're my favorite," Rob said.

"Really?" Bobby's eyebrows rose. "They're my favorite, too." He laughed. "Do you want to see some other toys?"

For the next half hour Bobby showed Rob his toys, one after another, carefully explaining their use. Rob saw a stack of books beside his bed. "Do you like to read?" he asked.

"I love to read," Bobby ran to the table and picked up a picture book. "This is my favorite, The Little Engine That Could. I can read it. Do you want to hear me?"

Rob sat on the edge of the bed beside Bobby and was surprised by the child's ability. He only had to help him with a few words. He looked up to see Gerri standing in the doorway. "That's amazing. He can read."

She smiled. "He's learning and he's heard that story about a zillion times." She took the book from Bobby and placed it on top of the stack. "How about some milk and cookies for you two?"

Bobby cheered and raced out of the room, Rob and Gerri right behind him. They sat at a round wooden table in the sunny kitchen. Gerri poured coffee for herself but Rob insisted on drinking milk with Bobby.

He had found what he had been looking for all his life and it felt like home.

# THIRTY-FOUR

A delicious euphoria buoyed Rob all day Tuesday. He thought of his son and Paige, the two people he loved. When he had left Gerri's last night, nothing was said about when he could come back. Bobby's last words to him were, "Will you come play with me again?"

"Absolutely," Rob had answered. He had looked at Gerri and saw her nod. On the way home he found himself laughing out loud.

Whole. That was the word Myrna had used and now he thought he understood what she meant when she said it. Was this wholeness, having a son, being a dad?

He wanted to tell someone. Paige. He wanted to share this wonderful news with her. He would call her as soon as he got home and go over to her house and tell her about his son. Too many lies between them. It was time to tell Paige the truth, all the truth. He would tell her about his involvement with Detective Adamson and Spud which meant he had to tell her about being in prison. She would understand. Somehow he would find the words to tell her he was her robber. He'd make her understand how much he had changed. And he would tell her about Bobby.

The idea that she might turn him in to the police crept into his mind and he cast it aside. Wishful thinking replaced reason, and he assured himself she wouldn't. She cared too much about him to send him back to prison.

*But what if she does?*

"She won't," he said aloud to the thought. He decided he would tell her about the Spud thing and prison and Bobby, and if he felt he could, then he would tell her the rest of the truth. She won't mind having Bobby in our lives, he told himself. It won't be like he would be living with us all the time. But he did want to have him as much as Gerri would allow.

Rob showered and changed into shorts and a tee shirt. He reached for the phone just as it rang. It was Adamson.

"I just wanted to let you know Smith hasn't fully regained consciousness."

Cold fear drowned Rob's elation. "What does that mean?"

"He's in and out and we haven't been able to question him. He's still in critical condition."

"What do you need to question him about?" Rob asked, the fear growing and creeping into his belly.

"We think he's been involved in quite a few burglaries in the past few months and we want to know who his fence is. Did he say anything about any of this to you?"

Voices were audible in the background. "No. He didn't mention doing any other jobs. At first he said he was going to hold up convenience stores but I think that was a smoke screen until he knew I was in with him."

"Probably," Adamson agreed. "Hold on a minute." To someone he said, "Okay, in five minutes." Then to Rob, "Sorry, I'm at the station and we have a meeting in a couple of minutes. You're right. It was probably a screen." He sighed. "We don't know if Smith'll live but we sure hope we can get something out of him pretty soon. He lost a lot of blood, and I'm told his heart stopped a few times in surgery, so we aren't even sure about his brain function now."

Rob hated to want someone to die or be brain damaged, but he knew that if Spud talked and gave up Benny, he would be next on the list. "You'll let me know?" he asked.

The detective hesitated. "Let you know? Sure." Another hesitation. "That gives me an idea. Do you think he might talk more freely to you if we let him think you have been arrested, too?" His voice quickened. "That might work. I'll talk to the chief."

Unable to disagree, Rob simply hung up when the detective said he would get back to him. He cursed himself for asking Adamson to let him know about Spud's condition. Obviously, it had given the officer the idea to involve Rob further. His life just went from one big mess to another.

No longer excited about calling Paige, he waited until he thought she would be home. He didn't leave a message when her machine came on and then he dialed her cell phone. He could tell she was busy by the way she answered.

"I'm sorry if I'm bothering you, Paige. I guess you're busy."

He heard a deep sigh. "I am but I want to talk to you. Just a minute." He heard some muffled words then the sound of a door shutting. "I'm back. I have some people in my office. I came out in the hall. I don't have long but how are you?"

*How am I?* He remembered he was supposed to have been sick. "Fine. I feel fine."

"Good. Is there something you wanted?"

"I wondered if we could get together tonight."

"Not tonight. I'm not sure how the rest of the week is going to go either. We've had a lot of accidents and I'm snowed under with family members. I was up here until eleven last night and won't get home until late tonight." He heard another sigh. "Is there something special on your mind?"

Well, not now, he thought. Disappointed, he told her to give him a call when she had time to see him.

"It may well be the weekend. How about planning for sometime Saturday?" He could tell she was in a hurry.

"Sure. Just let me know when," he said.

The let down from the high he'd experienced all day left him exhausted. He sat in the recliner for another hour. Hungry, he went to the kitchen and instead of cooking some of the food he had bought, he ate two bowls of cereal. He thought about calling Gerri and asking when he could see Bobby again, but he was so bummed he just sat and watched arena football before going to bed.

Thursday evening he called Gerri again and asked if he could take her and Bobby out for pizza on Friday night. Some of his excitement returned when she agreed and the anticipation of seeing his son stayed with him throughout the next day. He picked the two of them up at five o'clock, and they went to a well known kid-friendly pizza place.

Before their meal Bobby was allowed to go into the ball pit, a mesh enclosed room filled with multicolored plastic balls. Rob and Gerri watched from outside the meshed walls.

"Gerri, he's wonderful," he said.

She held her son's shoes, the fingers of one hand subconsciously twisting the strings that hung from them. "I know." She hesitated then turned to him. "Rob, he likes you. He asked when you'd be back."

Rob's heart thudded in his chest.

"In fact, he asked every day. He was so happy when you called and asked us to come here." She looked back at her son, her eyes shining with love. "There's one thing I have to ask of you, though."

"Anything, Gerri," and he meant it.

"When you leave, tell him when you'll see him again." She looked up at Rob, her eyes now serious. "Don't leave him hanging, wondering if you'll come back."

"I'll do it anyway you want. I'll come as often as I can. You tell me, Gerri. What do you want me to do?"

She looked back at her son, her voice so low he almost missed it, "I just want you to be his daddy."

"That's what I want, too." Rob watched his son jumping in the balls. "And I want him to know I'm his dad."

Gerri frowned. "I've thought about that." She faced him, keeping her voice just above a whisper. "I told you I haven't dated."

"Right. You didn't want a parade of daddies."

"Well, I still don't," she said.

Surprised, he leaned toward her, "I won't leave him, if that's what you're afraid of."

Her eyes narrowed as she looked at him and asked, "How can you be sure?"

He knew what she was referring to. "I know what you're thinking, but this is different. I'm different."

"You seem to be, but I'm just not sure. I have to be sure and so do you." She turned her back on the roomful of balls. "Rob, I refuse to allow my son to be hurt by you. If you want to spend some time with him now, I'm all right with that, but you do know you have no legal right to do so."

*No legal right. I'm just his father, that's all.* But he understood what she was saying. "I know. All I want is to be his father. I want to pay child support, back support for the years I've missed and I want to take care of him for the rest of his life." He touched her chin with his finger. "Gerri, I give you my word, I will always be here for him."

She stepped back from him. "Don't ever touch me like that again, Rob."

Shocked by her reaction, he apologized. "I'm sorry. I didn't mean…"

Anger danced in her eyes but she kept her voice low. "Yes, you did. You meant to draw me back in and I can't let you do that. We may have a son together but that's it."

He nodded. He wished he could tell her about Paige. Maybe it would help her to know he was in love with someone else and not a threat to her. "I thought you said you had forgiven me," he said.

She laughed, derision in the sound. "Right, but that doesn't mean I trust you."

He looked down at her and saw the determination in her eyes. "I understand."

Bobby bounced over to where they stood. He looked through the mesh siding. "I'm ready for my pizza."

"I'll meet you at the door," Gerri said. She looked at Rob. "If you can stay after I put him to bed, I think we need to talk."

He agreed and followed her to get their son from the roomful of balls.

Rob read to Bobby and helped Gerri tuck him into bed. "I'll be back soon," Rob said.

"When?" Bobby asked.

Rob thought about it. "How about Sunday afternoon? If it's all right with your mom, we can go to the park for awhile."

Bobby looked toward his mother, a big grin on his face. "Okay with you?"

"Sure," she said and kissed him on the forehead. She looked at Rob, "I like the park."

It had been Rob's hope that the two of them could go alone, but Gerri's expression told him otherwise.

Gerri left Bobby's door ajar and motioned Rob to follow her into the kitchen. He followed her lead and sat at the table. "Keep your voice low. I don't want Bobby to hear us talking."

He had misgivings about what she wanted to say and hoped he hadn't done something wrong.

"Rob," she began. "You have said you want to be included in Bobby's life. Child support, visitation, everything. Am I right?"

"I do. I want to do it all, Gerri. I want to be a real dad to him."

"You have no idea what all that will entail. It won't just mean coming to visit whenever you feel like it." She pointed her finger at him. "You have to make a commitment to be there whatever happens. Sometimes it might be good and sometimes not so good, but you can't come and go at whatever whim might strike you."

Rob leaned back in his chair. "Let me ask you a question. Are you thinking of the past?"

She nodded vigorously. "I am. I remember how many times I had to wait and wonder when you might show up. If you recall, you never made a date with me, just came and went whenever you wanted. No calls--ever." She leaned toward him. "Do you remember?"

"I do remember, but back then..."

She interrupted him. "Back then you were different?"

"Yes, I was." He leaned toward her. "Gerri, I am not the same man as I was then. So much has happened in my life. I wish I could tell you."

She sat back and crossed her arms. "Well, maybe some day you can. Right now, all I want to talk about is Bobby. This is the way it will be, Rob." She ticked one forefinger against the other, striking off an

288

imaginary list. "First, he will not know he is your son until I decide to tell him. I believe it would be hard enough for you to disappear from his life as just some guy but as his father? It would devastate him. He has asked me since he was two years old where his daddy is."

Rob groaned.

"Yes, in fact, after he met you he wanted to know if his daddy was like you." She waited for him to say something and when she saw he couldn't, she continued, "I said yes. I told him his daddy was a lot like you and that made him happy. He likes you-- more than you know. Maybe some place in his heart he knows you." She leaned back across the table. "Rob, more than anything in the world, I want Bobby to have a real dad--you."

"I'll do it, Gerri. I'll be his real dad." He wanted desperately to assure her he wouldn't run out on them again.

"Okay, Rob. She held up two fingers. The second thing is this. If the time comes when you're sure, and I know you're sure, then we go to a lawyer. We make it legal. You are Bobby's dad and the amount of child support will be determined by the courts." Gerri's eyes narrowed. "There won't be any getting out of it then or you'll go back to jail."

Tough words but he understood and was willing. "How will you know when I'm sure?"

She stood up, the conversation over. "I'll know." She pushed her chair back under the table. "And until then, it will be the three of us when you see Bobby. You won't see him alone until it is legal. What time Sunday?"

He couldn't keep it to himself any longer and on Saturday morning, over breakfast with Myrna, he told her about his child.

"A son. I can't believe it, Rob." She sat her fork on her half-empty plate and wiped her mouth with her napkin. "That complicates things, doesn't it?"

Rob pushed his plate away and leaned his crossed arms on the table. "A little."

"A little? What about Paige? Have you told her?"

"Not yet, but I'm seeing her this afternoon and I'll tell her then. I think she'll understand." His hope was less than it had been a week ago.

"Do you?" Myrna looked unconvinced. She leaned back in her chair. "What about the child's mother."

"Right now, Gerri doesn't want to tell him I'm his father. She wants to be sure I really want to be his dad."

"You do, don't you?" Myrna asked.

"Absolutely. There's no doubt in my mind, but I'm not sure I can be the kind of father he needs."

Myrna's face broke into a smile and she touched his hand. "You love him, don't you?"

Rob nodded.

"Then that's all he needs. He just needs to know his daddy loves him."

He knew she was right and when he thought of Bobby, his heart pounded with the love he felt, but when he tried to look at the future, fear blocked his vision. Complete joy eluded him because of the one secret still hanging in the balance. He could only see today and the next time he'd be with his son, the child his heart had desired for so long.

# THIRTY-FIVE

Weariness drew lines on Paige's face. Dark circles ringed bloodshot eyes and her shoulders slumped in the loose shift dress she wore. Her feet were bare. She had pinned her hair back but some of it hung in limp strands around her neck. She had a cup of coffee in her hand and gestured toward the kitchen. "Help yourself," she said and sat on the sofa, curling her legs under her. "I don't have the energy to be Miss Manners today."

Rob went to the kitchen and poured his own coffee then came back and sat beside her. He leaned over to kiss her but she didn't turn toward him and his lips landed on her cheek. She rested her head on the sofa back and sighed.

"I'm so tired, Rob. I probably won't be good company. You can leave if you want to."

He took her cup from her hand, sat it on the table with his and pulled her to him. "I'm soft. You can rest on me."

She patted his chest. "You're anything but soft. Your muscles are rock solid." She gave a tired laugh. "But it feels good to rest on them," and she nestled closer.

"Rough week. Tell me about it." Rob felt if he got her to talking it might open up for him to tell her what he came for.

She inhaled deeply. "Are you sure you're ready for this? It isn't pretty."

"Try me. Remember, I'm rock solid."

She laughed. "You know that hold up Monday where the man was shot by the police?"

Rob held his breath.

"Well, he's in St. E's. His mother and sister are there. That's all the family he has and both of them are …" She stopped. "Rob, you know I shouldn't be telling you this."

"I know but it's safe with me. I won't say anything to anyone and you know it." He needed to hear more.

"His mother is an addict. She comes to the hospital high then crashes and leaves.

"What's wrong with the daughter?" he asked.

"She has MS and Lord only knows what else. She has a bag; two bags, urine and feces, and they have to be emptied. The mother does it sometimes and sometimes she doesn't so someone has to. It's one holy mess."

"What do you have to do with them exactly?"

"Just about whatever needs to be done. I'm supposed to be trying to get this woman into some kind of drug program, and she says she will then she runs off and shoots up again. She says she can't leave her daughter then does when she needs a fix. The girl can hardly speak. We're talking to Social Services and some other agencies, may have to remove the girl from the home. It's enough to break your heart."

He hugged her closer to him. "And the man, the one who got shot?"

"Cop guarding him twenty-four seven. Kind of useless since he isn't conscious most of the time."

"Most of the time? You mean he's all right?"

"No, he isn't all right. But he wakes up off and on and hollers out, calls for his dad, shouts obscenities. They keep him sedated as much as possible."

"Is his dad around?"

Paige shook her head. "No, from what I understand he died in prison. Don't know how long ago."

"That sucks," he said. She agreed.

"Do you think he will recover?" This was the question he needed an answer to before he told her about his involvement.

"No, I don't think so. The doctors think he may have some brain damage from his heart stopping so many times, and one of the bullets hit him in the head. They didn't even find it for two days."

"How did they miss it?" he asked.

"They thought he had hit his head when he fell and the wounds to the body were life threatening, and they didn't x-ray the head immediately. I don't know. That's what I was told."

"How did they get it out?" Rob wasn't sure you could get a bullet out of the brain but maybe he was wrong.

"They didn't. It's still there."

The two of them sat in silence for several minutes. Knowing what he now did about Spud's family, Rob felt even worse about being the one who, in effect, put him near death. In all probability, his father may have not been much of a dad either. To have a drug-addicted mother and a handicapped sister must have been even worse on him. There was no turning back now, but he wished he had known more before he threw Spud to the wolves and got him shot. Still, what would he have done differently if he had known? He wasn't sure he had any other choice but today he did. It was a choice between telling Paige the truth and continuing with the lie.

This might not be the best time, but he needed to begin and the first thing was to tell her about his son. "I wanted to talk to you about something, Paige. Do you feel like it?"

"As long as I don't have to do the talking and can stay right here, I feel like it." Her head rested on his shoulder. "Shoot," she said. "I'm ready." She laughed. "I do hope this is something good."

"It is." How to say it? "You know I told you I didn't want to have any children because I was afraid they would die?"

"I remember."

"I don't think they would die and I've changed my mind."

Paige sat up slowly and looked at him. "If you are going to tell me you want to have children, then this isn't the time, Rob." Her tone hardened. "I'm going to tell you once more. I don't want any children in my life. Not now and maybe not ever."

No children in her life. That would include Bobby. Nothing more to say. For now the lies had to stand. She had left him no way out.

---

Sunday evening Paige phoned Rob. "I want to apologize for being such a grouch yesterday. I know you had something you wanted to talk about when I jumped down your throat. Want to talk about it now?"

Even though her voice gave him the impression she was more rested, he still didn't feel comfortable telling her about his son. "No, maybe the next time we see each other."

"Can you ever get away for lunch?" she asked. "We could meet somewhere tomorrow and talk awhile."

"I don't leave for lunch. Take a sandwich or something and eat on the job. I only have thirty minutes and Bull doesn't like for us to come back late."

They left it that if she could get away by five Monday, they'd have dinner together somewhere, and she promised to call him to let him know.

It was nearing noon Monday morning when Bull tapped him on the shoulder. Seeing it was his boss, he lifted his welding hood and faced him.

"Adamson needs to talk to you in my office," Bull shouted over the noise of the welding machine.

Rob laid the whip over the air conditioning pipe he was working on, slipped his hood over his head and set it beside the pipe. He followed Bull to the office, and when they got there, his boss motioned for him to go in then walked away leaving Rob and the detective alone. Rob removed his heavy deerskin gloves and shook Gene Adamson's hand. "What's up?" he asked.

"We think it might be time to try to talk to Smith. I called the hospital this morning and he's awake. I'd like for you to come with me and do what we talked about." Adamson stood with one foot on the seat of a wooden chair, his arms resting on his knee.

Rob hesitated, his mind racing to find a way out. When none came to him, he resigned himself to the inevitable and took off his leathers. He draped them across an empty chair and asked, "Do you want me to go home and change clothes?"

The detective looked him over. "You don't look bad to me. In fact, you look like you've been in lock-up for a few days." His smile was good natured and his voice held humor. "Seriously, you look all right. We don't have time to do any cleaning up. This shouldn't take long." He started for the door and said over his shoulder, "I'll drive you and bring you back here when we're done."

Rob followed him, his apprehension growing with each step. Outside the office Adamson hailed Bull. "We'll be back soon."

Before Rob could speak, Bull motioned toward where he had been working, "I'll take care of things."

On the drive to the hospital the detective briefed Rob on what he should say and how he should say it. Rob listened yet knowing in his heart they couldn't fool Spud. He would know he had been set-up from the beginning. The closer they came to the hospital, the faster Rob's heart beat. If Spud was alert and decided to spill everything he knew, this might well be the last time Rob saw the light of day. His next trip would be to jail then to prison. He covered his mouth and swallowed to push back the bile gathering in his throat.

All too soon St. Elizabeth's came into view. Paige would be in the building somewhere. Was it too much to ask, he thought, that they not run into her while they were there? A wave of nausea swept over him.

"Hey, Martin, you sick or something?" The detective had noticed the pallor of his skin.

"I'm all right," Rob said. "I just don't like hospitals much. This is where my brother in law died last summer." He met the detective's gaze. "And you know what happened when Spud was shot."

Adamson grinned and nodded. "Weak stomach? Don't worry, we won't see any blood."

The Intensive Care Unit was several floors above and in a wing beyond Paige's office. Rob's hopes soared that, at least, they wouldn't see her, and he wouldn't have that to worry about along with everything else. They went to a nurse seated behind a wrap-around Formica counter. The detective showed his identification. "We're here to see Royce Smith."

Royce. Spud's name was Royce. Rob had never heard it and it didn't sound right. It made him out to be a normal guy and he wasn't. He was scum, scum that had almost died because he insisted Rob go with him on a robbery doomed to fail from the start.

Before the nurse could answer, a man standing beside her spoke to them. He was dressed in blue scrubs, paper covers over his shoes and a disposable surgical cap covered his hair. He slipped a metal covered chart into the file on the counter. "You're here to see Mr. Smith?"

Adamson turned to him. "That's right."

The man moved closer to them and spoke quietly, "Would you come with me?" Without waiting for a response, he led the way to a small room. When inside, he started to close the door then looked questioningly at Rob and back at the detective.

"He's with me," Gene Adamson said.

The man nodded and shut the door. "I'm Dr. Bassett," he said and pulled the disposable cap from his head and tossed it into a waste basket. He extended his hand to shake those of the two men. "I'm surprised you came to talk to Mr. Smith. He's in critical condition and not conscious."

The detectives surprise was evident. "I called this morning and was told I could talk to him."

The doctor shook his head. "I don't know who you spoke to but there is no way that can happen. I'm surprised you're unaware of this patient's condition."

"I guess I am," Adamson said. "Can you bring me up to date?"

The doctor looked from one man to the other, obviously considering his words. "He has an internal infection. We think it's in the bowel area because his abdomen is distended and hard. We aren't positive because we can't get in there to see. We aren't sure he would survive more surgery at this time. He's getting massive doses of antibiotics to bring his fever down but his condition is grave."

"Does that mean he may die?" The question was out of Rob's mouth before he could stop it.

The doctor addressed him. "Of course, we can't say that with any degree of certainty but I'd say his chances of survival are slim."

"What are we looking at, doc?" the detective asked. "If the fever stays up, what might come next?"

"If he doesn't respond to antibiotics, his blood pressure may drop and he may have cardiovascular collapse, kidney failure. Any number of things can happen or all of them." He shook his head. "It doesn't look good for him."

The detective thanked him and he and Rob left the room, Adamson dejected and Rob relieved. As they walked down the hall a clamor of voices filled the air. A woman ran from a waiting room crying out, "No, dammit, you can't do that. Where is she? Where is my daughter?" Close behind her were two people, an overweight Hispanic man and an African-American woman. They each took an arm as she tried to wrest herself away from their grasps.

The small woman, rail thin with wiry uncombed brown hair, her skin a junkie's pallor was surprisingly strong and fought them off while screaming obscenities. Detective Adamson hurried to the scene, came up behind the woman and wrapped his arms around her holding her in a vise-like grip. She kicked and screamed more then finally dissolved into heavy sobbing. "Where is she? What have you done with Betty?"

The woman and man soothed her with their words. When she relaxed, the Hispanic man took her arm and said, "Come with me, Mrs. Smith. We'll take care of everything." Her reserves spent, she went with him.

The dark haired woman turned to the detective, "Thank y..." Then she saw Rob. Her head tilted to one side, questions in her eyes. "Rob?" she said.

The detective looked from one to the other. "Miss Lewis. I'm Detective Adamson. Do you remember me?" he asked and extended his hand to shake hers.

"Of course I do," she said. Her eyes remained on Rob.

"You know each other?" Adamson asked.

Rob nodded without smiling, waiting for Paige's reaction.

A slight flicker of her deep blue eyes. "Yes, we do," she said with an edge in her voice. "But I didn't know you two were acquainted."

The detective smiled. "Rob's been working on something with me for a few weeks."

"Is that so?" Paige said. "Well, I have things to do. I'll talk to you later." She turned abruptly and walked away.

Adamson's eyes followed Paige's departing figure. He turned to Rob. "I take it you two know each other." he said.

Rob didn't trust his voice and nodded.

"If you know her, you may know what happened to her a few years back."

To lie or not to lie? Rob released his breath in a deep sigh. "I know. She told me." He added, "but I didn't know you were the detective who worked with her on the case." A small lie. He hadn't known until she found Adamson's card at Myrna's and told him. "Can we go now? I need to get back to work."

The detective, openly suspicious, joined him as he walked away.

When they were in the car, Adamson drove quietly for several blocks. "She doesn't know about your past, does she?" he asked.

Rob shook his head. "No, I haven't told her." he admitted.

"You going to tell her?"

Rob wanted to tell him it was none of his business. Instead he answered, "Yes. As soon as possible."

The detective chuckled. "I don't envy you, brother."

---

Angry and hurt, Paige left the hospital at 6:30. She didn't call Rob at five as she promised nor had she heard from him. She vowed to herself to never speak to Rob again. It was bad enough that he had neglected to tell his own sister about her but then he had lied to her about being able to leave work for lunch, and then there he was with Adamson. And he'd lied to her about knowing him, too. Why?

Her curiosity got the best of her and she dialed his home number from her cell phone. When he answered, she said, her words clipped. "Come over now. We need to talk." She hung up as soon as she heard his "Okay."

She held her tongue until he was inside and the door shut. All the frustration and exhaustion she'd experienced the past few days threatened to erupt. Her face was pinched with anger, her eyes burned from lack of sleep, and she vented in sarcasm, "You've been busy, haven't you? I don't suppose you want to tell me about it."

Rob didn't speak quickly enough.

"Cat got your tongue? Oh, yes, the cat. Maybe Brad was right after all. You're one big fu...," she stopped, took a deep breath. Cursing wasn't what she wanted to do. She wanted to remain calm and if she let it all out, she might never regain control. "Coward," she said, as softly as she could. "I think it's time you tell me all about it." She couldn't bring herself to say his name.

He moved toward her, started to touch her and she drew back. "Don't." She held her arms out. "Don't touch me. Just talk."

"Sit down, Paige. Please." Rob sat on the edge of the sofa.

"I don't feel like sitting," she retorted, her mouth in a tight line but she sat in the chair across from him.

He cleared his throat, leaned forward, his elbows on his knees. "I've wanted to tell you this for a long time but it never seemed to be the right time."

"You lied to me about Detective Adamson. You weren't there to fix a gate," she said, her tone now dripping with scorn, "and you said you

300

never left work either. It's obvious you've been lying to me and I'd like to know why."

"Please, Paige. Let me tell you."

She leaned back in her chair and crossed her arms. "Sure, go ahead," she said with haughtiness. "Tell me all about it and this time," she stressed the last words, "make it the truth." Paige could see Rob was struggling with the words to tell her.

He cleared his throat again. "The truth is I have been in prison."

Prison. That wasn't what she expected to hear. Her shoulders drooped.

"It was a long time ago. I spent two years there for driving a stolen car and being part of a burglary gang." I was nineteen when I was caught and twenty-one when I went in," he said and looked away.

He sat back in the sofa and brought his eyes back to hers. She wanted to look away but couldn't. She detected an apology coming and was prepared to refuse it.

"Spud—Royce Smith found me a few weeks ago. He threatened to tell my boss who I am if I didn't help him rob a store. I went to my boss and told him the truth and he put me in touch with Adamson."

"That's why you had his card?"

He nodded. He rubbed the back of his neck and then touched the stud in his ear. "The cops worked it out for me to act like I was helping him and when we showed up, they were there. He shot and they shot back." He spread his hands. "End of story."

"And you didn't want me to know?" She uncrossed her arms and leaned forward. When he nodded again, she asked, "He threatened to tell who you are." She stood and put her hands on her hips. "And just who are you? Obviously you aren't who I thought you were."

"I'm not—I'm not Rob Martin. I changed my name when I was in Vegas." He stood. "That's not all I've changed, Paige. I'm not the same man. I'm not the man who was in prison. I'm…"

"Like hell you're not!" Her voice rose to a scream. "You're exactly the man who was in prison."

He took a step toward her and she stepped back. "No, stay where you are. What else have you lied to me about?" Her voice was shriller than she wanted but there was no turning back now. The volcano had blown.

When he started to speak, she stopped him, "Never mind. I don't want to hear any more. Just get out!" She pointed toward the door. When he didn't move, she shouted again. "Now! Get out!"

Without another word, he left. Paige stood where he'd left her, shaking. She hugged her arms around herself to stop her trembling. Her teeth chattered and tears fell from her eyes streaking her make up.

"Damn you, Rob Martin or whoever you are."

She sank to her knees and lay face down on the floor. Over and over she cried, "Damn you," until the words came out differently. "Damn you, Paige Lewis. You've done it again."

# THIRTY-SIX

The rest of the week went slowly for Rob. The happy time he had spent at the park on Sunday with Bobby and Gerri was buried beneath the pain of losing Paige. He tried to bring back the peace he had felt showing Bobby how to fly the NASCAR kite, seeing the excitement on his face when he held the string all by himself. All he saw was the agony and hatred in Paige's face, and all he heard were her words telling him to get out.

He had promised Bobby he would be back on Saturday. As the weekend drew near, he wasn't sure he had the strength to act like all was well with him. How could he face Myrna? Surely everyone would be able to see his broken heart, and he couldn't talk about it. Even if he could, there weren't any words to express his loss.

Friday afternoon he closed down his welding machine and hung up his leathers alongside his gloves and hood. When he turned to leave, Detective Adamson motioned to him from across the building's work area.

*What now? More bad news?* He hesitated before walking over to the man. *If he has come to arrest me, I'll run. If I have to I'll jump off this building...* Rob knew he would do whatever it took to escape prison at this moment. His life was in the toilet anyway, what more could go wrong?

The detective extended his hand and Rob shook it. "I thought I should come tell you in person, Martin."

*Martin. That's a good sign.* But he stepped back slightly, ready to run if necessary.

"Smith died this morning." He shook his head. "It's a mess. The man's life, his mother and sister. Sad."

"What happened?" Rob asked.

"The state took his sister away, put her in a state home and the mother committed suicide after she heard Spud had died. She went right out and overdosed. Don't really know if it was intentional. She was still alive when they found her but she didn't make it." He shook his head again. "That poor girl, the daughter. Handicapped the way she is and all alone. Seems some people just don't have a chance in life or don't try to better themselves." He heaved a deep sigh. "Sometimes I don't like my job." He turned to go. "Just thought I'd let you know it's over. Thanks for your help."

Rob watched him walk away, hands shoved deep in his pockets, his shoulders hunched against the tragedy he had witnessed.

Paige, he thought. This must be hard for her, too. He had seen how she tried to help this woman, how much she grieved over the lives she touched and now ... More than anything he wanted to call her, to tell her he understood, help her through it but it wasn't to be. As hard as it was for him to admit, their lives were now as separate as though they had never touched. But they had and a part of him was still with her, would probably always be with her.

Like the detective, he took a deep breath and let it out in an audible sigh, almost a groan, then went to his truck and drove home alone.

When he awoke Saturday morning, he heard singing and knew it was Myrna. Her joy was a knife in his heart. He turned over and covered his head with his blanket. If he stayed in bed, maybe she would leave. This one time, she wouldn't stay long enough to cook his breakfast, for them to have their weekly visit and he wouldn't have to try to be normal when his heart felt torn out of his chest.

A light tap on his door. "Rob. Sleepy head. Are you going to get up? Your breakfast is ready."

He threw the cover off and sat up, forcing himself to answer, "I'll be right out."

She met him in the kitchen, still humming happily to herself. "Pancakes this morning. With strawberries, too." Her smile slid by him and he knew he could pull it off. All he had to do was put on a slight act and she'd never notice what he was feeling. She was too wrapped up in her own happiness to see anything else.

He rubbed his hands together and said, "Great. Let me at 'em," then sat down and wondered how he would ever get the food beyond his throat. Myrna filled the kitchen with lively chatter about the kids and the wedding. She told him what Paul and the kids were wearing, but he heard no words, only her voice. He declined a second helping although the pancakes tasted surprisingly good since he hadn't eaten much since seeing Paige on Monday.

Myrna's voice brought him back from his own thoughts. "Well, will you?" she asked.

"Will I what?"

"Where are you this morning? Your head still in a cloud over your son?" She smiled as she cleared away his plate.

"What are you talking about?" His voice was harder than he intended and she flinched.

Myrna's smile faded. "What's going on with you? I asked a simple question. You don't have to bite my head off."

"I'm sorry," Rob said. "I guess I didn't hear you. I didn't mean to bite your head off." He forced a smile. "Ask me again."

"I asked you if you would bring your son and his mother over next week to Paul's for supper so we can all meet before the wedding. If you want, you can ask Paige, too."

Myrna leaned back on the counter, smiling again.

Head swimming, he looked down at the table. He tried to get hold of his thoughts but they were jumbled. Finally, he just looked up at her and said, "No. Not yet."

Her eyes narrowed and her forehead wrinkled. She pulled out the chair and sat across from him, hands folded on the table in front of her. Her hair was highlighted with golden streaks and Rob realized how pretty his sister was now that she was so happy.

"What's going on, Rob?" she asked.

How much to tell her? He started with Bobby. "Bobby doesn't know I'm his father yet and Gerri is very protective of him. I just don't think she would go for getting him together with… with…"

"His aunt and uncle and cousins?"

Surprised, he met her gaze. He hadn't thought of that. When Bobby finally knew he was his dad, he would find out he had some more family. "Yeah. Maybe later."

"Then you don't think they would come to the wedding either?"

He shook his head. "Sis, let it go for now. It'll happen soon enough." He paused to push down the pain his next words would cause him. "Paige and I broke up."

Myrna leaned back in her chair

Before she could respond a tune played from Myrna's red cell phone lying on the counter. Myrna jumped up and grabbed it.

His sister had become a part of the new age. She had given him her cell number a few weeks ago and suggested he get a cell phone. Paige had badgered him about it, too, and he had considered it, but now, what was the use?

He heard Myrna say, "That's wonderful." Then, "I'll come right now."

She turned it off and untied her apron. He saw she was wearing a navy blue dress instead of her usual Saturday garb of jeans and tee shirt.

"I'm sorry, Rob. I have an appointment at ten with the florist and now I have to run by the dressmakers for a fitting before then. My wedding dress just came in." She paused and came around the table and kissed the top of his head. "Will it be all right for you and Paige at the wedding?"

He nodded. "Don't worry about it, Sis. We aren't enemies. We'll keep it civil for you."

She smiled down at him. "Thanks." She gestured toward the sink. "I hate to leave you with a mess but will you take care of cleaning up?"

"Sure," he said as she went out the door. And to himself he muttered, "What else do I have to do?"

---

The sun began its long descent in the western sky. Paige watched the cars on Yale Avenue and thought of the people in them: Fathers going home to their families, mothers stopping to pick up children at day care then hurrying home to fix a meal for their husbands, or if they were single moms, taking the kids out for pizza at the end of the work day. So much hustle and bustle all the time. Hurrying to get to work then hurrying to get home. And during the day, the kids are separated from the parents and the parents involved in the stress of their jobs. No way would she ever put herself into that corner. If she worked, she worked and had no family to worry about, and if she ever decided to have a family, she would have to quit her job. Right now, that wasn't even an option.

When she and Rob were together, she had considered what it would be like to be married with no children, or to leave her job and have children, but neither felt right. As much as she liked Rob and as much as it hurt now to have him out of her life, there was always something holding her back. She couldn't quite give herself over to falling in love again. Or had she ever been in love in the first place? If she had truly loved Daniel, wouldn't she have given up everything for him? Even agreed to have a child?

No, that was her mother, not her. Bev Lewis had given up a promising journalism career to be the wife of a pastor. Paige was different. She couldn't see herself giving up what she felt she was called to do to become a wife and mother. Besides, Daniel had professed to love her but he hadn't been willing to give up what he wanted either.

Paige left the window and went to her desk. Mondays were hard days for her. The worst wrecks and sicknesses always happened over the weekend and the first of the week was filled with frightened, grief stricken people. Even the weekend hadn't helped her recover from the events of last Friday; Betty Smith being taken from her home and put into a nursing facility by the state. Her mother's anguish. Paige had tried to help the woman, had personally taken her to rehab but the woman couldn't do it. Refused to do it. Then her son dying. It had been too much for her. As long as she had Betty to care for, she had a reason to live. Without her or her son she had no one, no hope.

When they told Maureen Smith her son was dead, she left the hospital and no one could keep her from leaving, not Paige, not any of the staff, and heaven knows they had tried. Paige remembered how worried she was and knew in her heart something terrible was about to happen. She left the hospital as soon as she could and drove to the woman's house. It was she who found her close to death in her living room, the door standing open, the woman lying on the sofa clutching a photograph. Paige called for an ambulance and when she took the picture from the woman's almost lifeless hands, was shocked to see the images of a dark haired young man, a pretty woman and two small children, a boy and a girl, smiling at her. This had once been a normal family. What had gone wrong with them? How had they ended up so destroyed?

It was Paige who went to the nursing home and broke the news to Betty Smith. She held her when she cried and comforted her. When she left, she promised to return, but could she? Did she have the strength to face any more heartbreak?

She thought of Rob and wished she could feel his arms around her. He had given her so much of himself when she was hurting like this for her patients. But it was over, ruined by his lie. An ex convict. How could she not have suspected? Do they look any different? Should they wear a sign that tells everyone they meet? What would she have done in his place? Would she have been honest from the beginning?

Paige rubbed her forehead. Her head was beginning to ache again. She wasn't sleeping well—had had the dream twice during the week. For some reason it was more troubling than usual. When it awakened her, she hadn't been able to go back to sleep. If she knew who the man was, then would the dream go away? But the thought of seeing the man's face again frightened her more than she wanted to admit. No, it was better to let it go and never know.

She sank into her chair and opened her desk drawer, took out a bottle of white pills and popped two into her mouth. She drank the last of a bottle of water on her desk and cupped her face in her hands. Paige sighed when she heard the knock on her door. She wasn't in the mood to see anyone.

"Come in," she called.

The door swung back as Brad peered through the opening. When he saw the room empty except for his sister, he stepped in and quietly closed it behind him.

She didn't want to talk to him and said, her voice short and brusque, "What do you need?"

"I need to talk to you." He approached her desk and pulled a chair up to it. "I'm worried about my sister."

Tears formed and she stood quickly. "Your sister is fine." She turned her back to him as she walked to the window again.

He came up behind her and touched her shoulder. She moved away. If he was kind, she would cry and that was one thing she never wanted to do in front of Brad because he would have to know why and she'd have to tell him.

"Paige," he said softly, "please let me talk to you. We leave in the morning on the cruise and I can't go with things between us the way they are."

She struggled to hold back the emotion. He was being too nice. It would break her. "Okay," she said. "Let's sit."

She took a chair so she wouldn't be beside him and he sat on the sofa across from her. His expression was filled with concern and there was none of his old bravado.

"You were so quiet at lunch yesterday." He looked down at his hands and gave a slight laugh. "Ash and Mom and Dad had warned me to lay off you. They told me I'd been a real jerk lately, and I guess I have."

"You guess?"

"Okay, I have. But, I just didn't feel right about..."

"About Rob?" she finished for him. When he nodded, she looked away. "Well, you don't have to worry any more. We broke up." A tear rolled down her cheek and she hastily wiped it away hoping her brother hadn't seen it.

Brad didn't answer. There was no way she could hide her hurt right now. It consumed her. "I'm sorry, Paige. You must have really liked this guy. Is it--was it my fault?"

She shook her head. "No. It wasn't about you, Brad. But tell me, what was it about him that you didn't like? I'm just curious since you didn't like Daniel either."

He sat back in the cushions. She could see his thoughts at work and his expression changed from the kind one she had seen to the old Brad, the old arrogant Brad.

Before she could take the question back, he spoke through clenched teeth. "Are you sure you want to hear this?"

Her expression changed, too. The combative sister-brother battle was back on.

"I knew Daniel wasn't in love with you."

"Oh yeah? And how did you know that?" she asked skeptically.

"Because of what he said to me when we first met."

"And that was?" She wasn't sure she wanted to hear it, was afraid it would hurt more than she could bear at this time.

He sighed, "Because he said he knew the two of you would produce good children together. He knew it when he first met you."

His words stung.

"I asked him if that was what drew him to you, and he admitted it was. He liked the idea that you were part African-American and thought the two of you would make strong, handsome children."

Instead of allowing the hurt to penetrate her, she struck out at her brother. "Why didn't you tell me then?" She rose, her voice strident, "You—you--you jerk! Why didn't you tell me?"

He stood when she did and went to her. "Listen, Paige. I told Dad and asked him what I should do. He told me to keep it to myself, that it wasn't up to me to tell you because you'd find out soon enough yourself."

Even her father had betrayed her. She hated them all. She turned away from him.

"And Rob. What don't you like about him? Did he say something to you, too?"

He shook his head and followed her to the window again. When he tried to touch her shoulder, she moved away but faced him.

"He wasn't good enough for you, Paige."

Surprised, she asked, "Not good enough? What does that mean?"

"He's a welder, Paige, blue collar. He doesn't fit in with our family."

"You really are a jerk and a snob to boot. Blue collar!" She spit out the words. "He's a good man, a better man than you will ever be." Even when she said it, she was sure it was true.

Paige pointed her finger into her brother's face. "I think it's time for you to go. I hope you have a wonderful time on your cruise and I hope you listen to what you hear and maybe you will learn something. You aren't God and you can't make judgments about people based on your prejudices. Maybe you've never had anyone make unfair judgments about you."

Brad's expression changed. "Oh, yes, I have."

"Is that right?"

"Yes, it's right." He went back to the sofa and sank into the cushions.

Holding her anger but ready to explode, she sat across from him and took a deep breath to steady herself.

"Maybe you don't remember what it was like growing up in Georgia." His voice was quieter. "I was so glad to get out of there and out of being called names by people who just didn't understand our family." He looked at her. "It might not have been as hard on you because you were lighter than I was and you were pretty." Brad's hands became fists in his lap. "When I played football, the guys would call me names, ugly names and say things about my sister. Things they wanted to do to her."

She met his eyes. "What did you do?"

"I told Dad and he said they were just ignorant and that we should just pray for them, that I shouldn't be like them. Praying's all right but sometimes… He may have been right but it didn't make it any easier. That's why I left, why I came here when I got the scholarship to TU."

"And it was better?"

"Yes. I was accepted, but mainly because no one knew my mother was white and my sister was beautiful." A wry smile drew his lips. "I do have a beautiful sister and I care about her."

Anger spent, she said, "It's not about Daniel or Rob or what they say or what they do, is it? It's about skin color. You want me to marry a black man."

He nodded. "It would be better. Kids shouldn't have to go through what I did."

Paige understood her brother for the first time, his hurts and insecurities and his fears for his son and for her. "You know you can't make decisions for me. When—if I decide to marry, your opinion will not be a consideration. Do you understand that?"

Brad's eyes held hers for a long time before he nodded. "I understand."

"And I will expect you to be a gentleman and not act like a prick. Got that?"

"Did I just hear you say what I thought you did?" His eyes widened but he smiled.

"You did." A smile played on her lips, too.

Brad patted her hand. "You always surprise me." He stood. "I'll call you when we get back."

She followed him to the door. "I'll miss all of you."

He gave her a quick kiss on the cheek and chuckled. "I'll just bet you will."

313

# THIRTY-SEVEN

Rob was surprised when he came home in the middle of the week and found Myrna in her bedroom kneeling in front of her closet. "What's up?" he asked from the doorway.

She brushed a strand of hair from her eyes and pushed it behind her ear. "As you know, Brother-dear, I'll be moving soon and I thought it might be a good idea to get started cleaning. Paul's at home with the kids this afternoon," she added.

He sat on the end of her bed. "I guess we need to be talking about that--your moving and all."

She sat on the floor beside the closet and leaned against the wall. "I guess so."

"Do you plan to sell this house?" He looked around the room. This had been his home for almost a year, and now that he knew he would be staying in Tulsa, he hated to think about moving again. The thought had occurred to him that he might be able to buy it, but, with no credit, he wasn't sure he could get a loan.

"Paul and I have talked and if you'd like to stay here, we'd like to sell it to you, Rob. You would pay us directly, whatever you can." She joined him on the side of the bed. "I'm leaving all the furniture since Paul has everything we'll need, and," she reached out and touched his arm, "you'll have a place to bring your son. You can put up a swing set in the backyard.

It would be better than an apartment and cheaper. We wouldn't expect you to pay more than you can afford." Her voice rose with excitement. "What do you think?"

His own home, a place for his son to visit. "I think it sounds great," he said. "But, I don't want to take anything away from you and Paul. If you need the money..."

She shook her head, "Have you forgotten I'm marrying an attorney? Paul makes good money and his house is paid for." She stood up and began going through the closet again. "I'm not changing anything else in the house until the kids are all right with our marriage." She looked back at him. "It's their home and I don't want to destroy any of their memories of their mother."

"You're a good woman, Myrna Watson, De Luca-to-be." He stood up. "I'm going to take a shower. You think you might have supper with me tonight? I make great lasagna."

She laughed. "Absolutely. I told Paul he had to fend for himself."

An hour later Rob put the pan of lasagna into the oven and turned to find Myrna standing in the doorway, a small cigar box in her hands. Her expression of sorrow concerned him. When he asked what was wrong, she said nothing, just came into the kitchen and sat at the table.

"Oh, Rob. I feel terrible about this."

He sat across from her. "Tell me."

"This box. I was supposed to give it to you a long time ago. I forgot about it until I found it in the top of the closet."

"What is it, Myrna?" he asked.

She took a deep breath, her voice shaking. "It happened so long ago. It was right before our dad died."

*Mac McGruder? This has something to do with him? Maybe I don't want to know.*

"You know he and I hardly ever talked after--after you left--and after I gave my baby away. One night not long before he died I woke up and heard something in the living room. I got up and found Dad sitting on the floor with this box in his hands. He was…" she paused and took another shaky breath, "crying. Hard crying. It scared me."

It would have scared him, too. He didn't know his father could show any emotion except hatred. "What did you do?"

"I just stood there. I didn't know what to do. Finally I asked him if he wanted me to get him anything. At first he said no then he said he did. He asked me to sit down beside him and look in the box." Myrna's hands tightened on the box she held in front of her. "I was scared to look in it. I didn't know what he could have in it and I didn't trust him, but I opened it and found some things. He told me about them." She looked at her brother, tears shining in her eyes. "Rob, it was the first time he had ever treated me like a human being. And when he finished telling me about the things, he said if I ever saw you again, to give it to you." She pushed the box across the table to him.

Unbelieving, Rob stood. He moved the box back toward her. "I'm not sure I care what he said or what's in the box. If it came from him, it can't be good."

Myrna stood. "Just look in it, Rob." And she walked out of the room leaving the box on the table in front of him.

He didn't want to touch it. It had come from the person who was the cause of every bad thing that had ever happened to him and why should he care what this man had wanted to give him? But Myrna said he had cried, had treated her like she was human. It was hard for him to imagine his father like that.

The box loomed before him, an old beat up cigar box, the paper clasp torn.

Finally Rob pulled it toward him and opened the lid. He half expected some kind of cruel joke his father would pull on him from beyond the grave. But what he saw wasn't horrible. It was ordinary. A black and white photograph. Rob picked it up. The picture was of a man, stocky, strong looking. He had a dark mustache and was holding a small child in his left arm. The man wore a sleeveless undershirt and had a tattoo clearly visible on his right upper arm. The child, a boy, was wearing a hard hat too big for him. One hand held it back from his face as he looked into the eyes of the man holding him. Both of them were smiling.

Rob turned the picture over and in a scrawl on the back was written *My dad and me.*

Another photograph was under the one of the man and the boy. He picked it up. It was a grave. On closer examination Rob saw it was not one grave but two with a common marker. He wasn't able to see what was written on it because the snapshot was small and grainy.

The only other item in the box was a newspaper clipping.

> Robert Marion McGruder died Wednesday, April 6, 1956. Born January 15, 1922. Preceded in death by wife, Frances Bailey McGruder in 1950 and infant daughter, Mary Nell, that same year. He is survived by Robert Marion McGruder, Jr., age 9, of the home. Interment is at Forest Hills Cemetery.

His father was a junior, named for his father.

He looked at the picture of the man and boy again. The child must be his father. His father had never been anything except an ogre in his eyes. But he had a father, too, and that father had died when he was nine years old. Where had Mac McGruder gone after that? Where did he live? Rob had always been told his father had no family. He had asked his mother many times why he didn't have any grandparents and she told him they were all dead. She never told him how any of them had died.

He went into the bedroom where his sister was still working. Holding the box in both hands. She turned around. "Did you look?" she asked.

He nodded. His legs gave way and he sat on the bed again. She came beside him.

"What did he say that night?" It was something he had to know. "That night when he cried."

"He showed me the picture of him and his dad. He said it was taken just before his baby sister was born. He didn't remember everything about it but his father had told him his mother took the picture and because she was so pregnant, she didn't want to be in it. She said to wait until after the baby came and he could take a picture of her with her children. But she died in childbirth and so did the baby."

Rob's heart squeezed with compassion for the little boy in the picture. Three years old when his mother died. At least, he had known his mother for twelve years.

Myrna continued, wiping her hand across her eyes. "Then he showed me the picture of the graves, his mother's and father's. He said someone took the picture and gave it to him and that he had never gone back there. I asked him where he went since he was so young and he wouldn't tell me at first. Then he said he had been sent to live with some aunt in Kansas, someone he didn't even know, and she didn't want him. He would just shake his head and say things like, 'If I had been older, I would have told someone but no one would have believed what she did to me.'"

"How did his father die? Did he tell you?" Rob opened the box and took out the picture of the man and boy.

Myrna took a deep breath. "That was the saddest part. He told me he came home from school one day and found his father lying on the bed. He was dead. That's all he knew."

"Just like me," Rob said. "I came home and found Mama was gone."

Myrna touched his arm. "Like both of us, Rob. I was with you."

He faced her. "You were with me?"

She nodded. "We walked into Mama's room together and she was gone. You went right out and I heard you calling her name, but I think I knew that she was dead."

Rob rubbed his hand across the top of his head. "You were there. I don't remember that. All I remember was our dad telling me she was dead." He tossed the picture and the box on the bed. "He didn't say anything else, just looked at me like he wished I wasn't there."

Myrna stood beside him. "It wasn't like that, Rob. He was crying."

"Crying? Not him." He strode across the room to the doorway then back to where his sister stood. "I don't think he even cared."

"Rob, how can you say that? He did shed tears, not as much as when I found him that night, but I remember his tears at home and at the funeral."

"You went to the funeral?" Rob's eyes widened. "Why wasn't I allowed to go?"

His sister came to him; put her hands on the sides of his face. "Rob, you were there. Both of us were there, at the funeral home, at the gravesite. I was worried about you because you never cried. You just sat there and looked like you were far away."

Rob shook his head. "I was there? I don't remember any of that. I thought—I thought…" He sat down heavily on the bed. "How could I have forgotten?"

Myrna sat beside him, picked up the picture and held it lightly between her fingers. "I don't think either of us knew how much our father hurt when he lost Mama. Maybe he thought you didn't care."

"How could he think that?" Rob stood again. "That bastard knew how much I loved Mama. He knew and he didn't give a damn."

Myrna touched his arm to calm him. "No, he didn't know. You never cried. You never acted like you cared. That's all he saw."

"And how do you know that?" Anger seethed in Rob's chest. In that moment he wished he could hit his father. The very idea that he would think Rob didn't care.

"Because he told me."

Unbelieving, Rob asked, "Told you? When?"

"That night when he gave me the box for you." She pulled him down beside her to sit on the bed. "When he told me you didn't care about your mother, I told him that it wasn't true. I told him how hurt you were but that you just couldn't show it because it was so painful for you. I knew about that because I had to keep my own pain to myself." She turned his face to look at her. "Rob, our father was a mean man. I agree with you on that, but he was a man who was always in pain. Maybe he didn't know how to show anything except his pain."

Rob leaned his elbows on his knees and put his head in his hands. "I can't believe all this."

"After I told him how much you hurt, that's when he told me to give you the box. He said it might make up for the things he didn't understand about you. But I think he really just wanted you to know who he was, to understand him. Rob, if you could have seen him. It broke my heart, and I can't believe I just forgot it. I forgot about all of it." She leaned toward him. "I'm sorry. You should have had this from the beginning." She put the photo in his hands.

Rob held the picture before him then placed it back in the box. "It's all right."

"I guess I was so confused after he died and then being married to Leroy. It just all went away until I found it."

Rob stood. "Thanks for showing it to me." He went into his room and put the box in a dresser drawer. Why had his father waited so long to give the box to him? Did he know how much Rob hated him? Was he sorry for the way he had treated his son?

Anger rose up in him. *If that was true why couldn't he have told me himself?* He sat down heavily on his own bed and once again put his hands over his face. *He didn't name me Marion. Does that mean he cared too much for me to stick me with the name he hated?*

What did all of this mean? Rob massaged his temples. He stretched out on the bed. The face of the small boy in his father's arms wouldn't leave him. The imagined image of the child crying over the death of his mother and baby sister burned itself into his mind. As much as he tried to deny it, Rob could see the similarities between the angry, hurt father he hated, and the man he, himself, had become.

What do I do now, Mac McGruder? Forgive you?

For what? For being hurt all your life and taking it out on your wife and kids?

He stood up. "Not in this lifetime," he said.

# THIRTY-EIGHT

May came and went. Rob felt he was sleepwalking between the times he had with his son. He spent every Saturday morning with Myrna and every Saturday afternoon with Gerri and Bobby. Although he wished he could see his son every evening, Gerri had resisted when he broached the subject with her. Reluctant to allow her son to become too dependent on Rob until she was sure he could be trusted, she had decided their only time together would be Saturday afternoons.

Rob fought to keep his mind off Paige but somehow her face intruded on his thoughts. He would awake in the night thinking she was beside him and he'd reach out for her, his desire apparent. Then he would curse himself. They hadn't slept together before and never would.

The first few weeks he hoped he would hear from her, but he hadn't and after a time he knew it was hopeless. She didn't love him and whatever she had felt for him wasn't strong enough to overcome the truth she had finally learned. He knew that even if she did come back, he had more lies to clear up, and the one that would probably split them apart even more was one he wasn't sure he could ever tell.

One of those lonely evenings, the phone rang. It seldom rang and when it did, he always hoped it would be Paige calling him back to her. Usually it was a telemarketer but tonight it was Rico. He was excited to hear from his friend and told him about the Spud Smith event and about

Myrna's wedding. He asked how Rosa was, hoping she was doing better than the last time they talked.

"She is well. We will be parents again."

"I'm sure you will, Rico," Rob said, wondering again if he could tell his friend about his own son.

"No, mi amigo. We will be parents soon." Rico's voice wasn't as animated this time as it had been when he had told Rob the news of his wife's pregnancy the first time.

"You mean…"

Rico laughed, not the usual sound from the heart, but lighter and less jovial, "I mean in seven months, we will parents again."

"I'm glad," Rob said. "Rico, are you all right?" He didn't like the sound of his friend's tone.

"I am all right but I am also afraid." He laughed again. "Did you know your friend is sometimes a coward?"

Rob thought he would be scared, too, if he was in Rico's place. "I understand. I've been a coward in my life, too."

They talked a few minutes more then Rob told him about his son. When he did, Rico's exuberance was back. "I am happy for you. It is time you have happiness, Roberto. You have learned much from sadness."

Rob agreed. The sadness that had filled his life appeared to be lifting. Since the day he got the cigar box, as much as he didn't want to, he saw his father with different eyes. He couldn't get the picture of the man and the boy out of his mind. He tried to tell himself, so what if he was hurt? If his father wasn't to blame for all of Rob's failures and problems, then who was? How easy it had been for him to excuse his own behavior and not give his father the same tolerance.

The stories he had heard from John kept returning to his thoughts. He took responsibility for taking the steroids. And Rico didn't blame his brothers for trying to get out of Mexico and dying in the effort. Why did Rob have to blame someone for his mistakes? He knew the answer, because it was easier than taking responsibility.

John Taylor's words came back to him. "You have to forgive yourself." The man was right. That was the hardest part. When he was finally able to do that, John said he could go on with his life.

That's what I want to do, Rob thought. Put all that behind me and go on with my life. But even if he could forgive his father and himself, one secret still hung over him, and he had no idea if there would ever be a way to chase that one away.

# THIRTY-NINE

Bobby's birthday party was on a Saturday afternoon and Rob knew he would be meeting a lot of the parents of Bobby's friends. He wasn't sure Gerri wanted him to come to the party but it was Bobby who had invited him the weekend before. Rob believed that if Bobby hadn't mentioned it, Gerri probably wouldn't have. He had spent two afternoons at Toys 'R Us looking for just the right gift and had finally come up with a book about cars and a gift card. He would bring Bobby to the store later and let him choose his own present. Of course, Gerri would be with them since she still didn't trust him alone with their child. It was getting to him, but he felt the time was near when he could prove to her that he wouldn't walk out on Bobby the way he'd walked out on her.

He dressed in a blue sport shirt and Dockers and carried the wrapped book. Several cars were already parked on the street when he arrived. Nervous, he rang the doorbell. The woman who answered the door was shorter than Gerri and had long blond hair and green eyes. When she opened the door, she was smiling but when she saw him, her smile faded.

"You're Rob, aren't you?" She didn't step back.

"Yes." He wasn't sure she was going to let him in.

"I'm Lynn Abbott, Gerri's roommate."

He extended his hand but she didn't take it.

"You'd better come in. Bobby's been asking when you'd be here." She stepped back and he went into the living room. Bobby ran to him.

"You got me present?" The boy took the wrapped package and the envelope and put them on the coffee table beside other gift boxes and bags. "This is my happy birthday," he said smiling up at Rob.

Rob greeted Gerri and she introduced him to the other parents, simply telling them his name with no other explanation.

The children played a few games in the back yard and he helped Gerri with them while the parents stood in groups watching their kids and talking among themselves. One of the other men there was introduced as Lynn's fiancé, Jay Carter. The man was about his height with blond hair and was probably nice enough, but after Lynn's frosty greeting he kept his distance from them. Every time he looked Lynn's way, he found her watching him.

When it came time to cut the cake, Bobby took Rob's hand and dragged him to the dining room table. "You sit here," he instructed pointing to the chair beside his. Gerri started to light the candles and Bobby stopped her. "I want Rob to do it."

A look passed between Gerri and Lynn before she handed the matches to Rob. He lit the five candles then Gerri said. "Okay, Bobby, after we sing to you, make a wish and blow out the candles."

"Wait," Bobby said and leaned over to whisper in Rob's ear.

Embarrassed at the looks on Gerri's and Lynn's faces, he leaned toward his son. Bobby whispered, "Do wishes come true?"

He looked around the silent room, not sure if anyone else had heard the question. He spoke quietly in Bobby's ear. "Sometimes they do."

Bobby smiled and said, this time not quite a whisper, "Good, then I wish you were my dad."

Rob saw Gerri's face blanch, but she quickly recovered and led the birthday song. When Bobby blew out all the candles, he clapped his hands and looked at Rob. "My wish will come true," he crowed.

Gerri cut the cake, putting slices on colorful NASCAR paper plates while Lynn spooned ice cream beside the slices. After everyone had eaten, the party moved to the living room. Again Bobby insisted Rob sit right beside him while he opened his presents.

Then the party was over and the parents and children began to file out. Rob wasn't sure whether he was to stay any longer or to go, but Bobby made the decision for him.

"Let's go to the store now and buy my other present," he said, pulling Rob toward the door.

"Not now," Gerri said. "I have to clean up. We'll go later."

"Not you, Mom. Rob and me. We can go. You can stay here and clean up. We'll go by ourselves." Bobby continued his way toward the door.

Rob saw the blood rush to Gerri's face. He stopped Bobby and said, "Wait, Bobby. Let's wait for your mother. How about we help her clean up the party then we can all go together."

When Bobby hesitated, Gerri said, "Good idea. I need some help eating one more piece of cake."

Bobby's eyes lit up. "Another piece? Can we have another piece?"

"Sure can," she smiled. "You and Rob can eat some more cake while I get ready." She looked at Rob. "Thanks," she said as she and Bobby went into the kitchen.

Before Rob could follow Lynn came to where he was standing. "Rob, I have something to say to you. Will you give me a minute?"

He faced her and nodded.

"I was wrong about you. Gerri told me I was but I wasn't sure. I see how you are with Bobby. I think it'll be all right." Then she went out the front door where her fiancé waited.

---

Gerri left Bobby's door ajar and went into her bedroom. Wearily she sat on the white duvet covering her queen bed and hugged a forest green pillow to her chest. It had been more tiring than she thought possible having Rob at the party and facing the unasked questions of her guests.

She had made peace with her life for the last six years but since Rob had come back, that peace was elusive. As much as she had wished for male companionship she had put her desires on hold and seeing Rob brought back those buried feelings.

Surely I'm not still in love with him, she thought, and remembered how his touch had rocked her at the pizza parlor. The words to the song, "What Kind of Fool Am I?" ran through her mind.

"I would be a fool to fall for him again," she whispered.

A few minutes later Gerri tossed the pillow aside and left her bedroom. She pushed Bobby's door open and peeked into his room. The excitement of his party and the trip to Toys R Us had worn him out. He was sleeping, his open mouth emitting a soft snore. She went into his room and pulled the sheet over him. Love for her child overwhelmed her. When she saw him like this, she was aware of his vulnerability, his trust in her, and she knew she would move heaven and earth to keep him safe—even from his own father if it came to that.

Up to now Rob had done everything she asked. Today, when Bobby wanted to go to the store with him, Rob had gently turned it around so she was included. She wanted to say it was a masterful move on his part, but something in her knew it wasn't contrived. He had no ulterior motive in doing it but was honoring their agreement. How easy it would have been for him to make her look like the bad guy.

Gerri slipped out of Bobby's room, went into the living room and sat in the rocking chair, the same chair Rob had sat in the day he met Bobby. Sitting in the dark, she remembered how easily he had interacted with Bobby and how quickly they had bonded that day. Bonded like a father and son.

And today, when Bobby was going to blow out his candles, she had heard him clearly, "Then I'm going to wish you are my dad."

Gerri rested her head on the back of the chair and rocked gently. When could she tell Bobby his wish had come true? What was she waiting for? But in her heart she knew it wasn't time. There was something in Rob that had to be resolved before he was free to be the father their son needed. She would know when it had been done and then her son could know the truth.

She sighed deeply. And what would that mean to her? Maybe Rob was the reason she had never dated. Maybe it wasn't about Bobby at all. Even knowing what Rob had done hadn't diminished her feelings for him or her belief in him.

Her thoughts returned to her parents as they often did. She missed them and wished they could have known her son.

"One man's curse is another man's ladder," her father had told her mother shortly before he succumbed to lung cancer. But Georgia Harper didn't use her husband's death as a ladder out of her pain. It became her curse and she died of a broken heart a few months later. At age twenty, Gerri Harper had made her father's words her mantra and unlike her mother, she had taken situations in her life to higher ground. She was determined to never allow anyone or anything take away her ability to survive, and she planned to pass that truth on to her son. And now she was faced with another opportunity to put her dad's saying into practice.

Gerri rubbed her hand across her brow. Rob was on her mind a lot since he'd come into their lives. As much as she wanted to convince herself that his return meant nothing to her, in her heart she knew it wasn't true. Still this man was an ex-convict who had robbed a woman, left her to die and was hiding from the law. Not only was she allowing him to be with her son but she thought she still loved him?

She must be crazy!

# FORTY

*Blackness. Total, blackness*

*Face buried in something soft--.her head pressed down.....*

*Hard to breathe. Can't breathe! Help me! Someone help me!*

*No one can hear because there's no sound to be heard.*

*Push away from this suffocating softness.*

*My hands! Where are my hands?*

*No hands! No arms!*

*Kick! Get free from the weight! Can't move my legs! No legs!*

*Where are my legs? I can't see my legs!! Can't see them but I know where they are--on the floor beside me! I can smell the blood!*

*A movement above her--Hair pulled away from her neck lifting her head*

*He's going to cut off my head!!*

She awoke gasping, screaming.

The dream was back. Paige padded into the kitchen, turned on the light and shivered. Not from cold but from the dream. She drew a glass of water and went into the living room, curled her feet under her on the sofa and pulled a knitted throw over her. She sat in the dark with the light streaming in from the kitchen.

There was something different about the dream this time. What was it? She rested on the sofa back, closed her eyes and tried to remember.

331

The dream happened the same way every time. She was on her face and couldn't breathe. She had never been able to see the face of her attacker in her dream, only the eyes. This time it wasn't the same, but she couldn't remember. She drifted into a semi-sleep.

*She was standing in the kitchen of her brother's old house knowing something was about to happen, but she couldn't move. She waited, then he appeared in the doorway; a tall shadowy figure of a man. She saw the gun in his hand. Her eyes were stuck on the gun, but if she could pull them away, look into his face... He came nearer. Terror seized her, stampeded through her being and she screamed. In her dream she screamed, and then she heard his voice. It was familiar, but it wasn't cruel or menacing and she was no longer afraid. She easily moved her eyes from the gun and looked into the man's face. Long blond hair, scruffy beard and his eyes--then his face changed...*

Paige sat up and cried out.

# FORTY-ONE

The day before Myrna's wedding was a beautiful Oklahoma June day, sunny and warm. Albert and Carla DeLuca arrived Thursday afternoon to stay with the children while the couple went on their honeymoon to New York City and Niagara Falls.

Myrna spent Friday morning packing her bags and had everything ready by noon. She wandered around the house for awhile then stepped out into the back yard. Rob had mowed the lawn sometime during the week but the flower beds needed some early weeding. Being outside always energized her and she loved seeing her flowers bloom. This spring she hadn't even noticed if her bulbs had bloomed.

When Leroy was alive, she had been the one to mow the lawn and keep the beds weed-free and full of flowers. At Paul's she could still work in the flower beds but he hired someone to mow and trim the lawn. She wouldn't mind doing it but knew she would be busy with the children and keeping the household running.

On one hand the thought of her new life thrilled her. On the other she was aware there would be some problems. The girls appeared to accept her as a friend but what about when she took the role of a mother?

And Josh. He was respectful but still distant. Myrna and Paul had discussed all of it at length, how much of a role she should take and how much she should leave to him. She knew it had to be handled carefully and was willing to get outside help if needed. The only role model for a family had come from her mother and that hadn't been for long.

Myrna pushed the gate away from her and it held. Rob had fixed it sometime ago but she didn't know when. For years the latch had been broken and she had asked Leroy to have it repaired. When he never did, she had given up asking and simply tied a bit of twine around it to keep it from swinging open. Eventually the twine would break and the gate would be free again.

Leroy. Myrna leaned against the fence and looked at the back of her house. It wasn't her house now. It belonged to Rob. This is the place Leroy brought her the day they were married. On that day she had a small bag with a few belongings in it, and he had only given her one drawer in their dresser for them and told her she had to hang her clothes in the second bedroom closet.

Before they were married Leroy had been friendly and understanding. When she told him about her brother, he had sympathized with her. When he found her in an empty apartment crying after the death of her father, he had told her about the loss of his baby sister, Peg. That day he had offered to marry her.

Is that how it happened? Did he ask her or did he offer? After more than eleven years she wasn't sure. That same afternoon he had driven her to the court house where they got a marriage license. Three days later she quit her job and they were married at the same court house by a judge.

She had told Rob that he started being mean to her when she tried to be a grown woman instead of his child. Maybe that wasn't what had changed him. Now that she thought back on it, it began when Rob came around a few months after their marriage. It was subtle but Leroy made comments about Rob, never gave him a chance and always hated having him around. Could it have been because she had a sibling and Leroy didn't? He had never spoken of Peg again until Myrna brought her up a few years later.

They were driving somewhere, she couldn't remember now, but it was pleasant between them and they had been talking. She asked about his parents and how his sister had died, and Leroy went quiet. She remembered thinking he hadn't heard her and she touched his arm. He had jerked away from her and cursed. He told her to mind her own "damned business." She never asked again.

Rob. He had come home after five years to be with her when she needed him the most. All those years when she thought she needed him, but he came at the right time. Those first few weeks were a blur. She barely remembered meeting him at the airport but she did remember how angry she had been with him. When was it? In the car? In the hospital? It was because he left her but they had finally worked that out and she was glad she hadn't told what she knew about him. Why hadn't she?

She shook her head in bewilderment. He was a criminal but she had kept it to herself. How many other people knew? Would he and Paige get back together and if they did, what would she do when she found out the truth? It made Myrna sad to think that her brother could still go to prison when she knew how much he had changed. And he had a son, a son who needed his father.

Her pleasant thoughts had turned into fear and she didn't want anything but happy ones the day before her wedding. She would face the bad stuff when it came but until then she wasn't going to think about it.

---

It was the first time he'd seen Paige since they parted. Rob drove himself to the church for the rehearsal and Myrna rode with Paul, his children and his parents. He nodded to her when she came into the church, and she gave a slight nod in his direction after greeting Myrna and Paul and meeting Mr. and Mrs. DeLuca. Otherwise they didn't speak and avoided eye contact.

After the rehearsal the wedding party went to a restaurant for the dinner. Rob made it a point to sit with Josh. The two of them and the twins sat with Paul's parents, and Myrna, Paul, Paige and Paul's best man, Ron and Ron's wife, Janelle, sat together at the other end of the table. After the dinner, as quickly as was polite, he escaped.

He didn't go straight home but drove around Tulsa until eleven o'clock. When he got home, Myrna was already in bed. He had planned it that way. If she noticed his and Paige's discomfort, he didn't want to have to talk to her about it. He'd promised his sister their being together wouldn't disrupt her day, and he meant to keep that promise.

The morning of the wedding was as beautiful as the day before. A perfect day for a wedding, Myrna said, as Rob drove her to the church, and she didn't mention Paige or the fact that he had left early from the dinner.

On the way to the church she described her wedding dress to him in detail.

"It's an ivory peau satin and the top of it is beaded with small silk rosebuds that match the headpiece of my veil."

Rob laughed. "Those words don't mean a thing to me. Why didn't you just let me see it for myself?"

"Only Paige has seen it. I want it to be a surprise." She patted his arm. "You are absolutely handsome in your black tux and grey vest." She laughed. "I don't guess you've ever worn a tie of any kind, have you? And that bow tie is perfect."

336

Rob tugged at the collar of his shirt. "I wish I felt as good as I look."

"You look wonderful. Isn't it a great morning for a wedding? I always thought it would be better to get married in the morning instead of at night. That way the bride and groom wouldn't be so tired after waiting all day."

Myrna's excited voice melted into the background as his thoughts went to the day ahead.

Rob realized Paige had receded farther and farther from his memory as Bobby and Gerri moved to the forefront, but seeing her the night before brought back the feelings he had tried to bury.

When they got to the church, Rob went into the preacher's office with Paul and his best man until time for the wedding to begin. The wedding planner called the men from the room, Rob knew he would have to see Paige, and he didn't want to. He kept his eyes averted until he was in place beside Myrna.

Paige stood behind the flower girls and Josh, and she didn't look around when he came in. All he could see was her back, but he was acutely aware of the soft curve of her neck and shoulders in the off-shoulder dress. He looked away. It hurt too much.

He turned his attention to his sister. The wedding planner straightened Myrna's veil so it flowed down onto the train of her skirt. She handed her a bouquet of pale pink and yellow roses and instructed the two of them to stand to the side of the door.

The twins, dressed in yellow satin dresses, carried pink rosebuds, their hair entwined with pink and yellow ribbons were the first to walk down the aisle. Josh stood in the doorway of the sanctuary, a white satin pillow that held the wedding rings balanced on his hands. He looked over his shoulder at Rob and Rob winked at him. The boy smiled and winked back.

Rob took a deep breath and tucked Myrna's hand in the crook of his arm. "Good luck, Sis. You look beautiful." He kissed her lightly on the cheek.

The standard wedding march played. Myrna clutched a bouquet in one hand and gripped her brother's arm with the other. The small church was filled with friends, mostly Paul's, who stood and smiled back at the couple as they walked up the aisle. Rob could see the minister in his black robe and Paul in a dark tuxedo. It wasn't until they were almost to the altar that he saw Paige. Her dark curls were piled on her head with rosebuds laced through them. The flowers matched her butter cream satin dress. She held a bouquet of pink roses and smiled as they neared the altar. It took all his energy to look away from her and focus on the minister. Myrna kissed him on the cheek when he responded to the minister's question. Then he took his place in the front row and tried not to look at Paige.

It made a pretty picture, the colors of the dresses, the tuxedos, the flowers. Exactly what Myrna had always wanted and what she deserved. Even with his own discomfort, Rob was happy to be a part of it.

After the kiss and the couple walked down the aisle to the strains of the Recessional, Paige took the arm of the best man. Rob's eyes followed them out of the sanctuary but in the vestibule he stayed away from where the wedding party gathered.

Pictures were taken; the couple alone, the couple with the maid of honor and best man, with the children, with Paul's mother and father and the couple with Rob.

At the reception Rob stood in the background while Myrna and Paul cut the cake. Then they went to the head table and sat between the best man and maid of honor. On the left of the best man were

Paul's parents and his children. Paige sat on Myrna's right and the only empty seat was beside her.

Paul gestured toward Rob and pointed to the chair. Rob saw Myrna's expression change, and he knew she understood his reluctance to sit there. But, as usual, Paige's presence drew him to her. He wasn't comfortable but he couldn't stay away and he sat down without speaking or looking at her.

They ate in silence. Then Ron announced it was time for Myrna to throw her bouquet and he asked all the unmarried women to gather for the ceremony. Paige joined the group.

Rob started to leave but Paul stopped him. "You're going to try to catch the garter, aren't you?" he asked.

Rob had no idea what he meant but he nodded and walked away. He moved to the back of the reception hall and watched Myrna toss her bouquet back over her shoulder. He noticed most of the women were reaching up to catch it but Paige wasn't. She stood in the back and as soon as the rite was over, she disappeared.

A chair was brought to the center of the room and Myrna sat on it. She pulled her dress up and Paul slipped a blue garter from around her thigh. With that Rob went into the vestibule. Outside at the curb a long white limo waited for the couple, its driver leaning nonchalantly against the fender.

Rob's thoughts left the wedding and went to the evening when he would see his son and Gerri. Rob and Bobby had grown closer and more than anything Rob wanted his son to know he was his dad. He didn't know how to make it plain to Gerri that he would never walk out on Bobby and was ready to be his father. Every time he assured her, she said she would know when it was true. The last time they talked about it, she told him he had some baggage he had to take care of, but when he asked her what it was, she wouldn't say. She only said she'd know when it was gone.

In his heart Rob knew what that baggage was but he had no idea how he would ever rid himself of it. It was the truth about himself that Myrna and Gerri knew. It was only Paige who didn't know the truth. She, more than anyone, deserved to know. But how could he tell her now? And if he did, what would she do? Turn him in? At times he was sure that would be better than continuing to live with the secret.

He smelled her perfume and knew Paige stood beside him. Seeing her the night before had brought back the knowledge of what he had lost and that loss sat like a cold stone in the pit of his stomach.

A few moments of uneasy quiet passed before she spoke, "It was a beautiful wedding."

"Yes, it was."

"I'm happy for Myrna and Paul."

Rob's love for her flooded over him. "I am, too," he said.

Paige cleared her throat. "I'd like to talk to you."

"Okay."

"I'm not sure this is the place," she said.

Curious, he asked, "What's it about?"

"I think Myrna and Paul are about to leave. We can talk about it after."

The wedding planner announced the bride and groom were about to depart and called out, "Let's all give them a rousing sendoff."

The guests lined the sidewalk and threw birdseed on the couple as they ran to the limousine. Myrna stopped and hugged her brother, told him she loved him then embraced Paige and climbed into the car. As they drove away Paige turned to Rob. "If you don't mind, could we go to my house?"

Uh-oh, he thought. What's going on? But he just said, "Sure. I guess it's better than standing out here." She had already turned and was walking toward the parking lot.

---

Rob sat in his truck in front of Paige's condo. He wasn't sure what this meeting was about, but, some place deep inside, he knew it would bring changes in his life. He removed his jacket, unhooked his tie, rolled up the sleeves of his shirt and walked to the front door.

Paige let him in immediately. She had changed into jeans and a tee shirt. She said nothing, just motioned for him to sit down on the sofa then she took the chair across the room. She looked at her hands in her lap then spoke. "Myrna told me about your son. She thought I knew. I didn't tell her it was the first I'd heard about it." When she looked up at him, he saw her look didn't accuse him.

Myrna hadn't mentioned anything to him about talking to Paige and wondered if it was before he had told her they'd broken up.

Her eyes didn't waver from his face then she asked, "Will you tell me what you plan to do about him?"

"Him?" he repeated.

"Your son." Paige's voice was more businesslike than personal. *Why does she care?* "I plan to be his dad."

"How does he feel about suddenly having a father?"

"He doesn't know yet." *Is this some kind of therapy session?*

"Who does he think you are?" she asked.

"Just Rob, but he'll know soon." *What's your point?* he asked her silently.

"Oh," was all she said. She was thoughtful for a second then asked, "How does it feel, Rob? Having a son?"

341

*What does it feel like?* He couldn't help smiling. "It's wonderful, Paige. Better than I ever imagined."

She appeared to relax. "You love him." It was a statement needing no answer. .

He nodded. "More than I thought possible. When I think of him..." He stopped, his heart close to bursting with the thought of his child.

Her voice lost its edge. "And how about him? Does he love you?" A slight smile danced across her lips then, as quickly, vanished.

Rob saw her softening and wondered what was coming next. They weren't a couple any more and couldn't be unless something had changed with her. "Yes, we tell each other all the time. He's a great kid." He leaned forward. "Why are you asking about Bobby?"

"That's his name?" Delight filled her face. "I didn't know. Ironic, isn't it, that she named him for you."

This time he didn't answer. Knowing Gerri, he wasn't surprised at all.

"I mean, since you obviously weren't around when he was born." The edge was back in her tone.

He recognized her comment as a dig at his past but it still hurt to hear her put it into words.

"That was mean," she said quickly. "I apologize."

Rob shrugged. "It's true."

"Still..." she said. Paige took a deep breath. "What about his mother. How does she feel about you being back in their lives?"

Her apology didn't make him feel any better but he decided to overlook it. She had a lot more she could say about him if she knew the truth. "She seems to be all right with it," he said.

"How does she fit in with..." she paused. Her voice wavered. "With your life?"

"I'm not sure. She's a good woman, certainly didn't deserve the way I treated her before."

"Do you think there's a possibility --" she asked, her expression pained, "a possibility the two of you…"

"I don't know. I haven't thought that far." He didn't want to talk about Gerri with Paige, but he felt he owed it to her to answer her question honestly. "If you're asking whether I would marry her just for Bobby's sake, well, I can't say that." He paused before continuing. "But if I could love her? I'm not sure I can let myself feel like that about someone again very soon."

She nodded and looked down at her hands clasped in her lap.

"Paige, tell me why you wanted to talk to me. It's about more than my son, isn't it?" A glimmer of hope had risen in him; hope that she would tell him he was more important to her than a career. He could see the three of them, Paige, himself and Bobby together.

For a long moment she looked at him, her voice just above a whisper. She took a deep breath. "I just wanted to ask you about your son. Maybe I shouldn't have. I guess I was curious."

He watched her for a moment then knew this was the time. Whatever happened, he had to do it. "There's something I need to tell you, Paige. Something I should have said a long time ago." This may be it for me, he thought, but I can't keep it any longer. It's time I face the truth.

Rob looked at her face, the face of the woman he had hurt but, also, the face of the woman he loved. "I'm the one." He saw her confusion. "The one who robbed you six years ago.

Paige shook her head. Her brow furrowed. "What?"

He nodded and couldn't tear his eyes away. "I've always wanted you to know. In the beginning I was afraid of what you'd do. Then I fell…" His voice faltered. "I fell in love with you and didn't want you to hate me."

"Rob," she gasped as understanding dawned on her. Her face paled and her hands trembled.

"It's true and I think you know it."

She nodded slowly.

He waited while she took the truth in.

Finally she said, "I guess I do." Her mouth formed the word, her voice barely audible. "Why?"

Then the truth poured out of him, all the truth about his life of crime, about how he'd planned the robbery and waited for her to be alone. About his trip to Las Vegas and how he changed his identity. All of it until there was nothing left untold, and she listened. Even as he finished, he knew he had not only forgiven his father but he had done the impossible and forgiven himself. The weight lifted from his heart. Whatever she decided to do, he'd take it. He could finally handle what came even if it meant being locked up again. Prisons come in different versions, and he was free of this one. A jail cell could never change that fact.

He spread his hands. "None of what I told you is an excuse. I'm sorry I did it. Even when it was happening, I knew it was wrong. And since then, I've wished a million times I could go back and undo that night, but I can't. I wasn't going to leave you to die, Paige. I want you to know that. When I saw the housekeeper on her way to your house, I knew she'd find you. Still, just to be sure, I stopped on the way out of town and called the police."

"I always wondered who it was who called nine-one-one." She sat forward. "The police didn't tell anyone in the press about the call. They kept some things quiet that only the--criminal would know."

Rob blanched.

"They thought it might have been you, but I didn't believe it was." Looking away, she said, "I thought you were so evil, that you didn't care enough to do that." When she looked back at him, her eyes held a new revelation, "But, I always remembered something."

He waited.

"Before you left for good you came back."

He remembered.

"You said you were sorry." She smiled wryly. "I've never forgotten how you said it. It sounded like you meant it."

He laced his fingers together. "I did mean it but it was too late. I didn't know how to change it."

Paige sank back into the cushions of the chair. "I had the dream again the other night and this time I saw a face—your face."

"Then you already knew."

She shook her head. "I couldn't believe it. I thought it was because you had asked me if I wanted to find out who did it. I thought it was my imagination."

For a few minutes the silence was unbroken between them. "I deserve to go back to jail, and I'm ready if that's what it takes."

She took a deep breath and leaned her head against the back of the chair. She was quiet for several minutes, her eyes closed.

I've done the right thing, Rob thought. For the first time in my life, I've done something right. He knew he had finally crawled out of his pit.

Her voice broke into his thoughts. "What purpose would it serve to lock you up now?"

He had no answer.

"None that I see," she said. "I can't imagine you as the man who came into my brother's house. Bobby McGruder is gone. He died in Las Vegas." She looked toward the ceiling, tears pooling in her eyes. "When I think about you, all I remember is the hurt you've endured in your lifetime and how much you've wanted a child. I remember your desire to be a father and now you are." She reached for a tissue in a box on the table beside her and dabbed at her eyes. "I can't take that away from you and I can't take you away from your son."

He wanted to go to her, to take her in his arms and tell her how much he loved her, but he knew she didn't want that from him. Still, there were other people to consider. "And what about your brother?" he asked. "When you tell him, he won't feel the same way."

"I'm sure you're right." Paige compressed her lips into a thin line and said, "That's why I wouldn't tell him."

"What about all the things I took from him? How can I repay him?"

A slight smile tipped her mouth dimpling her cheek. "Don't worry about Brad. He got more than it was worth from the insurance company. He made sure of that." She sighed. "I wouldn't tell him because I know him and what he would do." She sat forward in her chair. "No, Rob. It's done. You've told me and it's over. Now I can really let it go."

"I don't know what to say, Paige. I didn't expect this." He stood and walked to the fireplace. He looked up at the picture, the barefoot woman in the red dress dancing with the man in the tuxedo on the beach, and he remembered how wonderful it had felt being with her the first time he saw the painting. "Thank you. I know that isn't enough, but thank you."

"It's enough," she said.

"Paige, I have to tell you I'm sorry, too, that I'm the reason you don't want to have a relationship." He leaned his elbow on the mantel and faced her. "I know, you love what you do and you've found your purpose, but I love you and if I hadn't hurt you, you wouldn't spend your life alone." Before she could respond, he continued. "I just hope that some day you can find someone who will have the same passion you do, someone you can love. If it isn't me, that's all right, but I want the best for you always."

"I have something to say about that." Paige balled the tissue in her fist. "You remember telling me my reasons for not wanting a relationship were, in your words, bullshit." She smiled. "It shocked me, the way you said it."

"I probably shouldn't have said it like that."

She stood and took a step toward him. "I'm not." Paige met his eyes. "And do you remember the day I tried to force myself on you?"

Rob shook his head. "Force yourself...?

She smiled and recited, " 'Rob, I want you to make love to me.' Surely you remember that."

He nodded and was surprised at her candor.

"When you rejected me, I was angry. Hurt. Ashamed. All of it, and it woke me up." She tossed the tissue on the table and took another step toward him. "I had to do some real soul searching, even talked to Dr. Fairchild about it, and I realized what I had been doing. I was trying to overcome my fear of losing my purpose. I was willing to give a part of me to you, and before you, to Daniel, but I was keeping the most important part to myself."

"And that was?" he asked.

"My heart. I was willing to give my body but never my heart because it belongs to my clients, the ones who need it."

Rob's arm dropped to his side. "I needed it, Paige. I needed your heart."

She walked to him and put her hand on his arm. "I know, but I couldn't give it to you; couldn't give it to anyone then. But now I can."

Rob's heart soared with hope once more.

"I know I can have a relationship, even want to have one. And I could have children, too." Rob knew she saw the hope in his face. "But not with you. Not ever with you now that I know."

It was done, had been done a long time ago and their life together had disappeared before it began.

"Go, Rob. Go to your child. Make a life for him." Tears ran down her cheeks again. She brushed at them. "You know, I really like you so much, maybe even love you. I wish things had been different."

Then she was in his arms. They held one another a long time. She turned her face to him and he kissed her. A long sad kiss. This one their last.

---

Rob stood on the porch. He squared his shoulders and rang the bell. Gerri opened the door and Bobby jumped into his arms.

"I'm ready, Gerri," he said.

And she knew what he meant.

# ABOUT THE AUTHOR

Barbara Leachman was in education for 23 years. When she retired from teaching, she worked as a chiropractic assistant and became a certified health care counselor. She was a widow for six years living in Broken Arrow, Oklahoma, when, in 2003 she married a widower she had known since sixth grade.

She and her husband together have six children and ten grandchildren with number eleven on the way. They have numerous grand-dogs, grand-cats and grand-horses. They are both retired and do a lot of traveling. They make their home in Albuquerque, New Mexico.

Printed in the United States
52433LVS00003B/21

9 781425 929787